SHEILA ROBERTS

A WEDDING
on Primrose Street

MIRA®

ISBN-13: 978-0-7783-1815-6

A Wedding on Primrose Street

For questions and comments about the quality of this book, please contact us at CustomerService@Harlequin.com.

www.MIRABooks.com

Printed in U.S.A.

For Karen

Dear Reader,

Is there anything more fun than a wedding? My characters Anne Richardson and Roberta Gilbert don't think so, which is why they're both in the wedding business. Anne is a wedding planner in Seattle and Roberta owns Primrose Haus, a lovely Victorian home in Icicle Falls where couples can say "I do" in elegant surroundings. Of course, their lives *must* intersect.

I enjoyed getting to know these two women who made similar life choices but in different circumstances and with different outcomes. As I wrote, I saw a lot of myself in both of them and in the relationships they had with their daughters. I also saw some of my mother and myself, and that brought back happy memories of my own wedding and how much she did to make that day special.

The mother-daughter relationship is so special, so important and, sometimes, so tricky. Throw in a wedding and things can really get interesting.

I hope you'll enjoy this tale of mothers and daughters, mistakes and new beginnings, and, most important, true love and all the ways we celebrate it.

I love hearing from readers! Find me on Facebook or visit me at my website, www.sheilasplace.com.

Sheila

A WEDDING
on Primrose Street

Chapter One

Anne, Wedding Planner and Mother of the Bride

"I don't care what my daughter thinks she wants. We are *not* having daisies at the wedding. They stink."

Anne Richardson pinched the bridge of her nose in an effort to stop the headache that was forming. She loved being a wedding planner...most days. But difficult clients did suck some of the joy out of her job. Everyone talked about Bridezillas, but in Anne's opinion Momzillas were ten times worse. And she was sure that Seattle had ten times more Momzillas per capita than any other city in the country.

"I mean, really," Laurel Browne continued. "Would you want daisies at your daughter's wedding?"

No, but if her daughter wanted daisies Anne would order them. Laurel was stepping over the line. Actually, she was stomping over the line.

Anne flashed on an image of Laurel as a giant mutant monster in a mother-of-the-bride dress, trampling a field of daisies. "Well," she began.

"I am *not* paying for daisies," Laurel said, her voice rising to a level that had Anne moving her phone away from her ear. "In fact, I no longer want to go with that florist at all. I thought I made it clear yesterday when we were in your office how subpar I think these floral arrangements are."

Oh, yes, more than clear. And that had started Wedding War III with her daughter. (Wedding War I had been fought the very first week over the colors the bride had chosen. Laurel had lost that one. Wedding War II had been over the venue and she'd come out the victor. Now she was pushing to win more wedding territory.)

"Of course, I understand your feelings completely," Anne said. But not her behavior. She had her daughter's special day in a choke hold.

"I should hope so," Laurel said huffily. "I am *not* paying you all this money to organize a wedding where I have to sit in a pew and smell daisies while I watch my daughter take her wedding vows. In fact, I sometimes wonder what I *am* paying you for."

To be your verbal punching bag? Anne ignored the jab about money. A wedding planner had to be thick-skinned. She also had to be a diplomat. Anne succeeded at both, which was why Memory Makers Weddings and Events was still in business after eighteen years.

"We do want your daughter to be happy on her special day," she said. At least one of them did. "So I'm going to suggest a compromise."

"What kind of compromise?" Laurel asked suspiciously.

"We could have the florist add daisies to the brides-maids' flowers and the bridal bouquet, and that would make Chelsea very happy. Then the flowers for the church and the table settings could be totally different, say yellow and white roses." She'd wanted to suggest that the day before when Laurel and Chelsea were in her office but hadn't been able to wedge in the words with mother and daughter going at it so vociferously. They'd left, still fighting.

"Hmm," Laurel said thoughtfully. "That might work."

"And really, this florist will do a lovely job for you. She's always open to suggestions." Or, as in Laurel's case, commands.

"Well, all right. Let's see if she can do that. Tell her we want something unique. Roses aren't enough. I want something with flair."

Flair. Who knew what that meant? But Anne promised flair to the max—for a reasonable price, of course—so she and the florist would have to become mind readers and translate the vague request into specific arrangements. Maybe Laurel would like her to spin some straw into gold while she was at it.

"Lord help me," she said with a groan after ending the call. "What did I do to deserve Laurel Browne as a client?"

"Happy Friday the Thirteenth," teased her younger sister, Kendra, who was busy making a spreadsheet for a new client.

"That woman is out of control." But then, this sometimes happened with younger brides whose parents were footing the bill.

"Sounds like you've got it handled," Kendra said.

"Yet another wedding crisis averted."

Kendra smiled. "Laurel has no idea how lucky she is that she has you for her wedding planner."

Obviously. "I *am* good."

And she'd proved it time and time again, organizing every imaginable kind of wedding, from medieval fairs to events in which the bride and groom parachuted onto the site where their vows would be exchanged. She never tired of planning weddings.

"Compensating," her mother had said when she'd first started doing it at church for free twenty years ago. If she was indeed making up for her own less-than-stellar wedding, she was doing a great job of it. She didn't plan weddings for free anymore, and her mother passed out her business cards as if they were chocolates. Even with her sister's help she often had to turn away business.

Too bad she hadn't turned away the Brownes, she thought, looking out her office window at the dripping Seattle sky. If Laurel reminded her once more that she was paying a lot for this wedding, she was going to pull out her eyebrows. And Laurel's, too.

The phone rang again. It was Marla Polanski, another Momzilla, wanting to know if Anne could change her daughter's wedding venue. It would be the third time. "We found a place up in Icicle Falls," Momzilla Marla raved. "It's a beautiful Victorian house with the most elegant gardens and a fabulous staircase Gwyneth could come down. I'm sending you the link right now."

"Okay," Anne said, "but you may have to adjust the size of your guest list." A house wouldn't hold as many people as the Kiana Lodge, the current venue of choice. A big, spread-out place across Puget Sound from Seattle with lovely grounds, it was a popular choice for many of her clients.

There was a moment of silence. Then Marla said, "Oh. Yes, that is an issue. Well, Gwyneth will simply have to pare it down a little because this place is exactly what we want—much more intimate and with so much charm. Anyway, I think they can handle up to a hundred."

That meant cutting their guest list in half. Anne hoped Marla would do the math. "Why don't you talk it over with your daughter?" she suggested.

"I will, but meanwhile book this place. I see they

have the second Saturday in August open, and I don't want someone else to get it. We can always change back to the lodge."

"I suppose so," Anne said dubiously. "Meanwhile, how about we keep the lodge booked until you're sure?" If they let go of their date they'd never get it back.

"I don't think we'll be needing it," Marla said in a confident voice. "I really want Gwyneth to be married up in Icicle Falls."

The customer was always right, even when she was wrong. "Of course," Anne said and hoped that was what Gwyneth wanted, too.

She'd barely ended the call when flowers from In Bloom arrived. "Cam's already begun the Valentine's Day spoiling," Kendra observed, looking at the huge vase crammed full of pink roses. "I wish he'd give lessons to Jimmy. All I'm going to get is my usual chocolate rose. Not even a box of chocolates."

"He's just trying to help you stay on your diet," Anne said.

Kendra frowned. "I don't want to stay on my diet on Valentine's Day." Or any other day, which was why she was still complaining about the extra twenty pounds that refused to fall off. "It's not fair that you got the skinny genes."

As if Anne didn't have to give those skinny genes a boost with regular visits to the gym. She decided now was not the time to mention that to her sister. Anyway, Kendra wasn't fat. She only thought she was.

"I bet Cam's taking you someplace fabulous for dinner tomorrow," Kendra said, her words tinged with sisterly envy.

"No, he's not. We're staying in and he's cooking."

Kendra heaved an exaggerated sigh. "Why did I pick such a Neanderthal?"

"Because he can fix a broken toilet?"

"There is that," Kendra admitted with a grin. "I guess I'll have to settle for ordering pizza since I'm sure Jimmy completely forgot about the big day." Her cell phone began to sing—"Born to Run," her husband's ringtone. "Hey, babe, what's up? Yeah? Are you serious?" Kendra gasped. "And here I was thinking you'd forgotten."

From the way her sister was smiling Anne could tell that Jimmy had managed to come through for Valentine's Day.

"Well, what do you know," Kendra said after she'd ended the call. "We're spending tomorrow night at the Four Seasons. I wonder which of the kids he had to sell to afford it."

"Probably both of them." Considering that the Four Seasons was one of Seattle's most luxurious hotels. "So I don't want to hear any more whining ever again about how your husband doesn't get it right on Valentine's Day," Anne said, pointing at her sister.

If she wasn't married to such a great guy herself she would've been jealous.

But she *was* married to a great guy, and come June they'd be celebrating twenty-five years together. They still hadn't settled on what they wanted to do, but at the moment an Alaskan cruise looked tempting to Cam.

Speaking of tempting, she thought the following day as she stopped by Le Rêve bakery on her way home from running errands. Their chocolate mousse cake would make the perfect finish to the steak and baked potatoes Cam was serving up.

Actually, the perfect finish had more to do with the lacy red bra and panties she was wearing under her black blouse and jeans. Eye candy that Cam would enjoy unwrapping.

Back at their 1906 traditional on Queen Anne Hill she found him out in the remodeled kitchen, comfortable in jeans and a T-shirt, putting together a tossed salad. Salad, grilled meat and baked potatoes—that was the extent of his culinary skills.

But he had other, more valuable skills, and he gave her a sample of what was going to happen later when he pulled her against him and kissed her. Oh, he was a luscious thing. Six feet of beautiful muscle, dark hair with a few silver highlights sneaking in to make him look distinguished and a mouth that could melt a girl with one kiss. She'd been hot for him way back in high school, and nothing had changed.

"Did you resist the urge to go by your office?" he asked.

"Yes, smart guy. After yesterday I need a break. I swear, Laurel Browne is enough to make me want to set my hair on fire with a unity candle."

He snickered. "Well, I guess you can't blame the woman. It's a big thing when your kid gets married. Speaking of kids, guess who called a couple of minutes ago."

"Laney." In spite of the fact that their daughter was ostensibly sharing an old house in the Fremont district with a girlfriend and no longer lived at home, she stopped by a couple of times a week and texted or called Anne every day. Sometimes to say hi but usually because she was experiencing a crisis or seeking advice or had news to share. She'd had a fight with her boyfriend, Drake. Or the tips at her barista job had been crummy. Or—and here was good news—she was going back to school next fall. Now she wanted to get a teaching degree so she could teach art as well as create it. Anne had smiled at that. Cam could finally quit worrying about whether Laney would ever be able to earn a decent living.

"Close but no cigar," he said. "It was Drake."

"And he was calling because?"

"To tell me he's going to propose tonight. Did you know they'd been looking at rings?"

"No." Anne felt the slightest bit hurt. Why hadn't Laney told her?

"He's taking her to the Space Needle to pop the question."

"He can afford that on an auto technician's salary?"

Cam shrugged. "Where there's a will there's a way. The guy is a saver. Anyway, don't be surprised if they show up here later."

Hmm. Maybe it was time for a plan B. Anne began to unbutton her blouse. "What if we had plans for later?"

Cam's gaze was riveted on her breasts, wrapped in red lace. His voice turned silky and he ran a hand up her arm. "Never put off till later what you can enjoy right now," he said, slipping off the blouse. "Red, my favorite color."

"I know," she said.

He tugged playfully on the waistband of her jeans. "What have we got under here? More red?"

She slithered out of her jeans and showed him.

"Oh, yeah. That's what I'm talkin' about." He pulled her close once again and nibbled her ear. "How do you do it, babe?"

"Do what?"

"Stay as beautiful as you were back in high school?"

"You're so full of it," she murmured, sliding her fingers through his hair.

"No, it's true. You're still the most beautiful woman I've ever seen."

Then he hadn't looked around much. Her nose was too thin and her feet were too long. Gray hairs were invading the brown ones at such a rapid rate she was having to increase her visits to her favorite salon on The Ave, and she had a colony of cellulite growing on her thighs. Those flaws didn't seem to bother him, though.

They sure weren't bothering him at the moment. He picked her up and hoisted her onto the kitchen counter. "Let's start with dessert tonight."

"You mean the cake?" she teased.

"I'm not dignifying that with an answer," he said and kissed her.

Oh, yes. Happy Valentine's Day.

Later, as they ate steaks off the grill and toasted each other with champagne, she was still feeling the glow from their lovemaking. Her husband had magic hands, and he sure knew how to make Valentine's Day memorable.

This one was going to be extraspecial. Cam was right; Laney would either call or come by to show off her new ring. What a perfect ending to the day, celebrating love with the next generation of family.

Her baby, her only child, was getting married, and to her high school sweetheart, just as Anne had done. Technically it was more a case of marrying a post–high school sweetheart, although the two had been friends for years. Anne and Cam had watched Drake change from a skinny, pimple-faced boy with tats and crazy-colored hair to a responsible young man who was ready to settle down. She could hardly wait to help Laney plan their wedding.

Of course, they'd talked a lot about weddings over the years. How could they not, considering what Anne did for a living? It had started when Laney used to play bride as a small child, dressed up with a pillowcase for a veil and a bouquet of some silk flowers Anne used for crafting. When Laney was in high school, she used to joke about wearing sneakers under her wedding dress like the bride in the old Steve Martin movie *Father of the Bride*. (Naturally, they'd watched that, along with *My Best Friend's Wedding*, *Runaway Bride*, *Made of Honor*, *27 Dresses*, *My Big Fat Greek Wedding* and any other wedding movie that came down the pike.) Hopefully, Laney had forgotten the tennis-shoe idea.

Anne could already envision Cam escorting their daughter down the aisle at Queen Anne Presbyterian, surrounded by flowers, Laney wearing a beautiful wedding gown, her long, chestnut hair falling to her shoulders in gentle waves. Anne's vision conveniently ignored the tattooed artwork running up Laney's neck and covering her right arm.

"There is such a thing as overkill," she'd said when her daughter went for her second tattoo, but Laney had just laughed and kissed her and skipped off to the tattoo parlor to commemorate her twenty-first birthday with more body art. Why, oh, why did her daughter have to take everything to extremes?

Because she was Laney. She'd always pushed the boundaries, staying out past curfews, cutting classes her freshman year in high school (thank God they'd broken her of *that* habit), dyeing her hair every color of the rainbow, adorning her ears with piercings. She'd gotten her nose pierced, too, but Anne had persuaded her to get a little diamond rather than the big stake she'd talked about, so at least that looked classy.

She's another generation, Anne constantly reminded herself, *and they have their own style.* Except style was such a subjective thing, and it wasn't only Laney's generation getting tattoos. Women Anne's age did it, too. One of her friends had a discreet rose on her ankle. It just seemed that the younger women, especially her daughter, never knew when to stop. It was enough to make a mother crazy. But then, she told herself, it was the duty of every generation to drive their parents nuts. Heaven knew, she'd done it to her own mother. Still...

"What are you thinking about?" Cam asked as he cut off a piece of steak.

She smiled at him. "Our baby's getting married." And that eclipsed fashion frustration. Fashion issues could be dealt with later.

"Yeah, I can't believe it. Seems like only yesterday that she had colic and I was walking the floor with her." He shook his head. "They're so young."

"So were we," Anne pointed out.

He nodded. "Our parents probably had this same conversation."

Anne was thankful she'd been spared hearing her parents' conversation. The one she'd had with her mother had been unpleasant enough.

"Drake's a good kid, though," Cam said. "They'll be happy."

"If they're half as happy as we are, they'll have a great marriage," Anne said and took a bite of her baked potato, which she'd slathered in butter and sour cream.

Sour cream, butter, chocolate cake. She'd have to eat nothing but salad for the next week.

They were watching a romantic comedy and eating their cake when Laney called. "Mom, can Drake and I come over? We've got something to show you."

"Sure," Anne said, playing dumb. "Come on by."

"Okay. See you in a few."

Twenty minutes later, her daughter was walking through the door, dressed for Valentine's Day in black leggings and a short denim skirt she'd probably scored at her favorite consignment store. Her curls peeped out from under a black tam and she wore red platform shoes and a matching red top under her black leather jacket. She'd accented the outfit with a long, red scarf.

She was followed by her boyfriend, a tall, skinny, tattooed drink of water wearing jeans and a black T-shirt under a black leather bomber jacket. Unlike Laney, he didn't have an ear full of hoops and cute earrings. Instead, he wore gauges that had stretched holes in his earlobes. Anne had to admit that if she'd gone boyfriend shopping for her daughter she would've passed him over in favor of a preppy-looking boy in law school. But what would Laney have had in common with that kind of boy? She and Drake loved each other and that was what counted. Just as Cam said, he was a good kid. Tonight he wore a smile that reached from ear to ear.

And Laney sported a ring with a diamond best viewed under a magnifying glass. "See what I got for Valentine's Day?" she crowed.

Anne took her daughter's hand and gave her ring the attention it demanded as Cam clapped Drake on the back and welcomed him to the family. "It's gorgeous," she said. Then she hugged both her daughter and her future son-in-law. "We're so happy for you two. Come on in and let's have some chocolate cake to celebrate."

"You'll never guess where we went to dinner," Laney said, following Anne into the kitchen. "The Space Needle."

"Pretty impressive. Did Drake rob a bank?"

"He's been saving for this since Christmas."

At least someone in their marriage would be good with money. "Well, how was it?"

"Oh, wow," Laney said. "The view from up there, you can see everything. Puget Sound, the city, the mountains. And the food was sooo yummy."

"Maybe you don't have room for cake," Anne teased.

"I always have room for cake. You know that."

Anne cut pieces and put them on plates, and Laney took them to where Drake and Cam sat in the living room. Meanwhile, Anne grabbed two more glasses and another bottle of champagne.

Once the glasses were filled, Cam raised his in salute to the happy couple squeezed together in an oversize armchair. "To Laney and Drake. May you both be as happy as we are."

"Thanks, Dad," Laney said, and she and Drake kissed each other.

"Have you set a date?" Cam asked.

"We're thinking June," Laney said.

The same month Anne and Cam had gotten married. "An excellent month," he said, winking at Anne.

But it didn't give them much time to pull together a wedding.

"We thought it would be really cool to go to Vegas," Drake added.

The two exchanged besotted smiles.

Anne hardly saw them. Instead, she was seeing her

daughter in some tiny chapel, all dressed up like a show-girl with a big, feathery headdress. And there was Drake, wearing a sparkly, white Elvis jumpsuit. To Laney's "I do," he responded, "Thank you. Thank you very much."

Vegas. Aaack!

Chapter Two

Roberta, Wedding Maven of Icicle Falls

Roberta Gilbert smiled as she surveyed the wedding guests dressed in their finery. This wedding had a Valentine theme, and Roberta had placed little heart-shaped boxes filled with chocolates on the linen-clad tables, along with the pink carnations and red roses the bride had requested.

It was the second time around for both bride and groom, who'd each been badly hurt by their exes. But that was behind them now, and the couple was clearly delighted with their new beginning as they swayed together in the center of the reception room.

It had once been two separate rooms, but Roberta had combined them years ago, making more space for guests. Every time she entered it she could feel the positive energy stored up from so many happy events. Tonight the chandeliers glowed in the antique gilded mirrors, reflecting the image of two beaming people, surrounded by forty well-wishers.

Roberta's eyes misted, partly from sentiment and partly because, darn it all, her bunions were killing her. Much as she loved these touching moments, she'd be very happy when midnight came and the party ended. Her daughter kept telling her she was getting too old for this, but what did Daphne know? Seventy-one wasn't that old. Anyway, Roberta couldn't imagine living anywhere other than her pretty, pink Victorian with the white trim here on Primrose Street. She did love weddings, and after thirty years of hosting as well as planning them, it was a hard addiction to break. So here she would stay until she keeled over and they carried her out, bunions first.

All right, maybe she could be tempted to pack in her business if some handsome older man who enjoyed Caribbean cruises and watching old doo-wop groups on PBS arrived on the scene.

The odds of that happening were about as good as the odds of Roberta winning the lottery…which she never played. Besides, she had several wedding years left in her.

"How are you doing?" asked a voice at her elbow, and she turned to see her assistant, Lila Kurtz, looking festive in a red dress and white apron decorated with red hearts.

In charge of the caterers, Lila always saw to it that everything ran smoothly. And tonight's food was especially elegant. It had been prepared by Bailey Sterling, who owned Tea Time Tea Shop and Tearoom on Lavender Lane, and the guests had raved about the three-cheese stuffed chicken, the pasta and tossed salads and the lavender cake. Roberta would definitely use Bailey again.

"Just fine," Roberta lied. Even though she had Lila and her crew, Roberta worked on the table settings, plated some of the food and did whatever else needed to be done. And no matter how much help she had, there was always plenty to do when a woman offered a full-service venue. Her bunions would attest to that.

"You could duck out now," Lila suggested.

She could. Once she was in her bedroom, she'd be oblivious to any noise coming from below or from the second-floor changing room at the front of the house reserved for the bride and her bridesmaids. Lila would see the revelers on their way and then lock up. But for heaven's sake, it was barely past nine o'clock. Only little old ladies went to bed at nine o'clock.

Still, she had her Vanessa Valentine romance novel waiting for her. "You know, maybe I will." She used to love watching the bride toss her bouquet but tonight her nice, soft mattress and a looming love scene were winning out over sentiment. "If you don't mind."

"Of course not," Lila said. Lila was a single mom with two grown children and she liked to stay up late.

"Well, then, I'll go upstairs. I have a few things to do," Roberta added in case Lila thought she was pooping out.

Lila nodded approvingly. "Take it easy tomorrow. Leave the mess for the cleaning crew on Monday."

"I will," Roberta promised. She had no desire to work any harder than she had to.

"And don't forget you've got Muriel Sterling coming over to do that interview for the paper on Monday afternoon," Lila reminded her.

Ah, yes. The interview. Roberta hoped Muriel didn't ask any nosy questions that would be awkward to answer, but if she did, Roberta knew how to dodge them. She'd been doing it for years.

The DJ was now spinning an upbeat song and the room pulsed with dancers. Roberta made her way around the edge of the crowd, ready to put her feet up and read her book. With her comfy flannel jammies on, she'd be free to let the story carry her away.

Suddenly it looked as if there wasn't going to be any carrying away—not considering who'd just arrived at the party. Roberta blinked, wondering if her eyes were playing tricks on her. But no, Daphne was still there, hovering in the doorway, her lovely face contorted with a scowl. What on earth was her daughter doing here?

She hurried over to where Daphne stood, wearing dark jeans and a leather jacket thrown over a plain, black sweater, a carry-on suitcase parked next to her. Her big blue eyes were bloodshot and her nose was red, probably from too many close encounters with a tissue.

"Daphne, darling, what are you doing here?" *On a weekend, looking like the bad wedding fairy. And with a suitcase?* Oh, wedding bell blues. Roberta could already guess what was wrong.

Daphne took in the crowd of happy revelers. "All that money wasted on champagne and cake. It never works out."

Sure enough. "Come upstairs," Roberta said, steering her daughter toward the staircase. "We'll get you settled and you can tell me what's going on."

Daphne didn't wait until she was settled. She started in right away, towing her suitcase up the stairs. "I knew something was wrong." *Thump.* "I've suspected for months." *Thump.* "I kept asking him and he denied it." *Thump, thump.*

Roberta sighed. Men were beasts. "So Mitchell's been cheating on you."

"You were right—he's slime," Daphne said, her voice trembling. "How could he do this to me?" she wailed. "Is it that hard to be faithful to someone?"

In Mitchell's case, obviously, yes. Poor Daphne. She

was so pretty, so trusting. She was like a man magnet. Sadly, she didn't seem able to attract anything better than the man equivalent of paper clips.

"I'm so sorry," Roberta said.

They'd reached the top floor now, and Roberta led her daughter to the back of the house, to the room opposite hers, the same room that had been Daphne's growing up. Here they were, together again, mother and daughter. And daughter was going through yet another romantic crisis.

Daphne was an underachiever when it came to relationships. Her first husband had been a lazy bum who spent as much time collecting unemployment as he did working. He drank too much and helped Daphne around the house too little. The only good thing to come out of that marriage had been Roberta's granddaughter, Marnie. (Unlike her mother, Marnie knew how to pick a man who had his act together and was now busy setting the world on fire, working in New York as an editor.) Husband number two had bailed on Daphne when Marnie hit her teen years. As for number three, Roberta had never liked him. She'd seen the way Mitchell ogled other women when Daphne wasn't looking. You couldn't trust oglers. She'd told Daphne as much but would she listen? Of course not.

Where was the ogler now? Back home, in Daphne's bed with another woman? "Did you kick him out?" Roberta demanded. Sometimes her daughter was too soft.

Daphne draped her coat over the bedpost and got busy unpacking her suitcase.

"Daphne," Roberta said sharply.

"I told him he had until next week to get his stuff out." Her face turned red and she pulled off her sweater. She opened the window and stuck her head outside.

A very convenient time for a hot flash, Roberta thought cynically. "So you left him in your house? Why?" She grabbed the coat and hung it in the closet.

Daphne pulled her head back in and scowled. "I didn't want to look at him. Honestly, Mother. Did you expect me to stay there after what I found out?"

"Yes," Roberta cried, exasperated. "That house belongs to you. He should be the one to leave, not you. When you go home, you call a locksmith first thing. Even if you have to take Monday off."

Daphne bit her lip, a sure sign that she was hiding something.

Oh, heavens, what now? "Daphne?"

Daphne pushed aside a lock of long, blond hair. "I'm not going home, not for a while."

"But you have to. Your job."

Not that it was a high-powered job. Daphne had used her college degree from the University of Washington to land a position as a receptionist for a seafood distribution company in Seattle, where she'd remained ever since as an underpaid fixture. In spite of her talents and her mother's high hopes, she had never felt the need to reach for the stars.

She could've been a fashion model or started her own interior decorating business or…something. Roberta had given her any number of suggestions over the years, but Daphne had preferred to stay on the bottom rung of the ladder of success. If Roberta hadn't been there for the birth she'd have sworn her daughter was some other woman's.

"I quit," Daphne said, breaking into Roberta's thoughts like a wrecking ball.

"You what?"

"I quit."

Roberta fell onto the bed. "Oh, Daphne."

"I can't stay in Seattle anymore," Daphne said, her lips trembling. "I just… I need a change."

"No," Roberta said firmly. "You need a job." Daphne couldn't jump off the high dive and assume there'd be water in the pool.

She couldn't, but she had.

"I'll find a job, but first I have to take some time off, get myself sorted out. Anyway, I have some money saved up."

"So do I, if you need it. But, oh, Daphne, what were you thinking?" Clearly she wasn't. Had Mitchell tipped her over the edge?

"I was thinking I need to make a new start," Daphne said in a small voice.

"You're fifty-three!" Who did she suppose was going to hire a fifty-three-year-old woman? It wasn't right, but age discrimination was a very real thing.

"Haven't you ever wanted to walk away from your life, start all over again?" Daphne pleaded.

Yes, and she had. So how could she discourage Daphne from doing the same? Now tears were leaking out of her daughter's eyes. "I thought I could stay with you for a while. Just till I get on my feet," she added, probably because she'd seen the consternation on her mother's face.

It wasn't that Roberta didn't love her daughter. It wasn't that she didn't want to see her. But living together? They were so different. They'd drive each other insane. Daphne herself had said so on more than one occasion.

Roberta always kept her house neat as the proverbial pin. Daphne's often looked as if it had been caught up in a tornado and then set down far from any store with cleaning supplies. On a good day you could find decorating magazines strewn on the couch and shoes scattered everywhere, coats hanging from the handle of the closet door rather than inside it. She had a flair for decorating, but what was the use of painting and purchasing expensive sofa pillows if you never dusted and your toilet was dirty? Roberta had never understood how her daughter could be so efficient at work and such a slob at home. Of course, to be fair, not one of the bums she'd married had ever helped her. Not that she'd ever asked them. She'd been far too easy on the men in her life.

And too easy on herself. Why she'd never wanted to improve in the areas where she was lacking baffled Roberta. But she didn't. She hated it when Roberta commented on her bad housekeeping habits or tried to offer advice. In fact, it seemed as if every time Roberta tried to help Daphne improve her life they wound up squabbling.

Still, she'd never turn Daphne away. She put an arm around her daughter's shoulders and gave her an encouraging squeeze. "Of course you can stay." She needed a plan, though. She needed to be proactive. "But, darling, you can't hide up here indefinitely and mope."

"I'm not going to mope. I told you, I'll find a job."

"In Icicle Falls?"

"There are businesses in Icicle Falls," Daphne said stiffly.

"Yes, of course, but you're not going to find anything with the salary or benefits you had at your job in the city." Not that her job in the city had paid *that* well.

"I don't need much to live on," Daphne said, raising her chin.

Roberta wasn't so sure. Her daughter had always had a husband to supplement her salary (although some were more reliable than others). She had no idea how difficult it could be to live on one small income.

"I'll have money when I sell the house."

"You're used to city life. You'll be bored," Roberta predicted.

"I can find plenty to do here in Icicle Falls. I could help you."

"With weddings?" Not only would they be living together, they'd be working together? Now Roberta's bunions weren't all that hurt. She felt as though her forehead was about to crack open. She rubbed her temples in an effort to stop the crack from spreading.

"Why not?" Daphne demanded, correctly interpreting her mother's body language. "In case you've forgotten, I helped with Marnie's wedding."

Roberta remembered. Daphne had forgotten to order the invitations and they'd gone out three weeks late. Giving her daughter a chance to regroup was one thing, but weddings...

"We'll see," she said, making Daphne frown. "For now, let's get some rest. Everything will look better in the morning." That was total baloney and they both knew it, but at least with a good night's sleep they'd be more able to cope.

Meanwhile, Roberta was going to bed with her romance novel. When she kissed her daughter good-night and wished her pleasant dreams, Daphne teared up and nodded bravely.

Roberta skedaddled across the hall to her own bedroom, where she fell on the bed. She should have been more supportive, listened more and said less. Daphne was in no mood for advice right now.

Her poor daughter wouldn't get a wink of sleep tonight. Roberta suspected she wouldn't, either. Not that she ever slept all that well anyway. Getting up two or three times during the night to go to the bathroom always interfered. Oh, how Mother Nature turned on her sisters after a certain age.

Well, there was nothing she could do now. And there likely wasn't anything she could do tomorrow. It was hard having grown children. A woman had so little control over her daughter's choices once that daughter was grown.

She got into her pajamas, picked up her romance novel and cuddled under the covers, ready—*finally*—to let the story carry her away. But she got carried only as far as the first kiss in the seduction scene before her mind wandered.

Kisses, seduction, Mitchell the ogler… Roberta frowned. If only Daphne had met a decent man, someone who'd treat her with respect and kindness. She was a good woman, tenderhearted and giving. She didn't deserve to have her heart broken. This was what came of being a poor judge of character.

Worrying about her daughter was exhausting. She set aside her book and went in search of sleep, but she didn't find it. Finally, she gave up, turned her bedside lamp back on and opened her romance novel again. At least there she could be assured that life would work out perfectly.

On Monday afternoon Muriel Sterling, Icicle Falls's resident writing celebrity, was knocking on the front door of Primrose Haus promptly at two. Just in time for tea.

"It's really kind of you to see me," she said to Roberta as she stepped inside, a gust of brisk mountain air following her in. "I hope it's not too much trouble after the wedding you had this weekend."

Muriel Sterling knew how to be gracious. "No trouble at all," Roberta told her. "I'm happy to see you. It's been ages since we've had a chance to chat."

"My life has gotten a little busy."

That wasn't a bad thing. Muriel had pulled away from her friends after the loss of her second husband. When she finally came out of mourning, she did so with a vengeance, helping her daughters run Sweet Dreams Chocolates and enjoying a blossoming writing career.

"Your mother would've been proud of all your success," Roberta said.

"You've been pretty successful, too."

She'd done all right. "I'm still not sure why you wanted to interview me, though."

"The editor at the *Gazette* approached me with the idea that it would be nice to feature some of our time-honored businesses run by local women, so of course we immediately thought of your wedding house."

"Come on into the parlor," Roberta said. "I have some lavender sugar cookies from your daughter's tea shop, along with a pot of Lady Grey."

"Those sugar cookies are impossible to resist," Muriel said and followed Roberta to the formal parlor at the front of the house. The room offered a fireplace and pretty antique chairs, some of which were even comfortable. Granted, the fireplace didn't put out a lot of heat, but on a cold February afternoon having a fire in it warmed the heart. Today the crackling logs enhanced the cozy feeling of the room.

She settled Muriel in front of the coffee table where Daphne had left a half-full coffee cup and a copy of *Better Homes and Gardens*. Roberta scooped them up and fetched tea and cookies. There were considerably fewer in the box than there'd been when Roberta brought it home that morning, which meant her daughter had gone on a cookie raid. Shades of her divorce from husband number two.

She returned to find that Muriel had taken a steno pad from her purse and flipped it open. "I was trying to remember. How many years have you been in business?"

"Thirty years." Had it really been thirty? Where had the time gone? "You may remember our first wedding in the house was my daughter's," Roberta added. "Daphne was the one who actually gave me the idea of opening it up to other people." Cleverness, one of her daughter's underused gifts.

And speaking of Daphne, here she came, wearing jeans, a sweater and a woebegone expression—a shining testimonial to the joys of wedded bliss. Roberta noticed the little watering can in her daughter's hand. Much as Daphne loved to decorate, she wasn't all that good with houseplants. Roberta guessed her sudden interest sprang more from a desire to search out some company than to water the plants. She couldn't blame Daphne. The pain of rejection was one that cut soul-deep and it was hard to be alone with that kind of hurt.

Although God knew Roberta had done it.

"Daphne, how wonderful to see you," Muriel said politely.

"Oh, hi," Daphne said, feigning surprise.

"Are you in town for a visit?" Muriel asked.

Daphne shook her head and got busy watering Roberta's ficus plant. "I'm up here to make a new start. I'm getting divorced." She studied the ficus, then moved it to the other side of the room, setting it next to the philodendron.

Muriel looked properly sympathetic. "I'm sorry to hear that."

Daphne shrugged. "It's for the best."

Which was more than Roberta could say for the new location of her houseplant. "Daphne, dear, what are you doing?"

"Hmm? Oh, I just thought this plant would look better over here beside the other one, in a group."

"That's a charming idea, but the ficus needs full sunlight," Roberta said.

Daphne's cheeks grew pink. "Oh." She picked it up and returned it to its original spot.

"Do you know what you want to do?" Muriel asked her.

"I figured I could help my mother with weddings."

"What a good plan," Muriel said, beaming with approval.

Yes, wasn't it? The very thought had Roberta reaching for a cookie.

"I'm sure your mother's delighted to have you home," Muriel said and helped herself to some cookies, as well.

"Oh, yes," Roberta lied.

"So, your daughter's was the first wedding held here, wasn't it?" Muriel asked, bringing them back to the interview.

Daphne gave a snort of disgust.

Roberta ignored her. "Yes, and then, a generation later, my granddaughter was married here."

"That was a beautiful wedding," Daphne said, her voice wistful.

"And you've had many in between," Muriel said to Roberta. "I still remember the lovely reception we had here when I married Waldo," she added.

"It was lovely. And who knows? Maybe someday

you'll get married again," Roberta suggested. Muriel's longtime admirer, Arnie Amundsen, would marry her in a minute if she ever gave him any encouragement. So far, though, she hadn't.

"I suspect not. After Waldo…" Muriel's smile faded.

"He was a sweet man," Roberta said.

"He was," Muriel agreed. "And you know how rare a good man is."

"You can say that again." Daphne tipped her watering can over Roberta's spider plant. The water spattered onto the antique music cabinet beneath it and Roberta tried not to grind her teeth.

Daphne frowned and mopped up the spill with the sleeve of her sweater.

"You never remarried," Muriel said to Roberta. "In fact, I remember when you first moved to Icicle Falls. You were a widow."

"I lost my husband in a car crash." Oh, how easily the lie slipped out after all these years.

Muriel looked at her with compassion. "I remember that. You never found another man to measure up."

Roberta was suddenly aware of her daughter's gaze burning into her. How many times growing up had Daphne wanted to know about her father, wondered why they didn't have any pictures of Daddy?

"Daddy's dead," Roberta had replied. Learning the truth when she was older hadn't sat well with Daphne, not until she heard the whole story. But even after that, she'd longed for more, tried to find a way to make what she had into more. Of course, it hadn't worked.

There were so many times Roberta had wished she could give her daughter a happy Ward and June Cleaver experience. Instead, Daphne'd had to settle for just June. But they'd done all right, the two of them. Anyway, family wasn't always what you were born into; it was the people in your life who cared about you, and in Icicle Falls they'd found plenty of people to care.

As for a man... "There wasn't exactly an abundance of single men in Icicle Falls back in those days," she said. "All the good ones were taken. Anyway, I've been happy on my own."

"Well, you've been an inspiration to a lot of women," Muriel said. "And your beautiful house is always in demand. What's the most memorable wedding you've ever had here?"

"Not mine," Daphne said bitterly.

Her daughter was not helping with the Primrose Haus image of happy brides and perfect occasions.

"It was a lovely wedding, though," Muriel said, clearly trying to be diplomatic. She'd attended that wedding. And Daphne's second one, as well. Fortunately, by the third try Daphne had narrowed her guest list considerably, so all their Icicle Falls friends were off the hook for wedding presents. "Is there any one that stands out?" Muriel asked Roberta.

"Oh, we've had so many it's hard to narrow down." Roberta waved a hand airily.

Now Daphne jumped in. "How about the one where when the minister said, 'If anyone can show just cause why this couple cannot lawfully be joined together, let him speak now or forever hold his peace,' and the best man spoke up? It turned out he and the bride had been sleeping together," she explained to Muriel.

That would make an inspiring story for the paper, Roberta thought, and frowned at her daughter, who became very engrossed in watering plants.

Muriel blinked in shock.

"They weren't from around here," Roberta assured her.

Muriel nodded and scribbled away in her steno pad. "What did you do after that happened?"

Roberta shrugged. "They'd paid for a party, so we served the food." Muriel's expression was disapproving, whether of Roberta's callous the-show-must-go-on attitude or the behavior of the unfaithful bride, Roberta couldn't tell. Maybe it was a little of both. "The only thing you can be sure of about people," she continued, "is that they'll surprise you."

"And not in a good way," Daphne muttered.

"I'm sure you had some weddings that *did* surprise you in a good way," Muriel prompted.

"Yes, of course," Roberta said. "Only last fall we hosted an impromptu reception for a couple who'd been sweethearts when they were young and found each other again on Facebook. They'd both lost their spouses and were so lonely. They started talking on the phone every night, and when he learned she was coming to Icicle Falls to celebrate Oktoberfest with friends, he came, too. They hadn't seen each other in almost forty years but they picked up right where they'd left off. They were married the very next weekend."

Daphne let out an unladylike snort. "I bet they're not together now."

Muriel smiled. "Oh, I bet they are. That's a beautiful story, Roberta."

"Sounds more like fairy tale to me," Daphne said.

Roberta sent her daughter another reprimanding look and Muriel feigned deafness.

She asked a few more questions, then wrapped up the interview.

Having known Muriel since she was a girl, Roberta asked about her daughters and was quick to tell her what an impressive job her youngest one, Bailey, had done with the food for the recent wedding reception. "We'll definitely use her again," she promised, and Muriel beamed like the proud mother she was.

She had a right to be proud. All three of her girls were lovely and accomplished young women who were doing interesting things with their lives.

Meanwhile, in another corner of the room, Daphne had managed to knock over a houseplant. It landed on the hardwood floor with a crunch as the pot broke and potting soil scattered in all directions.

"Sorry," she said and disappeared, hopefully to get a broom and dustpan.

"I hope everything works out for Daphne," Muriel said.

"I do, too," Roberta said with a sigh.

Her daughter had come home in Humpty Dumpty condition. What was it going to take to put her back together again? And would they be able to keep from killing each other in the process?

Chapter Three

Anne, Mother of a Bride in Need of Guidance

When the kids came over for dinner on Sunday it was plain to Anne that they didn't know what they wanted. Ideas had flown around the table faster than bats out of a cave.

And some of the ideas had been just as scary to Anne. They could get married at the coffee shop. Cute, but how many people could you fit in a coffee shop? Or on a ferryboat. If any guests were a few minutes late they'd miss the boat *and* the ceremony. Ferries ran on time. Wedding guests, not necessarily. Of course, they could always charter an Argosy cruise ship.

Before Anne could even bring it up, they were on to a new idea—a pirate ship. Apparently, you could do that at the Treasure Island Hotel in Vegas. (Back to Vegas again—nooo!) Or they could have a zombie theme. This was another suggestion from Drake. He was just full of ideas. (Who asked him, anyway?)

By the time they left, Anne was on her third glass of white wine and on the phone to her mother. "This is insane," she'd finished after delivering the bad news of her daughter's sudden poor taste in weddings.

"Frustrating, isn't it?"

She'd received the message in her mother's tone of voice loud and clear. *Yeah. How does it feel?*

Okay, so she hadn't let Mom throw her the super wedding she'd wanted. "That was different," she'd reminded her. And at least her mother'd had Kendra, who'd come through with the traditional wedding. Anne had only Laney.

"All you can do is make suggestions," Julia had said. "And if you think she's going to take any of them, you've been eating too much wedding cake."

"Ha-ha. I'm sure glad I called you."

"I am, too," Julia had said, ignoring the sarcasm. "This is happy news, and I know whatever kind of wedding Laney wants, you'll give it to her."

Of course she would. There was nothing she wouldn't do, no length to which she wouldn't go, to give her daughter the wonderful wedding she deserved.

"In the end, you want her to have the day she wants."

"Well, yes," Anne had agreed.

And she knew what Laney wanted. It was the same thing she'd wanted since she was a little girl. Anne could still remember, when Laney was seven, watching the wedding scene in *The Sound of Music* with her—the first movie wedding they ever watched together. Laney sat transfixed at the sight of Maria coming down the aisle to the nuns' chorus. "I want a wedding like that someday, Mommy," she'd breathed, and Anne had vowed then and there to make sure she got it. She was no less determined now.

Laney needed guidance. "I don't want her to wind up having any regrets." Wasn't it a mother's job to save her daughter from that? So far there'd been very little saving and a whole lot of running just to keep up.

* * *

Come Monday it was time to focus on other brides. In the morning Anne met with a bride-to-be, pinning down the details of her upcoming wedding.

"I love the idea of the treasure box," the bride gushed. "It would be great to fill that as part of the ceremony. What should we put in it?"

"Well, it can be anything you want. A copy of your wedding vows, for one thing. And didn't you say your bridesmaids were going to make tissue flowers to decorate the lodge? You could put in one of those, as well as your engagement picture. Also, a lot of couples put in something like a bottle of whiskey so they can toast each other on their one-year anniversary. You open the box again in another five years and another five and so on. Each time you can reread your vows. You'll have the flower as a keepsake and the picture to remind you how happy you are in this moment."

"And the whiskey to help us forget if we aren't," joked the bride-to-be.

"Or to congratulate each other on doing such a good job of building a life together."

Her client nodded vigorously, typing notes in her iPad. "We are so doing this."

Anne smiled. Happy brides were what made her world spin.

After lunch she spent two hours in the studio attached to her office with another bride-to-be, showing her table-setting options. Now it was time to book that venue Marla Polanski had requested.

Anne brought up the website for Primrose Haus in Icicle Falls and it was love at first sight. "Oh, this is beautiful," she said, and Kendra came to look over her shoulder.

The place was like something out of a fairy tale, with turrets and dormer windows and a front porch dripping with gingerbread trim. It was pale pink, the color of clouds at the end of a sunset, and the trim was white. The landscaping was just as charming, with lush lawns, a profusion of flowers, brick walkways and stone benches. And, of course, a fountain in the back. There was also a charming rose arbor where a bride and groom could exchange vows during a summer wedding.

"Wow," Anne breathed. She could so easily envision Laney and Drake standing under that arbor.

"Wow is right," Kendra said.

The inside of the house was as beautiful as the outside, all graceful furniture and chandeliers, and in the front hall a staircase with an elegantly carved banister that was perfect for a bride to come down. Gilded mirrors, vases filled with flowers—the owners knew what they were doing.

Anne clicked on the About Us button.

Roberta Gilbert has been hosting weddings at Primrose Haus for thirty years, but she never gets tired of opening her home to couples embarking on life's greatest adventure. Let her and her talented staff make your special day one to remember.

"I can see why my client wanted to use this place," Anne said.

"It makes me want to get married all over again," Kendra said with a sigh.

"Me, too. Want to go to Icicle Falls with me and check it out?"

"You bet. But only if we can stop at Sweet Dreams

Chocolates while we're up there. I mean, you can't visit Icicle Falls and not go to the chocolate factory."

"Gee, twist my arm," Anne said as she punched the number for Primrose Haus into her phone. A town with its own source of chocolate… What was not to like about that?

The little town had more going for it than chocolate. She and Cam had gone there years ago for the Christmas tree-lighting ceremony and been swept away by the Bavarian charm of the place. Everything from the European facades on the buildings to the overflowing flower boxes hanging from their windows said quaint Alpine village. They'd gone a couple of times when Laney was small, had even talked about taking up cross-country skiing, but then life got busy and weekends got full. Anne's business took off and Cam started coaching basketball and football. So the Bavarian-style town remained a pleasant memory rather than a destination. As for this wedding venue, somehow she'd missed it completely. Probably because her clients hovered around the greater Seattle area.

She could hardly wait to tour the house. If it was even half as spectacular as it looked in the pictures on the website, it could be a wonderful place for her daughter to get married.

A cheerful voice answered, "Good morning. Primrose Haus. This is Roberta."

Anne introduced herself and explained why she was calling.

"We often have people come over from Seattle," Roberta said. "And yes, I'd love to meet you if you'd care to visit on a weekday. I'm afraid our weekends are pretty busy around here."

Anne could imagine. The place was almost completely booked, except that she'd seen an opening for the last Saturday in June.

She and Roberta chatted a little longer, then set a date for the following Tuesday.

"Let's spend the night," Kendra suggested. "I just found a website for the Icicle Creek Lodge and it looks gorgeous."

"Great idea," Anne said. Girl-time with her sister, chocolate, a pretty place to stay… After the week she had ahead of her, a getaway sounded good.

It turned out to be the week from hell. One bride was unhappy with the job the photographer had done on her wedding and wanted a refund. Another decided she couldn't afford Anne and fired her. A mother of the bride called to scold Anne for not checking out all possible options for a florist. Momzilla Dearest had found one that was half the price of the florist Anne was recommending. Anne knew the florist in question and had rejected her because she wouldn't be a fit for the bride's vision. Still, Anne apologized and promised to get an estimate. The next day she learned that the vendor she rented linens from had gone out of business, leaving her scrambling for table linens for Saturday's wedding.

Saturday was the final stressor. Two dozen extra guests showed up, which meant she and the caterer needed to reportion the food. She was busy helping with this when Cressa, one of the caterer's assistants, came running up to her. "There's a table on fire!"

Sure enough. On the lower level of the tour boat where the wedding was being held, amid a sea of tables covered with white linen and set with candles and peach-colored floral arrangements, one table was a floating flambé. A very large flambé, shooting up flames three feet high. With visions of the entire boat catching fire, Anne grabbed the fire extinguisher she always brought along and dashed from the galley to the burning table, Cressa following behind.

Cheers from the upper deck where the ceremony was taking place told her the bride and groom were about to come down the aisle. All the bride needed was to see her reception area looking like a giant hot-dog roast.

At the table Anne fumbled with the extinguisher, misaimed and got a window, making Cressa squeal as if she'd just caught fire. "You missed," she informed Anne.

"I noticed." Anne tried again and this time hit her target, spraying goo all over the table.

"Yuck," Cressa said, frowning at the mess.

"What happened here?" Anne asked, setting down the extinguisher.

Cressa shrugged. "I dunno."

Anne surveyed the scene, getting in touch with her inner fire marshal. Her best guess was that a rose petal had fallen into the flame and then ignited one of the place cards.

She could hear people visiting up above. Any minute the guests would be wandering down in search of food. *(Please let there be enough.)*

She began pulling off plates, stacking them in her arms, covering her blouse with goo. Thank God she always brought along a change of clothes.

"Let's get this table cleared," she said to Cressa, who was still standing there, staring at the mess.

"What about the flowers?" Cressa asked, gathering up silverware.

The flowers were now decorated with fire-extinguisher glop. "I'll find something," Anne said and hoped she was right.

Five minutes later the table had a new cloth, and a few roses, stolen from the vases on other tables, were artfully laid around a fresh candle. Anne was sweating like a pig and her heart rate was through the roof. Oh, that was fun.

The guests never knew. With the bar open, everyone was happy. Meanwhile, Anne continued to run around behind the scenes, making sure the evening went smoothly, that the DJ didn't start the music until the plates had been cleared and that the photographer (who, it turned out, had a problem with motion sickness) was on hand to catch the bride and groom eating their cake.

This was worth all the headaches, all the stress, she thought as she watched the happy couple feed each other cupcakes. A wedding was more than a party. It was an event, a lifetime memory in the making, an important marker for the beginning of a new adventure.

Did her daughter understand that? Sometimes Anne wasn't so sure.

She said as much to her sister as they made their way up the mountains to Icicle Falls on Tuesday.

"It'll work out," Kendra assured her, "whatever Laney decides to do. And hey, I've seen the pictures on the Treasure Island website. Those wedding chapels are really elegant, and I think the ship sounds like fun."

"Oh, yeah," Anne said in disgust. "Maybe we can get Captain Jack Sparrow to officiate." She realized she had the SUV's steering wheel in a stranglehold and forced herself to loosen her grip.

"It beats being a zombie."

"Barely."

"What would you do if someone came to us and wanted a zombie wedding?"

Anne shot an appalled glance in her sister's direction before returning her attention to the snow-trimmed mountain road. "You have to ask? I'd tell them I'm not the wedding planner for them."

"I don't know. Planning a zombie wedding could be interesting."

"Good. Then when Coral and Amy are old enough you guys can have one."

"The zombie apocalypse will be over by then," Kendra said. "Anyway, you've done a lot of unusual weddings."

"Unusual, yes. Gross and tacky, no."

"One woman's gross and tacky is another one's fun and clever. Remember the wedding at Wild Waves?"

"That was a picnic, and the wedding itself was cute." Well, until the bride got sick on the roller coaster.

"Zombies can be cute," Kendra teased.

Anne groaned. "If Laney does that I'm going to disown her."

"I doubt it'll come to that, but you'd better resign yourself. Your daughter is an artiste and she's going to want to do something different."

"I can live with different," Anne insisted. "I just want her to think this through, that's all."

"She will. Everything's going to be fine."

Anne sighed. "I hope so."

The road leveled out and twenty minutes later the sisters were pulling into the town of Icicle Falls. There was a fresh dusting of snow on the main street and all the shops were thickly frosted. The mountains rose up behind, studded with evergreens. There was something restful and calming about this view, Anne thought. Now that they were empty nesters, she and Cam needed to invest in some cross-country ski equipment and come up here.

"It looks like the inside of a snow globe," Kendra

said. "Oh, there's a place that sells lace. And one that sells antiques. We have to get in some serious shopping this afternoon."

"Agreed," said Anne. "When can we check into the lodge?"

"Not until three."

"Well, we'll just have to kill time buying chocolate."

"Gee, what a shame."

But first they had an appointment with Roberta Gilbert at Primrose Haus.

Their GPS took them from the downtown area to a small street lined with older homes, all beautifully maintained. "This is it." Kendra pointed at the sign. "Primrose Street."

"I wonder if everyone has primroses in their flower beds," Anne said. It was hard to tell what anyone had right now, since the lawns were buried under a couple of feet of snow. She knew Primrose Haus had them because she'd seen them in the flower beds in one of the pictures on the website.

"There's the house," Kendra said.

Even under a blanket of snow, it was charming, and Anne felt herself overcome with house lust. "What would it be like to live here?" A quaint house in a charming little town…

"It would be work. Old houses always are," said her sister, the happy new-construction owner. "Remember all the money you guys poured into your place?"

"Think of the value," Anne retorted.

Kendra acknowledged that with a nod. "You lucked out. Finding a house on Queen Anne for under a million these days is next to impossible. If you ever sell it you'll make a fortune."

"We'll probably be there until we're old and gray,"

Anne said, getting out of the SUV. That was fine with her. She loved their Queen Anne house, enjoyed the neighbors, liked being near her family.

But then Roberta Gilbert opened the front door and they stepped inside and the house lust was back. This place was so…romantic.

"Your house is lovely," Anne gushed once Roberta had settled them in a front parlor where a fire blazed in a marble-trimmed fireplace.

"I'm fond of it," Roberta said. She was an attractive older woman, slender with short, gray hair and pretty brown eyes. Like her house, Roberta was a class act, dressed in black slacks and a pale blue cashmere sweater accessorized with a pearl necklace and matching earrings. She'd brought in a tray with teacups and a pot of tea and the proper accoutrements, as well as a small plate of cookies.

Kendra picked one up and took a bite. "Oh, my gosh. This is absolute bliss."

"Lavender cookies," Roberta said. "They come from the tearoom here in town and I must confess I have a weakness for them. We also have a bakery that specializes in gingerbread cookies. Cass, the owner, makes lovely wedding cakes."

"Do you have a florist in town, too?" Anne asked. They probably did. She'd seen some of the wedding pictures on the Primrose Haus website, and the floral arrangements were exquisite.

"Oh, yes. Lupine Floral does a wonderful job," Roberta said and then went on to tell them about the various vendors she used for weddings. The women discussed prices and exchanged wedding tales, and after an hour Anne felt she'd made a new friend.

"Would you like to tour the house?" Roberta asked.

"Absolutely," Anne replied. Looking at all the beautifully furnished rooms took her from lust to love. "This is such a great venue," she told Roberta as they walked back to the parlor.

"Thank you," Roberta said. "I enjoy hosting weddings here, although I have to admit it's beginning to feel more like work than it did ten years ago."

"I can imagine," said Kendra. "Keeping this place up looks like a lot of work."

"We manage."

"Do you ever do other events, like birthdays or anniversaries?" Kendra asked.

Roberta shook her head. "Rarely. We're too busy with weddings."

"I'd like to book this for my bride and bring her and her mother up to check it out next week if that's possible," Anne said to Roberta.

"Of course."

"And I see you have the last Saturday in June open. I wonder if I could give you a deposit to hold that for me. My daughter just got engaged. I really want her to see this place."

"Beats a pirate ship," Kendra joked.

Roberta was obviously too polite to comment, but she did cock an eyebrow.

"Right now we're exploring a number of ideas," Anne explained.

Roberta nodded. "Brides these days have some unique ones."

True, but if you asked Anne, unique wasn't always good.

"That could be the perfect place for Laney to get married," she told her sister as they drove away.

"It *is* great," Kendra agreed. She brought up Trip-

Advisor on her cell phone and pulled up the information on Icicle Falls. "Looks like there's lots to do there."

"Let's go by the chamber of commerce and pick up some brochures to take back," Anne suggested.

Maybe they could find some *unique* experience for Laney, like getting married in a mountain meadow. Then they could have the reception at the pretty house on Primrose Street.

Compromise. Life was all about compromise. So were weddings, and Anne was sure that here in Icicle Falls she and her daughter would come up with just the right one.

Chapter Four

Laney, the Bride-to-Be

She and Drake were getting married! Sometimes Laney could hardly believe it, even though they'd known each other, like, forever. They'd shared the same circle of friends since middle school, been in the same church youth group, taken the same classes. Funny how she'd thought he was such a goofball and no one she'd ever end up with. She was always crushing on guys who played in rock bands or high school sports heroes with their beefed-up muscles who swaggered down the hall on their way to class.

In middle school Drake had been skinny with a colony of zits on his face, and his highest ambition was to beat the video game "Halo." In high school his ambitions changed and he'd turned out for football. He was still skinny and spent most of his time warming the bench, and Laney had teased him about that. (Gosh, she'd been mean!) But he'd persisted, and as high school went on, he began to change from a scrawny goof to something a lot more interesting. She found herself stealing glances at him in English class; he was usually tapping his pencil or sneaking looks at his cell phone, bored out of his mind.

"I don't care about Shakespeare," he'd complained once when a bunch of them had gone to Dairy Queen for Blizzards. "I'd rather work a math problem or do stuff on my car."

"Everybody should read Shakespeare," Laney had argued.

"Why? Who understands that shit? It isn't even English."

"It is, too," she'd said, rolling her eyes. "It's early modern English."

"Well, they need to update it."

"Mrs. Krepps says you shouldn't try to update Shakespeare," Laney had told him. "You lose the beauty of the language."

"Bullshit," Drake had said, showing what he thought of their high school English teacher's opinion. "They have modern translations of the Bible. Shakespeare's not more important than the Bible."

Laney hadn't been able to find a good comeback for that. She'd had to settle for "You're such a loser."

That Christmas she'd given him an edition of *Romeo and Juliet* that put Shakespeare's language side by side with a translation into modern English. She'd given it to him as a joke, but to her surprise he'd actually read it.

"Not bad" had been his assessment. Then he went back to Dean Koontz and Stephen King on audiobooks when he tinkered with the old muscle car he'd found on Craigslist.

She couldn't give him too hard a time about that because, when it came right down to it, she wasn't that crazy about Shakespeare herself.

Come senior year, he finally made first string on the football team and became one of the guys who swaggered down the hall on his way to class. He barely passed English, but he aced his math and science classes.

He'd been happy when Laney was accepted at the University of Washington but equally happy that he was going to train to be an auto technician. "I don't want to sit in an office all day or make kids read Shakespeare. I want to do something hands-on," he'd said.

That had triggered a vision of him doing something hands-on with her. Yes, things had changed since middle school. The more Drake talked about what he wanted to do with his life, the more she wanted to share that life with him. Traveling, mountain climbing, kayaking in Puget Sound, visiting cities like San Antonio and New York and LA. He'd been to Disneyland when he was little. Now he wanted to go back and get his picture taken with Donald Duck. He wanted to go to Vegas and play craps and see Criss Angel. He wanted to volunteer with Habitat for Humanity, maybe go to Mexico and build houses for the poor. With his goofy smile, big heart and sense of adventure, Drake was special and Laney didn't want to see him fall for another girl. She wanted him to fall for *her*.

When he started talking about taking some new girl he'd met at the beach to the Fourth of July fireworks at Green Lake, Laney had gotten pissy, told him he had no taste in women.

"I don't know. She's pretty hot," he'd said.

"So am I. Why don't you take me to watch the fireworks?"

He'd looked at her oddly and said, "Yeah, why don't I?"

They had their first kiss on the Fourth of July as the fireworks exploded over the lake, and that was it. She knew, she just knew.

And now they were getting married. Squeee!

She'd been dreaming about her wedding day since she was a little girl. In fact, growing up, she'd been sort of a wedding addict. Her mom had hooked her the first time she brought Laney home a slice of wedding cake. She could still picture that piece of cake with its pink-frosting rose and small silver dragées, could still remember licking the frosting off her fingers. Mom subscribed to *Brides* magazine, and Laney had never gotten tired of looking at the pictures of all those models showing off gorgeous gowns. Every wedding movie she'd watched had sold her on the big "I do." She used to imagine herself getting married in some old English castle with glittering chandeliers, saying "I do" to a guy who looked like Prince Charming. As she got older, Prince Charming began to look suspiciously like Zac Efron or Orlando Bloom. Now, of course, Prince Charming looked exactly like Drake.

She had to celebrate. So on Wednesday, Drake's night for gaming with the guys, she invited her friends over for a girl party.

The revelers consisted of her longtime bestie, Autumn, who was actually always "over" since she and Laney shared a funky house in Fremont; Laney's friend from college, Ella; and Drake's younger sister, Darcy.

She'd just put out the fondue when Darcy arrived, bearing a gigantic bag of corn chips. "I'm so excited," she squealed, hugging Laney. "I finally get a sister."

"Me, too," Laney said, hugging her back. Her life growing up as an only child had been great, but she'd always wanted a sister. Now she had one.

Her friend Ella was next. "I'm so jealous," she said. "At the rate we're going, I won't be engaged until I'm fifty."

"I'm not getting married till I'm thirty. I've still got

things I want to do on my own," Autumn said as she took the salsa out of the fridge.

"What do you want to do on your own that you can't do with Ben?" Ella scoffed.

"Live in Paris for a year, study fashion design."

"You could do that with Ben," Ella pointed out.

"I can't flirt with Frenchmen when I'm with Ben," Autumn said with a grin.

Ella rolled her eyes and flopped down on the fake-leather couch Laney had bought at a garage sale. "So spill," she said to Laney. "How did Drake propose?"

"He took me to the Space Needle. I had a feeling he was going to propose."

"How'd you know?" asked Darcy. "He didn't even tell *me*."

"'Cause he was acting all nervous. He was checking his pocket every five minutes, like there was something in there he didn't want to lose, and when we were at our table he kept fooling with the silverware and drinking water."

"That's so cute," Ella said dreamily. "So did he get down on one knee and everything?"

Laney nodded. "Yep, just before dessert."

"And you said yes right away," Darcy prompted.

"You should've made him sweat," Autumn said and took a sip of her pop.

Darcy frowned at her. "That's mean."

"No, that's psychology," Autumn argued. "Make 'em sweat. That way they really appreciate it when you say yes."

"I still think it's mean," Darcy muttered.

"Have you set a date?" Ella asked Laney.

"We don't have the exact date yet, but we're talking about June."

Ella's eyebrows shot up. "Wow, that doesn't give you much time to plan the wedding."

"It's plenty of time, especially if we go to Vegas."

"Ooh, baby," said Autumn. "Slots and shopping and glitzy pools and big, huge fancy drinks."

"And hookers." Ella wrinkled her nose.

"Don't worry. Nobody's gonna proposition your man," Autumn said, and Ella stuck her tongue out at her.

"It's not for sure yet," Laney told them. "We might get married here."

Her mom had made a good case for that—a big guest list, catered dinner, getting married by Pastor Ostrom, who had watched her grow up. He was going to retire at the end of the year. She'd probably be the sweet old guy's last wedding.

But Vegas sounded like fun, too. She and Drake had already looked at the Treasure Island website. The packages weren't cheap, but were definitely cheaper than what they'd pay if they stuck around Seattle to get married. And she loved the idea of being down there in the center of all that excitement.

"Let's check out Vegas," Autumn said, grabbing her phone.

The images for Vegas weddings were all impressive. Her mother had thought a Vegas chapel would be tacky. Mom must have been thinking about the old days, because what Laney and her friends were seeing was totally glam.

"Drake thinks Vegas would be really cool," said Darcy. She frowned. "But I'm not twenty-one yet. I can't drink. At least if you end up getting married here, somebody will let me have a glass of champagne."

"Well, *there's* a reason not to go to Vegas," Autumn

cracked. "What do you want to do most?" she asked Laney.

A series of images flashed across Laney's mind—the royal wedding with all its pomp and splendor, the church weddings she'd attended growing up, images from the many websites she'd peered at over her mother's shoulder when Mom was working. Everything felt so wide-open she almost didn't know what to choose. But then she looked at those pictures on the Treasure Island site and smiled. "I want to go to Vegas."

Except Mom had called the other day to tell her about a place she'd found that would be perfect for the wedding. How the heck was she going to get out of that?

Chapter Five

Anne, Woman with a Plan

On Thursday Laurel Browne dropped by the office with her Pekingese, Rufus, cuddled in her arms. Anne had heard it said that owners and their dogs often resembled each other. Looking at Laurel and Rufus, she could believe it. Both had snub noses and blond highlights. And both wore a permanent scowl.

"Rufus and I were on our way to the groomer and thought we'd stop by," Laurel explained. "Didn't we, Rufus baby?"

Oh, goody. "Isn't he a handsome dog," Anne lied. "Hi, Rufus."

"Grrr," Rufus replied, showing her his teeth, and not in a sweet *Look, Mom, I floss every day* kind of way.

"I found some pictures on the internet of yellow floral arrangements," Laurel went on, holding up her finds.

Some? The sheaf of papers was the size of *War and Peace.* "Uh, thank you," Anne said. She could just imagine what Kate over at In Bloom would say when she saw this.

Anne reached to take it and Rufus snarled and snapped

at her. She yanked back her hand. Yikes! Were all her fingers still attached?

"Rufus, behave," scolded Laurel. "I'm afraid he doesn't like going to the groomer."

Or else, like his mommy, Rufus didn't like wedding planners.

"I'll put them here on the desk," Laurel said.

"Thank you." Anne hoped her smile looked sincere. She thought they'd settled the flower issue. Obviously, they hadn't. "I'll pass these on to Kate. And maybe next week you and Chelsea could come and see a few table settings," she said, raising her voice to be heard over Rufus, who was conveying his displeasure at being deprived of a finger sandwich by barking at her.

"Rufus baby, stop now," Laurel cooed. "That will be fine." No cooing for Anne. "We need to get this settled."

"Great," Anne said, pretending she and Laurel and Rufus were all BFFs. "I know we'll find something you and Chelsea are both going to love."

"With what I'm paying you, I hope so."

That again. "It's not nearly enough to cover the pain and suffering," Anne said as soon as the door shut behind Laurel. "And what's with that dog?"

"Little dogs can get aggressive when they feel cornered," said Kendra, who owned a Norwich terrier.

"Cornered? I'm the one who nearly lost a finger."

"She should've put the dog on the floor."

"So he could bite my ankle?"

"So he wouldn't feel threatened." Kendra shook her head. "You're such an animal-hater. The dog probably sensed it."

"I am not an animal-hater," Anne insisted. "Just because I prefer cats."

"You haven't had a cat in years."

It was true. After Pansy died she'd been too broken-hearted to even think about getting another pet. "I already have Cam, and one animal is enough," Anne said, making her sister snicker. "I need a caffeine fix. Want a mocha?"

"Sure, if you're buying."

"It's your turn but okay," Anne said, playing the martyr.

It didn't work. Her sister grinned and said, "Great. I'll take a large."

So off Anne went to the coffee shop on Queen Anne Avenue, where her daughter worked as a barista. It was midmorning and the place was humming with caffeinated drinkers and people waiting to get their hit. The smell of roasted coffee practically made Anne's taste buds spring a leak.

"Hi, Mrs. Richardson," her daughter's friend and roommate said.

"Hi, Autumn. I'll have my usual white chocolate latte and a large…"

"Coconut mocha," supplied Autumn with a grin.

"You guessed it," Anne said and dropped a dollar in the tip jar.

"Hi, Mom," her daughter called from her station at the espresso maker.

Under her bright red apron she wore a short-sleeved shirt to show off the mermaid swimming up her arm past seashells and starfish. Anne preferred it when her daughter wore long-sleeved tops. That way she didn't have to be reminded of the mermaid's existence. Laney loved mermaids and had designed the tattoo herself. Anne loved mermaids, too, as long as they stayed in movies, where they belonged.

It's her life, Anne had told herself when Laney got

her second tattoo, this one on her neck. A climbing rose. Like Laney herself, her tattoos were all about motion.

"It's your favorite flower," Laney had said. "Your favorite flower and your favorite daughter all rolled into one." Daughters—they were such a blessing. And such a source of irritation.

In spite of the tattoo irritation, Anne was proud of Laney. She had a nice guy, a college degree (something Anne had never gotten) and would soon be working on her teaching certificate so she could become an art teacher while she honed her silversmithing skills. She didn't do drugs or post naughty pictures of herself on the internet, and she was gainfully employed. She was creative and beautiful, and Anne loved her like crazy. She'd probably never love the tattoos, though.

Laney set out two to-go cups. "One small Americano and one double tall soy latte, no whip."

The two women who'd been waiting snagged their drinks and moved to a corner table.

Anne was next in line. She leaned over the counter. "So what did you decide about going up to Icicle Falls this weekend and checking out that place I told you about?"

Laney concentrated on putting a stainless-steel pitcher of milk under the steam wand, and for a moment all Anne heard was *whoosh*. Someone at a nearby table laughed.

"Hello?" Anne prompted.

"I've got that craft fair coming up. I've still got to make stuff for that."

"The fair isn't until Memorial Day weekend," Anne pointed out. "We need to get this venue nailed down. We don't have much time to plan your wedding."

"I know, but I think we want to go to Vegas. That won't take long to plan."

"You shouldn't make a snap decision until you've considered a bit more," Anne advised.

Laney shrugged and said, "I guess," a sure sign that she was underwhelmed by the idea of getting married in Icicle Falls.

"We can go up for a girls' weekend with Aunt Kendra and Grammy. What happens in Icicle Falls stays in Icicle Falls."

That made Laney giggle. "Mom, you crack me up."

"We can be wild."

"Where? There?" Laney set out the drinks.

"Let's at least go see it." They hadn't been to Icicle Falls since Laney was a little girl and she'd obviously forgotten what a special town it was. Once she saw the place, Anne knew she'd be on board. Laney and Drake liked to do outdoor things, and according to the brochure she'd picked up, there was plenty of that—hiking, river rafting, rock climbing. Laney just had to catch the vision. Then she'd be all over this.

"Okay."

It wasn't the most enthusiastic *okay* Anne had ever heard, but she'd take it. "I'll make reservations. It'll be fun. And this will give you another option to explore. Remember, your wedding's a big deal and you don't want to do something you'll regret later."

Laney gave her a you-might-be-right kind of nod, and since more customers were waiting for their drinks, that was the end of the lecture. Anne left the shop, feeling that they were getting somewhere.

"I don't know why you're trying so hard," her husband said over dinner that night.

Of course he didn't. She'd rarely complained about

their wedding. But even though she'd been a sport about it, she'd always wished she'd been able to have the wedding of her dreams, something that reflected the beauty of their love and the seriousness of their commitment. Not that what they'd opted for was bad; it was just… less. Could it have played out differently at the time?

No, she reminded herself as she relived that pivotal conversation and what followed.

1990

Anne and Cam sat in his souped-up truck outside her house in the late summer night with Michael Bolton on the radio asking, "How Am I Supposed to Live Without You?" Good question.

"I wish you'd never joined the army," Anne said, her voice as bitter as her tears.

"Come on, babe. You know we had a plan. This will pay for my college."

"If you live to go to college. If you come back." How was she supposed to tell him her news in light of this?

He reached out a hand and played with her hair. "Of course I'll come back, and then we'll get married just like we planned."

And by then… "I'm pregnant," she blurted.

His hand froze. "You're…pregnant? How could that be? We used protection."

"Well, I guess it wasn't very good protection," she snapped. "And now you're leaving for the Middle East."

"That wasn't exactly my idea," he said. "But…hey, a kid. This is cool."

"This is *not* cool," she informed him. He was going away. She'd be left on her own to deal with everything. They'd planned to have a big church wedding when he got out of the army. She'd work while he went back to school, and after he got his degree, she'd finish up hers. Then they'd have their two kids and a dog and a little house somewhere in the burbs and life would be perfect. Now nothing was perfect. "We should've waited."

"Are you serious? Babe, I've been taking cold showers since I was seventeen."

If she'd known this was going to happen, she would've kept sending him to the shower. Now look at the mess they were in. What would her youth pastor say? Never mind him. What would her mother say?

"We'd better get married."

"I don't have time to plan a wedding before you get shipped off to the Gulf." Everyone knew it took months to plan a wedding. She didn't even have a ring yet. Why did he have to go away? Why did this stupid war have to break out?

He stared out the window. There was nothing much to see on Tenth Avenue except tree-lined street and modest Queen Anne houses with their porch lights on. Then he began to tap his fingers on the steering wheel.

"We can go to the courthouse," he finally said.

"The courthouse?" Get married at the courthouse? That would be her big wedding?

He turned to look at her again, his face earnest. "I love you, Annie, and I want to spend the rest of my life with you. Let's make it official before I ship out. It doesn't matter where we get married just as long as we do. Right?"

Well, of course, that was the most important thing. But ever since she was seventeen, writing *Mrs. Cameron Richardson* in her high school notebooks, she'd dreamed of a traditional wedding with all the trimmings: the gown, the flowers, the church, the big reception afterward. Now reality was closing the door on that vision. She was pregnant; he was going off to the deserts of the Middle East, where who knew what would happen to him. They had to be practical.

She nodded but she couldn't talk. There was suddenly a boulder stuck in her throat.

Cam pulled her close and touched his forehead to hers. "Hey, I know this isn't what you wanted," he said softly.

She swallowed hard, forcing the boulder down. "I want to be with you," she told him. "That's what I want." If he didn't come back—horrible thought!—the only time they'd have together was right now. Was she really willing to give that up for a flower-filled church and a bunch of bridesmaids? Anyway, she wanted to start motherhood with a husband in the picture, even if that picture was of Daddy somewhere in a desert.

"Let's do it, then," he said. "Let's go downtown first thing Monday and get the license. Then we can get married next Friday."

She'd be with Cam. She'd be Mrs. Cameron Richardson. They wouldn't have much time before he left but it would be better than nothing.

"What do you say, Annie?" he prompted.

"I say yes!" She'd be crazy to say anything else.

"All right!" he crowed. And then he gave her a kiss that made her toes curl in her jelly shoes. Who needed a fancy wedding, anyway?

Not me, Anne told herself.

Not me, she reminded herself on Friday afternoon at four thirty as she entered the big, impersonal Seattle municipal courthouse wearing a white satin sheath and a small diamond ring, carrying a bouquet of red roses. She was flanked by her parents, her father smiling gamely, her mother smiling, too, although her smile didn't quite reach her eyes. Kendra trailed behind, the clueless younger sister, excited by the whole adventure.

And there, waiting for her, was Cam with his parents. His eyes lit up at the sight of her and he hurried over and kissed her. "You look incredible."

"You look beautiful, dear," his mother added and kissed her on the cheek before greeting Anne's mother. If she wasn't happy about the rush-job wedding, she didn't betray it.

"Well," said Dad, "let's get this show on the road, shall we?"

"Good idea," Cam said, smiling at Anne. He offered her his arm. She took it and they started down the hallway.

They made their way to the room reserved for weddings, passing lawyers busy conferring with their clients— sketchy guys in dirty jeans or angry women with naked ring fingers, probably in the process of getting divorced. This was her wedding march. No church filled with well-wishers, no big wedding reception after the ceremony, just a dinner at her parents' house with the two families and the small cake her neighbor Mrs. Hornsby had insisted on making for them. It was the world's ugliest cake, slightly lopsided ("I had a little trouble assembling it," Mrs. H. had confessed) with neon pink rosebuds that you needed sunglasses to look at and bride and groom toppers that must've been around since the fifties. But hey, it was a wedding cake.

An angry guy gave a man in a suit the finger and slouched away, knocking into Anne as he passed and telling her to watch where the hell she was going. It was all so different from what she'd dreamed of. *You're marrying Cam. That's what matters.* So why were tears springing to her eyes?

He looked at her with concern. "Are you okay?"

She nodded. "I'm just so happy."

And she had been all these years. Still, she'd always regretted the fact that she and Cam had taken their vows in such a sterile environment.

Laney could afford to wait and do things right, and somehow, Anne had to get through to her. When it came to her wedding, a woman shouldn't settle, even if her groom wanted to be a pirate.

Laney was going to have no regrets. Anne would see to it.

Chapter Six

Roberta, Woman of Mystery

"Nice write-up in the paper," Dot Morrison said when she stopped by Roberta and Daphne's table at Pancake Haus to say hi.

"Thank you," Roberta said, lining up the salt and pepper shakers. It *had* been a nice write-up, and sweet of Muriel to think of her.

"When are they going to do one on you?" Daphne asked.

"Next week," Dot said. "Looks like they're writing up all us old-timers first."

Old-timer. Sometimes it seemed like only yesterday that Roberta had arrived in town. Back then, Icicle Falls had been transforming itself from a struggling town on the verge of extinction to an Alpine village. The place was so full of hope you could almost taste it. Roberta had, and that was why she'd decided to settle here. She'd needed a good dose of hope. And a job.

She'd gone into this very restaurant when she hit town. Back then, before Dot had come to Icicle Falls and taken over the place, it had been nothing more than a greasy spoon catering to truckers and travelers crossing the pass, but to her it had felt like an oasis.

1961

Roberta got off the bus in front of the café and went inside. Summer was coming early to the mountain town of Icicle Falls and it was a relief to get inside and escape the heat. She ordered a cup of coffee that tasted like battery acid and a fried egg that upset her stomach, still delicate so early in her pregnancy. The toast that came with it, once she'd scraped off the burned part, helped with the queasiness.

"Honey, you look done in," said her waitress. The woman appeared to be the same age as Roberta's mother. Her hair was what Mother would have labeled "bottle blond," and the wrinkles around her mouth, along with the faint whiff of smoke coming off her, proclaimed her a smoker.

"I'm a little tired," Roberta admitted.

"We got a motel on the other side of town," said the waitress. "Nothing to write home about but it's clean."

Roberta couldn't afford a motel. She nodded and thanked the woman anyway.

"Course, pretty soon we'll have more going up, fancy ones like you'd see in Switzerland or Germany. This town is making some big changes. This time next year, it'll really look like something." She proceeded to tell Roberta all the plans in the works for putting Icicle Falls on the map. "My husband, Fred, and me, we're saving up to build ourselves a hamburger place. To pass on to the kids, you know?"

Roberta had nothing to pass on to her child.

No, she corrected herself. She had love. This baby would be well loved and well cared for.

If she could find a job.

And a place to stay. But her money supply was dwindling and she couldn't spend it on motel rooms. "Is there anyone in town who takes in boarders?" she asked.

Before the waitress could answer, someone new walked in, a pretty woman with brown hair wearing a white blouse and pedal pushers. She had an equally pretty little daughter with chestnut curls. The daughter stared at Roberta curiously as they approached the table.

She supposed she'd stare at herself, too, and wonder what someone her age was doing, traveling all alone. Soon she'd be showing, and with no wedding ring people would really stare. They'd do more than stare if they knew she was only seventeen. Well, she'd be eighteen in two months. Then she'd be an adult and no one could force her to do anything. She tried not to think about what a lonely birthday it would be.

"Hi, Flo," said the woman.

"Hi, Betty," the waitress said. "How's the cleanup going?"

"Great. The men have hauled those dead cars and car parts off for old Billy. And that's the last eyesore gone."

The waitress nodded approvingly. Then, remembering Roberta, said, "This young lady's looking for a place to stay. Do you know of anything?"

"Sarah Shepherd's taking in boarders," the newcomer named Betty replied. She turned to Roberta and introduced herself. "And this is my daughter, Muriel."

"Hi, Muriel." Roberta smiled and Muriel said a polite hello in return.

"So you're new in town?" Betty asked.

Roberta nodded.

"Where you from, dear?" asked Flo the waitress.

"California," Roberta lied.

Flo let out a low whistle. "You're a ways from home."

"I needed to make a new start," Roberta said. That was no lie. "I'm a widow."

"A widow," echoed Flo. "And you so young!"

"My husband was killed in a car accident."

"Oh, how sad," Betty said. "I'm very sorry."

Roberta murmured her thanks. "This seems to be a nice town," she ventured.

"You could do a lot worse than settle here," Flo told her.

"Hey, Flo," called a husky man seated a couple of tables down. "Are you gonna take my order or leave me here to starve?"

"You could live off that fat belly of yours for days, Hal," Flo retorted. She rolled her eyes. "Guess I'd better go take his order," she said and left.

"Mind if I join you?" Betty asked. Before Roberta could answer, she slid into the bench on the other side of the booth, her daughter following suit. "When did you lose your husband?"

"It's been…a while." Roberta could feel her cheeks warming. How many questions was this woman going to ask?

"I can't imagine losing a husband at such a young age," Betty said, shaking her head. "I hope he left you well provided for?"

"I'm afraid not," Roberta said. "We hadn't been married very long," she improvised. They hadn't been married at all, but that wasn't something she was going to share with a stranger. It wasn't something she was going to share with *anyone*. Ever.

"Do you know if anyone in town is hiring?" she hurried on. If no one was, there was no point in staying. She'd have to keep moving on. Where, she wasn't sure. When she'd first hit the road, all she'd wanted to do was put as much distance between herself and Seattle as she could. Now she realized she should have planned more carefully.

Except there hadn't been time to plan.

Across the table from her Betty was looking sympathetic. "I hear they need a teller over at the bank. My husband and the manager are friends. I'd be happy to put in a word for you."

"But you don't know me." For all this woman knew, Roberta could be a con artist. In a way she was.

"I'm pretty good at sizing people up. You seem like an honest young woman."

She was anything but.

"What do you think, Muriel?" Betty asked, smiling at the girl.

"I think she's pretty," Muriel said, then blushed.

"Thank you," Roberta murmured. Being pretty wasn't always an advantage. Sometimes it got a girl in trouble. "I'm a hard worker," she said to Betty. Not that she'd ever had any job besides babysitting. But she'd work hard for whoever hired her.

"I'm sure you are," Betty said kindly. "I tell you what. How about after breakfast I take you down to the bank and introduce you to Howard Mangle, the manager? Then I can show you where the Shepherds live."

The woman's generosity was almost too much. Roberta felt tears flooding her eyes. "You're very kind."

Betty cocked her head and studied Roberta in a way that had her cheeks heating again. "I suspect you're a woman in need of a little kindness right now."

* * *

If Betty had guessed Roberta's real story, she never let on. Instead, she'd taken Roberta under her wing and helped her get settled in town. Roberta had spent many a Sunday at Betty's house, enjoying dinner with her family. Betty and her husband, Joe, had helped Roberta move when, a few years later, she'd found her Victorian. Roberta had watched Muriel grow up and had been a regular customer of Sweet Dreams Chocolates ever since the day she got her job at the bank and splurged on a box of chocolate-covered cherries. She'd met new friends and made something of herself. Staying in Icicle Falls had turned out to be a good decision.

Maybe it would be for Daphne, too. Maybe here Daphne would finally get inspired to do more with her life. Open a shop, live up to her name and become a writer like Daphne du Maurier. Or Muriel. Something. Anything. So far all she'd been inspired to do was mope around the house.

"I hear you're back to stay," Dot said to Daphne.

"I've sure had enough of Seattle," Daphne replied.

"Well, I'm sorry your marriage didn't work out, kiddo," Dot said. "But sometimes a woman is better off on her own. Look how well your mom and I have done."

Daphne heaved a huge sigh. "You're probably right. I don't seem to do very well at picking men."

"It's hard to pick a good one when so many of the ones hanging on the branch are rotten," Dot said.

Daphne pushed back a lock of blond hair. "I suppose there are still some good men out there. I've just never been able to find one."

My poor daughter, Roberta thought. *Where did I go wrong?* Daphne should have been happily married. And successful. But here she was, rejected, dejected and living with her mother.

"Muriel sure knows how to find the good ones," Dot said. "In fact, you should talk to her daughter. Cecily used to be a matchmaker. Maybe she'll have some ideas for you."

"Like how to murder my husband?"

Roberta frowned at her, but Dot chuckled. "Things'll work out. They always do."

"Daphne!" Roberta scolded as Dot moved on to greet her other customers.

"Sorry," Daphne said in an unrepentant voice, "but I really could murder him. Stake him out in the sun covered with honey and let the ants have at him."

"There's an appetizing image," Roberta said in disgust. "Although I must admit, even that's better than he deserves." She'd never say it publicly, but she wouldn't mind getting a chance to put her hands around Mitchell's throat.

"Every time I think of him and that woman I want to…" Daphne crumpled her paper napkin.

Roberta reached across the table and patted her arm. "He didn't deserve you, dear. You're well rid of him."

Daphne's eyes filled with tears. "How could he do this to me?"

Quite easily, it seemed. But since that was obviously a rhetorical question, Roberta kept her answer to herself. She gave her daughter's arm another encouraging pat. "We're not going to waste any more energy talking about him. Instead, we'll focus on you. We need to come up with a plan for what you're going to do next. You can't just mope around the house all day."

"I don't want to mope. Let me help with the next wedding."

"There's really nothing left to do," Roberta said. "Everything's under control."

Daphne looked at her, reproach in her eyes. "You don't want me to help."

Yes, that was part of it.

"You should let me," Daphne urged. "You may as well plug me in now. You've got bunion surgery coming up in May. You'll need the extra help."

She probably would. She'd planned to delegate more work to Lila. "Darling, you're going to be busy with your divorce."

"Not that busy."

"Well, then, you should be busy job-hunting. You don't want to work on weddings, not in your present state of mind."

"I want to help you. I want to be useful."

"You're being useful." Daphne had cleaned the whole house the day before, even transferred her dirty breakfast dishes from the sink to the dishwasher without being nagged.

"I could do more if you'd let me. If you'd believe in me," Daphne added softly.

Was that what Daphne thought? That she didn't believe in her? If she hadn't believed in her daughter, why would she have wasted her breath all these years suggesting things Daphne could do to improve her life?

"I'm fifty-three and you still don't see me as anything but a failure," Daphne said.

"That's not true." Except it was. Oh, dear.

The waitress arrived to take their orders, ending the conversation for the moment. Roberta found she didn't have much of an appetite. "Coffee, please," she said.

Why did everything have to be so difficult between mothers and daughters? Or was it just her and Daphne?

Maybe it *was* just her. She was always encouraging Daphne to try more, do more, be more, but whenever Daphne offered to help with the business, Roberta put her off.

Daphne wanted Roberta to be proud of her, possibly even more than Roberta did. She needed to give her daughter a chance to earn that pride, something Roberta's mother had never done for her.

"Would you like to assist with setup for the next wedding?" she asked after their waitress left. There was a task Daphne could manage just fine.

"I'd be happy to," Daphne said and smiled.

Roberta smiled, too. It wasn't too late to make some changes. Daphne needed to feel useful, and Roberta could use the extra help. Really, she was a lucky woman to have such a sweet daughter who wanted to be part of her life. This could be a win-win situation.

Or a disaster.

Chapter Seven

Laney, on the Bridal Trail

"What do you want to do this weekend?" Drake asked as he dragged a French fry through his ketchup.

Laney stared out the car window at the row of customers standing in front of Dick's Drive-in in the University district, waiting to order burgers and shakes. "Uh, I have to go to Icicle Falls this weekend."

"Huh?" The look he gave her was both surprised and accusatory.

Suddenly the hamburger she'd been eating didn't taste so good. She should've told him. She'd had all week to tell him. They always hung out on the weekend.

"I'm sorry," she said. "I should've told you."

"Yeah, that would've been nice."

Now he was frowning and she felt like a rotten girlfriend. People who were in love should spend their weekends together. "My mom wants me to go see a house up there that she thinks would be great for us to get married in."

He stuffed a handful of French fries in his mouth and digested that information.

"It can't hurt to look," she went on. "Since we haven't actually decided what we want to do."

"Well, I know what I want to do, and I thought you did, too."

"I do. I did. I don't know." Eloping to Vegas had sounded like fun. She'd never been and was dying to see the fountain at the Bellagio, eat in one of those fancy restaurants and play the slot machines. But then her mom had talked about how important her wedding was and how Laney didn't want to do anything she'd regret and she'd had second thoughts. And Mom kept talking about that place in Icicle Falls, as though it was so special. "I just want to go up there and see. Okay?"

"Sure, but…" He frowned.

"But what?"

"If you're going up to look at a place where we might get married, I should go, too."

He should, but nobody had invited him. Oh, that hamburger really wasn't sitting well. "It's a girls' trip. My aunt and grandma are going, too." As if that was supposed to make him *not* feel left out? "You'd be so bored," Laney added.

Now he was looking out the window and frowning.

"Don't be mad," she said, laying a pleading hand on his thigh. She hated it when he wasn't happy.

"I'm not mad. I'm…" The frown got bigger. "Well, okay, I'm kind of mad."

"I probably won't like the place anyway." But maybe she would. If Mom thought it was such a wonderful place, she needed to at least check it out. After all, Mom was the wedding expert.

He took a deep breath and expelled it, then reached over and gave her the little one-handed neck massage that always made her melt. "It's okay if you do. I want you to be happy."

"Hey, I'm marrying you. How can I not be happy?"

That took away the last of his frown. And the kiss she gave him put a smile back on his face. "We could go to Vegas for our honeymoon," he said. "We were gonna hang around there after we got married anyway."

It seemed like a good compromise. Laney set aside the vision of herself standing on the deck of the wedding ship in Siren's Cove at Treasure Island. If they had a more traditional wedding, they could have a big party with a ton of guests. That would be way better. Not very unusual or interesting, though. Kind of…boring.

She realized she was the one frowning now. A more traditional wedding didn't have to be boring, she told herself. She could give it flair, add her own personal touch. Besides, a wedding with lots of family and friends would be fun and would make her parents happy, especially her mom. Everyone would be happy.

Well, maybe not Drake. Oh, man.

"Would you really mind if we had a more—" *Oops, almost said "boring"*—"traditional wedding?" she asked.

He shrugged. "Hey, it's all about the bride, right?"

But he was disappointed; she could tell. His smile wasn't lighting up his eyes. "It's all about *both* of us."

"I'm cool with whatever you decide," he said.

"No, you're not."

He drew her to him and touched his forehead to hers. "Yeah, I am. So go up to Icicle Falls with your mom and have fun. And send me pics."

Okay, that settled it. Sort of. For now. Part of her still wasn't sure. She reminded herself that she didn't have to say yes to the house in Icicle Falls if she didn't like it.

Although if she didn't, Mom would be disappointed. Grammy, too.

Aunt Kendra, on the other hand, would say, "Do what you want." Only problem was, Laney wasn't sure what she wanted anymore.

That was both atypical and unsettling. Laney always knew what she wanted, and it was often very different from what her mom wanted for her. She still remembered the first time she and her mother had disagreed. She'd wanted to wear her princess jammies to kindergarten, and Mom had insisted on play clothes. She'd whined, cried and finally thrown herself on the floor, refusing to get up. And she'd won a major battle. Sort of. She'd gotten to wear her princess jammies, but she'd done it at home because Mom refused to take her to school. Even in kindergarten her mother hadn't approved of her sense of style.

Some things never changed. First princess jammies, then piercings, then tats. Mom thought she was with it, but she was really kind of a conformist. She didn't like coloring outside the lines. Literally. "Inside the lines, sweetie, like this," she'd said whenever she colored in Laney's coloring book with her. "That's right. A purple cow? Now, how about we make the next one brown?"

Like Dad, she'd worried when Laney decided to major in art that she'd never be able to support herself and had quit worrying only when Laney decided to go back to school in the fall and get a teaching degree. She thought Laney's place in Seattle's free-spirit Fremont district was dumpy and hated the way Laney and Autumn had decorated it. Not that she'd come right out and said so, but Laney could read her mother as easily as a graphic novel. Mom didn't do well with extremes. She had one piercing in each ear and wore the same small diamond earrings almost every day. She dressed conservatively and drove a Volvo because it was supposed to be the safest car on the road.

All of that was okay. For Mom. But Laney was different from her mother, and much as she loved Mom, she had to be true to herself. She'd look at the place in Icicle Falls but she wasn't making any promises.

A good thing she hadn't, she thought when they pulled into town. *This is so not Vegas.* Still, she had to admit it was cute. It was almost as though she'd stepped into another country, with the frescoes painted on the buildings and all the flower boxes under shop windows. Then there was the river running alongside the town. She could see herself and Drake rafting on it. She took a picture with her phone and sent it to him.

Let's go on it, he texted back.

"The river would be perfect for your wedding party to go inner tubing on before the rehearsal," Mom said.

Inspiration hit. "We could even get married on the river, on a raft." She texted Drake. Want to get married on it?

Sure, came the reply.

"It might be hard to get on a river raft in a wedding gown," Grammy said from the backseat.

Did she want a traditional wedding gown? Maybe not. "I could wear shorts and a bikini top. And a bridal veil," Laney added, picturing herself in white shorts and a white bikini top.

"Shorts?" Mom said weakly.

Okay, maybe that wouldn't work, either. "It was a thought." Suddenly she was remembering the princess jammies. "But if we get married on the river..." She needed to keep her options open.

"Let's get checked in and then go buy some chocolate," Aunt Kendra said, pulling them back from the river's edge.

"Great idea," Grammy said.

"I'm all for that," Mom agreed. "How about a trip to Sweet Dreams before we see the house?" she asked Laney.

"Great idea," Laney repeated. They might not see eye to eye on fashion trends; they might not see eye to eye on wedding venues, either. But there was one thing they always agreed on, and that was chocolate.

They all checked into the Icicle Creek Lodge, which, according to Mom, was the best place in town. "They've got a honeymoon suite," Mom said.

If you asked Laney, it looked like a place her grandmother would stay in with its old-fashioned carpeting and the ornate, old European-style furniture. But the beds in the room she was sharing with her mom were comfy with their crisp, white comforters, and the view out the window was killer awesome.

Mom joined her at the window. "It's gorgeous up here, isn't it?"

"Oh, yeah," Laney said.

"And there's a lot to do. Hiking, rock climbing, shopping, inner tubing."

She could get into all of that. Laney nodded.

Mom turned from the view to look at her. "What do you think of the town?"

"It's cute."

"If you don't like it, we can have the wedding in Seattle," Mom said. "But the house really is beautiful."

Laney nodded. It probably was.

"Well," Mom said, "let's go get some chocolate."

They went to the room next door and collected Aunt Kendra and Grammy, then went to the Sweet Dreams gift shop. Oh, yeah. It was worth coming up here just for the salted caramels. Laney bought some to take home to Drake.

Then they were off to check out Primrose Haus.

"This is charming," Grammy said as they parked in front of the pink Victorian.

Yeah, Laney would give it that. She snapped a picture and sent it to Drake.

Once inside, they met the owner, Roberta Gilbert, and her daughter, Daphne, who gave them a tour of the place. Laney could see why her mother had fallen in love with this house. With its fancy mirrors and decorations, it was impressive, almost like a museum.

Could she see herself in here in a long, lacy gown? Not sure, she texted Drake.

Your call, he texted back.

The outdoor space was impressive. It looked like the set of some PBS movie. And the mountains rising in the background were impressive. Maybe they could get married on the river and have the reception here. Laney took a picture with her phone and sent it to Drake with the subject heading This is cool.

Mtns, he texted back. Rock climbing?

Sure, she replied. They could find enough to do here.

Meanwhile, Mom, Grammy and Aunt Kendra were all firing questions at Mrs. Gilbert and her daughter.

"As I mentioned when I talked to you, we have a wonderful florist in town," Mrs. Gilbert was saying to Mom.

"But we can also think outside the box when it comes to decorations," her daughter said. "Like balloons."

Laney smiled. "That sounds fun."

"Weddings *should* be fun," Daphne said with a smile. The smile soured. "Considering what you have to deal with after the wedding's over."

Mrs. Gilbert cleared her throat. "We also have a caterer here in town and an excellent baker."

"Can she make cakes like the ones you see on *Cake Boss*?" Laney asked.

"She can make anything you want."

"Including cakes made of donuts," added Daphne. "That's a new trend we've been seeing."

"I like that." The image of a big tower of donuts made Laney smile. "I'm thinking of actually getting married on the river."

"We have a lovely park there," Mrs. Gilbert said diplomatically.

"And having the reception here," Mom put in.

"We cater to whatever the bride wants," Mrs. Gilbert said. "We'll show you the reception room."

It was certainly bigger than the deck of a pirate ship. Laney looked around, picturing herself dancing there with Drake and their friends. Okay, a wedding on the river, followed by a reception here. They could do that.

"So, what did you think?" Mom asked as they drove away.

"It could work," Laney said.

"I can see you getting married under that rose arbor," Mom said.

There was something in her voice, as though she was talking about what she'd do if she won the lottery. It left Laney biting her lip and looking out the window.

"Or coming down that staircase in a long, white gown," Grammy added dreamily.

"Or princess jammies," teased Aunt Kendra.

"You'll be such a beautiful bride," Mom said, smiling at Laney as if they'd already settled everything.

"I haven't decided on anything yet," Laney said, determined not to get pushed into a snap decision.

"Of course, you need time to think," Mom said.

Yes, she did. Still, Laney felt outnumbered and out-gunned, as if no matter what she said, she was going to end up at the house on Primrose Street in an old-fashioned, lacy gown.

Maybe that was what she wanted, deep down, to look like Kate Middleton. Mom had been glued to the TV, watching the whole royal extravaganza and drool-ing over it. But it was hard to shake the excitement in Drake's voice out of her memory or the little thrill she'd felt when he said, "Let's get married in Vegas."

"What did you think of the house?" Aunt Kendra asked her as they stood in line at Herman's Hamburgers, wait-ing to order cheeseburgers and garlic fries for everyone.

Laney shrugged. "It's fancy."

"Yeah, it is. Is it you?"

Laney chewed her bottom lip. That was the problem. The house was beautiful. Any wedding held there would be like a storybook wedding. But *was* it her? She'd al-ways thought she wanted to look like a Disney princess at her wedding, but she wasn't sure she was really prin-cess material. So far no Disney princess had tattoos. Would it be the wedding of a lifetime or the mistake of a lifetime? Having a wedding reception in a house seemed so… *No, don't use the B word.* Anyway, her reception didn't have to be boring. A house that old, maybe it was haunted. Maybe they'd see a ghost. Maybe they could have the guests come as ghosts.

Maybe that was a dumb idea.

"If it isn't calling to you, don't do it," Aunt Kendra cautioned just as Mom joined them.

Mom's brows drew together. She looked like the bad

fairy Maleficent in *Sleeping Beauty* right before she changed into a dragon. "What are you telling her?"

Oh, boy. Laney braced herself.

"Only that she needs to be sure she really wants to get married at Primrose Haus," Aunt Kendra replied calmly.

Okay, here it comes. Mom was going to breathe fire now and turn every chocolate shake in the place into hot chocolate. "Well, of course she does," Mom snapped. She smiled at Laney. "You do like it, don't you?"

"Yeah. It's nice." If they had the reception there that would make everyone happy.

Mom nodded. "I knew you'd love it."

It could work. She and Drake could make this wedding fun. Somehow...

Ten minutes later they were all seated at a booth, working their way through gigantic burgers, fries and shakes and throwing out wedding ideas. Neither Grammy nor Mom seemed very excited about Laney getting married on a raft on the river.

"What if you fall in?" Grammy worried, dabbing at her mouth with a napkin. She wore her gray hair in the same oversprayed helmet she'd worn in her own wedding pictures. There'd been no getting married on a raft for Grammy.

Or Mom.

But it appealed to Laney. "If I did, it would be something to remember," she joked.

"Not in a good way," Mom said.

"Oh, she wouldn't fall in," said Aunt Kendra. "That only happens in movies."

"And on *America's Funniest Home Videos*," Mom said with a frown. "You don't want your wedding to be a joke."

No, she didn't. And her mom was the wedding organizer, the specialist. Of course Mom would work with her to make sure she had a perfect wedding.

But would it be hers?

Chapter Eight

Daphne, the Warrior Princess

Daphne was back in Seattle, in her old house, on special assignment. Her job was to gather tax returns, financial statements and pay stubs.

"Don't worry," her new lawyer, Shirley Schneck, assured Daphne when they met. "We'll see that both of you get exactly what's coming to you." And the glint in her eye didn't bode well for Mitchell.

"She's a barracuda," Dot Morrison had told Daphne. "Thanks to her, I lost my best waitress. The girl got such a good settlement she was able to quit. Went back to school and became a dental hygienist. Shirley's divorced herself. She thinks all men are spawn of Satan. The woman will make sure your cheating husband gets pounded into the ground."

Looking at Shirley, it was hard to imagine her pounding anyone into the ground. She was around Daphne's age with a plump, motherly face and figure to match. When they'd met, she'd been dressed in black slacks and a pale pink sweater accented with a fringed scarf—hardly the kind of apparel lawyers on TV wore. Her office was like something Martha Stewart would have designed with mint-green walls and antique (no leather!) furniture and paintings of flowers hanging on the wall.

But the sweet face had suddenly turned menacing. It had made Daphne glad that Shirley was working *for* her and not against her, and she'd left Shirley's office fired up and ready for battle.

Returning home to the scene of the crime had doused the fire. Mitchell's time to pack up his things was long gone and so was he. No more husband.

She stood in the living room, looking around at the house she'd worked so hard to turn into a home. She'd redone the living room only last fall, using a soothing tan palette. She'd paid a fortune for that deep chocolate mohair couch. And she and Mitchell had repainted the kitchen this past summer. "Yellow's such a happy color," she'd said, and he'd smiled and agreed. It had been so cozy, the two of them in the kitchen, painting.

He'd actually seemed to enjoy that project, even though he hadn't been very excited about it when she'd first brought up the idea. Mitchell, obviously, had been very good at faking it.

But he couldn't have been faking *every* happy moment they had together. He sure hadn't faked enjoying the sex; that much she knew.

And he'd sounded so sincere when he insisted, "I love you, Daph. That thing with Stella meant nothing."

Men said that in movies all the time. Apparently, they said it in real life, too. "How long have you been with her, Mitchell? How long has she meant nothing?" she'd demanded. Probably as long as he'd been "having to" work late, which made it about three months. For three months her husband had been pretending to love her while he hooked up with another woman. For three months she hadn't been enough. Or maybe longer. Maybe there'd been other women, too.

She ran a hand along the back of the couch. They'd made love on that couch on New Year's Eve.

She'd sell the thing. Or set it on fire. With Mitchell strapped to it.

She sighed and moved into the office, where she spent the first part of the afternoon pulling together the information requested by her lawyer. Then she packed up the rest of her clothes. That done, she went to the garage to get her golf clubs. She could spend some time at the Mountain Meadows Golf Course.

The sight of them and her golf shoes brought tears to her eyes. She and Mitchell had taken lessons together. She'd envisioned them wintering in Arizona when they retired, playing golf, relaxing at the club and drinking iced tea. *Oh, Mitchell. Why did you have to be such a weasel?*

She grabbed the bag. She'd sell the stupid clubs on eBay. She really wasn't very good in spite of the lessons.

And there were his clubs, sitting right next to hers. She'd told him to get his stuff out of here. Maybe she'd sell his clubs, too. In fact, looking around, she saw quite a lot of stuff that should've been gone by now. Well, then, she'd make a little run to Goodwill. *You snooze, you lose, Mitchell.*

Into her car trunk went not only her cheating husband's golf clubs but his drill and toolbox. Oh, and his tennis racket. He was much too busy banging Stella to play tennis these days. He'd be furious when he found that stuff missing but, oh, well. He'd had more than enough time to get it gone. Anyway, what was he going to do, sue her? Ha-ha.

She was finished by five. A good day's work, she

thought, pleased with herself. She was shocked to see that he still had a few clothes in the closet. Perhaps he'd moved in with Stella and was running around her place naked.

The idea of Mitchell running around some other woman's house naked sent a tear streaking down Daphne's cheek. *No, no, no*, she told herself. There would be no more crying over Mitchell.

She showered, put on fresh makeup and then went to meet some of her old friends from work for dinner at Anthony's Home Port in Shilshole. There she treated herself to a Dungeness crab salad and some chowder and plenty of bread, and washed it all down with white wine and encouragement from the girls.

"You're well rid of him," said her friend Ellie Meyers. "What a creep."

"He's lucky you don't Bobbitt him," put in Carrie Anne Hodges, the office manager.

"Bobbitt him? What does that mean?" asked one of the younger women.

"Look up Lorena Bobbitt on Google and you'll see," one of the older women said.

"You cut off his troublemaker," Carrie Anne explained. "I would."

"Whoa," Ellie said, "does Terrence know this side of you?"

"You bet," Carrie Anne said and stabbed her salmon fillet.

Carrie Anne had been married for twenty-nine years. No doubt fear and intimidation was how she kept her man.

Susan the bookkeeper shook her head. "You're so full of it. I've seen you two together. You're, like, soul mates."

Daphne sighed. She'd thought Mitchell was her soul mate. He loved romantic comedies as much as she did. And fine wines and travel. Although they hadn't done much traveling—mostly weekend trips to San Diego or Vegas. Mitchell had an ex-wife and he had child support to pay. Now Daphne couldn't help wondering about that ex. He'd said she was a real witch, insecure and possessive. Jealous. Had he given her reason to be? And what had he told Stella about Daphne? She didn't want to know.

From appetizers to dessert, dinner was a pep rally for Daphne. "You can do it.".…"Divorce him.".…"You'll be so much happier."

That was hard to believe, she thought when she came back to her house for a good night's sleep before returning to Icicle Falls. The place felt so…empty. Just like she did. She sighed and flopped onto the couch, staring at the lifeless TV. No sense turning it on since she'd discontinued the cable. She was in no mood to watch TV anyway. She much preferred to sit there and mope, remembering the good years she'd had with Mitchell. Like that time a friend lent him his sailboat and they went out on Lake Washington. It had been a perfect day, even though there'd been no wind. They'd motored around the lake, eating Brie cheese and crackers and drinking white wine. Then there'd been that weekend trip to Astoria last summer. They'd had so much fun walking along the waterfront, dining in that cute seaside restaurant. And that night…

She grabbed a sofa pillow and hugged it. How could a man make love so sweetly and not love a woman? Maybe the thing with Stella really didn't mean anything. Everyone made mistakes, right? He'd been so sorry, so upset, when she confronted him. Perhaps she should give him a second chance. She'd sleep on it.

She climbed the stairs to the master bedroom, changed into an old nightgown and went to bed. A hot flash hit her and suddenly the covers were too much. She kicked them off.

Even the simple act of kicking off the covers triggered a memory—Mitchell fetching an ice cube from the freezer and rubbing it all over her, the feel of the ice melting on her skin, then the touch of his lips as they followed its wet trail. She hated being in bed all by herself, hated being in this house all by herself. She'd never liked being alone. There was something so forlorn and unsettling about it. And she never felt safe. Every little noise set her nerves on edge.

She wished she'd gone ahead and driven back to Icicle Falls after her evening with the girls. She wouldn't have gotten in until late, but at least she wouldn't have been all alone in a big bed in a small house.

Don't be silly, she told herself. Her Ballard neighborhood was perfectly safe. *Think about something else.*

Well, that was a dumb idea. She lay there, staring at the ceiling, thinking about something else—her third divorce. Third time's the charm, right? Wrong. With her and Mitchell it had been more a case of three's company. She scowled. She shouldn't give him a second chance. That was just crazy.

But what they'd had together was good…

Until it wasn't. She punched her pillow and rolled over onto her side. She probably wouldn't sleep a wink.

At midnight Daphne was jerked out of a sound sleep by a noise. Downstairs. Someone was in the house. Here in her safe neighborhood in Ballard. She scooped up her cell phone and dashed to the bedroom door to lock it. And when it wouldn't lock, she remembered that the lock was broken. Why, oh, why hadn't she gotten it fixed? She could hear the soft rumble of a male voice downstairs. Was it getting closer? Was the intruder coming upstairs?

Her heart was banging against her chest, crying, "Let me out!" She dashed into the bathroom. Maybe she could jump out the bathroom window. She shut and locked the bathroom door. Then she called 9-1-1. "There's a burglar in my house," she whimpered as she slid open the window. She gave the woman on the other end of the call her address and added, "I'm alone." *Again. For the third time. And now I'm going to get burgled. Alone.* This was so unfair! So sick and wrong. Mitchell should be here getting burgled along with her.

"The police will be there right away," said the nice lady. "I'll stay on the line with you until they arrive."

A lot of help a voice on the phone would be. *Go away, burglar, or the lady on the phone will yell at you.* Daphne stuck her head out the window and looked down. A second story didn't sound that far up until you contemplated jumping from one. She'd break a leg. Or her back.

"Meanwhile, have you got a safe room, someplace where you can go and lock the door?"

"I'm in the bathroom." *Thinking about jumping.*

"Good. Lock the door and stay there until the police come."

A flimsy lock on a bathroom door probably wouldn't stop a burglar. But maybe the burglar wouldn't care about the bathroom. Well, unless he had to go potty.

Daphne looked around for a weapon she could use in case the intruder had a weak bladder. Snapping him with a towel wouldn't help much. Too bad the mirror was screwed into the wall. She could've broken it over his head. The toilet plunger! She grabbed it and braced herself against the wall.

The voice was in the bedroom now. Aaaaah! Daphne's heart was going to explode. She was going to pass out right here on the bathroom floor.

She heard another voice. The burglar had an accomplice. A female.

Wait a minute.

She tiptoed to the door and pressed her ear to it.

"Baby, you make me so hot."

The burglar was having sex in her bedroom? Of all the nerve!

"There's no one like you, baby. Oh, yeah, that's what Daddy likes."

Daphne's eyes narrowed. She knew that voice and that pathetic no-one-like-you line. "Never mind," she told the woman on the phone. "The burglar is my husband. I'll take care of this on my own."

Now Stella was saying, "Mitchell. The bed's unmade. Has someone been here?"

Daphne unlocked the door and threw it open. "As a matter of fact, someone has."

"Daph," he gasped in shock. There he stood with his pants pooled around his ankles. His partner in infidelity already had her blouse off, her boobs wrapped in a black lace bra. They weren't even that big. Mitchell had left her for…that?

Daphne was across the room before you could say "dirty, rotten cheater." She gave Mitchell a whack with the toilet plunger. She'd been aiming for his head but missed, catching him instead on the shoulder. Still, the yelp of pain it produced was hugely satisfying.

It was like playing Whack-a-Mole. Only better.

Whack-a-Rat. She took another swing, this time catching his arms, which were raised in self-defense.

"Daphne, cut it out," he protested, trying to both protect himself and get his pants back up.

"You were supposed to be out of the house," she growled and took another swing. He ducked and she missed. *Strike one.*

"I came back to get some things," he explained, hopping away and yanking his pants up.

"I can see what you came back to get. You came back to get laid." Daphne swung again as Mitchell jumped onto the bed. *Strike two.* Next time she was going to connect and hit a home run...with his head. "In our house, Mitchell. Our bed!"

"Daph, stop," he begged, struggling to dodge the toilet plunger and zip up his pants.

Stop? Not until his head was flatter than a pancake.

Meanwhile, his partner in romantic crime had her hands in her fake red hair and was screaming like a character in a horror movie. Daphne turned on her. "And you," she said in disgust. "You must be Stella."

"No!" the woman cried. "I'm Lydia."

"Lydia?" He'd moved on to yet another woman? Lydia, Stella, Rumpelstiltskin—Daphne didn't care who the woman was. She was toast. "Whoever you are, that's my husband."

"We're separated," Mitchell protested as Daphne raised the toilet plunger.

Lydia didn't stick around for any more details. She fled the room, screeching all the way.

Before Daphne could pursue her, Mitchell jerked the plunger out of her hands. *Strike three. Go back to the dugout.* Three was *not* her lucky number.

"Daph, calm down," he commanded.

"Calm down? Are you serious?" He'd scared her half to death and then humiliated her. Again. She was ready to expire from adrenaline overload and he was telling her to calm down? "Why are you here?" she demanded. "And give me back my toilet plunger."

"*Our* toilet plunger," he corrected her. "Not a chance."

"Fine. You want it, you can have it. And you can have that…that bitty-boobed fake redhead, too. You deserve each other. And the toilet plunger." Tears were spilling from her eyes now and she took an angry swipe at her cheeks. "I trusted you, Mitchell. I gave you my heart."

He hung his head. "I know. I'm sorry."

"You are. You're a sorry excuse for a man." To think she'd been stupid enough to entertain, even for one moment, the thought of taking him back. "Get out."

"Daph, I haven't found a place to live yet."

She couldn't believe her ears. "What, you want to stay here? With her? Not on your life. I told you to leave and I meant it. Go live at what's-her-name's place."

"Her place is too small," he protested, then had the grace to look chagrined.

"Small, just like you," Daphne snapped.

"Daph, I'm sorry. I made a mistake."

A mistake. So that was what you called cheating on your wife. Daphne shook her head. "Were you always such a waste of love and I didn't see it?"

His cheeks flushed russet. "I'm sorry. I really am. I never meant to hurt you."

"Oh, really? So you didn't think having another woman on the side would hurt me? Oh, Mitchell, I'm well rid of you."

"Mitchell?" the new Stella called from downstairs. "Are you all right?"

"I'm fine," he called back.

"As fine a rat as I've ever seen," Daphne snarled. With his George Clooney face he was almost prettier than she was. People had often remarked on what a beautiful couple they were. "Just like Ken and Barbie all grown up," someone once said. And, as it turned out, what they had was about as real as those plastic dolls.

The rat slipped by her and out the bedroom, taking the toilet plunger with him. She stood there in the middle of the bedroom and listened to the murmur of their voices while her heart settled back down. Then the front door slammed shut and she was alone again.

Chapter Nine

Anne at Work

Pulling together a wedding could be like going out to sea. You planned for it as best you could and then hoped for good weather. When you started, the sea could look calm, but there was always a chance that a typhoon would hit. Pirates might find you. Anything could lurk beneath the waters. Sometimes people didn't bring the right clothes for stormy weather or thought they'd packed enough food and then ran out. Or brought along someone who should've been pushed off the dock before they set sail.

Such was the case with the wedding Anne was coordinating this particular weekend. Teddy, the bride's nephew, should have been, if not pushed off the dock, at least left on it. Teddy was four and a bundle of energy. He had the attention span of a gnat and was as spoiled as a child could get. This did not make him a good candidate for ring bearer.

But Teddy was the only child, the only grandchild, the only nephew, the only…everything, and the bride was on board with having him in the wedding party, along with his mother, who seemed completely incapable of controlling him. At the rehearsal he ran up the aisle with the ring pillow, the ribbons with the rings swinging wildly. Positioned on one of the carpeted steps leading up to the podium, he soon became bored with the adult conversation and began to hop up and down the stairs. When he wasn't doing that, he was trying to look under the bridesmaids' skirts or making faces at Anne, who was getting things ready for the big day. He finally wore himself out and collapsed on the lowest stair for an impromptu nap, allowing the minister to finish walking the bride and groom through their vows.

"Maybe we can drug him," muttered his grandfather.

Anne suspected it would take more than drugs to tame Teddy.

The afternoon of the wedding it looked as if someone had, indeed, drugged Teddy...with speed. Or too much sugar. He bounced around the foyer like a kangaroo looking forward to an extra helping of Marmite until his exasperated grandfather finally took him by the arm and growled at him to stand still.

"You walk down the aisle like a gentleman," Grandpa cautioned just before Teddy's big moment.

The dose of sternness seemed to work. Or maybe it was stage fright. Whatever the case, Teddy did an admirable job of getting the rings down the aisle.

All right, Anne thought, taking in the scene. So far everything was going according to plan.

The bridesmaids did their stately walk, sophisticated in navy blue dresses accented with red shoes. Then it was time for the father to walk his daughter down the aisle. Anne gave them the cue and sent them on their way, daughter smiling and father teary-eyed.

Anne felt misty-eyed herself, watching them go. There was something about this moment in the wedding ceremony that always got to her. It was such a sweet tradition, the man who had raised the young woman, who'd been there to hear her nighttime prayers and sample her first baking efforts, who had fretted every time she was late coming home from a date, who had, in short, taken care of her and guarded her, now publicly declaring that he was willing to share her love with a new man, to let her start a new chapter in her life.

Anne stayed long enough to see the father kiss his daughter and join her hands with the hands of her groom. Then she went to the fancy old historical home in Seattle where the couple was having their reception to make sure all was in readiness.

She knew it would be. Everything had made it there safely. The cake was standing in place, a lacy tower of elegance, surrounded by tiered plates of cookies shaped like tuxedo clad hearts; the tables were all set, draped in navy tablecloths and topped with green vases filled with gerbera daisies and ferns, while a giant swan sculpted in ice presided over the buffet table. The caterer was busy setting out the food—appetizer trays with everything from brûléed goat cheese to asparagus wrapped in prosciutto, Caesar salad and pasta salad, crab legs, crusty rolls, teriyaki chicken and rice pilaf. Soon the elegant room would be filled with a new Mr. and Mrs. and all their friends, ready to help them celebrate.

Soon happened in twenty minutes, with families starting to trickle in. Then came some of the younger couples, the women all lovely in heels and party dresses, their guys equally dressed up, their suits a traditional contrast to their piercings, gauges and tats. Two couples were talking and snickering, a sure clue that Teddy had put on a show at the wedding.

Next came the bride's parents. "Everything looks beautiful," Greta, the mother of the bride, said to Anne.

Anne murmured her thanks and asked Greta how the ceremony had gone.

"It was lovely," Greta said, tears in her eyes.

"It would've been better if Teddy hadn't been in it," her husband muttered.

Greta shrugged. "Little boys."

Her husband shook his head.

"Teddy went under one of the pews with the rings and my son had to get him out," Greta explained. "It'll make a funny wedding story someday."

"Yes, and it'll make a funny story when I tie him up and stick him in a corner," her husband said darkly.

"Now, Theodore," his wife scolded.

Obviously, Theodore wasn't happy with his namesake.

"These things do happen," Anne said. Especially when the Teddys of the world weren't left on the dock.

"Well, that better be all that happens," said the bride's father.

But it wasn't. Teddy was on a roll. As the guests milled about or found seats at the tables, he darted in and out of the crowd, chasing a little girl with red ringlets. In the process he managed to run into a tall, willowy woman whose height was accentuated by six-inch heels, knocking her off balance. She grabbed for the nearest person, who happened to be another woman in equally high heels, and that woman, too, lost her balance. Down they both went, taking a bowl of Caesar salad with them and sending a tray of teriyaki chicken flying.

This was the final straw for Grandpa, who took off after Teddy. In an effort to escape, the child dived under the elegantly clothed table with the cake and cookies on it. Several people gasped, "Oh, no," and one of the groomsmen jumped to save the cake, which, thanks to the movement of the tablecloth, was in danger of sliding off the edge. He caught it in time, setting it back in place, and everyone heaved a sigh of relief...until the redheaded girl decided to join the mischief-maker under the table, taking the tablecloth with her, bringing down the cake and sending cookies flying just as Grandpa reached under the table and grabbed Teddy.

There was much howling as Grandpa took the young man to another room for a stern talking-to and the bride saw what had become of her cake.

"Not to worry," Anne told her. "We'll fix this."

"But my cake," the bride protested.

"I can't duplicate the cake, but I can make sure you have something."

And while the caterers cleaned up the mess and Teddy probably got tied up and stuck in a corner, Anne raced to the neighboring chain grocery stores, buying the prettiest layer cake she could find as well as all manner of cupcakes. Forty minutes later, a slightly less elaborate cake sat on the table, surrounded by tiered plates with a selection of cupcakes. Some strategically repositioned candles and flowers added elegance. The rest of the reception went off without a hitch, and after drinking champagne and dancing with her new husband and her doting father, the bride was smiling once more.

"You saved the day," Greta said to Anne later that evening.

Anne smiled modestly and shook her head. "Even when things don't go the way you plan, a wedding is always a happy event."

Laney's wedding would go perfectly, though. She

was going to make sure of that. Thank God they didn't have a Teddy to mess everything up.

They still had a lot to do to see that everything went smoothly on Laney's big day, so Anne called her daughter on Monday when she had a few minutes between clients. The call went straight to voice mail and Anne sighed. It was after lunch. Laney would be off work now, and since the sun was out, she was probably running around Green Lake. Anne settled for a text. We need 2 talk. Call me.

She'd just finished conferring with her favorite caterer about food for an upcoming wedding—pulled-pork sliders, savory cupcakes, sushi and a dessert buffet—when Laney checked in. "What's up, Mom?"

Was it Anne's imagination or did her daughter sound wary? Maybe Anne's text had seemed a little…imperious. "Oh, nothing," she said airily. "I was thinking we should lock in Primrose Haus for your wedding reception, that's all," she rushed on and then held her breath. *Please, God, don't let Drake have talked Laney into Vegas*.

There was a moment of silence on the phone that shot Anne's heart rate up. Finally Laney said, "Okay, let's do it."

She seemed hesitant. Suddenly the buzzard of guilt perched on Anne's shoulders. *Way to go*, it said. *Pressure the poor kid*.

Oh, crud. The buzzard was right. She was forcing her daughter to do something she wasn't excited about.

But Laney had always wanted a fancy wedding, ever since she was a little girl. Deep down, she really did want this and if she settled for something else she'd regret it later.

Still, Anne had to ask, "Are you sure?"

"Yeah, I'm sure," Laney said.

"You don't sound sure."

"Mom. I'm sure. It'll be great for the reception. I still want to get married on the river, though."

"Okay." *Hopefully, in a wedding gown. No shorts and bikini top.* "Great. Tell you what. Why don't you come by the office and we can talk about your vision for the wedding."

"I need to get a shower first. I just finished running."

Laney loved to run. She'd been on the swim team in high school and had added running to her regimen in college.

She'd tried to convince Anne to take it up, but Anne preferred a brisk walk on the treadmill at the gym or a walk in the snow on a wintry day. She would just have to live without experiencing that mystical runner's high, because she'd never be caught running unless she was being chased by a bear. And since she didn't do camping, either, there was no danger of that.

Her daughter loved to tease her about her poor excuse for a sense of adventure. So she didn't like rock climbing or sleeping in leaky tents. If she was going to enjoy nature, she wanted to do it from the comfort of a cozy, little cabin.

"That's fine," she said. "See you whenever you get here."

Funny how a mother and daughter could have so much in common—a love of parties and romantic comedies and card games—and yet be so different. That wasn't a bad thing, she reminded herself as she ended the call. Her daughter was her own woman. And that was how it should be. Still, when it came to weddings...

"You're frowning," her sister said.

Anne blinked. "What?"

"You're frowning." Kendra studied her. "She's not even here and you're already worried."

"No, I'm not," Anne lied.

"You know, it *is* her wedding."

"I know that."

Kendra raised an eyebrow. "Do you? Really?"

Anne made a face. "Of course I do. The bride always gets the last say."

She punched in the number for Primrose Haus in Icicle Falls. She'd tell Roberta Gilbert they were definitely a go for that Saturday in June before her daughter could change her mind. This was the right decision, she knew it. Laney would have no regrets.

"We'll be looking forward to helping you create a wonderful memory," Roberta said when she and Anne had finished talking business.

A wonderful memory, Anne thought. Yes, that was what this was all about, a wonderful memory for her daughter.

Not just for her daughter, but for everyone who loved her, as well.

"I can hardly wait to see our Laney get married," her mother had said after the family dinner on Sunday, when it had been the two of them lingering over one last cup of coffee once everyone else had left. "Drake is such a nice boy."

"Yes, he is," Anne had agreed.

"It's the first wedding we've had in the family in a long time. And who knows? Maybe there'll be a baby soon."

"I don't think they're in a hurry for that, Mom. Anyway, they're young. They've got time." The words had barely left her mouth when Anne realized how false that statement could be. She and Cam had thought they'd had plenty of time to have another. How wrong they'd been.

Laney had ended up being their only child. Fortunately, she was a wonderful kid, but Anne would've liked a couple more.

As if reading her mind, her mother had veered away from that verbal path. "Well, we'll enjoy the wedding. You know," she'd added, toying with her mug, "we all assume weddings are just about the bride and groom, but so many people get so much out of them. I'm sure you've seen that over the years. A wedding gives those of us who are older a chance to share in the couple's happiness and to relive that special time when we found the person we wanted to spend our lives with. Of course, for the kids it's a party, but don't you think it's also an example?"

"Of what?"

"Of commitment. A wedding, no matter where it is—" Julia had reached out to cover her daughter's hand with hers "—is a sign of loyalty, of responsibility." She bit her lip, as if hesitating to continue.

"What?" Anne had prompted.

"I don't think you understood at the time why I was so upset about your hurried affair. I wonder if you can see now, after having planned so many weddings for so many brides. It's an important event for the whole community."

Anne could only nod in agreement. Of course, given the options she'd had at the time, she'd do the same thing all over again. Still, if the situation had been different, if she hadn't gotten pregnant...

Some things in life you couldn't redo. But her mother had a point. You could relive. With Laney's wedding she and Cam could celebrate both their daughter's union and their own. They'd celebrate love, family and friendship. Yes, her mother was right. A wedding was a big deal for a lot of people.

But mostly for the bride. She could hardly wait until Laney arrived and they could start planning the details of the momentous occasion that lay ahead for all of them.

An hour later Laney was in the office, comfy in jeans and a long, black sweater, accented with one of her necklaces, a silver creation featuring her signature mermaid carrying a silver heart. She and Anne sat at the computer, discussing color themes and decorations, with Kendra tossing in the occasional comment.

"What's wrong with purple?" Laney asked with a frown.

"Nothing," Anne said quickly. "It can make for striking decorations." It also made Anne think of the red-hat ladies and the popular poem about a woman wearing purple when she was old. Of course, there was nothing wrong with being old *or* wearing purple, but it didn't seem like the right color for Laney's wedding.

"Purple might be kind of cool," Kendra put in.

Who asked her? "If that's what you want, that's what we'll go with," Anne said, reminding herself that her daughter got to make the final decision. Still, she wanted to make sure Laney would be happy with it. "Let's look at some other colors, too, though."

"Okay, fine," Laney said irritably. Her phone dinged and she checked it, then spent a moment thumbing a text.

"Who was that?" Anne asked. They were trying to get this wedding planned. Did Laney really need to stop in the middle of their meeting and text someone?

"Autumn. I told her I was coming over here to pick out colors. She's gonna be my maid of honor."

Not surprising, considering that they'd been friends since high school.

The phone dinged again.

Oh, great. "Honey, at this rate we're not going to get anything done," Anne chided.

"Autumn thinks purple would be ugly."

Well, then. That decides it.

"We should look at other colors," Laney said.

Obviously, Autumn's opinion did decide it. Anne wasn't sure whether she should be grateful or annoyed. "Tell her we'll keep her posted," she said and hoped Autumn would get the message and go have a latte.

They checked every imaginable color theme and style from red to pink polka dots. Finally, Laney said she wanted green and brown. All right. Progress. Ten minutes later, they found something new to disagree on. "Why can't I have balloons?" Laney demanded.

"I didn't say you couldn't have balloons," Anne insisted. "But in all different colors? That'll look odd." It made her think of circuses and clowns or state fairs. Might as well throw in some pigs and a Ferris wheel. And what was the point of using different-colored balloons if Laney had picked a specific color scheme? "Anyway, I thought you were going with green and brown."

"They don't make balloons in green and brown," Laney pointed out.

"Somebody must," Anne said and brought up yet another image on the internet.

"Eew," said Laney, frowning. "Lime green. That's gross."

Yes, lime green wouldn't work. They'd been talking about forest green. But Anne had an alternative suggestion. "You could have ferns and chocolate mint, and crystal votives on the tables would be gorgeous."

"But what about the balloons?"

"Honey, we can't find any in the color you want. You're going to have to bag the balloons."

Laney frowned, obviously unhappy with the idea of giving up on balloons.

"The ferns and mint will be pretty. And both you and Drake enjoy the outdoors, so it would be bringing something you love into the wedding theme."

Her argument produced a thoughtful nod.

"Let's look at cakes," Anne said and moved them on to new territory before Laney could argue for a rainbow of balloons again.

They found one on Pinterest—a beautiful green fondant with tasteful brown swirls. "Wow," Anne breathed.

"That's pretty," Laney conceded. "But I want a donut cake."

Okay, donut cake. That took them to a different set of images. The donut cakes were cute, Anne had to admit, but they weren't very elegant. She remembered feeding Cam some of the tacky cake their neighbor had made, telling herself how wonderful it was that they had a cake at all, yet wishing for one with a froth of white frosting and pastel-colored flowers from the bakery. She hadn't had time to budget for a cake, and she hadn't wanted to ask her mother to pay for one. Her parents had paid for her gown and bouquet, and under the circumstances that had felt like plenty. Looking back now, she realized Mom would happily have sprung for a cake and anything else she wanted if she'd only asked.

"Hey," she said, pointing to one image. "You could have a donut bar. What about a donut bar and a traditional cake? Something for everyone."

"Including Mom," Kendra added snidely.

Anne ignored her.

"A donut bar isn't the same as a donut cake," Laney said stubbornly.

"Not all of your guests are going to want to eat donuts," Anne pointed out. "If you do the donut bar *and* the cake, then everyone's happy."

Everyone except the bride. Laney's mouth slipped into a half frown.

"Don't you think that's a good compromise?" Anne nudged.

"Yeah, I guess it is."

One more thing settled. They were moving right along.

Next they chose invitations. This, too, involved much discussion. The save-the-date cards Laney finally picked were cute. They'd be trimmed with Laney's colors and feature a picture of her and Drake with conversation bubbles over their heads saying "I do" and "Me, too!" Underneath, block printing would say "How about you? Save the date to celebrate." It was a little unconventional, a perfect fit for her daughter.

"We'll need to go up to Icicle Falls to visit the florist next," Anne said. "When can you get away?"

"I'm not sure," Laney hedged. "I'll let you know."

Not sure? Let her know? They needed to get this planned. "Honey, we can't drag our feet. June's not that far away. There's still so much to do."

"I get that, Mom." Laney checked the time on her cell phone. "Oh, wow. I've gotta go."

"But we still have to talk about napkins and what kind of food you want and…"

"I know, but I've got company coming for dinner tonight and I haven't even shopped yet."

Anne felt deflated. They were just starting to have fun and her daughter had to leave? "Oh. Well, okay."

Laney gave her a quick kiss, hugged her aunt Kendra and then was out the door before Anne could suggest another day to get together.

"That went well," Kendra said after she left.

"It did." Anne ignored both her sister's sarcasm and the feeling that things could have gone better.

"Right. That's why she left at three thirty in the afternoon to get ready for dinner."

"She had to shop."

"Uh-huh. And you believe that? Hey, I've got an oil well in New York City for sale. Wanna buy it?"

Anne frowned and swiveled her desk chair to face her sister. "Okay, what exactly are you saying?"

Kendra swiveled her chair, too. "I can put it in one word. *Momzilla.*"

"I am not a Momzilla!" Anne protested.

"True," her sister agreed. "Not a full-grown one yet, anyway. Right now you're just a baby one."

"Oh, very funny," Anne snapped.

"I thought so," Kendra said and turned back to her computer.

They worked in silence for twenty minutes before Anne asked, "How was I being a Momzilla?"

"Well, let's see. You want to start with the great debate on the invitations or go back to the battle of the colors?"

"There was no battle over colors. I was simply making suggestions."

"Mmm-hmm. Like you did with the balloons. And how about the donut cake?"

"She's getting donuts," Anne said, choosing the most solid ground to stand on.

"She's getting a donut bar. And you're getting the cake."

"This isn't for me!"

"Are you sure?"

"Of course. I'm trying to make sure Laney has the perfect wedding she deserves."

"Everyone has a different definition of *perfect*," Kendra said.

Anne couldn't argue with that. So she decided not to. Instead, she got busy researching party favors for a client who was getting married at West Seattle's Golden Gardens, a favorite beach of many Seattleites. Can coolers would be just the thing for a beach wedding. And baseball caps. Yes, her bride-to-be would love those. Darn, but she was good.

And since she *was* good and had been doing this for years, there was nothing wrong with guiding her daughter. So there.

Still, the thought that maybe she was taking too much control moved into her brain and set up a broadcast tower. So that night over dinner with Cam, she recapped her session with Laney, hoping for a different verdict. "Do you think I was being a Momzilla?"

He took a last bite of ice cream and pushed aside his bowl. "Nah. You were giving her advice. That's what you do, right?"

"It is. And I just want her to have a lovely wedding, something memorable."

"Understandable," he said with a nod. "Don't worry about it. She gets the final say."

"True." Laney did want a donut bar, didn't she? And there was nothing wrong with having cake, as well. She could have her cake and eat it, too. Ha-ha. Anyway, Anne and Cam were paying for the wedding, so if they wanted to throw in a cake as a bonus, why should Laney care?

Except Anne had talked her into having a donut bar instead of a donut cake. She'd talked her into a lot of things. She flashed on a sudden image of Laurel Browne insisting, "We are not having daisies at the wedding."

No, no. She wasn't anything like Laurel Browne. Laney was the one who'd settled on green and brown for her colors, and Anne wasn't about to rock that boat. And the balloons, well, they simply weren't the right color. That was hardly Anne's fault.

But the cake? Okay, they'd go with the donut cake. She grabbed her cell phone from the kitchen counter.

"Who are you calling?" Cam asked.

"Laney. I'm going to tell her we'll do a donut cake *and* a regular cake."

Cam made a face that plainly said "I'm a long-suffering husband" and got up to take their bowls into the kitchen.

Dinner was their time and they didn't take calls then. But they were done with dinner now. Anyway, this was important. Her call went to voice mail, and she remembered that Laney was having company tonight. Still, that never stopped her from answering her phone. She was one with her phone. Was she mad about the cake thing?

"Hi, honey," Anne said as soon as voice mail gave her the all clear to speak. "So, I'm thinking if you really want a donut cake, there's no reason you can't have one. Pick the one you like and email it to me and then I'll send it on to the baker. Hope you're having fun at your dinner party. I love you," she added.

There. No one could accuse her of being a Momzilla now, not even a baby one.

"Feel better?" her husband asked.

She nodded. "The donut cake will be cute. It's going to be a lovely wedding."

"They all are," he said. "Hey, and speaking of special events, we should talk about what we want to do for our anniversary."

An excellent idea. But after her busy workday and sorting out the issue of the cake, Anne was suddenly out of steam. "Could we do that tomorrow?"

"Yeah, sure."

He sounded the slightest bit disappointed.

"I'm too tired to think," she said. Anyway, they had plenty of time to plan their anniversary.

He came back to the table, bent over and wrapped his arms around her. She could still smell a hint of the woodsy cologne he favored. He put his face next to hers and she felt the brush of five o'clock shadow. "What do you want to do instead?"

Bury the baby Momzilla and cuddle on the couch. "Let's see what we've got in our Netflix queue."

"Okay," he said, and they moved to the living room.

Cam preferred action flicks, but he found a romantic comedy for her. "We don't have to watch this," she told him as they settled on the couch.

"Sure we do," he said, kissing the top of her head. "Tonight it's all about you."

It's all about you. Had that been the case this afternoon?

Of course not, she assured herself. Laney got to make the final decisions. Anne was there only to help her make the right ones.

She smiled and snuggled up against her husband. No Momzillas here.

Chapter Ten

Daphne, Starting Over

Daphne changed the locks on her house, but not before making sure Mitchell got the last of his clothes. She piled them all on the front lawn. "Feel free to come by and get them whenever you want," she said to his voice mail. Maybe, if he was lucky, there'd still be some left by the time he got to the house. Hee hee.

She merged onto I-90 eastbound and watched as Seattle got increasingly smaller in her rearview mirror. "Goodbye and good riddance," she muttered.

Not the city, just the last two men she'd found in it. What was wrong with her that she couldn't seem to get this love thing figured out? She was nice. And attractive—men had been telling her that all her life. She was responsible, didn't nag too much, and she never ate crackers in bed or complained when her man wanted to watch football, although she detested the sport. Surely that deserved better than she'd gotten so far. Why did she attract so many losers?

Oh, who cared? She was going to start a new life in Icicle Falls, help her mother run weddings and laugh behind the backs of all those delusional brides who paraded through Primrose Haus in their overpriced gowns on their way to happily-ever-after. Ha! There was no such thing. Sooner or later that Cinderella castle always crumbled. Disney should be sued.

On and on the bitter thoughts went as she drove up the mountain highway to Icicle Falls. It took seeing the Willkommen in Icicle Falls sign to pull her out of her funk. The town looked like something out of a movie back lot with its charming Bavarian shops, its town center with the gazebo and skating rink, which during summer would get used for everything from outdoor art fairs to folk dance festivals. Church spires pointed heavenward, reminding the faithful that there was a God who cared about their troubles. And above it all, the mountains in their snowy majesty stood guard over the residents of the little burg. Here was a welcoming place where she could start over with people she'd known all her life, people who'd be genuinely interested in her, who wouldn't just pretend. So she'd be celibate forever. By the time a woman was in her fifties did she really need sex?

Except fifty was the new forty. And that put her at forty-three. A forty-three-year-old woman still needed sex. She frowned. She wasn't sure she wanted to go the rest of her life without physical intimacy.

You can do it, she told herself. Her mother had managed fine on her own.

She wasn't her mother.

Okay, she'd be like Mitchell and have sex whenever she wanted with whomever she wanted. There were probably plenty of single men her age in Icicle Falls. Plenty of men, anyway, but her age? Hmm.

Well, then she'd find a boy toy. Or a lonely old geezer. Her frown deepened. She didn't want to be like Mitchell and break hearts. That wasn't kind, and she wouldn't wish a romantic heart attack on anyone. With a sigh she concluded that she'd have to rise above her circumstances, look for the silver lining, cast her fortunes to the wind… know when to hold 'em, know when to fold 'em. Whatever. In short, she'd build a new and better life. She still had a lot of years left to carve out some happiness for herself and find fulfillment.

Without a man. She'd do it all without a man. And she'd never watch another romantic comedy again. Pandora selected a new song for her car radio and Barry Manilow began to croon, *"When will I see you again?"* She shut off the radio and shut Barry up. The next time she saw Mitchell it would be in divorce court.

Oh, how she wanted someone to love.

She *had* someone to love, she reminded herself when she walked into the Victorian on Primrose Street, carrying the surprise she'd picked up on her way home. She'd stopped at the local art gallery that also did framing. There was her mother, asleep in an armchair, one of her romance novels open on her lap. She looked… old. When had that happened?

Daphne had always thought of her mother as invincible, tireless. When she wasn't working she'd been at church, tending to the flower beds, at a committee meeting or seated at the portable sewing machine she'd bought when Daphne was in first grade, putting together an elaborate Halloween costume for Daphne or making her a dress. Saturdays had been cleaning day and Mother had worked herself into a fever sweeping, dusting and scrubbing. She'd made sure Daphne did the same. Long after Daphne had had enough, her mother would still be going at it. Even on Sundays there was little rest. Starting in spring, Sunday afternoons were for weeding. Once the yard was in shape, it was time for Sunday dinner, which often meant company. And more work, because after the company left the dishes had to be done. Finally, when it was only the two of them and *Bonanza* on TV, the embroidery would come out.

Once, when Daphne was in high school, she'd asked her mother, "Don't you ever want to just sit back and do nothing?"

Mother had been disgusted by the very suggestion. "I have too much to do. I'll rest when I'm old."

Today she looked like a woman who was losing the race against Father Time, the wrinkles carving deeper into her face, her hands small and heavily veined. She looked vulnerable and the sight pulled at Daphne's heart-strings.

Daphne leaned the present against the wall, then tip-toed over to where her mother slept. She was in the process of replacing the book with an afghan when Mother woke with a start.

"Daphne, you're home."

"Sorry I woke you."

"I wasn't sleeping. I was just resting my eyes."

Of course, a woman always snored when she was resting her eyes. "You look tired," Daphne said. *And old. When did you grow old on me?*

"I'm not," Mother insisted. "What time is it?" She squinted in the direction of the cuckoo clock in the kitchen.

"A little after one." Daphne walked toward the kitchen. "Have you had lunch?"

"Not yet." Her mother began to get up.

"Stay put. I'll make it."

Of course Mother didn't stay put. She joined Daphne in the kitchen and started taking bowls out of the cupboard. "We have chicken soup left over from the other night. Why don't you heat that up?"

Sounded good to Daphne. Soup was perfect for a blustery day and she'd loved her mother's homemade soup. Once Daphne became a teenager, Mother taught her to make it. *Cut the carrots smaller, darling. Big carrots in soup are the sign of a lazy cook. You don't need a lot of salt. A pinch of garlic. Basil. Well, let's try it. Hmm. Very nice. I think you might have a flair for cooking. Who knows? Maybe you'll have your own restaurant someday.*

Daphne had not gone on to have her own restaurant. She'd preferred working in an office where she could have regular hours and get evenings and weekends off. Cooking was a hobby she'd enjoyed. She hadn't wanted to take the fun out of it by doing it for a living.

Mother had been disappointed that she'd opted for such an ordinary life, but the life she'd chosen had suited her. She liked being an employee, liked being part of a team. She wasn't sure where she got that—certainly not from her mother—but she was wired to be a helper.

Seeing her mother asleep in her chair had driven home to Daphne how much she wanted to help out here. Roberta Gilbert would never admit she was slowing down, even a little, and yet obviously she was. She needed her daughter.

"How did things go in Seattle?" Mother asked.

No way was Daphne telling anyone about this latest Mitchell escapade. Ever. Especially not Mother. She'd go into I-told-you-so mode, and Daphne wanted that about as much as she wanted adult acne. (Although adult acne might be preferable to hot flashes.) "I got what I needed out of the house and changed the locks." Everything else she'd sell or give away. Or burn, she mentally added, thinking of the living room couch.

Mother nodded approvingly. "Good." She leaned against the kitchen counter and studied Daphne. "You didn't see him, did you?"

Define "see." Daphne decided her mother meant in the sense of doing something dumb like going out with Mitchell. "No." At least she hadn't succumbed to that stupidity. She supposed she should be grateful for the episode in the bedroom.

The studying grew more intense. Daphne could feel her mother's gaze on her as she heated the soup. "Are you all right?" Mother asked.

"I am now." Daphne dug out a package of crackers and stuffed one in her mouth. Ah, carbs, a girl's best friend.

"Daphne. What happened in Seattle?"

"Nothing," Daphne lied even as her cheeks burned. Why was it that every time she and her mother discussed her love life, she felt fourteen? She loaded another cracker into her mouth and turned up the heat under the soup.

"What kind of nothing?"

Daphne's tender feelings began to toughen up. Mother would've made a successful attorney. *I'm not letting you off the stand until you crack.* "No kind of nothing. Honestly, Mother. I'm a grown woman." Who was back where she'd started, once again living at home. She set aside that humiliating fact. "Do we really need the third degree?" she demanded, infusing her words with as much wounded dignity as possible.

Roberta shook her head. "No. Not at all. It just seems…" She clamped her lips together, killing the sentence. "I only want to make sure you're okay."

"I am," Daphne assured both of them as she poured their soup. "I will be."

It seemed as though all the men she'd chosen had done nothing but make her feel bad about herself. She was through with that. She was through with men. Period. Even if fifty was the new forty, which meant she was only forty-three. She could go the rest of her life without sex, and if she wanted someone to love she could get a dog. She flashed on a sudden image of a big, woofy dog wandering around Primrose Haus, jumping on the guests. Okay, maybe a cat.

Her mother smiled faintly. "Well, good for you."

Yes, good for her. Meanwhile... "I have something for you," she said. She hurried to where she'd left her gift, then brought it back to the kitchen and presented it to her mother.

"Now what's this?" Roberta asked, taking the wrapped picture-shaped package.

"Open it and see."

She pulled off the wrapping and her eyes lit up in delight at the framed article from the *Gazette*. "Oh, Daphne, how thoughtful."

"Do you like it?" Of course she did, but it was so nice to hear the pleasure in her mother's voice, Daphne couldn't help wanting to prolong the moment.

"I love it, darling. Let's hang it here in the kitchen, where we can see it every day."

As if Roberta Gilbert needed to be reminded of her success? But Daphne was happy to comply.

"Don't worry about the dishes. I'll do them," Mother said after Daphne had hung the picture and was disposing of the wrapping paper.

Actually, she hadn't been worried about the dishes at all. Naughty her.

Later that day her daughter, Marnie, called to check in.

"I'm sorry you're going through this, Mom. You deserve better."

Evidently not, but she appreciated her daughter's support. "Thanks, honeybee."

"I love that nickname," Marnie said, a smile in her voice. "And I love you. I wish you'd come out for a visit."

"I will soon," Daphne promised. "I need to get my feet under me first, though."

"Um, how's that going, staying with Grandma?"

"It's going fine." *Sort of.*

"You can always move out here, you know."

She knew. Marnie would have liked nothing more than to have her nearby. "You don't need me underfoot. You're busy with your own life." And dealing with her father, who liked to invite himself to New York for a visit whenever he was drying out (which was rare) or wanted a cheap vacation (which was less rare).

"I'd never be too busy for you."

"Thanks, honeybee. I appreciate that." She wasn't interested in moving to the East Coast. She liked it fine here on the western side of the States. But it was good to be wanted by someone, especially when that someone was her daughter.

"I brought everything you need," Daphne said to her lawyer the next day.

Shirley Schneck nodded as she took the fat sheaf of papers. "Thanks. How are you doing, by the way?"

"I hate men," Daphne informed her. "I'm going to become a lesbian."

"You have no idea how many women have told me that," Shirley said with a smile. "You'll change your mind at some point, though, and be ready for another man."

"I doubt it." Daphne scowled. "I'm going to get a kitten."

"Good idea," Shirley said. "Keep the anger going for now. You'll need it for the battle ahead."

A battle. She was going to be battling her former best friend and lover. She could feel a little spring of tears bubbling up. Then she thought of Mitchell and his latest Stella and the spring went dry.

"You'll get through this," Shirley told her and proceeded to get down to business. The business of war.

War was exhausting. By the time Daphne left the office, she felt like a dish towel after a round with the washing machine agitator. Divorce was awful. After her second divorce she'd vowed to be careful, pick more wisely, never find herself in this position again. Yet here she was.

Okay, she needed chocolate. It was almost lunchtime anyway. Chocolate for lunch, maybe not the most nutritious choice, but, oh, well. Right now her soul was more in need than her body.

Five minutes later she walked into the gift shop of Sweet Dreams Chocolates, a veritable cornucopia of treats. Display racks and tables offered everything from various-size boxes of chocolates to snack items such as chocolate-dipped potato chips and caramel corn drizzled with white and dark chocolate. Lovely smells drifted over from the adjoining factory, making her mouth water.

Heidi Schwartz was working the counter as usual. She greeted Daphne with a friendly hello. "Anything special you're in the mood for today?"

Sex. "What do you have that's new?" Daphne asked.

"Our big seller is the dark chocolate–chipotle truffles. I can put some in a box for you."

Daphne nodded. "Put in some of those white chocolate bonbons with the rose-flavored filling, too. And a couple of salted caramels."

Heidi got to work. "I hear you're back in town to stay. Are you going to help your mom with weddings?"

"That's the plan." Daphne supposed Heidi had also heard that she was getting divorced. News traveled fast in a small town. If Heidi saw the irony of a divorcée helping with weddings, she kindly didn't say anything.

Daphne was getting out her charge card when Samantha and Cecily Sterling made an appearance, probably on their way to lunch. "Hi, Daphne," Cecily said. "How are you doing?"

There was no need to ask what Cecily meant by that. "I'm fine, glad to be home."

"Have you found a job yet?" Samantha asked.

Good grief. Was there anything anyone didn't know about her? Oh, yes. One thing. No one knew she'd discovered her husband with yet another woman and attacked him with a toilet plunger. No one was ever going to know about that.

"Not yet," Daphne said. "I only need something part-time. I'm going to be helping my mother with weddings."

"Our mom's been talking about hiring an assistant," Cecily said. "I think you two would work well together."

"Yeah?" Daphne liked Muriel Sterling. Well, who didn't? Muriel was eternally sweet, perpetually positive. She'd make a great boss.

"You ought to go see her," Samantha urged.

Maybe she would.

She stopped by Herman's Hamburgers and treated

herself to a fat Herman's burger loaded with fried onions. Then she decided to swing by Muriel Sterling's rented cottage and convince her that hiring an assistant would be an excellent idea.

She went there by way of Johnson's Drugs, where she picked up some mints to disguise her onion breath. Not that Muriel would care. She'd known Daphne all her life. Still, if a woman was going to talk jobs, even with an old friend, she needed to be professional.

Hildy Johnson was on the cash register. She was as tall and homely as Daphne remembered, only she'd put on some weight. Her breasts now stood out like cannons.

"I'm sorry your third marriage didn't work out," she said as she rang up Daphne's purchase.

Hildy, the soul of tact.

"It's hard to find a good man, especially once you get older."

Fifty is the new forty. "It's hard to find a good man, period," Daphne said and handed over a five-dollar bill.

Hildy nodded. "Yes, it is. But you're still a beautiful woman."

"Thank you." Much good it did her.

"I'm sure you'll have men lining up at your door. Or rather, your mother's door. You're living with your mother now, aren't you?"

Hildy made it sound like the hallmark of failure. Okay, Daphne wasn't exactly a success story so far, but her story wasn't over yet.

"I'm helping her run Primrose Haus," she said.

Hildy's eyebrows went up at that.

"I may be getting divorced but I can still plan a wedding reception," Daphne said, her Miss Congeniality smile disappearing.

"Oh, well, yes. Of course you can. It's not like you've never had your own reception before."

Three of them, but who's counting?

Hildy must have realized what that implied because her cheeks suddenly flushed red. "Your mother must be happy to have you back. And everything will work out fine," she added, handing over Daphne's change along with her breath mints.

"Thank you," Daphne murmured.

She left the drugstore, the memory of her romantic failures keeping her company. That was enough to depress even the most optimistic of women.

It was starting to drizzle and she drew her coat tight against the cold March air. Instead of popping a breath mint, she pulled out a dark chocolate–chipotle truffle from her Sweet Dreams candy box and gave her taste buds a treat. There. Life wasn't all bad. It was darkest just before the storm and every cloud had a chocolate lining. And she was taking her new life one day at a time, one step at a time. And the next step was to convince Muriel that she needed an assistant.

Maybe, while she was helping Muriel, Muriel could help her.

Situated next to a vineyard, Muriel's cottage was a Thomas Kinkade painting come to life. White with green shutters, the cottage was hugged by azaleas and rhododendrons. A dried-flower wreath hung on the front door in anticipation of spring.

Daphne's heart rate picked up as she knocked on the door. The very thought of trying to convince a potential future employer that she was worthy of being hired stressed her out. Which was probably one reason she'd stayed at the same job all those years. That hadn't gotten her very far, but when it came to moving up the ladder of success, she was afraid of heights. And all her mother's nagging had only increased her fear. Performance anxiety, she supposed.

This was an old family friend, though; she didn't need to be nervous.

Muriel opened the door and, at the sight of Daphne, broke into a delighted smile. "Daphne, what a nice surprise!"

Her delight was a balm to Daphne's wounded spirit. "I should have called. Are you busy?"

"Just editing some pages. I'm happy for the distraction," Muriel said. "Come in. How about a cup of chocolate mint tea?" she asked as she ushered Daphne into the small living room.

Mint…breath mints. She should've taken one before she got out of the car. Did her breath smell? "That would be great," she said, taking care not to stand too close to Muriel.

"Have a seat. I'll be back in a minute," Muriel said and disappeared into the kitchen.

Daphne settled on a floral love seat and dug out a mint. She popped it in her mouth as she looked around. The place was half the size of Muriel's old house, but it was homey. In addition to the love seat, it held two matching chairs and an ornately carved coffee table. In the far corner, off the kitchen, sat a small mahogany dining table and four chairs. A vase filled with green carnations brought spring into the house and served as a reminder that Saint Patrick's Day was right around the corner. A buffet stood against one wall, topped with a mantel clock. One large painting of a garden entrance blooming with wisteria hung over the love seat, and framed photographs of mountain scenes—her daughter

Samantha's work—occupied space on other walls. The house smelled faintly of lavender.

Now Muriel was back bearing a tray with a chintz teapot, cream and sugar and two china mugs, plus a small plate with finger sandwiches and one with some of her daughter Bailey's famous lavender sugar cookies.

Daphne smelled something new, the enticing combination of chocolate and mint. "That tea smells delicious."

"It is," Muriel said with a smile. "Just the thing for a cold afternoon."

"It's sweet of you to feed me," Daphne said, helping herself to a cookie.

"I was getting hungry. I thought you might be, too." Muriel poured tea into a china mug and handed it to Daphne. "How are you settling in?"

"Pretty well. I'm glad to be back." Even if the whole town did know she'd failed at love. Again.

Muriel nodded. "This is a good place to come and heal a broken heart."

"I'm hoping it's a good place to build a new life," Daphne said.

"It is."

It was now or never. Daphne took a sip of tea for courage. "As I'm sure you've heard, I'll be working with Mother at Primrose Haus, but I'm also looking for something I can do part-time to bring in a little extra money. Cecily said you might need an assistant. I have a lot of experience in that area."

"I could certainly use the help," Muriel said. "It seems that these days an author has to do so much more than simply write a book, and I do find mailings and organizing blog tours to be very taxing."

Daphne knew what a blog was, but what on earth was a blog tour? Whatever it was, she was sure she could handle it. "I'm good with a computer and I'm very good at organizing."

Muriel looked at her eagerly. "Even paperwork?"

"Especially paperwork." She might not have inherited her mother's cleaning gene but she could certainly file.

"Let me show you my office."

Daphne followed her into a tiny bedroom that was serving as her office. It had a filing cabinet, several bookshelves crammed with books and a huge desk... piled high with papers. There was barely room for the computer. The filing cabinet was covered with more papers and so was the printer that sat on a little table next to the desk. A stack of books lay on the floor next to the desk, and in another corner a wicker basket overflowed with still more paperwork and magazines. Muriel Sterling definitely needed help. She'd written a book on simplifying your life. It obviously hadn't included a chapter on simplifying your office space.

"Between my personal life and my writing life, I'm afraid it's all kind of...overwhelming," Muriel confessed as if reading Daphne's mind. "I got rid of a lot when I moved, but managing my business is becoming too much for me. I think hiring an assistant would really bring some order to that part of my life."

"I think you're right," Daphne agreed. "I'd love to help you," she said. "And you'd be helping me, too."

"It's hard starting over, isn't it?" Muriel said kindly.

Daphne's eyes suddenly prickled with tears. "Yes, it is."

"But it can be done." Muriel opened the closet, revealing more clutter—shelving filled with everything from printer paper to sachets and soaps, candles and gift baskets. And more books. "When I do author events I always bring a basket full of goodies as a door prize," she explained. "I love giving things away. And speaking of giving things away…" She selected a book from one of the many stacks. "You might find this helpful. I like to think it helped Bailey when she came home to make a new start."

Daphne took in the book cover. It was simple and striking, with a single long-stemmed red rose against a blurred black-and-white garden. The title was gold embossed. *"'Starting Over,'"* she read. "That's me. Thank you."

"No, thank *you*. You're going to make my life so much easier."

Now, if Daphne could just find someone to make *her* life easier. Maybe a genie. Or a fairy godmother. Or a Jiminy Cricket to warn her every time she was about to make a dumb decision. No, never mind. She made dumb decisions only when it came to men, and since she was done with men she didn't need old Jiminy.

She left Muriel's place feeling far more positive about her life and her future. She could hardly wait to earn a paycheck again. She and Muriel had agreed on a fair salary for three mornings a week, and Daphne was going to start on Friday. That was fine with her. Cash flow was a good thing, and working only three days a week, she'd still have time to get her affairs in order, as well as take some of the load off her mother's shoulders. And prove she was capable of doing so.

Daphne sighed. Maybe that would never happen. Her mother was a perfectionist and an overachiever. Not content with her job at the bank and having a pretty house, she'd started her own business and turned herself into one of the grande dames of Icicle Falls. In the past, Roberta Gilbert had chaired any number of committees, seeing to everything from town beautification to organizing the Oktoberfest parade. She still rode in it every year on the Primrose Haus float, along with any of the local brides who'd gotten married or held their receptions at the house that year. Oh, yes, she was a hard act to follow. Not to mention an exhausting one.

But Daphne was determined to do it.

This job was a hopeful beginning. Her mother might not have thought highly of her skills but Muriel Sterling obviously did, enough to hire her. Who knew where she might go from here? Today Muriel Sterling's loyal assistant, tomorrow the organizer of some new Icicle Falls festival. She wouldn't always be a loser.

She smiled. Once she was free of Mitchell and had money from the sale of the house, she'd be sitting pretty. Heck, she was sitting pretty now.

She was so busy thinking about how her life was going to improve, she almost didn't see the dog darting into the street in front of her. She stomped on the brakes and just about throttled herself with her seat belt. The animal dodged out of the way, then romped back to the side of the road to give a huckleberry bush the sniff test.

"You are not going to last long if you do that," she muttered.

The dog, some sort of yellow Lab mix, still seemed to be a puppy. She got out of the car and called, "Here, boy," and the dog came bounding over, tail wagging.

The animal had on a flea collar but appeared to have slipped its dog collar. It looked well fed and happy, and she suspected, judging from the muddy paws and legs, it had dug out of someone's yard. "We'd better take you to the animal shelter," she said. She opened the back door of her car. "Wanna go for a ride?"

The dog happily jumped into the backseat. Her mother would have had a heart attack over the mess, but Daphne liked dogs, and she'd rather have a little mess to clean up than see this animal get hurt.

Dr. Wolfe, the town vet, was volunteering at the shelter. Although she hadn't met him, she'd heard about him and knew he'd recently married one of the local women.

"Hello, there," he greeted her as she came in with her new friend prancing by her side.

"I found this dog wandering loose. I think he got out of someone's backyard."

"That looks like Bandit."

The dog confirmed the vet's deduction with a tail wag.

"Well, Bandit, you little sneak," Dr. Wolfe said, squatting down to pet the animal. "I see you've made the great escape again." He smiled up at Daphne. "I'll make sure he gets back to Mrs. Little. She's probably out searching for him."

"Thanks," Daphne said.

"No problem. Maybe this will finally convince Mrs. L. to get an invisible fence. By the way, I'm Ken Wolfe," he said and smiled at her.

He seemed like a nice man. Too bad he was taken.

You're not looking anymore, ever again, she reminded herself. Mitchell had seemed like a nice man when she first met him, too. She wasn't going to waste any more time looking for nice men. If she wanted something to love, an animal was the best bet…the four-legged kind.

"I'm Daphne Gilbert," she said, reverting to her maiden name.

"Roberta Gilbert's daughter?" Daphne nodded and he said, "She's great. My wife and I got married at Primrose Haus. It's pretty impressive."

"Yes, it is." Daphne gave the dog a goodbye scratch behind the ears. How she'd love to have a dog, but she knew better than to even suggest it. She'd just turned to leave when, from out of nowhere, a small black cat trotted over to her and began rubbing against her legs. "Well, who's this?" she asked, bending down to stroke its soft fur. She hadn't had a cat since her sweet tabby died. And that was shortly before she'd married Mitchell. Mitchell had been allergic to cat dander, so no cats for Daphne. But Mitchell was gone now and Daphne wasn't allergic to cat dander.

"That's Milo. We got him a couple of days ago. His owners are getting divorced and neither one wanted him."

Poor guy, she thought. *I know how you feel, little fella. It's awful not to be wanted.* "He looks young."

"He is, under a year, so he's got energy to burn. But he's been neutered and he's had all his shots."

Daphne picked up the cat and he began to chew on her hair. It made her giggle. She couldn't remember the last time she'd laughed.

She'd love to take Milo home with her. A cat wouldn't be any bother. He'd probably run and hide when they had wedding guests. And if he wasn't prone to hiding, she could always shut him in her room for a few hours. She had a comfy bed with a homemade quilt (another of her mother's many talents), perfect for catnaps.

Except…she couldn't simply bring a cat home any more than she could a dog. The house on Primrose Street had been her home growing up but it wasn't now. In fact, it was more a business than a house—her mother's business. It would be selfish and inconsiderate of Daphne to do such a thing, especially considering the fact that her mother wasn't particularly fond of animals.

She sighed. "He's awfully cute. I hope you find a home for him quickly." Somewhere from the back of the build-

ing she heard a dog howl. Leaving without an animal…
it felt wrong.

Never mind, she told herself as she drove away from
the shelter. *You won't always be living with your mother.*
Down the road she'd get a little place of her own here in
town, a place like Muriel Sterling's that she could doll
up with rustic furniture and gingham curtains. Then
she'd get a pet. Or two.

She found her mother seated at the kitchen table,
going over bills. "Where were you all this time?" Roberta asked.

"I had some errands to run." Daphne set a box of the
chocolates she'd bought on the kitchen table.

Her mother cocked an eyebrow. "Should you be
spending money on chocolate?"

Daphne sat down opposite her and nudged the box
in her direction. She couldn't help smiling as Mother,
unable to resist, selected a white chocolate truffle. "I
think I can afford it. I got a job."

Her announcement produced a smile of approval.
"You did?"

Daphne nodded. "Starting Friday, I'm going to be
working for Muriel Sterling three mornings a week. I'm
going to get her organized."

"That's a great beginning. But it surely won't be
enough to live on."

Daphne's own smile curdled. Leave it to her mother
to see the dark clouds instead of the rainbow. "If I'm
working part-time I'll still be able to help you here,"
she pointed out.

Her mother's expression changed from approving
to…wary. Hard to believe only a few days ago she'd
suggested Daphne help her. Now it looked as if she was
having second thoughts. What a surprise.

"Something else might come up," she said. "You don't want to be tied down here."

"Or you don't want me to be."

"I didn't say that," her mother said stiffly.

She didn't have to. Daphne had never had an aptitude for foreign languages, but she had no problem with body language, especially her mother's. "I really am capable of helping you."

"I know. Let's not talk about that right now, though. Let's talk about what you did with the rest of your day. Or have you been at Muriel's all this time?"

"No. I also went by the animal shelter."

Daphne got no further. "You brought home a dog?" Her mother's horrified gaze roamed the room as if she was looking for a Saint Bernard to suddenly dash out from around the corner or behind the curtains.

"No. I didn't think you'd want one here."

"Certainly not. They make huge messes and they smell."

Which was why, growing up, the only pets Daphne had were parakeets and goldfish. "Dogs are high maintenance. Cats not so much," she ventured.

Mother didn't seem any happier about the prospect of a cat. "Don't tell me you got one."

"I was strongly tempted. They had the cutest black cat there."

"Cats may be cute, but they scratch furniture."

"Not if you get a scratching post."

"I suppose," her mother said, and Daphne could almost hear her thinking, *And where, among my antiques, would that go?*

It was just as well she hadn't adopted Milo. Daphne sighed. "Don't worry. I won't bring one here. I wouldn't do that to you." She loved her mother dearly, but sometimes she wished the woman would loosen up a little.

"Darling, it's not that I wouldn't love you to have a cat. However, this place doesn't really work for pets, not with all the receptions we host. Some people are allergic."

"Of course," Daphne agreed. "There's something about pets, though. Animals love you unconditionally." Sometimes she wasn't sure she could say that about her mother.

"Down the road, when you get your own place…"

It was the same thing she'd told herself, but hearing her mother say it stung. "And I know you're in a hurry for that to happen."

Mother frowned. "I didn't say that, and I wish you wouldn't put words in my mouth."

She didn't have to say it. Daphne was nothing but a big inconvenience. What kind of mother wouldn't be happy to have her daughter back with her? Everywhere Daphne turned these days, she found rejection.

That's not true, said her brain. *Your mother's not rejecting you. She's rejecting having a cat. And she's probably assuming you'll want your own place.* Of course she was being oversensitive and unreasonable. Still, her wounded heart wouldn't listen. She felt that prickle in her eyes again, signaling the arrival of tears. She pushed away from the table. "I'm going up to my room for a while. I need to check my email."

"Daphne." Her mother's voice softened, taking on that pleading don't-be-a-pill tone Daphne was all too familiar with.

"I'll be down later," she said, striving to keep the hurt from seeping into her words. She went upstairs to her old room and shut the door behind her, putting distance between them. Not too different from her teen years when they quarreled. Except she'd outgrown door slamming.

She settled on the bed with her old laptop and brought up her email. One of her neighbors in Seattle was inviting her to a party. Actually, she was on more of a fishing expedition. *Are you two still together? I haven't seen you around much. Or Mitchell. And what was with the sacks of clothes on the front lawn?*

Daphne gave a snort of disgust. "You'll figure it out soon enough."

A friend had forwarded a collection of cute animal pictures with clever captions. Oh, she thought again, how she'd love to have a pet. She did need to get her own place. It was ridiculous living with her mother at her age.

Maybe it wouldn't be if her mother could ever admit she needed her, if they could work together and help each other. But her mother didn't want her help. Roberta Gilbert didn't need anyone's help.

Daphne shut the computer and looked out the window at Sleeping Lady Mountain. The view had always inspired her. Today it didn't.

She reached for Muriel's book and began to read. It was almost as good as actually being with Muriel, having a heart-to-heart talk.

Wherever you are right now, you're there for a reason.

Daphne frowned. *Yes, because I'm a failure at love.*

And whatever choices or mistakes brought you to where you are, know that you're in this place at this moment to learn something, to go somewhere new or to encourage someone else. The door is open. All you have to do is step out.

Easy for Muriel to say. She didn't have Roberta Gilbert for a mother.

Chapter Eleven

Roberta, the Expert on Love

Roberta suddenly had a headache. It happened a lot when dealing with her daughter. This time she couldn't lay the blame at Daphne's door, though. It belonged solely to her. In the space of a few short minutes, she'd managed to devalue Daphne's new job and insinuate that she wanted her gone.

Truth be told, she did. Not far away, of course, but far enough so she wasn't in such close proximity, constantly worrying and aggravating Roberta. Someplace like Seattle. Or even Wenatchee. Daphne had her own life to live, and she could make her own decisions, but when she made poor ones, Roberta had to grind her molars. Actually, if that was all she did, things would go so much better between them. But she never could settle for simple molar-grinding. She always had to say something.

Honestly, though, wasn't it a mother's job to give her daughter advice? And Daphne needed advice. On a regular basis. She did such impetuous things, and this job working for Muriel was the latest example. Roberta didn't see how a part-time job was going to be of any benefit to Daphne's bank account. Of course, at this point Primrose Haus could support both of them, particularly since Roberta owned the house free and clear. Not that Daphne had ever hinted at getting a paycheck from her. Roberta knew her daughter just wanted to help. But at the rate they were going, Roberta would be buying aspirin by the case.

She took one of the chocolates from the box Daphne had left behind. It was too bad Daphne's marriage hadn't worked out. Roberta had known it wouldn't and tried to warn her. But would she listen? No. When it came to men, she was entirely too trusting. Well, the apple didn't fall far from the tree, did it?

Ancient past, she told herself. Yet she could remember it all as though it was yesterday.

1961

Gerard was the best-looking boy in school. Everyone said so. He arrived the summer before their junior year and made an instant impression on the football coach. And from the very first day of school, he also made an impression on every girl in school, including Roberta. He dated enough of them, skimming the cream from the top of the social tier. That meant she didn't have a chance. She was a straight-A student and on the debate team, but that didn't carry the clout that being a cheerleader did. Come senior year, he was captain of the football team, which should have put him even more out of reach.

Remarkably, it hadn't. He'd fallen for her after she'd tutored him in English. He thought she was wonderful. She was the only girl for him. He told her so every time they parked in some dark, deserted spot, his hands trying to sneak places they didn't belong.

He was the only boy for her, more addictive than a hot-fudge sundae, more exciting than any of the boys she'd gone steady with her sophomore and junior years. All two of them. It wasn't that she was homely. She was pretty, she knew that; the problem was that she was also smart, and that scared off a lot of boys. So, when it came to boyfriends, she'd been happy to take what she could get.

Andy the math genius had been shy—so shy, in fact, that he'd needed half a dozen dates to work up the nerve to kiss her. And that first kiss had been chaste and disappointing. The ones that followed weren't much better. They were always tentative, just enough to stir up her teen-girl hormones, certainly not the kind of kisses she'd seen on the movie screen when she went to the matinee with her girlfriends. She'd seen a few of those scenes at the drive-in with Andy, too, but somehow they never seemed to inspire him to greatness. She wasn't too upset when his father got a job transfer and the family moved to Maine.

Leonard wasn't any more interesting. He preferred making model airplanes and going to comic book conventions to movies or dances, and they parted by mutual consent. She decided to spend the rest of her junior year concentrating on her studies. And loving Gerard Jones from afar.

What a thrill it was when she entered her English class September of her senior year and found him in it. And how perfect that the teacher stipulated on alphabetical seating. Gilbert before Jones. She wound up in the desk in front of him, which finally put her on his radar. He wasn't intimidated by her smarts, probably because he had so much confidence in himself, and he loved playing with her long, dark hair when the teacher wasn't looking. Then came the tutoring sessions at the library. He'd say things like "You smell so good I can't concentrate" (this was thanks to Roberta getting into her mother's Chanel No. 5) and "Has anyone told you that you have beautiful eyes?" (She did, actually, and it was about time he noticed.) Then one day, as they were leaving the library, he said, "There's a new movie at the drive-in. Want to go?"

Of course she did.

At the drive-in he didn't give her an insecure, short-lived kiss. Oh, no. It had been a full-on force-of-nature attack, an assault with his lips. And tongue.

"What are you doing?" she demanded, pushing him away.

He gaped at her. "You don't know how to French-kiss?"

Obviously not. She felt like a fool.

"Never mind," he said, pulling her back toward him. "I'll teach you."

And what a teacher he was. His kisses left her breath-less, and as they became increasingly more intimate with each date, she had difficulty remembering her mother's words of caution. *Never let a boy take liberties. He won't respect you.* But Gerard seemed to respect her just fine. He always opened doors for her, and the corsage he bought her for the Christmas Ball was the most beauti-ful one she'd ever had.

Still, she did what all good girls did. She kept her legs crossed. After a while he got frustrated with her crossed-leg syndrome and broke up with her. He started seeing a cheerleader, and to show him she couldn't care less, she started dating a boy on the debate team. But he was no Gerard, and by spring they were back together.

One evening, as the windows of his daddy's Buick became more and more foggy, she let him take off her bra. When he unclasped those little hooks he pretty much undid the last of her resolution. The thrill of what he was doing with his mouth and hands was unlike anything she'd ever known. But what would her mother say if she saw Roberta with her skirt up to her waist and her top missing?

"Bobbi, I want you so bad," he murmured against her neck.

"I can't," she moaned, but she didn't remove his hand from her breast.

"I love you—you know that. That's why I couldn't stay away."

She conveniently forgot that she'd been the one who'd gone crawling to him, hinting that she'd give him what he wanted.

"You love me, too, don't you?"

Now his hand was someplace it had absolutely no business being. She tried to find her willpower. "My mother would kill me."

"Who cares about your mother? She's old. What does she know?"

He had a point.

"We've been going together all year."

Except for that short time they'd been seeing other people. That had been a mistake. There was no one like Gerard and she didn't want to lose him again.

"You've got my letterman's jacket. I wouldn't give that to just any girl."

The cheerleader had worn it for three weeks.

But it was hers again now. Ooh, she was melting.

"If you loved me you'd let me."

Of course she loved him. "I can't," she said, trying to squirm out of his arms. He knew good girls didn't go all the way. Oh, but she wanted to.

He pulled back his hand and moved to the other side of the seat, leaving her feeling rejected and unsatisfied. "Fine. I guess you don't love me, after all. I don't know why I'm bothering to be with you if you don't love me."

His words were like some horrible magic wand, bringing tears to her eyes. "I do love you."

"No, you don't. You haven't proved it."

She knew what she had to do to prove it.

You shouldn't do this. The thought wasn't strong enough to overcome her desire and the need to show Gerard that she did indeed love him. She slipped out of her panties and closed the distance between them. "Don't stop, Gerard. Let's not stop."

So they didn't. And from that night on, every date ended with a sexual encounter. They took precautions. Gerard got her some spermicide he said was guaranteed to prevent pregnancy and she believed him. It wasn't until almost the end of the school year that she missed her period.

"I'm late," she told him as they sat in a booth at the Dairy Queen with their burgers and shakes.

He looked momentarily confused. "What do you mean late?"

"My period," she said, blushing.

His face turned as white as his vanilla shake. "Are you sure?"

Her periods had been as regular as clockwork since seventh grade. "I'm sure."

Now his brows drew together and his mouth dipped in an angry scowl. "You'll have to do something about it."

What, exactly, did he want her to do? "What do you mean?"

"Get rid of it, Bobbi. I can't get married. I have a scholarship to Stanford. Remember?"

"You can still go to school. I'll work," she offered.

"While you're preggers? Use your head."

This wasn't the reaction she'd hoped for. She'd dreamed of him hugging her, telling her not to worry, it would be all right. He'd take care of her. She'd even hoped he'd say that he'd marry her, postpone school and get a job. Instead, look what he was asking her to do! She had no idea how to get rid of a baby and no desire to learn.

"Well, I can't get rid of it. I won't."

He pushed away his shake. "Suit yourself." Then he was scooting out of the booth. "Come on. I'm taking you home."

The ride back to her house was a silent one. "Are you mad?" she finally asked in a small voice.

"Yeah, I'm mad," he snarled. "And I'm done. I want my letterman's jacket back."

"You're breaking up with me?" No, this couldn't be happening.

"What do you think?"

"I think you're a jerk," she shot at him, hot tears stinging her cheeks.

"And I think you're a slut."

A slut. He'd called her a slut when he was the only boy she'd slept with? She hadn't even known how to French-kiss when she first met him. "I'll teach you," he'd said. Oh, yes, he'd taught her a lot. But just about sex. He hadn't taught her anything about love.

Of course, her mother hadn't taught her much about love, either. Her grandma had been the only one who really cared about her, but Grandma had been helpless to turn Roberta's mother from her plan once Roberta's secret was out. "You can't keep it. This is for the best," she'd insisted. Whose best, she hadn't specified.

No one could accuse Roberta of being like her mother. If anyone here had known the woman, which, thankfully, no one had. Roberta had actually cared. She'd loved Daphne with a passion, had wanted her beautiful little girl to have a successful and satisfying life. She'd done everything in her power to make that happen. Growing up, Daphne had it all—Girl Scouts, art lessons from a local artist, piano lessons, a lovely wedding, the kind Roberta herself had dreamed of. And then another. And another.

Through it all, Roberta had stoically stood by her daughter, watching her stumble from one romantic failure to the next, reminding herself that it was Daphne's life and she was free to choose her own destiny...if you could call such a bumbling mess a destiny.

Where had she gone wrong? Unlike her mother, she'd been supportive, constantly trying to bring Daphne up to her full potential.

Roberta sighed. Mothers always wanted their daughters to be perfect, and their daughters always disappointed them. It never changed from one generation to the next. The only thing that changed was the expectations.

Enough wandering around in the unpleasant past, she told herself. She had a darned good present and that was what mattered. She put the teakettle on the stove to freshen her tea, and as she waited for the water to heat, she gazed out the kitchen window at the grounds.

The grass was getting shaggy. She needed to have

Hank Hawkins come over and start getting the yard in shape for spring. She picked up the phone and punched in the number for Hawkins Lawn Service. Not surprisingly, it went to voice mail. Hank and his boys were already busy.

Hank had moved to Icicle Falls seven years ago, which meant he was still considered a newcomer. His arrival had coincided with Roberta's knees getting tired of all the weeding she had to do. She'd hired him and been pleased, and he'd been working for her ever since. She'd recommended him to Pat York and Janice Lind and several other people, and now he was always in demand. Lucky for her she was a highly valued client.

"Hank, I think it's time to start cleaning up for spring around here. When can you fit me in?"

It turned out that he couldn't help her right away, even though she was a valued customer. "Sorry, Roberta, I can't make it until Friday afternoon," he said when he called her back.

She didn't like having Hank or his men there on Fridays. She often had clients coming in on Friday afternoons or evenings, or events to set up for.

This weekend was clear, though. "I'll take it," she decided. Then, after that, they could get back on schedule and do midweek maintenance.

An unwelcome thought entered her mind after she ended the call. Daphne would be home Friday afternoon. This would not have been a problem if Daphne was happily married. But now...

Hank was a good-looking man, tall and broad-shouldered, but divorced and a bad risk. Daphne was a beautiful woman, a *vulnerable* beautiful woman, with poor taste in men. Roberta could envision her daughter and her gardener encountering each other by the azaleas and falling madly, stupidly, in love.

She'd have to make sure she found some time-consuming errands for her daughter to run after work; that was all there was to it. Daphne fell in love as regularly as some people ordered coffee at Bavarian Brews.

There would be no ordering up of a certain tall drink of water here. No, sir. Not on Roberta's watch.

Chapter Twelve

Anne, Wedding Planner and Shrink

"We want to get married at the beach, and we'd like our dogs, Cutie Pie and Commodore, to be in the wedding, too," said the excited bride. Rika Washington had hired Anne two weeks ago and called her every day since with a new question, concern or inspiration. Today was inspiration day.

The customer was always right, Anne reminded herself. Still, she couldn't help remembering some of the doggy disasters she'd seen over the years when brides included their pets. There'd been the irritable pooch who'd bitten the groom's hand when he went to put the ring on his bride's finger, and the happy mutt who'd done a mating dance with the leg of the bride's father as he stood waiting to give his daughter away.

The worst one was Bismark, the German shepherd who ran away with the flower girl. The bride had thought it would be adorable to have Bismark tow a flower-bedecked wagon holding the flower girl down the aisle during her garden wedding at Seattle's Washington Park Arboretum. Her father happily complied and got busy in his wood shop, producing an adorable little wagon.

Bismark seemed more than willing to do his part at the rehearsal the evening before. The day of the wedding, however, he spotted another dog at the far end of the park, and instead of walking sedately down the aisle with five-year-old Olivia, he took off at a gallop, the little girl clutching the wagon rails and screeching at the top of her lungs.

"No, Bismark!" yelled his mommy and took off after the dog, her veil flying behind her. Of course, the groom and the groomsmen went after the dog, too, who had a head start since he'd bolted before he'd barely begun to go down the aisle. Half the guests joined in the pursuit as Olivia and Bismark hurtled across the lush lawn, Bismark barking and Olivia screeching.

The wagon tipped, spilling Olivia onto the grass, flowers and all, but Bismark kept going. The owner of the other dog, a highly energetic mixed breed, pulled on his leash, keeping him tightly reined in, while the woman with him made shooing motions and yelled at Bismark to scram.

Bismark had no intention of scramming, and doggy mayhem broke out. After much growling and swearing and threatened lawsuits, not to mention a torn tuxedo, the groom got him and hauled him back.

Other than a grass-stained dress and a missing hair wreath, Olivia was none the worse for wear, but she was still shrieking even after her mother picked her up and carried her back.

The child was eventually calmed and the dog was, well, in the doghouse, on his leash and made to sit with the groom's father. It didn't seem to bother Bismark, though, because he spent the remainder of the wedding barking at the other dog, who'd long since departed.

Anne recounted the story of Bismark and Olivia and

cautioned Rika that while animals could add a lot to a wedding, they could also be unpredictable.

Rika was unfazed. "Cutie Pie and Commodore will be well behaved. They're basset hounds. They don't have the energy to be bad."

Anne's family had owned a basset hound when she was growing up, and she knew exactly what the woman meant. "You're probably right."

"We're going to get Commodore a tux and a boutonniere and Cutie Pie a little veil."

Anne could see the wedding pictures now. They'd be cute…or ridiculous. Anne leaned toward ridiculous, but she wasn't the one getting married.

"I'm so excited," gushed the bride-to-be. "This is going to be a beautiful wedding."

Every wedding was. Even ones that involved flower girls getting unexpected wild rides.

She'd just had time to share Rika's latest idea with Kendra when her next client arrived for their lunch meeting.

Lisbeth Holmes appeared to be somewhere in her thirties. She worked as a buyer for Nordstrom, and with her cashmere sweater, black pencil skirt and expensive shoes (not to mention the high-end costume jewelry and that Coach purse), she looked like a walking advertisement for the store. She was a tall, svelte brunette, the kind of woman who would make a gunnysack look good. Put her in a bridal gown and she'd be breathtaking.

Her groom was six inches taller, with a football player's build. He was dressed casually in jeans and a sweater (not cashmere). Maybe he worked for some company that wrote computer software or games and had a more casual work code. Or maybe he was an escaped Seattle Seahawk. But no. It turned out the future groom wrote murder mysteries for a living.

His name was Tad, and he and Lisbeth had been together for the past two years. He'd finally popped the question, and now Lisbeth was ready to start planning the wedding of her dreams. Judging by the modest diamond in her engagement ring, murder didn't pay all that well. Anne hoped the woman wasn't dreaming too big.

"We're talking about February, Valentine's Day," Lisbeth said.

They'd have a terrible time getting a table when they went out to celebrate their anniversary, but at least they'd have no trouble remembering it.

"That sounds lovely," Anne said. "What's your vision for the wedding?"

Sometimes a bride-to-be would seem a little confused by this question. Not Lisbeth. "I want a traditional church wedding," she said. "Red and white for my colors. And I'd like to have the reception somewhere with a pretty view."

Anne nodded, taking notes as Lisbeth talked. And now, before they went any further, she had to ask. "What's your budget?"

"I've been saving for this for the past two years," Lisbeth said, beaming, and named a figure that pleasantly surprised Anne.

"She's really good with money," Tad bragged, helping himself to one of the tea sandwiches Kendra had set out on the desk. "Considering what I make, it's a good thing."

"You'll make more," Lisbeth assured him. "He's going to be the next Stephen King," she predicted.

"But I don't write horror. And speaking of horror, my parents as well as Lisbeth's are divorced, and we've got a lot of exes and steps, and some of them aren't talking to one another. How do you work around that?"

"We'll find a way," Anne told him. She usually did, although sometimes it was a challenge.

She could see her sister, over at her desk, trying to hide a smirk and tried to forget the time she'd pulled aside an ornery grandma who hated her grandson's bride and was making a ruckus. Anne had threatened to lock her in the church broom closet if she didn't behave. Elder abuse, not one of her finer moments. The bride was grateful, though.

"Let's talk a little more about the big picture," Anne said, ignoring Kendra.

An hour later they'd made a good start. The bride had given Anne a clear idea of what she wanted. She'd also given her a check.

"When you have a chance, go to the website and download our timetable and checklist. You'll find them both very helpful," Anne said. "I'll get some ideas together and email you a few helpful links."

"Great," said Lisbeth. She smiled at her future husband, and he grinned back and took her hand.

"Man, I can't believe we're actually doing this," he said.

"It took both of us a while to decide," she confided in Anne. "We don't want to end up..."

"Like our parents," he finished. "I don't want to spend a bunch of money on a wedding just to end up in divorce court."

"You're not spending anything," his bride said, her voice slightly condescending.

His cheeks flushed. "Well, I'm paying for the honeymoon."

She rolled her eyes. "I can hardly wait to see where that'll be. Tukwila probably."

The flush deepened. "Hey, I've been saving, too."

Oh, boy, here was a chink in the armor. Financial inequality could be a recipe for disaster. Anne hoped they'd also been saving for premarriage counseling.

"It's okay," said his bride. "Someday, when you're really successful, you can take me to Italy."

If they lasted long enough.

But what happened after the wedding wasn't her responsibility. She couldn't promise a couple a perfect marriage. Her job was to create the perfect wedding. And that she could do.

She was feeling happy about her calling in life until Laurel Browne walked into her office. And Laurel wasn't smiling. Which meant that soon Anne wouldn't be, either. Mothers of brides should be caged until after the wedding. Well, okay, not all of them, just some of them. Laurel in particular. Why was she here? She didn't owe Anne money, and any question she or her daughter had at this point they could ask via phone or email.

Anne forced her lips to turn up at the corners. "Hi, Laurel. What brings you here?" *I wish I didn't have to ask.*

"My daughter has a new idea. She saw it online. Or read it in a book. Or something."

"Oh, boy," said Kendra under her breath.

"Sit down." Anne took a seat behind her shabby-chic desk and motioned Laurel to one of the chintz chairs across from it.

"I think I've been more than reasonable," Laurel began as she sank into the chair.

Compared to what? Anne schooled her face into a supportive expression.

"But I draw the line at goldfish swimming in vases on the tables at the reception. What am I supposed to do with all those goldfish afterward? And what if one of them dies and…floats? That'll be appetizing for our guests."

"I do see your point," said Anne. This happened sometimes. Brides spent too much time on Pinterest and pretty soon they wanted to incorporate every idea they saw into their weddings.

"Well, I put my foot down. I had to. But…" That was as far as Laurel got. Her face crumpled and her eyes were suddenly awash in tears. "We're not speaking. My daughter and I are not speaking," she repeated on a sob.

Oh, dear. Now Anne knew the real reason Laurel had come to the office. She didn't need a wedding planner. She needed a shrink. Or just a sympathetic ear.

Anne reached across her desk and laid a comforting hand on Laurel's arm. Kendra, thinking in practical terms, placed a box of tissues in front of Laurel and murmured, "I'll get some coffee." And with that she disappeared, leaving Laurel in Anne's capable hands.

Capable as she was, seeing Laurel's meltdown unnerved Anne. Her own mother-of-the-bride mantle was still new, with no rips or tears, but here was Laurel, living proof that anything, even something as small as a goldfish, could rip that mantle to shreds.

Everyone had mother-daughter disagreements, as she well knew. She and Laney certainly had when Laney was growing up. There'd even been a time when they weren't speaking. The fact that it was short-lived hadn't made it any less horrible.

Anne had said no to Laney staying out all night after her senior prom. Of course she'd been accused of being the meanest mother on the planet, the only mother unfeeling enough to ruin her daughter's big night. Anne had insisted Laney come home after the post-prom cruise, threatening dire circumstances if she didn't. Voices rose to the point that Anne was sure someone in the neighborhood was going to call the police. Anne had the last word. Literally, because then the stony silence fell.

It turned out that Laney's life wasn't ruined, but an entire week of Anne's was when Laney stopped talking to her. Cam convinced her to cave and Laney to apologize and life finally settled back down. But now, listening to Laurel, Anne could still remember that sick feeling in the pit of her stomach, the irrational fear that she and her daughter would never speak again, all over a prom-night curfew.

Mother-daughter relationships were a complicated mixture of love, loyalty, irritation and resentment, and there was nothing like a wedding to stir that pot. Seeing Laurel sitting here in her office weeping gave Anne the uneasy feeling that she was looking at the Ghost of Wedding Future. No, she told herself. She and Laney might have had their differences over the years—what mother and daughter didn't?—but she was no Laurel.

"We never fight," Laurel was saying. "This is not like my daughter." She looked at Anne with tear-drenched eyes and a trembling lower lip. "What should I do?"

Anne sighed. "Let her have the fish."

Laurel dabbed at her eyes with a tissue. "Chelsea's out of control, Anne. I can't keep giving in to every crazy thing she wants."

"Sure you can," Anne said gently. "I know it all seems a little silly to you, but it's something she really wants. And honestly, a few fish won't cost much. We'll handle it so you won't have to worry about what to do with them after the reception." Anne had a couple of friends with ponds. They'd love more goldfish.

Laurel blew her nose. "Fish, Anne. It was…the final straw."

"I know," Anne said. "But think of all the presents you've given your daughter over the years, all the birthday presents, the Christmas presents, graduation gifts."

Laurel sniffed.

"This is the most important gift, maybe the last big one, you'll give your daughter. You want it to be special, to be what she really wants."

Laurel bit her lip and nodded.

Kendra returned bearing coffee in a ceramic cup with the company's logo on it—two entwined hearts dusted with confetti. Laurel took it and stared into it as if contemplating whether to drink the coffee or try to drown herself in it. "You're right, of course." She frowned at the cup and set it on the desk. "This is all becoming so…stressful."

"Don't worry. We're here to make it as easy as possible for you," Anne said.

Now Laurel did something she hadn't done since she'd first walked into Anne's office with her daughter. She smiled at Anne. "Thank you. Thank you for being so understanding."

"I have a daughter, too," Anne said, "and we're planning her wedding right now."

"Good luck with that," Laurel said cynically. She sighed. "I just want Chelsea to be happy."

"That's what we all want for our children."

"She doesn't always know what's best."

"They don't," Anne agreed. "But they have to live their own lives, and after a certain point, all a mother can do is guide her daughter."

Laurel nodded sadly.

"The fish will be lovely."

"Yes, I suppose they will." Laurel frowned. "What if they die?"

Worse things had happened at weddings. Anne decided to keep that bit of information to herself. "Trust me," she said. "It'll be fine."

Laurel took a deep breath. "All right. The fish stay." She rose, once more in control of her emotions, in control of the wedding. Or so she thought. "I'll be in touch," she said and sailed out of the office.

"Well, that was exciting," Kendra muttered after she left.

"Never a dull day in the wedding business. You know that," Anne said.

"I bet she's on the phone to her daughter as we speak."

"I bet you're right. I would be."

"Me, too," Kendra said. "Kids turn us into such softies. By the way, Coral wants to start wearing makeup."

"What did you say to that?"

"I said, 'Heck, no. We'll talk when you turn fifteen.'"

"I'm sure that went over well." Anne could envision her nine-year-old niece flouncing out of the room, hurling threats that ranged from running away to hunger strikes as she went.

"Oh, yeah. She told me I was a heartless monster. Then she went straight to her father and asked him.

Anne grinned. "And what did *he* say?"

Kendra grinned back. "'Ask your mother.'"

"He's either the smartest man alive or he's a big chicken."

"Yeah. Which do you think?"

Anne chuckled and went back to her computer.

But even as she looked at the screen she couldn't get

the image of a tearful Laurel out of her mind. Would that be her a week or a month from now? No, of course not. Laney was a grown woman now, not a temperamental teenager, and they had a great relationship.

And Laney knew that anything Anne suggested would be in her best interests. After all, Anne did this for a living. And she could be diplomatic; she could steer her daughter in the right direction.

Couldn't she?

Chapter Thirteen

Daphne, Wedding Hostess in Training

Daphne's first morning working for Muriel Sterling went faster than a plate of chocolate chip cookies at a family picnic. She got overheated organizing Muriel's messy supply closet (thank you, hot flash) and then, since she still had time left, dealt with a backlog of emails from readers who'd been inspired by Muriel's latest book.

"I hate not replying personally," Muriel had said, "but I tend to get bogged down when I'm writing back, and then I don't get any work done on my new book."

So she'd delegated, giving Daphne a series of stock phrases she could use. "Thank you for taking time to write me."…"So glad you found the book helpful."… "Remember, new beginnings can be difficult but they can be made."

Daphne caught herself reciting that last line whenever an image of Mitchell's handsome, smiling face came to mind. She'd thought they'd be together for the rest of their lives. The rest of their lives had lasted only six years.

It was oddly comforting to read the emails from readers

who one moment had been riding high and the next found themselves in life's recycle bin, having to create something new out of what had become garbage.

I lost my job, but after reading your book I know another door is going to open, wrote one reader. My husband died. Reading about how you coped after losing yours was so comforting, wrote another.

Still another emailed, I thought life couldn't get any worse when I got breast cancer, but then my husband couldn't deal with it and left me halfway through my chemotherapy. That was when I didn't want to live anymore. Thank God a good friend gave me your book. After reading it, I decided no way was I going to let all the bad stuff define who I am as a woman. I got a wig and I've been taking piano lessons. I already feel better about my life and hopeful for my future.

Wow, and I thought I had it bad, Daphne mused. She began her reply using one of Muriel's stock phrases, but then her fingers insisted on typing more. Your hair will come back lovelier than ever, I'm sure of it. Congratulations on all the positive things you're doing.

She was suddenly aware of Muriel reading over her shoulder and she gave a start. "Sorry. I got carried away."

"Don't be sorry. That's exactly what I would've told her," Muriel said. "I knew you were the right woman to work for me."

The right woman, Daphne thought with a smile as she walked home from Muriel's cottage. Yes, things were looking up. From now on, her life would be better. Manless and better.

She went to the bank and opened a new account, then picked up the groceries her mother had requested. And because it was past lunchtime and, after all, a girl had to eat, she went by Gingerbread Haus to treat herself to a latte and a gingerbread boy.

Cass Wilkes, an old-time acquaintance, was still there and happy to wait on Daphne.

"Is business as good as usual?" Daphne asked as Cass rang up her order.

"Sure is. But I'm putting in fewer hours these days, hiring more help. Life's too short to work yourself to death. The kids are growing up fast, and I want to be able to spend more time with them. Did your mom tell you Dani's expecting her first in September?"

"No. Congratulations." Daphne would love to become a grandma, but that was waiting in the future, since her daughter was currently too busy with her career to think about babies.

"How about you? I hear you're about to join the ranks of the single. Are you doing okay?"

"I am. Who needs men, anyway, right?"

"These guys are your safest bet," Cass joked, handing over a gingerbread boy.

Daphne pretended he was Mitchell and bit off his head. Very satisfying.

"If you ever want to go to Zelda's for a huckleberry martini, let me know," Cass suggested.

Daphne was both touched and encouraged by her kindness. Who said you couldn't go home again? "Thanks. I will."

She returned to Primrose Haus to find a metallic-blue truck filled with lawn care equipment parked outside, the words Hawkins Landscaping Service emblazoned on the side of the cab. Mother's lawn guy was here. Daphne had seen him only once, when she'd come up to visit the year before, but she remembered him as a brawny man with a great smile. Not that she was interested. She didn't care how brawny he was.

Anyway, who had time for a man? She was going to be much too busy rebuilding her life to bother with the opposite sex. Tonight she'd read more of Muriel's book.

But first she had to make dinner. Like her mother, Daphne enjoyed cooking. She loved trying new recipes, experimenting with different herbs and food combinations and seeing what she could come up with. Mostly, she liked the fact that she could control what happened in the kitchen, and these days, that was more than she could say for the rest of her life. Her mother wasn't always easy to cook for, especially as she got older. Daphne had heard everything from "It's a little too salty for my taste" to "I can't eat garlic anymore. It gives me heartburn." For the most part, though, Mother actually liked what she made and complimented her on it. And cooking was one way she could do her share in the household and not feel like a burden.

Mother had complained about her bunions hurting that morning, so Daphne had offered to make tonight's dinner. Three-cheese stuffed chicken (light on the garlic) was on the menu, along with fresh asparagus and rosemary bread.

Mother was taking a break with a cup of tea and a book by Vanessa Valentine, her favorite author. She looked up from the book when Daphne entered the parlor, grocery bag in hand, and seemed almost startled to see her. "You're home earlier than I expected."

"Oh?" She was working only part-time. Had Mother been hoping she'd stay away until five?

Before she could ask what, exactly, that meant, her mother had moved on. "How was work?"

The job Daphne wasn't going to be able to earn a living at? *Okay, let it go.* Things had been a little strained the past couple of days. They didn't need to continue in that vein. She certainly didn't want them to.

"Great," she said and gave her mother a kiss on the cheek. "I like working for Muriel." Muriel was positive and encouraging. She probably never found fault with any of her daughters.

"I'm glad. She's lucky to have you."

In light of her earlier reaction to Daphne's new job, it was the proverbial olive branch. Daphne had no problem taking it. "Thanks."

She went to the kitchen and put away the groceries, then started out the back door to get some rosemary.

"Where are you going?" Mother called. She sounded almost panicked. What was that about?

"Just getting some rosemary for my bread. I'll be right back."

"You don't need to bother with that. Plain bread will be fine."

"No bother," Daphne said and slipped out the door. Her mother loved rosemary bread. What had gotten into her?

Daphne stepped onto the back porch just as Hank Hawkins came around the corner. In addition to his oh-so-manly build, he had brown, curly hair with a few wisps of gray hanging over a craggy brow, deep-set brown eyes and a superhero-size chin, square and… manly. His arms were like mini tree trunks. If he'd been a firefighter he would surely have been chosen to pose for a calendar. *Mr. July Hot.* Whew. She could feel the waves of testosterone coming at her.

"Hi," he said. "Daphne, right?"

She nodded. Gosh, he was…manly.

"Don't know if you remember me. I'm Hank." He pulled off a leather garden glove and held out a huge hand.

"I remember." She held out her own hand and his swallowed it. His hand was warm and slightly rough, and she was suddenly sizzling in spite of the chill in the air.

Great. Of all the times to have a hot flash. That was all this was, she informed herself. Nothing more. Except she was hot where she didn't normally get hot...

Cooling down would've been a lot easier if he wasn't looking at Daphne as if she was a bottle of cold beer waiting for him in the desert. She knew that look. She'd gotten it often enough over the years.

And right now he looked to her like the last chocolate chip cookie on earth. *Stop that! You are done with men.* Even if she wasn't, she wouldn't take up with this specimen. He was probably still in his forties. And if fifty was the new forty, then forty was the new thirty, and that made him too young for her. *Boy toy, boy toy,* chanted her hormones. She told them to shut up.

"How long are you here?" he asked.

"I'm here to stay. I'm getting divorced." Now the heat on her face was pure embarrassment.

"I'm sorry."

She shrugged. "It happens." *To me. A lot.*

"So, what are you going to do?"

"I've started working for Muriel Sterling, and I plan to help out with my mother's business."

That sounded good, and at least her mother was willing to give it a try, but Daphne knew Roberta still didn't trust her not to screw up. Daphne supposed she had reason. While she'd been perfectly competent at her job in Seattle, there was something about being under her mother's watchful eye that made her performance level sink like the *Titanic.*

Hank, ignorant of the mother-daughter dynamic, nodded. "She could use it. Roberta's a firecracker, but she's starting to slow down. Even so, she can still run circles around most of us." He'd probably said that to be polite. Big and strong as he looked, Daphne suspected Hank had plenty of staying power. Staying power…sex. *Don't go there!* Too late. She'd gone. With Hank. *Well, just pull yourself back, fool.*

"Are you settling in okay?" he asked.

"Yes. This is an easy town to settle into."

"It is. I imagine you know everyone here."

"I know a lot of people," Daphne agreed.

"So, how full is your calendar?"

Oh, boy. He wasn't wasting any time. The hot flash got hotter and she peeled off her jacket. "Pretty full."

"Too soon, huh?"

"You could say that. Or you could say I'm through with men," Daphne added. *Might as well stop this plane before it takes off.* And parts of her were ready for take-off.

He nodded, absorbing that information. "Guess I can't blame you. I've got an ex. I understand the feeling."

"I've got two. This will make number three."

His eyes popped wide. "Whoa."

"Yeah, whoa." How pathetic. She bent over to break some needles off the gigantic rosemary bush by the back porch, hoping he hadn't noticed the five-alarm fire on her face.

"Sometimes it takes a while to find the right person," he said in a chivalrous effort to put an optimistic spin on her failures.

"And sometimes you never do." She stripped a small branch and stood up. "I've decided to become a lesbian."

Now his eyes were as big as golf balls.

"Nice talking to you, Hank," she said and went back inside the kitchen. She almost ran into her mother, who was hovering by the door.

"Were you talking to Hank just now?"

It was the same tone of voice Mother had used when she was a little girl. *"Were you in the cookies?"* Come to think of it, she'd used that tone of voice plenty of times when Daphne was an adult. *"Are you seriously thinking of marrying that man?"*

"Just visiting," Daphne said, depositing the rosemary on the kitchen counter.

"He's divorced, you know."

It was hard to imagine any woman wanting to get rid of a man like that. Uh-oh. Here came the heat again, fast as a gas-stove burner. Daphne blotted her forehead and got busy digging around in the cupboard for yeast.

"The last thing you need is another man in your life," Mother said. "You don't have good luck with men."

As if she needed it pointed out to her? "I'm aware of that," Daphne said stiffly.

"I just don't want you to make another mistake." Mother ran a hand over Daphne's hair, pulling it away from her face, the same motherly gesture Daphne had often used on her own daughter when they were having a serious conversation.

"I know," Daphne said, trying to erase the irritation from her voice. "I'm not planning on it."

"Sometimes things happen that a woman doesn't plan on," Mother said. "You're better off not even talking to him."

"I'm not going to be rude." What was she supposed to do, hide in the house when he came over? *If you had any sense you would.*

"Daphne," Mother said sternly.

"Mother, I think I can decide for myself who I will and won't speak to."

"I'm just cautioning you," Mother snapped.

"Thank you. Now I've been cautioned." Daphne took out a pan to scald her milk and slammed it on the stove. That put an end to the conversation.

There wasn't much conversation at dinner, either. A compliment on the bread, which was obviously supposed to mollify her. A prediction that they might get some rain tomorrow. The chicken could use some salt—this from the woman who was trying to cut down on her salt intake. Oh, and Daphne wasn't going to leave the kitchen in a mess, was she?

After they'd finished eating and Daphne had cleaned every pot and pan, Mother announced that she intended to watch a rerun of *The Rockford Files* on her favorite classic-TV channel and invited Daphne to join her.

She passed on the invitation. Cozy mother-daughter evenings were highly overrated. She went for an evening walk instead and found herself at Zelda's. Maybe she'd visit with Charley Masters, the owner, ask her how her relationship with *her* mother was. Heck, maybe she'd go around the restaurant, take a survey, get some tips on how to be the ideal daughter.

Daphne settled in a booth and ordered a piece of huckleberry pie and a Chocolate Kiss martini. She drank the martini and pushed the pie around her plate.

She was playing with a chunk of crust when Charley stopped by to say hello. "Daphne, I heard you were in town."

"Is there anyone who hasn't?" Daphne frowned and pushed away her plate.

"Small town."

Where everyone knew everyone else's business.

Daphne had heard Charley's story, as well, and realized she'd been down the same hurt-strewn road. Her first husband had cheated on her with one of their restaurant employees. If anyone could empathize, it was her.

Charley slipped into the booth opposite her. "I'm sorry. It sucks being betrayed like that, even when it's by a loser."

"Thanks," Daphne murmured. "My mother thinks I'm a failure." Oh, no. Had she said that out loud? One Chocolate Kiss and she had the loosest lips in town.

Her horror must have registered on her face because Charley smiled and said, "Moms always expect more from you. It's in the job description."

Daphne moved her empty glass away. "I can't believe I just said that."

"You probably needed to. And you know what else you probably need? Another Chocolate Kiss. I'll get you one."

True to her word, Charley fetched it herself and gave Daphne a free shrink session. "You didn't do anything wrong," she concluded. "You trusted the guy. You believed in him. That's what we're supposed to do. It's what we all *want* to do. Nothing wrong with that. And, you know, things have a way of working out. I'm living proof. I've got the best guy in the world now."

"Well, if you've got the best, there's no point in my looking," Daphne said, managing a smile. "Anyway, I'm done with men." She could hardly count the number of times she'd said that—to herself and others.

Charley rolled her eyes. "I've heard those words before. Hey, I said them." She slid out of the booth. "Stay for an hour or two. It's karaoke night in the bar, always good for a laugh."

"I could use a laugh."

She could also use a life, so she hung around the bar for a while, watching the locals warble to their favorite pop songs. Then, when she knew her mother would be asleep, she returned to the house and took Muriel's book to bed.

One of the best things about starting over is that the possibilities are endless. Don't worry about where you've been. It's where you're going that counts. The slate is clean. What gets written on it is up to you.

Daphne smiled. Her future wasn't dark and hopeless. It was filled with possibilities. And she was going to take advantage of every one of them. She was going to write a new story on that clean slate.

Muriel's inspiring words and Daphne's determination to do well combined to give her a very good week. The days she worked with Muriel, she came home energized and pleased with herself. She cooked dinner every night and her mother not only complimented her, but had second helpings of everything from mushroom lasagna to salmon loaf, an old classic Roberta had taught her to make when she was a teenager.

"I swear, Daphne, I've gained five pounds," she said and took another bite of caramel cream pie. "This is incredible. Darling, you could have your own restaurant."

"Not here," Daphne said. "Too much competition."

Mother frowned at her pie. "Really, Daphne, sometimes you give up before you even start."

"I didn't know I was starting anything," Daphne retorted. It was more a case of her mother, as usual, concocting some grand scheme for her and then expecting her to follow through. Rather ironic, considering that Daphne practically had to beg to be allowed to help with weddings. Owning a restaurant would be twice as challenging as assisting with receptions.

Her response produced a long-suffering sigh. "I worry about you, Daphne. I don't know what you're going to do with the rest of your life."

Obviously not partner with her mother in the wedding business. "I don't, either," Daphne said, "but I'm going to figure it out. Let me get my ducks in a row first."

Mother sighed again and nodded, and they left the discussion there, with the ducks swimming about, trying to line up.

A wedding was scheduled for Saturday, and Daphne was on hand to assist with the setup. She'd enjoyed doing this for her daughter's wedding five years earlier. It had been such a lovely affair, and she'd had so much fun helping. Granted, she'd messed up on the invitations, but in addition to work, she'd been taking a neighbor to chemo and preparing meals for the woman's family. Plus Mitchell had been starting a new job and that had put them under a lot of stress. Still, the invitations had finally gone out and the wedding had been well attended.

Now she was ready to shoulder part of her mother's load and, yes, enjoy the vicarious thrill of a happy event.

"Thank you, dear," Mother said after everything was arranged and ready to go. "You've been a huge help."

Music to Daphne's ears.

"Would you like to serve during the reception? It's only appetizers."

This was like getting invited to sit at King Arthur's Round Table. "Sure," Daphne said.

And so she did, passing through the crowd of wedding revelers with a platter of hot wings the bride was particularly fond of. Why on earth anyone would pick something with barbecue sauce for a wedding was beyond her. It was so messy, and the guests were going through napkins as though there was no tomorrow.

Daphne wished Lila had given her the shrimp platter instead as she nervously made her way between revelers. She gave the mother of the bride an especially wide berth, since the woman was wearing a pale blue dress that would not go well with barbecue sauce.

The father of the bride waylaid her and helped himself to several. *Eat 'em all*, she felt like saying. *Then I can get rid of this ticking time bomb*. She'd barely finished that thought when two kids darted at her from out of nowhere. They were on a collision course and Daphne took a step away to avoid them, which had her backing into the bride's grandmother.

"Pardon me," Daphne murmured and turned to avoid getting her with the deadly wings. Sadly, just as she turned, the bride passed by in all her wedding-gown glory. This might not have been a problem except that the bride had been indulging in a lot of champagne and was now weaving like a passenger on the deck of a storm-tossed ship.

Daphne tried to dodge her, but then an equally tipsy bridesmaid laughed at something one of the groomsmen was telling her and took a step back, bumping into Daphne, nudging her right into the bride. There was an "Oomph" and an "Eek," followed by a wail and a "Look what you've done!" and an "I'm so sorry." And then there were tears. Loud, copious tears. And then... there was Mother.

"Oh, dear," she said.

"My dress is ruined!" screeched the bride.

"Let's go to the powder room and see if we can fix this little spot," Mother suggested.

"Spot" was an understatement. It was more like a stream. No, make that a river, a river of sauce wending its way down the bride's front.

"I'm so sorry," Daphne repeated.

"You should be!" spat the bride.

And now here was Mom's assistant, Lila, with a rag and a small plastic bin, silently cleaning up the mess that had fallen on the floor. Lovely. How many women did it take to clean up a Daphne mess?

"We can fix this," Mother said again. "We have a wonderful dry cleaner here in town, and of course we'll pay for the cleaning."

"That won't help me now." The bride looked down at her stained dress and burst into a fresh chorus of wails.

"No, but baking soda will," Mother said, taking the hysterical bride by the elbow. "Daphne, fetch the bottle of white vinegar and the baking soda," she commanded and led the bride to the powder room.

Daphne hurried to the kitchen, trying not to cry, Muriel Sterling's words mocking her with every step. *The slate is clean. What gets written on it is up to you.* She was a disaster, the backward mirror image of King Midas. Nothing she touched turned to gold. It all turned to poop.

She got the baking soda and the vinegar and a dishcloth and dashed out of the kitchen, nearly colliding with Lila, who was coming in.

"That wasn't your fault," Lila said.

"Yeah, well, tell that to my mother."

"I will," Lila said firmly.

As if it would do any good.

The bride was still hysterical and threatening to sue

when Daphne arrived at the powder room. The mother of the bride was hovering outside, begging her daughter to calm down. Too late for that.

Daphne squeezed inside (three was definitely a crowd in a powder room, especially when one of them was wearing a voluminous gown) and then stood by like a surgical nurse assisting in a delicate operation, handing over cleaning supplies. All the while the patient kept up a tipsy tirade, but Mother had nerves of steel and continued to work.

Finally she said, "I think we've got it." The operation was a success. "Daphne, run upstairs and fetch me the hair dryer."

Daphne dutifully fetched the hair dryer and watched as her mother blew away most of the stain.

"You did it," the mother of the bride gushed happily when her daughter finally emerged, and all the guests who'd been hovering nearby applauded.

Roberta Gilbert to the rescue. How embarrassing that the mess had been caused by her very own daughter.

"It could happen to anyone," she said to Daphne later that night as she and Daphne and Lila unloaded trays of champagne glasses onto the kitchen counter.

"It wasn't Daphne's fault," Lila put in. "The woman ran right into her."

"I know," Mother said, patting Daphne's shoulder. "I saw."

Vindicated. She wasn't done writing on that slate, after all.

There was another wedding scheduled for the following weekend, and her mother was actually giving her a second chance and allowing her to help with it. Maybe they *could* work together. Then someday, when Mother was tired of all this, Daphne could take over.

Weddings could become a family tradition. Perhaps that would make up for the fact that a successful marriage didn't seem to be.

No, she corrected herself, Marnie was breaking that pattern. She was happily married. Marnie was, simply, Daphne's magnum opus.

The next Saturday dawned bright and sunny, with blue skies and fat, fleecy clouds floating over the snow-tipped Cascades. A perfect day for a wedding. And this was going to be quite the affair. Not as big a deal as the upcoming wedding for the mayor's daughter, which would take place in May, but a big one nonetheless. In addition to a cake worthy of a Food Network TV show, the bride had ordered swan-shaped cream puffs from Gingerbread Haus and a full-course dinner that was to be catered by Schwangau, the priciest restaurant in town. She'd spent a fortune on flowers at Lupine Floral and had ordered enough wine and champagne to get the entire town of Icicle Falls snockered. Not content with a DJ, she'd hired a five-piece band. Guests were all receiving small gift boxes of Sweet Dreams chocolates. Everyone was setting up when Cass Wilkes from the bakery arrived with the cake still in layers.

"We don't have the table quite ready yet," Daphne told her.

Cass checked the time on her cell phone. "I've got to get back to the bakery pretty quick. We're shorthanded today."

"Tell you what. Let's unload it in the kitchen, and Lila and I can put it together," Daphne said.

Cass looked frankly worried by this suggestion. "I'd better wait."

"We can manage," Daphne assured her. She'd seen

enough cakes put together in her time, and she'd seen the picture of this particular model. Very traditional, with layers held up by vintage champagne flutes. She and Lila could handle it.

Cass gnawed a corner of her lip. "I don't know."

"It'll be okay," Daphne promised her. "Anyway, it's our fault things aren't ready for you."

Cass yielded. "All right. Thanks, Daphne."

"No problem." And it wouldn't have been a problem if the lace on Daphne's tennis shoe hadn't come undone. Or if she'd even seen that it had come undone. Or if Lila had seen it. But the sneaky lace worked its way loose and dangled under her feet as she bore the top layer of the cake, walking behind Lila, who had the middle layer. They'd already set up the bottom one on the cake table. When they were done, it would rise like a fondant tower from a bower of roses and orchids. It was going to be lovely. They were almost at the table when the wicked shoelace played its joke, tripping Daphne, making her lurch forward. She tried desperately to keep the cake from going down with her, but only succeeded in bumping into Lila. For a moment they did a little dance, both balancing their cakes in the air. The Dance of the Wedding Cake, tra-la, tra-la. And then the dance was over, and the dancers were down on the floor, one of them with her face in the frosting. Filled with horror, Daphne sat up, parting the sea of frosting on her face. The sea parted and there came her mother.

And that blank slate had fresh writing on it. It said *You're toast.*

Chapter Fourteen

Anne in Charge

Some weddings came off like well-rehearsed plays. Most weddings, though, like the humans who participated in them, had flaws. Some of those flaws were small—maybe not quite enough food, the bride and groom trying a fancy dance move and collapsing on the floor, the flower girl sitting down and taking off her shoes in the middle of the ceremony. Some of the flaws were a little bigger—the best man losing the ring or getting drunk and making a completely inappropriate toast at the reception. Some flaws were huge, like the bride or groom not showing up.

That last flaw had marred only one of Anne's weddings and it had happened the year before. The groom failed to show. The bride had been in tears and her father had gotten into a shouting match with the groom's father and finally punched him in the nose, maybe figuring that was as close as he was going to get to the errant groom-*not*-to-be. The church was emptied, the caterers were sent home and the parents of the bride wound up paying for food nobody ate. Anne had waived her fee. She learned that, later on, the groom returned, begging for a second chance, and he and the bride had a quiet ceremony and then got out of town before his father-in-law could take a swing at him. Someday, hopefully, they'd all look back on the wedding disaster and laugh. Or at least not come to blows.

At today's wedding, nobody was going to take a swing at anyone, unless it was one of the caterers, slapping an amorous grandpa.

"He pinched me," an outraged Cressa told Anne. "I was walking past with a platter of cheese cubes and the geezer pinched me!"

"Let Renaldo go to him from now on and stay on the other side of the room," Anne advised.

Cressa frowned. "The old guy moves around a lot. I think he's following me."

Her and every other girl in the room. Anne watched as he put an arm around one of the bridesmaids and gave her a decidedly ungrandfatherly squeeze while attempting to look down her dress, then proceeded to hit on the mother of the groom.

There were other problems besides Grandpa. One twelve-year-old boy was systematically emptying every nut and candy bowl in the reception hall, gobbling the contents without restraint. Anne had already seen several adults chase him away, to no effect. His older brother, who was obviously too young to drink, was enjoying himself equally, sneaking into the champagne punch when no one was watching (not an easy feat, considering how many people were dipping into the punch bowl).

The male members of the party weren't the only ones out of control. Two of the bridesmaids were already tipsy, and one of them was cozying up to the groom.

At the rate this gathering was going, there would be much to remember, and not in a good way. Anne always tried to caution her brides to think carefully about their guest lists. There was a direct correlation between the kind of people a bride invited and the kind of wedding she had.

Anne couldn't do anything about the tipsy bridesmaids or the lecherous grandpa. She did, however, diplomatically point out a potential problem with the underage tippler to the mother of the bride, and a few minutes later she saw the young man being hauled away by his father for a chat.

The gluttonous twelve-year-old was making for the nut bowl again and Anne decided to stop the little squirrel before any more nuts or candy were put out. She suspected nature was eventually going to take its course and he would pay. But by the time retribution arrived there'd be nothing left for the guests.

She got to the cake table just as he was scooping out another handful. "They're good, aren't they?"

The boy gave a start and looked over his shoulder, the picture of guilt. "Uh, yeah."

"I love nuts, too," Anne said and chose a couple of pecans, making them partners in nut thievery. "But, you know, you've got to be careful with nuts."

He looked at her suspiciously.

"Yeah. Too many of them give you—" she lowered her voice "—the runs. And it comes on really suddenly." She looked furtively around and hunched down, a woman about to share a secret. "I went to a wedding once where a boy ate too many and he…" She bit her lip. "All over everything, in front of all the wedding guests."

She had the squirrel's attention now.

"Everybody laughed," she added for emphasis.

The boy dropped the nuts back in the bowl. Lovely. But it looked as though a cure for gluttony had been found. "Aren't you going to have any more?" Anne asked innocently.

He shook his head. "I've had enough."

She watched as he slipped through the crowd, heading in the direction of the restrooms. Ah, the power of suggestion, she thought, and went to fetch more nuts.

The rest of the reception went well. The tipsy bridesmaid stopped hitting on the groom after she threw up in the rhododendron bushes and then passed out, the punch and nut thieves settled down and Cressa got a marriage proposal from Grandpa.

All in a night's work.

Watching the bride and groom, strolling from guest to guest with their arms around each other, left Anne feeling that same sense of accomplishment she always felt upon seeing another couple happily wed. Soon she'd be experiencing the thrill of her own daughter's reception...

It was a long and busy night, but that didn't stop her from getting together with her family the next day. Anne's family liked to gather once a month at her mother's house for Sunday dinner. Julia usually cooked a roast of some kind, with plenty of vegetables, and her daughters brought the rolls, salad and dessert. This Sunday the whole gang was there—Kendra and her husband, Jimmy, and their two daughters, Coral and Amy; Anne and Cam; and Laney and Drake, family member in training.

When it was football season the men often drifted off after dinner to watch the game on TV, while the women either visited or played cards. The same thing happened during baseball season if a Mariners game was being aired. But since none of the men were big basketball fans, during basketball season they joined the women for conversation or some sort of game.

This afternoon it was Trivial Pursuit, and the women

were behind, struggling to answer the sports-and-leisure questions.

"This is hard, Mommy," said Coral, Kendra's oldest.

"It sure is," Kendra agreed. "Who knows this stuff?" she protested, throwing up her hands.

"Men," Jimmy said.

"They should have cooking questions in here," Kendra grumbled.

"Talk about a sexist remark," Cam teased her. "What makes you think men don't know anything about cooking?"

"The greatest chefs in the world are men," put in Dad.

"Not anymore," Kendra said. "And there certainly aren't any at *this* table."

"That's because our women are such great cooks." Dad grinned at their mother. "Why try to compete with perfection?"

"I wouldn't object if you tried," Julia said, grabbing a handful of bridge mix.

"Aw, Julia, you know you love to cook," he said.

"Not all the time."

"All you have to do is say the word," Dad told her.

"Fine. Tomorrow night *you* make dinner."

He frowned. "You can't just spring that on a man."

"Sam Wellington, I've been trying to spring that on you for years."

Anne doubted her mother had tried very hard. Her parents had always had a traditional relationship, with her father working and her mother staying home and running the house. Still, she knew that after forty-five years in the kitchen, her mom was getting tired of KP.

"Daddy, tomorrow night's the perfect night to cook," Anne said. "All you have to do is put the leftovers in foil and stick them in the oven."

"Maybe we'll have sandwiches tomorrow night." Julia waggled a finger back and forth from Laney to Drake. "Make him cook some of the meals when you two get married. If you don't train them right from the beginning, they never learn."

"Don't worry, Mrs. W.," Drake said. "I know how to cook."

"He already makes dinner for us on Fridays and Sundays," Laney said proudly.

Her grandfather shook his head. "Young men today, they're all henpecked."

"Is that so?" asked his wife, cocking a disapproving eyebrow.

"Hey, I say do whatever works." Cam clapped Drake on the back. Then he looked at Kendra. "So, are you girls going to answer the question or not?"

"Not," Kendra muttered. "Who hit the most home runs for the Yankees? Who knows?"

"I do," Jimmy said with a smirk.

"Oh, go ahead and answer and then shut up," Kendra told him, turning his smirk into a grin.

The men won, and after much good-natured grumbling, it was time for pie and ice cream and more visiting.

"Have you two figured out where you're going to live after you're married?" Julia asked Laney.

"At Drake's place," Laney said, smiling at him. "His roommate's already moved out and I'm going to use the spare bedroom as a studio."

Julia smiled. "That sounds like an excellent idea. And how are the wedding plans coming?"

"Good," Laney replied.

Slower than a dying slug, Anne felt like saying. "We still have so much to do."

"At least you have your venue," Julia said. "That house is lovely."

Drake frowned. "I thought we were getting married on the river."

"We are," Laney assured him and leaned over to kiss his cheek.

"The house is for the reception," Anne reminded her mother.

Julia's eyebrows took a disapproving dip downward. "I thought you decided against the raft."

If Anne had her way, her daughter would be getting married under the rose bower in the garden at Primrose Haus. It would be in full bloom by June and so lovely. But she hadn't convinced Laney yet.

"That's still up for discussion," she said hopefully.

"No, it's not." Her daughter glared at her.

Drake looked from mother to daughter, and he wasn't smiling, either. "If we're gonna stick around here, we should at least do something cool like get married on the river."

"I thought you guys were going to Vegas," Jimmy said. Obviously, Kendra hadn't been keeping him in the loop.

Laney and Drake exchanged a look that was—what? Regretful? Oh, no. Anne had to be misreading that. "This will be better," she said quickly. "More people can come."

"I don't know. Vegas sounded like fun," Jimmy said. This was followed by a pained expression and an "Ouch" as his wife kicked him under the table.

"Anyone for more pie?" Anne asked with brisk cheer-fulness.

Seconds on pie was a good distraction, and the conversation drifted into new avenues, but Anne felt discontent coming from her daughter and future son-in-law's corner of the table like a miasma. Surely they weren't changing their minds. No, they couldn't be. She was just imagining it.

"Drake doesn't seem all that excited about the new wedding plans," Cam observed as they drove home. "Are you sure they're both okay with this?"

"Of course I am," Anne said. "Primrose Haus will be great for the reception and they'll love getting married on the river." At least she'd talked her daughter out of wearing a bikini top—she hoped. "This will be something she can remember proudly all her life."

Cam shot a quick look in her direction. "As opposed to?"

"Well, having regrets."

He nodded and kept his eye on the road. "Like her mother."

She'd never complained, never said anything. "I don't have regrets."

He grunted.

"What's that supposed to mean?" she demanded.

"I know you wanted a big, fancy church wedding."

"I wanted you more," Anne said, and that was the truth. "Anyway, we're not talking about me."

He shrugged, ready to drop the subject.

Anne wasn't. "If Drake was in charge we'd all be wearing eye patches, walking around with parrots on our shoulders and saying, 'Aargh.'"

"I'd be fine with that," Cam said, smiling. "Just as long as nobody asked me to walk the plank."

"Who knows what they'd ask you to do." No, the direction they were taking now was the right way to go. Her daughter would thank her for this.

Planning a wedding was such a special time for a mother and daughter. That was another thing they'd be cheated out of if Laney just went off to Vegas. It was one last mother-daughter adventure to enjoy before Laney embarked on her new life. They would look back on this with such fond memories.

The next day, Laney's day off, they hit the road for Icicle Falls for some of that special mother-daughter time, armed with lattes Laney had made for them and a to-do list. Blue sky and sunshine promised an early spring.

"We've got appointments with the florist and the baker," Anne said. "The caterer couldn't meet with us today, but she's going to email some sample menus to look over. Oh, and I heard there's a local guy who DJs for weddings."

"We already have a band," Laney said as they exited I-5 for I-90 eastbound.

"You do?"

"Drake's friend Anders has a band. The Flesh Eaters."

"The Flesh Eaters," Anne repeated weakly. "Um, what kind of music do they do?"

"Some grunge, some progressive, some new wave. They're versatile."

That was versatility? Anne tried to picture her parents dancing to the earsplitting wall of sound produced by the Flesh Eaters and failed. "Sweetie, are you sure that's a good idea?"

"What do you mean?" Laney's voice was defensive now.

"I'm just wondering if that's really the best choice for your wedding music."

"I think it is."

"Well, yes, of course. But you'll have other generations at your wedding. You want them to enjoy themselves, too. If you have a DJ he can play a variety of music, something for everyone."

Laney chewed her lip. "But he's Drake's friend. We already told him he could play."

Ah, here was the crux of the matter. Laney didn't want to disappoint a friend. "Just tell him it didn't work out." Heartless, maybe, but that was the wedding biz.

"Yeah, like everything else so far," Laney grumbled.

Okay, that hurt. "That's not true," Anne said. "You're getting married on the river."

Laney frowned at the stand of evergreens they were passing. "I can tell how much you guys approve of that."

"It's your wedding," Anne said.

"Glad you remembered."

Ah, mother-daughter bonding. Nothing like it.

Once they got to Icicle Falls, Anne let her daughter have free rein. Laney picked out the biggest, boldest wedding cake possible at Gingerbread Haus and ordered a donut cake as high as the Trump Tower. By the time they added the groom's cake, a chocolate mountain complete with a rock climber to celebrate Drake's favorite hobby, they were over the cake budget by five hundred dollars. Anne didn't blink.

"The donut cake will be an excellent addition," said Cass, the bakery owner, which brought a big grin from Laney.

"Whatever my daughter wants," Anne said. As long as it didn't involve a pirate ship or zombie musicians.

"Thanks, Mom." Laney threaded her arm through Anne's as they walked away. "I love our cakes."

"You're welcome," Anne said and patted her hand. Her daughter's gratitude was worth an extra five hundred dollars.

Then it was on to Lupine Floral, where they met with Heinrich Blum, the shop's creative genius. He greeted them warmly and predicted that Laney would be the most beautiful bride Icicle Falls had ever seen. Anne suspected he said that to every bride who came through his doors, but Laney ate it up.

"And what's our budget?" he asked.

Anne told him and he nodded appreciatively. "We can give you something very nice for that. What are your colors?"

"Brown and forest green," Laney replied.

"Very tasteful," he said, and it was all Anne could do not to remind her daughter who had suggested those colors.

"We thought perhaps you might be able to do something with brown roses, ferns and some chocolate mints," Anne couldn't help adding.

"Chocolate mints. Love it!" Heinrich said, confirming Anne's good taste.

He showed Laney several pictures of past Lupine Floral creations and then they spent some time surfing the net and discussing ideas. Finally it looked as though they had a plan. "How does that sound?" he asked.

Laney shrugged. "Pretty good."

He held a hand to his chest in mock horror. "Only pretty good? I'm crushed."

Laney quickly corrected herself. "I mean, it's beautiful."

It just wasn't a pirate ship. Anne didn't want her daughter to be disappointed with the flowers at her wedding. She didn't want Laney to be disappointed with anything. "Maybe we could throw in a little more," she said.

"A little more...pizzazz?" Heinrich guessed.

"Well, yes."

"Of course. But you do want to stay in your budget, right?"

"Well, let's expand the budget."

"Okay, then," he said with a smile. "We'll see what we can do." What he could do was incredible. He put together a plan that would turn the beautiful Primrose Haus into an enchanted castle, employing everything from the flowers and greens they'd already selected to twinkle lights and lanterns for the garden, and crystal vases stuffed with more twinkle lights for the inside. Table centerpieces would be branches (surrounded by flowers and greens, of course) with candle lanterns hanging from them. By the time he was done, Anne was practically drooling.

Even Laney looked impressed. "I love it," she said, a huge smile on her face.

Anne's savings account was probably in trouble, but so what? She'd find the extra money somewhere. And anyway, they weren't *that* far over budget.

Yet. They still had to order food, had to buy the wedding dress, the favors and the gifts for the bridesmaids.

Anne saw the proverbial writing on the wall and it was all in dollar signs. Okay, so she'd be paying for this wedding for the next five years. She'd gladly do whatever it took to make sure the day turned out to be exactly what her daughter had always dreamed of—especially after shooting down the Vegas idea.

Ah, guilt. The perfect present for the mother of the bride.

Chapter Fifteen

Laney, Having to Choose

"I don't get why you don't want me to come," Drake said as he and Laney jogged side by side around Green Lake on Saturday after her shift at the coffee shop.

"I told you, it's not that I don't want you to come, but it's just girls." Guys never went along when their fiancées went bridal-gown shopping. She'd watched enough episodes of *Say Yes to the Dress* to know that. "Even my dad isn't going." And if anyone should be there, it was Dad, since he and Mom were paying for it. "Anyway, it's bad luck to see me in my wedding gown before the wedding." That was a silly superstition and not very practical for taking pictures, but the drama of waiting until the big moment appealed to Laney.

"My brother saw his wife. They had their pictures taken before the wedding."

Laney tried another tack. "You'd be bored."

"Seeing you all dressed up? No way."

"You're so sweet."

Drake always said stuff like that. She was marrying the best guy ever.

"So, come on. Let me go with you."

Laney grinned over at him. "Uh-uh. You need to be surprised," she added with a teasing smile.

He shook his head. "I don't get why you're looking for a wedding dress anyway. I thought you were gonna wear shorts."

"I changed my mind."

Actually, her mother had changed her mind, but Mom was probably right about this. Getting married was major, and she might regret it if she went for casual.

Drake was frowning now. They weren't going to fight about this, she hoped.

"Come on. Don't be mad," she coaxed.

"I'm not mad. I'm just…"

"What?"

"I don't know."

Guy-speak for *I don't want to talk about it*. "What?" Laney pressed.

"I hate being left out of everything like I don't matter."

She stopped running. So did he. A cyclist whizzed past them.

"You do matter," Laney said. "You should know that. You're the most important person in my life."

"Yeah? Then how come I don't get to be involved in anything? How come you don't even ask me what I think?" He wiped his sweaty brow and looked away.

Two women jogged past them, laughing about something.

"I haven't even seen the place where we're getting married," he continued.

"I've shown you pictures."

He gave a snort of disgust. "Big deal. I thought we were gonna go up there. You've gone up twice without me."

She moved closer and put a hand on his chest. "Come on, babe. That was to order flowers. What guy is into flowers?"

"And cake. You ordered the cake. I'm into cake."

"Okay, I'm sorry. I didn't think it was that important to you."

"Well, it kinda is. I mean, *I'm* getting married, too. Someplace. Someplace I haven't seen."

Now Laney's stomach hurt. She hugged him and laid her head on his chest, hoping that would take away the hurt for both of them.

"It's not that I want to tell you what to do or anything," he said, wrapping his arms around her. "I just want you to care what I think."

"I do care," she protested.

"Yeah, right," he said sullenly.

They were getting married! This was supposed to be fun. Why wasn't she having fun? Maybe because her period was right around the corner. She always felt bitchy before her period.

That was it, of course. She'd be back to normal in a few days.

Meanwhile, though, she had to get back to normal with Drake. "How about we go up there the first weekend in May? I think they have some festival then. It'll probably be lame, but we can check it out, maybe do some rock climbing. I'll show you the park on the river, and we can go to the rafting place and talk to them about renting a raft for the wedding."

Mom had forgotten to add that to their list of things to do when they'd gone to Icicle Falls. She'd probably be glad to see that Laney had taken care of it. Not that she was worried about Mom right now. It was Drake she wanted to please. She looked up at him, hoping to see the smile back on his face.

It wasn't yet, but he nodded in agreement. "Okay. Fair enough."

"And to make things even, I won't go with you when you and the guys pick out your tuxes."

Now he did smile. "I'm not doing that without you. I don't wanna screw it up."

"It's hard to screw up renting a tux. But you'd find a way," she teased and started jogging again.

"That's why you have to come with," he said, falling in step with her.

They completed their jog in perfect harmony, so she should've been in a great mood later that afternoon when she picked up her best friend, Autumn, to go wedding-gown shopping. But she found herself feeling mildly grumpy. What bride felt grumpy about shopping for a wedding gown? Oh, yeah, one who had PMS. Oh, well. Trying on wedding dresses was bound to put her in a good mood.

It *was* just PMS, wasn't it? "It's not that I don't like everything we decided on," she said as she and Autumn drove to meet her mom and aunt and grandma at the bridal shop in the U district that her mom had suggested.

"What's with this 'we' stuff?" Autumn scolded. "It's your wedding. Who's in control?"

"I am," Laney insisted. She was. She was having her donut cake and she was getting married on the river.

"I guess," Autumn said dubiously. "Your mom's really sweet, but sometimes she kinda takes over."

"Well, she's not taking over today. *I'm* the one wearing the wedding gown. And the bride is always right. That's what Mom says."

"Sure. If you say so."

She did say so. And yeah, okay, maybe her mom was a little controlling. But Autumn should talk. Her mom still got on her about cleaning their house, even came over every other week with her Pledge and dust rag to check that it was done right. Mom never did stuff like that. She hadn't told Laney what to do since she moved out.

Only since she got engaged.

No, she hasn't, Laney reminded herself. *She's just made suggestions.*

Well, she wasn't going to be making any suggestions about Laney's wedding gown. Laney wanted the decision to be hers and hers alone. She wanted to fall in love with the perfect gown for her big day.

Autumn dropped the subject, and they picked up the two other bridesmaids, Drake's younger sister, Darcy, and Laney's other close friend Ella, who'd recently gotten engaged.

"I don't know how you guys are pulling this together so fast," Ella said to Laney as they drove down Forty-Fifth. "There's so much to do."

"It helps when your mom does it for a living."

"I'm impressed," Ella said. "Gordy and I aren't getting married until next February, and I'm about to have a nervous breakdown."

"Go to Hawaii and get married on the beach," said Autumn. "That's what I want to do when *I* get married."

"That's what I want to do, too," said Darcy. She was the youngest of them all and had just broken up with her boyfriend, so Laney suspected a wedding on the beach at Kauai would be a ways off.

"Too expensive," Ella said. "Half the family wouldn't be able to come, and my mom would have a shit fit."

"It's not about your mom," Laney told her, and Autumn pretended to choke on the Diet Coke she was drinking.

"Tell that to her," Ella retorted as they pulled up in front of Here Comes the Bride. Even though they were ten minutes early, Mom's car was already parked in front of the shop. They walked in to find her standing in front of a rack of size-six gowns along with Aunt Kendra and Grammy, in earnest conversation with the saleswoman.

"Let's set this one aside," Mom was saying, pointing to a low-cut gown with sheer sleeves.

"Not taking over at all," Autumn said under her breath.

"Shut up," Laney whispered back, and Autumn smirked.

Having heard the little bell over the door, Mom looked over her shoulder and smiled at Laney. "Hi, sweetie," she called. "Are you ready to play princess?"

That was what they'd called it when Laney was a little girl and dressing up in pillowcases, lace and bits of organza and anything else Mom had lying around. This time she'd be dressing up and it would be for real. The last time they'd done anything like this was when they'd gone shopping for her prom dress. The dress shopping had been fun but things had gone downhill fast.

She remembered how Mom had tried to control her prom night and ruin all her big plans with Drake. "Someday you'll understand," Mom had predicted right before the fight got really ugly. She was an adult now, and she still didn't understand.

The memory of the prom-night battle didn't exactly sweeten her mood. But she smiled and went over and dutifully kissed everyone.

"Hi, girls," Mom said to the bridesmaids. "I'm so glad you could join us today. Maybe we can find your dresses, too."

"Wow, you are efficient," Ella murmured.

"We don't want to put it off too long in case we need alterations," Mom told her. To the saleswoman, she said, "This is my daughter, Laney."

"Hello, Laney," said the woman. "I'm Glenda. My assistant, Rose, and I will be happy to help you find the perfect gown today."

The perfect gown. Laney's bad mood melted. "Thanks."

Mom held up the one she'd been looking at. "What do you think of this one?" she asked Laney.

It was okay, but... "I don't like the long sleeves," Laney replied.

"Up in the mountains it could still be chilly in the evenings," Mom said.

Grammy pulled out a gown weighed down with ruffles. "Here's a nice sleeveless one."

Laney wrinkled her nose. "Too ruffly."

"Oh," Grammy said, surprised, and put it back.

"Told you," Aunt Kendra said to her.

"This is nice." Autumn lifted a simple satin gown with a sweetheart neckline and a full skirt from the rack.

"Nice" didn't come close. It was freakin' awesome. "I love that," Laney breathed.

"How about this one?" Aunt Kendra asked, pulling out a gown with cap sleeves.

It was pretty, too, trimmed with lace and sequins, but she didn't love it the way she did the first one.

"Why don't we set you up in a dressing room and you can try these on," suggested Glenda. She called over her assistant, who took one of the gowns. Then she smiled at everyone else. "Ladies, if you'd like to go on over to our seating area, we'll bring your bride out in a minute."

"Try this one on, too," Mom said, handing over the long-sleeved gown.

Laney frowned. She'd already said she didn't like it. "No, I don't want that one."

"Just try it on," Mom urged.

"Okay." But she wasn't taking it.

"Hey, here's one," said Ella, holding up a lacy number with seed pearls, a full skirt and a long train.

"I'll try that one on, too," Laney decided.

So, off she went to the dressing room, with Glenda right behind her.

The first gown she tried on was the one with the sweetheart neckline. She felt like a princess in it. Glenda fluffed out the skirt and Laney turned and smiled at her reflection. Drake would love her in this.

Glenda ushered her from the changing room to where her family and friends sat in a grouping of comfy chairs.

"Oh, wow," said Aunt Kendra. "You look great."

Grammy's expression was slightly pained and Mom was half smiling.

Laney would never fight with her grandma, but Mom was a different story. "What?" she demanded. As if she didn't know.

Mom almost jumped. "Nothing."

"You don't like it."

"No, it's very nice," Mom said and managed a long-suffering smile.

"You don't like my tat showing." And if she wore her hair up, the one on her neck would show, too. But so what? She happened to like her body art, even if her mother didn't.

Mom sidestepped the issue. "We don't have to buy the first dress you try on. Let's see what the others look like."

"Fine," Laney snapped. With a swish of her skirt she whirled around and marched back to the changing room.

Next came the gown with the capped sleeves. "I like the first one better," said Autumn.

"Me, too," Ella chimed in.

"Yeah, me, too," said Laney.

"It's a very pretty gown," Grammy said, and Laney noticed her grandmother didn't say *she* looked pretty in it.

The third gown got slightly more positive reviews but Grammy still wasn't oohing and aahing and neither was Mom.

"Let's see the long-sleeved one," Mom said.

Keep an open mind, Laney told herself as she returned to the dressing room.

One look in the mirror confirmed it; this wasn't the gown for her. It was definitely a princess gown, but one a dated Disney princess would wear.

"My goodness, she's beautiful," Grammy gushed when she came out to model it for the others.

She shook her head. "It's too old-fashioned."

Grammy disagreed. "That's not old-fashioned. That's classic."

"The tat will still show," Laney said. So if that was Mom's issue, what was the point of getting it?

Her mother studied the gown and tapped her finger to her lips thoughtfully. "It's not bad."

Oh, just what she wanted, a gown people would look at and say, "It's not bad."

"Don't do it," cautioned Autumn.

Autumn was right.

"We've got all afternoon," Aunt Kendra said. "I say try on every gown they have in your size."

And so she did, with Glenda and Rose scurrying back and forth, their arms full of lace and organza and satin. None of the gowns did it for her like that first one. "I want to try that on again," she said to Glenda as her assistant bore away yet another gown.

The woman nodded and helped her into it. She looked at her reflection. Oh, yes, this was the gown she wanted. She went back out. "This is the one."

"It *is* nice," said Grammy.

"If that's the one you want, that's the one you should get." Sadly, it wasn't Mom who said this. It was Aunt Kendra.

"Let's look a little more," Mom suggested.

"I've tried on every friggin' gown in the place," Laney growled.

"I know. But there are other shops."

"Mom, my tat's gonna show. There's nothing you can do to hide it." Maybe her mom would like her to get married in a white body bag.

"Sweetie, you want to be sure," Mom said.

"I am sure." She loved the gown. She could see herself in it, walking through the woods to that raft on the river. This was what she wanted to be wearing in her wedding pictures.

"I still think we should look around a little more."

"Until we find something *you* like. I thought this was my wedding." Why was Mom being like this? She was spoiling everything.

"It is, but I don't think that's the best gown for you."

"This is the gown I want."

Mom sighed, and in that sigh was a world of disapproval.

"Oh, never mind." Laney stormed off to the dressing room. Never mind the friggin' gown. She'd get married in shorts (lowriders!) and a bikini top. Maybe she'd even get another tattoo before the wedding. A tramp stamp. Mom would love that.

Just as she was leaving, she met her mother coming into the changing area with still another gown. "Here's one we missed," Mom said. It had a sweetheart neckline… and a long-sleeved lace jacket to go with it. Yet another attempt to cover the hated tattoos.

"I don't want to try it on," Laney snapped. "I don't want to try on any more wedding gowns. In fact, I don't want to get married in a gown, after all," she added.

"Oh, come on, Laney. Don't be like that," Mom said, following her out of the changing area.

"Like what?"

"Stubborn," Mom said, irritated. "Just try this on."

"No. I'm done." Laney grabbed her purse. "Let's go, you guys," she said to her bridesmaids.

"Laney, quit acting like you're twelve," her mother scolded.

"I'll quit acting like I'm twelve when you quit treating me like I'm twelve," Laney called over her shoulder as she made her way to the door.

"Oh, boy," Ella said.

"That went well," added Autumn. "But hey, I don't blame you. It's your wedding."

Somebody needed to explain that to Mom.

Chapter Sixteen

Anne, Mother in Crisis

"Really, Anne," Julia said as they trooped back to Anne's car. "What were you thinking?"

"What do you mean what was *I* thinking?" Anne countered. "I wasn't the one who threw a fit in the bridal shop."

"No, you were the one who caused it," Julia said sternly.

"I certainly was not." Anne unlocked the car and they got in, her mother riding shotgun in the front passenger seat. "Laney was being stubborn and uncooperative," Anne said and shut her door with a bit more force than necessary.

"She found the gown she wanted," Julia pointed out.

"Mom, do you want her parading down the aisle with that tattoo sleeve showing? Not to mention the one on her neck." Although, actually, the one on Laney's neck was kind of cute. Not that Anne would ever tell her.

"The sheer sleeve didn't hide it anyway," Kendra said from the backseat. "You'd need heavier material, and you're not going to find that in any summer wedding collection."

"We could look online," Anne said. "Or..." Oh, she didn't know. And right now that wasn't the issue. Her daughter was mad at her. No, make that furious. Well, darn it all, she wasn't exactly happy with Laney, either. This should've been fun, a memorable outing. It hadn't been fun and it'd been memorable in the worst kind of way.

"I hate to say it, but the baby Momzilla is growing," said Kendra.

"I am not a Momzilla!" Anne almost shouted.

"What on earth is a Momzilla?" Julia demanded.

"It's what we call an out-of-control mother of the bride," Kendra explained.

"Momzilla," Julia said, trying out the word. She nodded. "Yes, Anne, I think you were a bit of a Momzilla today."

"I was not! I didn't tell my daughter what wedding gown to buy or refuse to pay for a gown I didn't like."

"Only because you're not a full-grown Momzilla yet," Kendra said.

"You may not have done that but you certainly balked at getting the dress your daughter picked out," said Julia. "You might as well have told her you wouldn't buy it."

Anne frowned at her mother. "So, you want her to walk down the aisle with the mermaid in full view of everyone?"

"What does it matter?" Kendra argued. "It'll be family and friends at the wedding, and they all know she's got a sleeve. Heck, half the women at the wedding will have tattoos."

"Call her and tell her to get the gown," commanded her mother.

Anne scowled at the traffic in front of her crawling

down Forty-Fifth. "I don't see what's wrong with going to another shop and seeing if there's anything else."

"Well, then, your eyes are closed," Julia said shortly. "Laney loved the first gown, and none of the ones she tried on lit up her face like that one did. Your sister made a good point. Everyone coming to the wedding knows about Laney's tattoo. They've all gotten used to it. So you may as well let her have the dress she wants."

"Twenty years from now, when she looks back on her wedding pictures, what's she going to think?" Anne asked.

"That she got to have the dress she wanted," Kendra answered. "Come on, sis. Give it up."

"Easy for you to say. You haven't gone through this yet," Anne grumbled.

"Well, *I* have," said Julia. "And if you think I wanted to see my oldest daughter married in the courthouse, you can think again."

"I *know* you didn't want me getting married in the courthouse."

"*You* didn't even want you getting married in the courthouse. But you married the man you loved in the dress you picked out, and I was there to support you. It was your decision and I had to live with it. In the end, that's all a mother can do. Unless, of course, she wants to become a Momzilla," Julia added, obviously enjoying her new word.

"It's a gorgeous dress," put in Kendra, "and Laney looks beautiful in it."

"She didn't even try on the one with the jacket," Anne muttered.

"If I get like this when my daughters get married, somebody shoot me," Kendra said from the backseat.

"You will," Anne predicted. Maybe it wouldn't be

over a gown, but it would be about…something. Suddenly she had empathy for the Laurel Brownes of the world. Being the mother of the bride wasn't easy.

Both her mother's and her sister's final words to her when she dropped them off were to call Laney and tell her she could have the dress, which left her feeling self-righteous and misunderstood.

She drove home, her eyes stinging with tears. She hadn't actually said not to buy the dress. All she'd wanted was for her daughter to be open to different options. How was that so bad?

Laurel Browne's words haunted her. *"We never fight."* But they had, and over something as inconsequential as goldfish.

When it came to mother-daughter disagreements, Anne had seen it all. She'd seen mothers and daughters get into it over everything from whom to include on the guest list to what flavor cake to serve. She'd always watched with smug tolerance, assuring herself that when they planned her daughter's wedding, there'd be none of that. She and Lancy were too close for such nonsense, and although they might not have had the same taste in fashion, they certainly shared the same taste in weddings. They always had.

Until now. Now it felt as if every choice was a challenge and every decision her daughter made a surprise. And not necessarily a pleasant one.

Okay, so Laney was her own woman now. And Anne had no problem with her daughter making her own decisions. This was her wedding, a once-in-a-lifetime event (well, theoretically), and she wanted only to make sure Laney got it right, that she had no regrets later. Was that so wrong?

She came home to find Cam grading papers. "How'd it go?" he asked.

"Not good," she said and proceeded to give him a blow-by-blow account of what had happened.

"Not good," he agreed. "What are you going to do about it?"

She knew what she wanted to do. She wanted to implant a chip in her daughter's brain so she'd make the best choices.

No, she was trying to make her a Stepford Bride. She was trying to make Laney not be Laney.

The realization was horrifying and humiliating. Laney loved her mermaid tat, considered it part of her artistic expression. If Anne was ashamed of that, wasn't she also ashamed of her daughter?

She was proud of Laney, proud of how well she was doing, what a talented young woman she was. Did the tattoo matter so much? Obviously, it bugged her, but why? Because she thought people would judge her for her daughter's extreme tattoo and consider her an inferior mother? And what did that say about her? She suddenly felt selfish and small. This was her daughter's big day. It was about Laney, not Anne, and if Laney wanted a sleeveless dress, then she was going to get a sleeveless dress.

Anne called the dress shop and caught Glenda just as they were closing. "We're going to take that sleeveless dress with the sweetheart neckline."

"It is a lovely dress," Glenda said encouragingly. "And your daughter will look beautiful in it."

"Yes, she will." Laney would look beautiful in anything.

"My daughter has a tattoo," Glenda said. "She went

sleeveless with her wedding gown, and you know, it looked fine."

Anne sighed and gave the woman her charge-card information.

"Good decision." Cam nodded in approval when she hung up.

"It *is* all about her," Anne said as much to herself as him.

"Yes, it is."

"I guess I'd better call and tell her she can pick up the dress." Compromise. They all had to compromise. Hadn't she told herself that a while back?

She called Laney's cell but, big surprise, her daughter wasn't picking up. She was probably off somewhere with a voodoo doll marked "Mom," sticking pins in it. Hopefully, she'd listen to Anne's voice mail message.

"Hi. It's Mom. I just wanted to let you know that I've paid for the wedding gown you liked." Loved. Laney had loved it, and every bride deserved to have the wedding gown of her dreams. "You can pick it up anytime. I'm sorry we quarreled, sweetie. I want you to be happy and have the wedding you want." And there was still so much to do between now and the big day. She added a verbal PS. "Oh, and by the way, have you sent out the save-the-date announcements yet?" Okay, that sounded a little…critical. "If you haven't, I'll be glad to help you."

"Interesting way to end an apology," Cam observed as she ended the call.

"We have to stay on top of things."

"Yeah, I see how well we're staying on top of things for our anniversary."

She decided to ignore that remark. They'd get to it

eventually, when she wasn't feeling completely wrung out. Planning a wedding had never been so stressful.

Of course, she'd created much of the stress herself. How tangled mothers' and daughters' lives got! She could still see her own mother's face when she announced that she and Cam were getting married at the courthouse ASAP.

1990

Julia stared at Anne as if she'd just announced a death in the family. "You what?"

It was only the two of them, seated at the breakfast table with cups of coffee and banana bread left over from the day before. Anne gripped her mug tightly. "Cam and I are getting married next week at the courthouse," she repeated, smiling insistently.

"Anne," her mother protested, "that doesn't make any sense. You wanted a church wedding and a big reception. You don't even have a ring yet."

As if she didn't know. "We're going to look at rings tomorrow."

Julia shook her head. "I don't understand. You two have been an item since high school. Why the rush all of a sudden?" And then a disapproving look took over her face. "Anne Marie Wellington, are you pregnant?"

Anne was still trying to compose her answer when her mother said, "You are," in tones that were just as disapproving as her expression. "Oh, Anne, what were you thinking?"

That I love him. Obviously, she hadn't been thinking about getting pregnant. They should've waited until they were married to have sex. Too late now. Anyway, she wanted Cam's baby, wanted to have something of him to love while he was so far away.

"How am I ever going to tell your father?"

Anne bit her lip. She had no idea, but she hoped it was when she wasn't around. He'd be as disappointed in her as her mother was. "I'm sorry," she said in a small voice.

Julia expelled her frustration in a long sigh. "We raised you better." Now she was shaking her head. Okay, so they'd messed up, but her mom didn't need to carry on as though she'd committed the crime of the century. Women who weren't married got pregnant all the time. They even moved in with their boyfriends.

"Mom, I'm sorry, but I love him."

This inspired another long sigh. "I know. Still, there's still no need to rush like this."

"Yes, there is. He's shipping out in a few weeks. We want some time together before he goes. If he doesn't come back…" Her throat tightened and she couldn't finish the sentence.

"You're going to regret this haste." Her mother went on as if she hadn't spoken. "All those dreams you had, those plans, all the times we talked about your wedding. All these years your father's dreamed about walking you down the aisle."

That was when Anne realized she wasn't the only one who'd had to give up a dream. Her mother had been anticipating a wedding, too.

This was not how she'd planned to start her married life, but she couldn't turn back the clock. Anyway, she'd meant what she said. She did want as much time as possible with Cam, wanted to give him some happy memories to take with him. Maybe things hadn't turned out according to plan—the old plan—but they'd make the new plan work.

She said as much to her mother and Julia came around the yellow Formica kitchen table and hugged her. "You're right. We love you, and we love Cam, too."

"And what about the baby?" Anne asked.

"Of course. We'll love the baby to pieces." Her mother frowned again. "I just wish... Oh, never mind," she said brusquely. "We'd better go shopping for a dress this afternoon."

And so they got right down to the business of getting Anne ready for her courthouse wedding. Her mother said nothing more about her disappointment and helped her pick out a dress and bouquet. Her father hugged her and told her he'd be happy to give the bride away, and so they made the best of things. On her wedding day her parents hosted a family dinner featuring standing rib roast and baked potatoes. And that horrible cake the neighbor made. *At least it's a wedding cake*, she thought.

Her parents gave Cam and her two entire place settings of fine china and a check for a hundred dollars. Other friends and neighbors, upon hearing the news, sent gifts, as well, but Anne's courthouse wedding hung over the day like a black cloud. She'd disappointed her mother; there was no denying it. Still, if she had it to do over, she'd probably make the same choices. The bottom line was that she loved Cam and he loved her. And later that night, when they were in their motel room at Ocean Shores, wrapped in each other's arms and listening to the crash of waves on the beach, she was able to sigh happily. Thank God, she thought, that even when life wasn't perfect, when daughters weren't perfect, there was usually a plan B.

In the end, weddings were about the bride and groom, Anne reminded herself now. Yes, she planned weddings for a living, but she had no business telling her daughter what gown to wear.

No more Momzilla, she vowed. From now on she'd back off—but there was nothing wrong with offering guidance.

Chapter Seventeen

Roberta, Mother of the Year

It had taken a while after the last wedding mishap for mother-daughter relations to return to normal. Roberta had not reacted well when Daphne dropped the wedding cake; she'd be the first to admit it. But honestly, what grown woman tripped over her shoelace? Anyone would've reacted the way Roberta had.

Maybe not. Muriel Sterling, Daphne's new guru, would've hugged her and kissed her frosted face, told her accidents happened. But Muriel Sterling wasn't running a business where cake was a necessity. And Roberta thought she'd shown considerable restraint, all things considered. All she'd said was "Oh, Daphne." All right, she'd also tagged on "For heaven's sake!"

With one little phrase she'd hurt Daphne's feelings. Again. It seemed she was always upsetting her daughter. But that same daughter kept her in a near-constant state of upset, as well. Years of worry over Daphne's relationships and her future security had grown every gray hair on Roberta's head.

If she didn't accomplish anything else in this world,

Roberta needed to get Daphne's life sorted out. Then she could stop worrying.

Somewhere along the mother-daughter timeline, Daphne had turned from a well-loved child to an obsession. Obsessions were exhausting.

This day was going to require yet more emotional energy. Hank Hawkins would be arriving soon to put the fishpond in order and do some planting, and Roberta needed to find a way to get her daughter gone. It shouldn't be too hard, since this was Daphne's day off. Surely she'd want to go have a latte or something.

Roberta had already taken her morning walk, eaten her granola and was on her second cup of coffee when Daphne made her appearance in the kitchen, wearing a ratty old T-shirt, the circles under her eyes testifying to a poor night's sleep. Even in her rumpled state she was a beautiful woman.

"You look tired," Roberta greeted her.

"I didn't sleep well last night," Daphne said, pouring a cup of coffee. "I kept having these awful dreams. I was back with Mitchell and he wanted me to have a threesome with him and Betty White."

"Betty White?" What was happening to her poor daughter's subconscious?

"And Betty dragged me to Macy's to shop for a black negligee for her. We couldn't find one and Mitchell got mad and said he was leaving. But he came back and set the house on fire with me in it." Daphne rubbed her forehead. "I hate him, Mother. I truly hate him."

"Well, you'll soon be rid of him," Roberta said, hoping that was a comfort.

Daphne frowned into her coffee cup. "The sooner, the better."

"Meanwhile, there's nothing to take your mind off your troubles like a day of shopping."

"I don't feel like shopping. There isn't anything I need."

"Well, I need something."

"Like what? I asked yesterday if you needed anything and you said no."

"I forgot I'm almost out of Metamucil," Roberta improvised, "and we could use some more double-A batteries. And maybe while you're at the drugstore, you could pick up my prescription." She was bound to have some prescription or other waiting. She always did. "Oh, and why don't you get us a couple of lattes."

Daphne was looking at her with a mixture of perplexity and irritation. "Anything else?"

Nothing Roberta could think of. She wished she'd sent something to the dry cleaner. "That should do it." She hoped.

"All right," Daphne said. "I'll go as soon as I have breakfast."

Her daughter took forever with breakfast, putting together an omelet and then sitting down to eat it while reading the copy of *People* she'd brought home the day before. Hank would be here any moment.

"You're not done yet?" Roberta said, coming into the kitchen to check on Daphne's progress for the third time.

"What's the hurry?"

"I'd like to get my prescription as soon as possible."

That worked. "I guess I'd better get dressed, then," Daphne said, shutting the magazine.

"I'll clean up." Roberta took her plate. "You go get ready."

Daphne had just left the house when Hank arrived.

Whew, Roberta had gotten her daughter away from temptation in the nick of time.

And a good thing, too. Hank Hawkins was a fine specimen of manhood; he was also polite and hardworking. But he would never do. Being divorced made him a very poor risk, especially for Daphne. Honestly, at this stage any man would be a poor risk for Daphne.

She must have run her errands on winged feet because it seemed Hank had barely started working and she was back. With plants.

She handed Roberta her usual plain latte. "They didn't have a prescription for you at Johnson's."

"I forgot—I already picked it up," Roberta lied. "What's this?" She pointed to the box of pansies Daphne had set on the kitchen table.

"I stopped by the nursery. They were on sale. We've got a few spots in the flower beds where they'll fill in nicely."

Roberta wasn't sure if she was pleased or irritated that her daughter was making landscaping decisions for her.

She was still trying to decide when Daphne said, "Since Hank's here he can get them in the ground for us right away."

"I'll do them later," Roberta said.

"Mother, you don't want to be out there on your hands and knees. That's why you hired a gardener. Remember?"

Roberta wished she'd never confessed how tired she was of yard work.

"Don't worry," Daphne said. "I'm just going to take him these plants. I'm not going to ask him for a date."

Roberta scowled at her daughter's departing back. Really. When had Daphne become such a smart aleck?

And why had she returned home so quickly? Had she known that Hank was coming over? Roberta certainly hadn't said anything. She hadn't known he'd be coming by herself until the day before, when he'd called and told her he had to change his regular day due to a dental appointment. She'd automatically agreed to the change, forgetting that it would be Daphne's day off.

She should've called him first thing in the morning and canceled. Or asked him to send someone else. All this forgetfulness. Perhaps she had a subconscious desire to match her daughter up, a longing for one of them to grab the romance brass ring.

No, no, no. Everything Daphne grabbed turned into something smelly. There would be no grabbing going on here at Primrose Haus, especially with a man who already had one strike against him. That made four strikes between the two of them—a very bad combination of numbers.

Roberta could hear voices outside the kitchen. She stole over to the back door and opened it a crack. Then she leaned in for a listen.

"Met any interesting lesbians yet?" Hank asked.

Roberta blinked and shook her head. She must have misheard. She pressed her ear closer to the door.

"I saw someone at Zelda's who looked interesting," said Daphne.

What? Since when did Daphne decide she preferred women to men?

"Uh-huh," Hank said. Even through the door Roberta could hear his skepticism.

"You know, I was where you were. Emotionally, I mean."

"Oh, really?"

"Yeah. After my wife told me I was too boring to bother with and left me for another man."

"Your wife left you for another man?"

Daphne sounded shocked. So was Roberta. She'd always thought Hank was a nice man. How sad that his wife hadn't appreciated him, and it was a pity he and Daphne hadn't met earlier, before Mitchell the ogler came on the scene.

"Yep," Hank was saying. "Some cowboy she hooked up with when she went to the Ellensberg rodeo with her girlfriends. I guess he gave her a wilder ride than I could."

Daphne said something, but it was so soft Roberta couldn't be sure what. It sounded like "I'm sorry."

"I used to think it was all on me. Then I realized it wasn't."

"My husband left me for another woman. Well, more than one. He was a rat and I already know it had nothing to do with me. Except for the fact that I picked him in the first place. When it comes to men, I'm not a good chooser."

"What makes you think you'll have any more success with women?"

Roberta shook her head again. Honestly, what kind of conversation *was* this?

"Okay, the truth is, I don't want to be with anyone," Daphne said. "I like being on my own."

No, she didn't. Poor Daphne. Cupid had given her a raw deal. She deserved better.

Maybe Hank Hawkins was better.

Oh, but a fourth husband? Was that even worth considering? Roberta was still mulling it over when the kitchen door opened suddenly, taking her by surprise and nearly toppling her onto the back porch.

"Mother! What are you doing?"

Roberta willed away the guilty flush on her cheeks. "It was hot in here. I was opening the door for a little fresh air."

"You were eavesdropping," Daphne said in disgust.

"I was not."

Daphne crossed her arms. "Really, Mother."

"I don't know why you're getting after me," Roberta said, opting for wounded dignity. "I simply happened to be passing by the door. I must say, I didn't know Hank's wife left him for someone else."

"There's a lot of that going around," Daphne said bitterly.

"It's too bad you didn't meet someone like him sooner."

She could have if she'd listened to Roberta and used one of those online dating services everyone was talking about. From what Roberta understood, you filled out a detailed questionnaire and then were given any number of perfect matches. But, as usual, Daphne had to do things her own way. And look where it got her.

Daphne frowned. "We're not going to start talking about my horrible taste in men, are we?"

Roberta had no desire to go down that long and winding road. "I have no intention of talking about your past mistakes."

"Good," Daphne said with a nod, "because that's a subject I'd rather not discuss if you don't mind." With that she picked up her latte and walked out of the kitchen, leaving Roberta feeling frustrated.

As usual. She'd made a verbal misstep somewhere in the conversation and now Daphne wasn't happy with her.

Well, she wasn't always happy with Daphne, either, but at least she cared, which was more than she could say for her own mother.

"I'm only doing this for your own good." The words came back to haunt her. Oh, yes, her mother had the right words for every occasion—not that learning her daughter was about to become an unwed mother was much of an occasion—but her actions spoke so much more loudly.

1961

"If you're going to refuse to tell me who the father is, then I have no choice," Roberta's mother snapped. "Although I can guess, and that young man should be held accountable."

"You can't guess anything," Roberta said, determined to be stubborn. There'd been that period of time she'd been with another boy. The baby could be his, couldn't it? And just now, she wished it was. Any other boy would have done the right thing.

They were in the living room, the perfect living room with its crushed-velvet furniture and expensive drapes, the living room where her mother liked to entertain friends for coffee. (If you could call the rich, snobby women she cultivated *friends*.) Roberta huddled in a chair, her tummy churning. Her grandmother, who'd been summoned from her little house up on Tenth Avenue, perched on the couch, trying to calm Roberta's mother with phrases like "These things happen" or "Helen, darling, please try to get hold of yourself."

Nothing could calm her mother. She paced the room like a caged animal while Roberta sat in a wingback chair, her hands tightly clasped. If her father had been alive he might have tempered her mother's wrath. He certainly would have hugged Roberta and told her he still loved her and that it would be all right. But Daddy had died when Roberta was ten. Her mother had played the brave, grieving widow to the hilt, although Roberta sometimes wondered if she even missed him. Had she ever really loved him? Did she know what it was to love someone? Did she know what it felt like to have your heart broken?

Not that Roberta loved Gerard anymore. She hated him for being so selfish, hated him for leaving her in this mess. She'd rather be alone the rest of her life than forced to marry such a selfish creep.

Of course, her single state made it oh-so-inconvenient for her mother, who worried more about what people would think than her own daughter's broken heart.

"Well, you can't keep it."

"What do you mean?"

"The baby. If you won't tell me who the father is, then you'll have to give it up for adoption."

Give up her baby? She might have hated Gerard, but she already loved this little life growing inside her. How could she give it away? "No," she protested.

"What are you planning to do?" her mother asked contemptuously. "Waddle around town with a big tummy, a walking advertisement for what not to do? Do you want people laughing behind your back? Do you want every respectable man to cross you off his list? Men don't marry girls who get themselves into this kind of mess."

"Then maybe I don't want to get married," Roberta shot back. Brave words but she did want to get married. She'd never imagined herself alone.

"Don't talk foolishly," her mother scolded.

"This is a short time in your life, dearest," her grandmother put in. "I know it's…awkward."

Was that what you called this horrible feeling of rejection?

"But we can get past it," Grandma finished.

"There's a home outside Seattle, in Dunlap," her mother said. "They take in girls who find themselves in this situation. Your father was from California. We'll say you've gone to visit family down there. No one will be the wiser."

"I don't want to go to some…home and stay with strangers."

"You can't stay here, Roberta. How would it look?"

Roberta didn't have an answer for that.

"I'm only doing this for your own good."

They were going to turn her out, send her off to some jail for unwed mothers, hide her away like a leper. "I won't go," Roberta said stubbornly. "And you can't make me."

"Oh, yes, you will," her mother said, pointing a finger at her. "You've gotten yourself into this mess and now you'll have to deal with the consequences."

Roberta jumped up. "I won't! You can't make me." And with that she ran from the room. Upstairs she slammed her bedroom door to emphasize how strongly she felt.

But slamming doors and protestations did no good. Her mother swept everything aside and made the arrangements. And if that wasn't bad enough, she kept Roberta home under virtual house arrest.

The following week, as she and Roberta sat at the kitchen table, she broke the silence by announcing, "It's all arranged. You'll be going to the Florence Crittenton Home for Unwed Mothers. Your grandmother and I will take you the day after tomorrow."

The day after tomorrow, she was getting shipped off to some…place, to live with strangers, other girls who found themselves in the same mess. Well, she wouldn't do it. Her mother could make all the arrangements she wanted, but Roberta wasn't going to go along with it, like…like a sheep headed to the slaughter.

Except what choice did she have? Only one.

"Roberta?"

She looked up to find her mother regarding her with a stern expression. "Did you hear what I said?"

"Yes, Mother." Let her mother think she was going along with this.

"Good. Pack a few clothes tonight. I'll bring you more as you need them."

Maternity clothes, of course. Oh, she'd done this all so wrong. She should be married, sitting at her own kitchen table, talking about the baby, making plans. Gerard had cheated her out of that. But he wasn't going to cheat her out of being a mother. Neither was her own mother.

"May I go out tonight to say goodbye to my friends?"

"You may go out and see your friends as long as you stick with our story. You'll be visiting your father's relatives in California."

"Yes, Mother."

Roberta told her friends she was leaving, all right, but she told them the real reason. She and her best friends, Nan and Linda, sat on Nan's canopy bed and discussed what Roberta should do.

"I have ten dollars in my purse," Nan said.

"And I have six," added Linda. She frowned. "That's not enough for bus fare and a place to stay."

"Or food," Nan added. "I know! I'll tell Daddy that Linda and I want to go shopping tomorrow. He'll give me some money."

"Jilly just got her allowance. Let's call and ask her to come over and bring what she can," Linda said.

"We can't let too many people know about this," Roberta cautioned. "Someone will tell my mother."

"Jilly won't," Linda said. "I've got the car. I'll go pick her up. Oh, and she's the same size as you. She can put some clothes in her train case and tell her mother she's spending the night with me."

Meanwhile, Nan was up and rummaging through her jewelry box. She came back holding a gold locket. "Take this. If you need to you can pawn it. If not, keep it to remember me by."

Roberta's eyes filled with tears. She had such good, caring friends. If only she had a mother who cared as much. She took the necklace and hugged Nan. "Thank you," she managed around a throat constricted with emotion.

Once the money was collected, there was nothing left to do but say goodbye to her friends at the bus station.

"Don't forget to change buses," Nan told her. "In case the police come looking for you."

"Or your mom hires a private detective," Linda said.

"And if anyone asks, remember all I told you was that I was going to visit family in California."

Nan was crying now. She pulled Roberta into a fierce hug. "Oh, Bobbi, I'm going to miss you. Are we ever going to see you again?"

"I don't know," Roberta answered.

One thing she knew for sure—she'd never see her mother again.

She'd relented and gone back to visit when Daphne was two, hoping that once her mother saw her pretty blue-eyed granddaughter with her golden curls, she'd repent her heartless behavior. But her mother had refused to even come to the door. Roberta had stood on the porch of the large brick colonial, her daughter's hand in hers, knocking and then ringing the doorbell, telling herself that her mother simply hadn't heard her knock. But then she'd seen the living room curtain twitch. Her mother knew she was there, knew it was her standing on the front porch. She still didn't let Roberta in.

"She's ashamed," said Roberta's grandmother, who'd been overjoyed to see her. Grandma had fed her tea and ginger cookies and held Daphne on her lap, exclaiming over what a sweet child she was. She'd listened with interest as Roberta told her about her new life in Icicle Falls, how well she was doing at the bank. Grandma had even said she was proud of Roberta.

Her mother never did. Oh, she finally heard from her. Grandma had passed on Roberta's mailing address, and Roberta had received a letter a month later. But it hadn't been filled with kindness and forgiveness. Instead, it had been a diatribe, all about how Roberta had disappointed and humiliated her. She'd tried to help her and Roberta had thrown that help right back in her face. And then she came waltzing home, bold as brass with a baby in tow, and expected her mother to welcome her with open arms? Wicked, ungrateful girl!

The very memory of that letter could still open the dam of emotion. Her mother had been the most selfish creature alive. At least she'd had her grandmother, who sent presents every Christmas and chocolate bunnies at Easter. Grandma had even come to Icicle Falls to visit once before she died, bringing a handmade dress for Daphne and pictures for Roberta of when she was a little girl and her father was still alive.

"It's important to hang on to the good things from the past," she'd said. "Your mother... Well, I'm sorry. She's my own daughter but sometimes…" Grandma didn't finish the sentence. No need. Roberta understood.

And now she *really* understood. Daughters didn't always turn out the way a woman wanted. But all daughters deserved to be loved.

And helped. Even when they drove their mothers nuts.

Chapter Eighteen

Daphne, the Wiser Woman

Today she was going to court to finalize her divorce. Again. For the third time. There would be no haggling over child custody or fighting over who got the cat. Mitchell had his things and Daphne had hers. The house was in her name, so she'd keep that to do with as she pleased. As for the time-share they'd bought two years ago, against her lawyer's advice, she'd told him he could have it. She didn't want to go anywhere that would remind her of Mitchell.

"We're ready," Shirley had said on her last office visit.

Yes, as far as all the paperwork went, they were. But Daphne wasn't ready emotionally. She didn't want to go to the courthouse and see her failure officially recorded.

Still, to the courthouse she went. Into Room 3 with its rows of hard, wooden benches and the judge's throne of judgment looming above it all. She saw two people, each on opposite sides of the room, conferring with their lawyers in whispers and scowling at each other. Another lone man in a three-piece suit didn't seem any happier to be there. But she saw no sign of Mitchell. She didn't know whether to feel angry or relieved. She'd seen him at the pretrial conference, and that had been enough. She never wanted to see him again. Still, what did it say about her that he couldn't even bother to show up for their final court date?

She sat at the back of the courtroom, waiting her turn, watching as other people stood before the judge alongside their lawyers and officially ended what had started as happy unions. Ages ranged from twenties to fifties. How many church weddings were represented here? Had these couples lit a unity candle, poured sand into a glass vase? Promised to love, honor and obey, stay together in sickness and in health? Had any of them tried three times and failed?

Three weddings, three disasters. She probably held the record in Icicle Falls for more romantic failures than anyone else. And yet, each time she'd started out with such hope, such an air of celebration.

Her first wedding had been fit for a princess; her mother had seen to that. Even though Mother had her doubts. Why hadn't Daphne herself had any doubts? Oh, yes, because she was an idiot.

"You're still so young," Mother had said. "Why don't you wait a little longer?"

The answer to that had been simple. She was tired of waiting to have sex. Her mother had warned her about jumping into bed, telling her that often ended badly. When Daphne decided to jump into marriage instead, Mother flipped on the caution light again, and that was when she'd finally shared the truth about her own mistake and Daphne had learned that the daddy she'd always thought was dead was very much alive.

Daphne had tried to contact her birth father, wanting to see him, maybe develop a relationship with him. He couldn't have been as awful as her mother had said.

It turned out that he *was* as awful as her mother had said—a selfish man who didn't want to be reminded of his youthful indiscretion, as he so kindly put it. So she'd decided that, after all those years, she didn't need a father anyway, not when she had Johnny. He was more than enough for her.

Johnny was good-looking and fun and she could hardly wait to start their new life together. He had a job with a construction company in Seattle and a line on a cute little apartment in Magnolia. He was ready to go and so was she, so she plunged heart-first into marriage.

Her bridesmaids had dressed in pink, her favorite color, and she'd carried pink tulips. She'd read that tulips signified passion and that had certainly described her relationship with Johnny. Even the cake had been a mass of pink—pink frosting, pink roses, pink doilies underneath. Roses for a rosy future. But that rosy future lasted only five years, which was probably longer than it should have taken for Daphne to realize that her husband loved booze more than he loved her. Or their daughter.

So then came Fred, good solid Fred. And once again, there'd been a wedding on Primrose Street, a June wedding with lots of flowers and candles and a fancy sit-down dinner. The guest list was a little smaller than for wedding number one, but it had been lovely all the same. Daphne had gone with blue this time, the color of trust and peace, and she and Fred had vowed to be faithful all the rest of their days, to stay together in sickness and in health, for better or worse.

Somehow they'd neglected to add "in boring times and through the everyday grind" and Fred had started drifting like a sailboat with no anchor. And speaking of sailboats, he'd had to go and buy one. At first it was expeditions to the San Juans. Next thing she knew, he was talking about sailing around the world.

"But Marnie's in middle school," she'd protested. "We can't pull her out of school. And I have to work."

"We can homeschool her. You can quit your job."

"Fred, what will we live on?"

"We've got some money in savings, and I'm going to write a novel."

This was what came of marrying a man who was twelve years older. He'd been ready for a midlife crisis and she hadn't. He filed for divorce and sailed off without her. She was still waiting to see his novel on bookstore shelves or the internet.

Single parenthood was no fun, but she managed. Then Marnie graduated from college and moved out of the house and the place seemed so…empty. When Marnie moved to New York, Daphne figured she'd learned her lessons in love. She was ready to try again. And, lo and behold, along came Mitchell, charming lovable Mitchell. They got married in Seattle, at her house. Just family. She wore a gold cocktail dress because she'd read that gold was the color of success and triumph, and she'd carried a small bouquet of orchids and stephanotis to represent joy and marital happiness.

As she stumbled down memory lane her eyes began to leak tears, not so much for the loss of Mitchell but the loss of hope. *Don't cry*, she told herself, but somehow her tear ducts didn't get the message. In fact, they began to produce tears at an alarming rate. *Don't cry, don't cry, don't cry.*

Her lawyer passed her a tissue, and that small kindness made the tears flow all the harder. She slipped out of the courtroom and rushed to the women's bathroom. It was old-fashioned, with black-and-white tiles on the floor and ancient windows, and her wails echoed like a banshee's. *Don't cry, don't cry, don't cry.*

Another woman came into the bathroom. She was wearing jeans and a T-shirt and a scowl. She smelled of smoke. It could've been from cigarettes or plain old anger. "Whoever he is, he ain't worth the tears," she growled at Daphne.

Daphne wanted to explain that she wasn't crying over Mitchell. She was crying over lost love, over the sad fact that she'd probably be alone the rest of her life and never have sex again, even though fifty was the new forty and that made her forty-three. Instead, she swallowed a sob and nodded. Then she splashed cold water on her face, took a deep breath and went back to Room 3.

"Are you okay?" Shirley whispered when Daphne slid back onto the chair beside hers.

"I will be," Daphne whispered.

She spent the next half hour watching other people's marriages dissolve, and then it was her turn to go stand in front of the judge. Still no Mitchell.

Nobody seemed to need him anyway. It took less than ten minutes for the state of Washington to put its seal of approval on the end of her marriage.

Outside the courtroom she hugged Shirley and thanked her for all her help.

"Now, get out there and enjoy your single life," Shirley said.

"I will," she promised.

The first thing she did to enjoy her new single state was to sit by the river and have a pity party. She didn't need any noisemakers. She was making enough noise herself boo-hooing. It was wrong; it was unfair. She'd never wanted to be single.

But, she finally reasoned, being single and happy

(she'd get there eventually!) had to beat being married and miserable. She wished she felt happier about no longer being miserable, and she said as much to Muriel Sterling when she went to her house later to put in a couple of hours. She set up some signings for Muriel's upcoming release, a book of chocolate recipes and small-town reminiscences. Muriel had told her she could take the day off, but Daphne realized she needed the distraction, needed to do something to feel good about herself.

"Transitions are hard," Muriel said as she and Daphne settled at her little dining table with mugs of chocolate mint tea and a plate of brownies.

"After this many divorces I should be used to it," Daphne said with a grim smile.

"It's a loss. I don't think anyone ever gets used to loss."

"When it comes to men, I don't seem to be very smart," Daphne confessed.

"Oh, I wouldn't say that." Muriel nudged the plate of brownies closer to Daphne.

She'd been eating way too many carbs lately. She shouldn't.

Wait a minute. Why not? So what if she'd gained a couple of pounds since coming home to Icicle Falls? Who cared?

She took a brownie and bit off a good-size chunk. "Oh, wow. These didn't come out of a box."

Muriel smiled. "They're my own special recipe. Chocolate—it's one of life's small pleasures."

Small pleasure was better than no pleasure. Daphne took another bite.

Muriel picked up a brownie and examined it. "You know, a lot of life is about starting over."

"I've got that market cornered. But no matter how

many times I start over, I can't seem to get it right." Daphne sighed. "I hate being a failure."

"We all fail. It doesn't make us failures. You're only a failure if you quit trying, and I suspect you're a long way from quitting. In fact, I think you have a very good future in store."

"I wish I could believe that."

"You can't judge your future by your past, Daphne. You know, there's a Bible verse I recently discovered. It talks about not calling to mind the things of the past, about God wanting to do something new in you."

Forget the past? How did someone do that? Her past was like a big neon sign flashing Loser.

Muriel studied Daphne for a moment. Then she said, "Would you be willing to do something for me?"

Daphne looked at her suspiciously. "What?" Was Muriel going to suggest she take some self-improvement course, or stand up in the middle of a service at Icicle Falls Community Church and ask everyone to pray her out of loser purgatory? Go on *Dr. Phil* and get psychoanalyzed? Become a marathon runner?

"Start telling yourself, 'From now on, every choice I make will be the best choice for me at this time.'"

Daphne made a face. "I don't know."

"Just try it," Muriel urged. "It'll take the pressure off. Every decision doesn't have to be perfect. It just has to be right for you at that particular moment. You're a kind, intelligent woman, Daphne. I think the only thing stopping you from living a happy life is that you've programmed some wrong information into your brain. It's chipped away at your confidence. A lack of confidence makes us not want to try anymore, and I don't want to see you give up trying, not when you still have so much life to live."

Was Daphne's big problem a lack of confidence?

"What can it hurt?" Muriel asked.

Nothing. Daphne gave an assertive nod. "You're right."

"Everything you've experienced, both good and bad, has taught you things, made you wise. Now you need to draw on that wisdom," Muriel finished with a smile. She offered Daphne the plate of brownies.

Okay, she didn't need to keep self-medicating with carbs. "No, one was enough," Daphne said.

Muriel smiled. "Probably a wise decision."

"It's the best choice for me at this time," Daphne said with a grin.

After finishing up with Muriel, she made another wise decision. She was going to do something positive to celebrate her freedom from the rat of the Western world. She'd buy herself a present.

With this in mind, she made her way to Hearth and Home, one of her favorite shops in Icicle Falls. Daphne had always loved decorating and prettying up her house. Granted, she wouldn't have her house much longer, but she had a room, and she'd find something to put in it to remind her of new beginnings.

The shop wasn't large, but Gigi Babineaux, the owner, had stocked it with lovely things—an eclectic selection of unique and vintage furniture, candles, paintings and statuary.

"Daphne, I heard you were back in town," Gigi said.

Like everyone else, she'd probably heard why. "It's nice to be home."

"You look good."

"I feel good." Daphne was shocked to realize that was no lie. She walked by a gilded mirror and caught herself smiling. This was the day her divorce was final. She shouldn't have been smiling.

Oh, yes, she should. She was done with being miserable and brokenhearted. That was the old Daphne. The new Daphne was truly free to begin again.

Suddenly she saw just the thing to commemorate her new life. She drifted over to an ornate buffet where an amethyst glass vase imprinted with butterflies beckoned. Butterflies. Was there any better symbol of transformation, of new beginnings?

Daphne looked at the price tag. Whoa. Would purchasing this be a wise decision, the best decision she could make in that moment?

Yes, she decided. It would. This was a landmark day, a turning point in her life, and buying the vase would be a good way of reminding herself that she was indeed capable of making wise decisions. No more falling for the wrong man, no more letting neediness or loneliness rush her into a relationship she'd live to regret. She picked up the vase and marched to the cash register.

"I almost took this home myself," Gigi said as she rang up the purchase. "I love butterflies. And fairies."

Gigi herself reminded Daphne of a fairy queen with her long, white hair and diaphanous blouse worn over her jeans. She was older than Daphne, probably nearing retirement age, a slim, small woman who favored bangles and dangly earrings.

"My divorce was final today," Daphne confided to the fairy queen. "I wanted to get something to mark that I'm starting over."

Gigi approved. "Great choice," she said. "How are you settling in?"

After her shrink sessions with Muriel... "Fine."

Gigi nodded. "Good. It's not fun having to pick up

the pieces, but you will. I did. Moved here ten years ago after getting rid of my abusive husband. I've never been happier. Still, it's an adjustment. If you ever want to talk, let me know. I'm always up for a break at Bavarian Brews."

"Thanks. I might take you up on that," Daphne said. She'd take Cass up on her offer to go out for drinks, too. She needed to start hanging out with more people.

Gigi wrapped her purchase in several layers of tissue paper and Daphne went on her way.

But she didn't go home. She wasn't done celebrating yet. The mention of Bavarian Brews made her realize she needed to toast her new beginning.

She'd just picked up a blended coffee drink oozing with caramel and topped with toasted coconut when a male voice rumbled, "Yours looks better than mine."

She knew that deep baritone. The butterflies on the vase she'd purchased migrated to her chest. She glanced over her shoulder to see Hank Hawkins standing behind her with a to-go cup of coffee.

He held it up. "I take mine plain."

She would *not* allow herself to be interested in how Hank Hawkins took his coffee (or anything else about him), but it would be rude not to make some polite conversation. "I like black coffee now and then, too, but it's more fun when you dress it up. Is this coffee-break time?" she asked, noting his grass-stained jeans and the flannel shirt he wore over a T-shirt. He sure knew how to fill out a T-shirt.

"Yup. How about you?"

"I'm finished working for the day. Just stopped by to celebrate." Or did she mean medicate? No, no, no. She was celebrating. Mitchell and the heartbreak he'd caused were going to be nothing but a distant memory.

"Celebrate the end of work?"

"Nope, the end of my marriage."

He took a step closer. "So, you're a free woman."

She backed up. "Free forever."

"Forever's a long time."

It was getting hot in here. She undid the buttons on her sweater. She noticed him watching, and that made the hot flash hotter. She took a big sip of her cold beverage. "So is being in a bad marriage."

He nodded. "I know what you mean, and I don't blame you for not wanting to try again. I sure didn't want to."

She noticed his use of the past tense but decided not to comment on it.

"But a bad marriage is a little like hitting your thumb with a hammer."

Or your head.

"It hurts like the devil at first, but after a while your thumb recovers and you forget the hurt. Then you're back swinging the hammer again."

"Have you forgotten the hurt?"

He smiled. He had a very sexy smile. It was definitely hot in here. She took another gulp of her drink.

"It's in the past. No sense living there. I'm ready to pick up the hammer again."

She knew what that translated to. He was ready for another relationship. She wasn't. The time would never be right for her. *From now on every choice I make will be the best choice for me...* The best choice she could make right now would probably be to scram.

"Not all men are jerks," Hank said.

"No. Only the ones I'm attracted to."

But Hank Hawkins didn't seem like a jerk at all. He seemed like a nice, trustworthy man.

Looks could be deceiving, Daphne reminded herself. It was time to go. "I'd better get home."

He saluted her with his coffee. "Have a good one."

She would. Her life had no way to go but up. *I'm not going to worry about past mistakes, no matter where I've made them,* she told herself.

Her mother must have seen her coming. She opened the front door for Daphne as she came in bearing her new vase. "How did it go at court?"

"Fine," Daphne said, walking in. "I'm a free woman, and from now on I'm going to make better choices."

Mother gave a satisfied nod. "I know you will, dear. What's that you've got?"

"I'll show you." Daphne started for the back parlor where they did all their living.

"No, no. Show me here."

What on earth was that about? Was her mother getting eccentric in her old age? But Daphne complied, setting down the bag and pulling her vase out of the tissue paper.

"Oh," Mother said, her voice filled with awe. "How lovely."

"It's my divorce present to me," Daphne said.

"Butterflies," Mother said softly. "How appropriate."

"I thought so," Daphne said, pleased that her mother got the symbolism.

"Well, put that away where it won't get knocked over and then come on back to the parlor. I have something for you. It's an early birthday present," Mother added, suddenly looking like a woman who'd just learned where the Easter bunny hid his cache of Cadbury eggs.

Very mysterious. Daphne put her vase on the dresser in her bedroom and went back downstairs to see what her mother was up to. She entered the back parlor to find

Mother bent over some kind of animal carrier. "What on earth?"

Mother stood up and turned around. She was holding a black cat.

"That looks like…" No, it couldn't be.

"Milo," Mother said. She walked over to Daphne and placed the cat in her arms. "I know your birthday isn't until later in the month, but I thought you should have him now."

The animal purred and snuggled up against her shoulder. Oh, yes, they were meant to be together. Still, her mother's views on pets had been pretty clear.

"But we don't want animals here." So, was this gift another subtle nudge for Daphne to find her own place? "And you were worried about people with allergies."

"I'm aware of what I said," Roberta said crisply. "But I reconsidered. We'll find a way to work around the allergy problem. Anyway, I think we could use the company around here, don't you?"

Daphne didn't know what to think.

"This is your home, too," she added.

It was such a simple statement but it meant so much. Once more she found herself with tears in her eyes, but these were the best kind of tears, the kind that sprang from a healing heart.

"Thank you," she said, giving her mother a one-armed hug and a kiss on the cheek. Milo seconded her thanks with a loud meow.

"You've had a rough time of it these past few months, but things will get better now. A strong woman can get through anything."

Her mother was testimony to that. She never spoke much about her own mother, but the lack of communication between the two of them had said it all. Roberta

Gilbert had single-handedly carved out her successful life here in Icicle Falls.

Daphne wasn't her mother, and yet she must have inherited that independence gene. All she had to do was find it. And she would, because from now on she was making wise choices, the right choices—for her.

Chapter Nineteen

Anne, Queen of Disaster Relief

Outdoor weddings were lovely…as long as it didn't rain. Anne looked at the cloudy sky covering Lake Washington like a dome of doom and sighed. It had been sunny all day and Anne had begun to hope that the weatherman was wrong. Why couldn't the rain have held off a little longer? She'd reminded the bride and her mother that end of April was not a good choice for cooperative weather. In Seattle anything before the Fourth of July was a risk.

But Felicity had her heart set on an outdoor wedding, and her mother, Trina, had her heart set on giving Felicity anything she wanted. "She's my only baby," Trina had said. "I want her to be happy."

Anne could understand that. Although she did encourage the bride to have a plan B.

"It won't rain," Felicity had said blithely.

"If it does, I guess we'll have to squeeze into the basement," her mother had said with a helpless shrug. Later she'd confided to Anne. "I don't know how we'll fit everyone in the house."

"That's something to consider," Anne had responded diplomatically.

Mother and daughter did consider it, and the bride-to-be stuck to her plan for an outdoor wedding. They cut the guest list, but not enough, since even after that her mother worried about where they'd put everyone.

Planning the event had been easy. Both mother and daughter had been delighted with all of Anne's ideas, making it a snap to take care of ordering the cake and flowers and finding the DJ and caterer, renting the chairs and the tent and the dishes and linens. Now all sat in readiness waiting for the bridal party to finish with photos in the garden and on the dock.

Anne blinked as something wet hit her in the eye. This was followed by another something wet splashing her cheek. Oh, no. Here came the rain.

The photographer was finishing up, and Felicity and her groom and their posse began horsing around on the dock, the guys pretending to push the girls off and the girls squealing in mock horror. Ah, the energy of youth. They seemed oblivious of the darkening gray clouds and the spatter.

The mother of the bride wasn't, though. She hurried over to Anne, her face a study in motherly concern. "Oh, Anne, you were right. This was a bad idea. I wish I'd never let Felicity talk me into this."

Anne was never one for I-told-you-so. "What would you like to do?"

"Felicity will want to wait and see if this blows over."

Maybe it would, but not in time for the wedding to take place outdoors. They'd have to move the ceremony inside. Anne looked over to where Felicity stood on the dock, laughing. A speedboat decorated with flowers bobbed next to it, ready for the father of the bride to motor the couple to an undisclosed wedding-night location. She felt sorry for Felicity and her mom. They'd taken a gamble and lost.

Trina shook her head. "She wanted an outdoor wedding so badly, and she wanted it this weekend."

Anne knew why. Trina had told her. Felicity had wanted to honor her older sister, who had died in April twelve years earlier from childhood leukemia. Later in the evening the wedding party planned to toss their flowers on the lake in honor of her.

When Anne had brought up concerns about the weather, Felicity had insisted that the day she'd picked would be sunny. It had to be. The universe couldn't be that cruel.

It had been all Anne could do not to say, "Oh, yes, it can. In fact, the universe doesn't care two figs about you or any of us."

1997

Anne burrowed under her blankets on the couch and turned up the TV, ignoring the ringing phone. She knew it would be her mom calling to check up on her, but she didn't want to talk to anyone, not even Mom. All she wanted to do was stay here forever watching soaps on TV and feeling sorry for herself. She'd been doing a pretty good job of it, too. So far, forever had lasted three months. She barely cleaned; she served sandwiches and canned chili for dinner, and let her business slide, leaving Kendra, who'd only recently come on board, scrambling.

"We can try again," Cam had said after her first miscarriage, holding her in his arms and kissing the top of her head.

But now she was convinced it didn't matter how many

times they tried. They were never going to have another baby.

"It's a blessing in disguise," her grandmother had said after each miscarriage. "Something must've been wrong with the baby. This is nature's way of telling you to start again."

No, it was nature's way of taunting her. She'd always thought they'd have at least two children, maybe three, or even four. She'd longed to hear the thunder of feet as her children raced up and down the stairs, longed to hear giggles and see sisters and brothers playing together in the backyard. She felt cheated and angry, and she felt especially angry at God. This was her third miscarriage. How could He let this happen?

"How is it that any bad thing happens?" her mother had responded earlier in the week when Anne was venting her anger. "There are no guarantees in this world. You know that. All we can do is enjoy the good things that come our way and accept the bad."

Well, Anne didn't want to accept the bad. Her arms ached to hold the little one who'd tried so hard to hang on inside her. She felt the loss as surely as if she'd carried the baby to term. Now she was in deep mourning, her husband and daughter mere figures, blurred and moving at the dark edges of her grief.

The phone rang again. She turned the volume on the TV even higher.

Later in the day she was still on the couch when her mom let herself in with the spare key Anne and Cam kept under the flowerpot out front. "I don't want to see anyone," Anne greeted her and burrowed deeper under her blankets.

"I know." Her mother sat down on the opposite end

of the couch, settling Anne's feet in her lap and starting a foot massage.

"It's not fair," Anne said bitterly.

"I know. But you still have a living daughter."

Anne pulled her foot away. "What's that supposed to mean?"

Her mother calmly took back her foot and resumed rubbing. "I'm only agreeing with you."

"No, you're not. You're trying to teach me a lesson."

Julia smiled. "Things always had to be fair when you were growing up. I had to make sure you and your sister both got the exact same number of cookies for your after-school snack, the exact same number of gifts at Christmas. And, oh, the complaints when she was allowed to stay up as late as you on special occasions."

"I don't know where you're going with this."

"Going? I'm simply agreeing with you. It's *not* fair. It's not fair that you still have a healthy, happy child when so many women all over the world wind up with none. Come to think of it, it's not fair that you have such a kind, loving husband who's always there for you. Or such a nice house. And plenty of food on the table."

"Now you're going to lay a guilt trip on me for feeling the way I do?" Anne demanded, incredulous.

Julia stopped the foot rub. "No, sweetie. Remember, I had a miscarriage between you and Kendra and it broke my heart. But I couldn't stay brokenhearted forever. I still had a child who needed me. And after losing the baby, well, you became even more precious."

Anne had been too wrapped up in her grief to remember what she still had.

"I'm not saying you shouldn't mourn this loss," her mom continued. "All those hopes and dreams, gone, the little one finished before even getting a chance at life.

It's horrible. But at some point you have to go on. You can't lie on this couch forever. And you can't let yourself become bitter. It's not fair to your husband and the child you have."

Anne chewed her lip, taking that in and yet wishing she didn't have to.

"You still have so much to be thankful for," Julia said gently.

"I don't want to be thankful, damn it!" This was followed by a storm of tears and a maternal shoulder to cry on. And hugs. And a quiet prayer together.

An hour later, Anne got up and made a real dinner for her family for the first time in three months.

Dinner wasn't all she made. She made an attitude adjustment, too. She reentered life with a vengeance. She and Cam took tango lessons and started scheduling a monthly date night.

On their first night out, as they sat in a little Italian restaurant in lower Queen Anne, enjoying pizza and Chianti, she thanked him for being so patient and understanding. "I know you always wanted to have more kids."

"But I've got you and Laney, and I'm okay with that, Annie. In fact, I'm more than okay. I think I'm a pretty lucky guy."

"And I'm a lucky woman," she said.

He raised his glass to her. "We've got a lot to be thankful for, babe."

Yes, they did, she thought as they clinked glasses. Cam and her mother were right. In spite of what she'd lost, she could still be thankful for what she had.

Now the wind had arrived, whipping the water on Lake Washington into whitecaps and tearing at the pretty white tent. While the groom and his groomsmen carried chairs into the basement, Anne, the bride and her mother and aunt all went into a wedding huddle.

The bride began to cry, her eyeliner running. "I can't believe this! Where are we going to put everyone?"

"We'll make it work," Anne promised her. The basement was roomy and finished and had a fireplace, perfect for a floral arrangement. The bride and groom could take their vows in front of it. They'd have to forgo the tables and squeeze chairs along the walls. A number of guests would have to stand, and in the interests of squeezing everyone in, the bride would have to don a raincoat and make her entrance via the patio door.

"Good idea," said the aunt after Anne had shared her ideas. "We can do this."

"Go fix your makeup," Trina said. "We'll take care of everything."

And they did. With Anne supervising, everyone got busy preparing for plan B. The bride patched up her makeup and found her smile again, even as the rain beat on the windows.

The guests came and the basement got hot with all the bodies in it. So hot, in fact, that the bride fainted just before saying, "I do." Father fretted while the groom carried her to the nearest chair, and a friend of the family who happened to be a doctor helped revive her. A door was opened and a gust of wind blew in, along with a neighbor's dog, who insisted on greeting one of the guests with his muddy paws. In spite of all that, the bride and groom finished their vows and the guests enjoyed their salmon, getting their food from the upstairs kitchen and spreading throughout the house to eat with their plates on their laps.

As the evening continued, the wind blew away the

clouds and the night cleared up enough for dancing on the soppy lawn and, most important, for the bride and her bridesmaids and the groom and his groomsmen to cast their flowers on the water in memory of the bride's sister.

"For a while there I wasn't sure I'd be able to say this," Trina said to Anne, "but it was a wonderful wedding."

"Your daughter's a wonderful girl."

They turned to watch as, in the middle of the lawn, the groom spun his new bride in a circle, both of them laughing.

Bride and groom happy, mother of the bride happy—mission accomplished.

Chapter Twenty

Laney the Tour Guide

"**I** was thinking we should get together on Saturday after you're done with work and wrap up a few more things for the wedding," Mom said.

Laney found herself suddenly clenching her cell phone and walking faster on the treadmill at the gym. "I forgot to tell you. Drake and I are going up to Icicle Falls this weekend."

Normally, she would've told her mother. She told her mother practically everything and they talked every day. But lately all they talked about was the wedding, and she was tired of talking about the wedding.

What was wrong with her? What kind of daughter didn't want to talk with her mother about her wedding?

If only Mom wasn't acting quite so…in charge. It had taken a fight in the middle of the stupid bridal shop for Laney to get the gown she wanted. Of course they'd made up, but things hadn't felt quite the same since. Autumn's words kept sneaking back into her mind every time Mom called to go over stuff. *"It's your wedding. Who's in control?"* Sometimes it didn't feel as though she was at all.

Not that her mom didn't ask what she wanted or what she thought. She did. But then when Laney told her, Mom seemed to find a way to shoot it down or change her mind.

And poor Drake—he'd really been left out. It seemed as if somehow things got decided and were a done deal before he even heard about them. That wasn't right. A lot of guys couldn't care less, but he wanted to be involved.

Well, this weekend he would be. It would be their time together. They'd check out the river, go dancing and, if the weather cooperated, get in a little rock climbing on Sunday before coming back to Seattle.

"That's a good idea," Mom said, bringing Laney back to the moment. "I'm sure Drake will love it up there."

Laney hoped so. It was his wedding, too, and she wanted him to be excited about it. Actually, she wanted them both to be excited about it.

She *was* excited. Yes, she was!

"We can do more next week," Mom said. "We need to get out those save-the-date cards."

"I already sent them out," Laney said. Her mom had almost made her crazy pushing to get those done. She hadn't been this much of a slave driver since back in Laney's junior year of high school, when Laney was applying at colleges. *"It's your wedding. Who's in control?"*

"And now people will be expecting invitations. You know they should go out two months in advance. We don't want to wait too long."

Everyone already had the date on their calendar, so Laney didn't see what the big deal was, but she said, "Don't worry, Mom." She shouldn't be dragging her feet like this. She should just sit down and do it. And she would. Next week. Or…when she had time. "I gotta finish my workout, Mom."

"Oh. Well. Okay."

They said their I-love-yous and then ended the call. Laney turned off her cell phone and upped the speed on the treadmill. She and Drake were going to have fun this weekend. He'd love Icicle Falls. Everything would get done and her wedding would be perfect. And she'd never been happier in her life.

She reminded herself again how happy she was once she and Drake were in his truck and on their way up the mountains to Icicle Falls. There were still some patches of snow on the ground but the evergreens were in their full glory. The sun was the center of attention in a cloudless, blue sky. In short, it was a beautiful day to be heading for the mountains.

She'd taken the day off, so they'd left at nine, which put them in Icicle Falls in time to have lunch at a burger place called Herman's Hamburgers. They passed by a life-size wooden figure of a woman in a traditional German dirndl as they entered. She was holding a platter bearing a hamburger. The little sign hanging from her neck said Willkommen in Herman's.

"Okay, what's with that?" Drake asked.

"It goes with the theme," Laney explained. "You know, it's supposed to look like a Bavarian village up here. That's what Mom says."

"Whatever."

He might have been unimpressed with the German theme of Herman's but he loved the burgers and garlic fries. After that they moved on to Gerhardt's Gasthaus, where Laney had found a bargain. This time they encountered real people wearing dirndls and lederhosen.

"Weird," Drake said under his breath.

The lobby was all dark wood and carved wooden chandeliers with lights made to look like candles. A mounted deer's head hung on one wall, watching them with glassy eyes. Another wall bore a coat of arms with a lion on it. Stepping into their room was like going back in time, with old furniture and some ornate wooden... things that reminded Laney of *The Lion, the Witch and the Wardrobe*.

"Where's the closet?" Drake asked.

"I think this is it." Laney opened the doors on the thing and found a rack and hangers. "Yep."

He came to stand behind her. "You don't see that at Motel 6."

"It's kind of cool."

"I guess." It wasn't hard to tell from his tone of voice that he didn't agree with her. "Let's get out of here."

On their way out, they poked their heads into the little bar, taking in the huge wine casks and the decorative steins on the wall. Two old guys sat on bar stools, talking to another old guy who was pulling beer from the tap. "A real hot place," he observed.

"We're not gonna be here tonight," Laney assured him. "There's dancing at the Red Barn."

"The Red Barn? I'm guessing they don't do rap there."

"Uh, country?"

"Yee-haw," he mocked.

"I've heard it's a fun place."

"There's gotta be someplace here that is," Drake said.

They made their way down the main street through the throng of tourists, watching the goings-on at the center of town. The aroma of sizzling bratwurst drifted over to them from the hot-dog place farther down the street, mixed with the tempting smells of waffle cones from the nearby ice cream and candy shop. A German oompah band was set up in the gazebo, playing accordions and yodeling, and in the middle of the street a gigantic maypole had been erected. Performers in traditional German costumes danced around it, wrapping it in colorful ribbons.

"Seriously weird," Drake muttered as they passed.

"I saw this online," Laney said. "It's to celebrate May Day."

"I thought that's what people say in airplanes when they're gonna crash," he joked, eyeing the dancers as if they were some strange species. "I guess."

So far he wasn't exactly in love with the town. She shouldn't have let her mother talk her into getting married in Icicle Falls.

Mom didn't talk you into this, she told herself. *You decided you wanted to get married on the river.* And wait till Drake saw the river. Once they got down to the Wenatchee, heard the whoosh of water speeding past and saw the swirling, white eddies crashing around the boulders, his smile grew. Visiting Adventure Outfitters was like going to guy playland. They had kayaks stacked outside the building, river rafts and giant inner tubes down by the river, and inside she and Drake found all manner of outdoor sports equipment and toys.

"Oh, yeah," Drake said with an appreciative smile. "That's what I'm talking about."

There was only one person in the store, and he was pulling life jackets out of shipping boxes and stacking them on a display table. He was older than them, maybe toward the end of his thirties, dressed in jeans and a flannel shirt. His hair was long and shaggy, and he was already getting some wrinkles, probably from spending too much time on the river.

He gave them a friendly nod. "Hi, there."

"Cool stuff," Drake said, gesturing around him.

"We try. You interested in booking a river rafting trip?"

"Actually, we came to talk about booking a raft for June," Laney said.

"Smart to do that now," said the guy. "June is a high-demand month."

"We want to get married on one," she explained.

"Serious?"

"Serious."

"Hey, Mick, come on out here!" he called. He thrust a calloused hand at Drake and then Laney. "I'm Darrell."

A man who looked her grandpa's age emerged from a back room. He was tall and skinny and he had dark hair shot with gray. Judging from the salt-and-pepper stubble on his chin he hadn't bothered to shave that morning.

"These guys want to get married on one of our rafts," Darrell told him.

The old man nodded. "Never had anybody get married on a raft before." He rubbed his grizzled chin, contemplating. "You wanna go down the river on it afterward?"

"Sure," they both said.

"Well, come on down and I'll show you what we've got."

The rafts were definitely rustic. Laney could almost see her mother cringing. But they could fix one up with flowers and it would look great. Anyway, it would be fun to shove off on the raft after the ceremony, better than a horse-drawn carriage. They could meet everyone at the reception after.

Details were discussed, and Drake laid down a deposit, and then it was time to visit Primrose Haus.

He wasn't quite so enthusiastic about that. "It's kind of old-lady looking," he said as they pulled up in front of it.

"It's a Victorian. It's supposed to look old," Laney said, and suddenly she was aware of the garlic fries gurgling around in her tummy.

"Hey, I'm okay with it," he said. "It's just, well, it's not Vegas."

She sighed. "You're right." Obviously, he was still stuck on Las Vegas.

"It's not too late to change your mind, you know," he said.

Yes, it was. "This will be great," she insisted.

"Which one of us are you trying to convince?"

"I don't need convincing," she said and rang the doorbell. Nobody came. "That's strange. There are cars out here." One of them was a PT Cruiser with a gingerbread boy and girl painted on the panel, along with the words Gingerbread Haus, the bakery that was going to do her cakes.

She rang the doorbell again. A moment later the door was opened by Daphne, one of the women she'd met when she came up with her mother. She was somewhere around Mom's age, a little bigger in the butt and boobs but really pretty with perfectly highlighted hair and perfect makeup. She reminded Laney of those older models you sometimes saw on the cover of *People* with headlines like She's Turning Fifty and Still Turning Heads.

The woman gave her the kind of friendly uncertain smile people used when they were sure they should know you but couldn't remember who you were.

Laney introduced herself. "Hi, I'm Laney. My mom and I were up here last month. June wedding."

"Oh, of course, and this must be your groom."

"This is him," Laney said, hugging Drake's arm.

Drake reached out and shook her hand. "Hi, I'm Drake."

"I'm Daphne. Come on in."

"I thought maybe I could show Drake around," Laney said.

"Oh, sure. We're setting up for a wedding this evening, so things are a little crazy, but I'd be glad to give you the tour," Daphne told her.

"Super. Thanks," Laney said and followed her inside. Behind her she was aware of Drake looking around, and she began to see the decor through his eyes. Fussy girl-stuff like you might find in a museum or on an episode of her mom's favorite show, *Downton Abbey*. Laney had liked it when she and Mom came up, but now she couldn't help wondering how comfortable her groom and his friends were going to be here.

"This is where we usually have our receptions before the nice summer weather hits," Daphne said, opening a pocket door and showing them a huge room with a crystal chandelier. Fancy chairs were scattered around the room, and there was a fireplace with a marble mantel at one end.

A table clad in white linen and edged with flowers had been set up in another corner, and the older lady Laney and her mom had met earlier was helping the woman who owned the bakery set up a wedding cake on it.

"It's like a castle," Drake said, and Laney wasn't sure whether or not he meant that as a compliment.

Their voices echoed across the room, catching the older woman's attention. She smiled and made her way over to them. "Well, hello. I do believe this is one of our brides."

"It's Laney," said Daphne. "And Duke."

"Drake," Drake corrected her, and she blushed.

"Of course. Drake. Great name."

"Thanks," he said in a tone of voice that asked if it was so great why didn't she remember it.

"Let me show you the grounds," Daphne said next and led them outdoors.

It was too early for much of anything other than the primroses to be in bloom; even so, the grounds were impressive, with statues and a fishpond and that rose arbor Mom had wanted them to get married under. The rose arbor would be nice once it had flowers blooming but Laney preferred something more exciting.

Like a *Pirates of the Caribbean*–style ship.

No, like a raft on the river. "By summer it'll be gorgeous out here," Daphne said, "with the lavender and honeysuckle and the lilies and peonies."

Drake didn't say anything, so Laney filled in the empty conversational space. "It's really pretty."

"The whole house is," Daphne said with a smile. "My mother's held a lot of weddings here, including mine." Her lips slid down at the corners. "And my daughter's," she added, bringing the smile back full-force.

Her wedding must not have turned out so well. Laney sneaked a look at her left hand. No ring. That sucked.

That won't ever be Drake and me, she told herself. They'd been together long enough to feel confident it would last. He was kind and fun. He knew that she was grumpy in the morning, that she could get pissy when she was PMSing and that she wasn't very good with money. And he loved her anyway. He knew what turned her on and what turned her off. And she knew what turned him on. (Anything!) She'd learned that he was easygoing but also anal about saving money, and they'd already talked about having a budget when they got married. Ick. But it was probably a good idea because he wanted to budget for big things, like cross-country camping trips and a house. And if it made him happy, then she was willing to write down how much money she spent at her favorite clothing consignment shop. Right now he was trying to act all chill, but she could tell he wasn't excited about having their reception here. "You don't like it," she said once they were back in the truck.

"It's okay."

"Just okay?" How could they have the reception here if he didn't like the place?

"I don't think that house is really us."

What *was* really them? Tents and log cabins and houses with modern colored-glass lights hanging from the ceilings. Old leather furniture and flea-market coffee tables.

And mountains and rivers. "Did you like the idea of the raft?"

"Oh, yeah!" He turned to face her and pulled her to him. "Hey, if you want to get married up here and have the reception at that house, then that's what we'll do. I want you to be happy."

"I want you to be happy, too."

"You know what—you're the bride and it's more important for you to be happy." It was such a Drake thing to say.

She hadn't sent out the wedding invitations yet. Like he'd said, it wasn't too late to change her mind. Two different images battled there—one of her stepping off a raft in her beautiful dress and coming to a big reception with all her friends and family at the fancy Victorian, the other of her and Drake in Vegas. The two of them, their parents and a couple of friends, no one to clap when they walked down the aisle or dance at their reception or blow bubbles as they ran for their car. But there would be glitz and glamour and excitement. She gnawed on her lower lip.

"Hey," he said, touching his forehead to hers. "If this is what you want, this is what we'll do."

It *was* what she wanted, what she'd always wanted. She'd gotten sidetracked with the idea of going off to Vegas and getting married on the Treasure Island wedding ship. But this was the wedding she'd dreamed of when she was a little girl. Mom was right. If she abandoned that vision, she'd be sorry.

Still, she didn't want Drake to have any regrets, either. She gave him one last chance. "Are you sure?"

"I'm sure. I love you, babe. I want our wedding to be your dream come true."

How had she lucked out, finding such a great guy? She thanked him and kissed him, then said, "Okay, let's do it."

With the issue finally settled, they went on to enjoy the amenities of Icicle Falls, eating dinner at Zelda's, one of the town's most popular restaurants, going dancing at the Red Barn and learning how to two-step. Although Drake had poked fun at country music, he'd enjoyed himself and even talked about getting a cowboy shirt, which made Laney laugh.

"Yeah, gauges and cowboy shirts really go together," she teased.

"They could," Drake insisted. "Why not?"

That was Drake, always full of crazy ideas. Was getting married on a raft going to be enough for him?

Chapter Twenty-One

Roberta, Letting Go

Mayor Del Stone dropped by on Monday to discuss his daughter's wedding, armed with a last-minute to-do list from his ex-wife in Oregon. "Mandy wanted me to check on a few things," he said as they sat down in Roberta's parlor with coffee and raspberry coffee cake. (Del never turned down a treat and he had the girth to prove it.) "She said she sent you an email yesterday, but hadn't heard back."

Roberta checked her emails twice a day. "I didn't see anything." Of course, Del's wife had sent her so many over the past few weeks she wouldn't have been surprised if one had fallen through the cracks.

"She changed the recipe for the nonalcoholic punch." He handed over a piece of paper with a recipe printed on it.

That had been in a previous email, and Roberta already had it in the Stone-Woodhouse file. "Yes, I've got that," she said politely.

He nodded and consulted his list. "My daughter changed her mind about the flowers. She wants stargazer lilies and…" He squinted. "Stepha—"

"Stephanotis," Roberta supplied.

"That's it." He beamed as if he was a teacher and she an exceptionally bright student.

"Stephanotis symbolizes marital happiness." Daphne had carried it in her bridal bouquet at her third wedding. Obviously, it took more than flowers.

"Anyway, can you let Heinrich know?"

"Certainly."

"Mandy wants to make sure we can all get here for pictures at two instead of three. She thinks three will be cutting it too close."

"That's fine," Roberta said.

"And she wants to make sure all the decorating will be done by then."

"That won't be a problem."

"Okay, what else?" He consulted his list. "Oh, and you're ordering an extra case of champagne, right?"

"Yes, Del, that's been done."

He nodded, looking the slightest bit sheepish. "Mandy is a perfectionist. I tried to tell her you've got everything under control, but she doesn't listen to me."

Roberta could understand why. Del was something of a blowhard and it wasn't worth listening to two-thirds of what he said. And, if you asked Roberta, he wasn't the most competent mayor the town had ever had. If he was, the potholes on Pine Street would've been fixed by now.

Still, he'd managed to glad-hand enough people to get himself reelected. And his daughter's wedding was going to be the social event of the season. Every member of the Icicle Falls Chamber of Commerce had been invited as well as the mayor of Portland, all the Icicle Falls town councillors and even a state representative. This was definitely an important wedding.

"Del, you know you're in good hands with us. No need to worry."

At least, she hoped not. Her bunion surgery was scheduled for Wednesday and there was no way she'd be up and around by the wedding. But Lila would be covering for her. Daphne was going to help, too.

Daphne. Was she ready for prime time?

Roberta thought back to the mishaps that had occurred since her daughter had come aboard the *SS Wedding Special*. She'd better postpone her surgery. Daphne wasn't hopeless, of course, but if she was going to be helping with the business as she kept insisting, she needed a few more weddings under her belt before taking on one of this magnitude.

Roberta assured Del again that everything would go smoothly and, after one more serving of coffee cake, showed him to the door. Then she got on the phone to the surgeon's office, informing the receptionist she'd like to postpone her surgery.

Wouldn't you know? Daphne picked that very moment to come home. "What are you doing?" she demanded as she set a bag of groceries on the kitchen counter.

"Let me call you back," Roberta said and ended the call. She felt like a child caught doing something naughty, which was ridiculous.

"Why are you canceling your surgery?" Daphne asked. "You've been waiting to get this done for a month."

"I don't think this is a good time."

"Why on earth not?"

Here was where it got sticky. How did she tell her daughter she didn't trust her not to make a mess of this wedding without sounding as if she didn't trust her? "There's simply too much going on."

Daphne's big blue eyes narrowed. "I saw Mayor Stone driving away just now. Was he here talking about the wedding?"

"Er, yes."

"You don't think Lila and I can handle this alone."

"It's an important wedding, Daphne. I think I should be there."

Daphne sighed in disgust. "Mother, we can handle this."

She would have Lila there, and Lila was the soul of efficiency. But if Daphne happened to spill appetizers on the mayor's daughter…

"I promise not to go anywhere near the bride with food," Daphne said, reading her mind. "Or anyone else, for that matter. I'll stay in the kitchen and help the caterers plate the dinner. And I won't go near the cake," she added, managing to smile at her mishap.

Roberta could smile now, too, although at the time she hadn't been smiling. They'd had to call Cass and make a slapdash substitution. But Cass had pulled it off. Besides, anyone could trip. Although Roberta never had.

"Mother, you need this surgery. There'll never be a convenient time. You'll always have weddings booked and each one will be important."

But probably not as important as this one.

"I know it's hard to delegate, but if you could bring yourself to trust me, I promise it'll all be fine. Everything's already ordered and organized. What could go wrong?"

Any one of a hundred things. However, Daphne was right. It wasn't easy to get in with the surgeon Roberta had scheduled. If she gave up this date, she'd probably be sorry.

"You can't do everything yourself," Daphne said gently. "It's not good business. That's why people have assistants."

"All right," Roberta said. "I'll let you girls handle it."

"Good." Daphne's tone of voice implied that it was about time Roberta came to her senses.

As if Roberta had no grounds for concern. Well, then, let Daphne demonstrate her efficiency. "You can start by checking with Ed York to make sure he got my message about ordering another case of champagne."

Daphne already had her phone out and was typing on it. "Done," she said a moment later.

The quickness of it made Roberta blink. "And I'll need you to go over to Lupine Floral and see what they can give us that incorporates stargazer lilies and stephanotis instead of roses."

"I can do that."

Wait a minute. What was she thinking? She could do this herself. "On second thought, I'll look after the flowers."

"Mother," Daphne said sternly. "I can go over there. You must have other things to do."

Actually, she did. She had a pile of paperwork waiting for her and several calls to make.

"Trust me," Daphne urged.

"All right. I do have several other things I need to take care of today."

"Then take care of them. I've got this covered," Daphne said. She kissed Roberta on the cheek and then went back to putting away groceries.

"Thank you, darling," Roberta said.

As she went to her little office, she reassured herself

that Daphne could indeed handle this, then tried not to think about how she'd neglected to order the invitations for her own daughter's wedding on time.

That was then. This is now, she told herself. Her daughter had emerged from her latest romantic rough patch and had her wits about her once more. All would be well.

But maybe Roberta should still postpone that surgery.

In the end, Roberta had her surgery on the original date. Daphne drove her over the mountains to Virginia Mason in Seattle and brought her home again, where she did an excellent job of caring for Roberta, as well as keeping the house running smoothly. They set Roberta up in the back parlor on the sofa with her foot propped on pillows (and Milo to keep her company) so she wouldn't have to use the stairs.

"I'll be happy to bring food up to you," Daphne had offered, but Roberta had nixed the idea.

"I'd feel too isolated stuck up there." She didn't want to feel so cut off from what was going on in the rest of the house. And she wanted to be within hearing distance when Daphne was on the phone, handling last-minute wedding details.

This arrangement created almost as much work for her daughter as if they'd ensconced Roberta in her room, but Daphne never complained about having to run up and down stairs fetching fresh clothes, toiletry items or whatever book Roberta wanted. Could a mother ask for a better daughter?

And Daphne was certainly proving to be helpful, especially in the kitchen, Roberta thought as she enjoyed a shrimp salad Daphne had made for lunch. Maybe it wasn't such a bad idea having her daughter live with her. For the most part they'd settled into a comfortable routine and were getting along quite well. Maybe having her more involved with the business wasn't a bad idea, either. Perhaps someday she could take over. Perhaps now Daphne would, at last, come into her own and shine. Yes, Roberta should have suggested this long ago, groomed her daughter from the start. Or at least after her second divorce.

Well, it wasn't too late. Daphne could learn the ropes now. Roberta smiled at the pleasant vision of Daphne becoming one of the town's movers and shakers, working with the chamber of commerce, helping plan festivals. Even running for mayor someday. There was so much she could do if she'd develop a little more confidence in herself.

The girl could succeed if she had a mind to. All she needed was some motherly assistance, which Roberta was happy to offer every time the phone rang.

"Mother!" Daphne said after Roberta had insisted on talking to a woman who called about having a fall wedding at Primrose Haus. "I'm perfectly capable of answering questions about price and availability."

"Of course you are," Roberta agreed, "but I'm not helpless here. I don't want to sit around like a lump watching TV all day." Her foot was beginning to hurt and she popped another pain pill. And she was getting sleepy. The surgery had really taken it out of her. She needed a nap. "I think I'll shut my eyes for a few minutes, though. I know you'll see to everything while I do."

"Good idea," Daphne said, placated. She kissed Roberta on the forehead. "Have a good rest. I'll take care of everything."

And she did.

So when the day of the mayor's daughter's wedding

came, Roberta wasn't the least bit worried. Lila had things well in hand, and Daphne had sworn that every detail had been attended to, including shutting Milo in her room so he wouldn't get underfoot.

That didn't stop Roberta from putting on the special boot the doctor had prescribed for her and hobbling out to the reception room to see how things were coming along. Daphne had run to the store to pick up some Sweet Dreams chocolates (a last-minute request by Del), and Heinrich, the creative genius from Lupine Floral, had arrived himself to fuss with the flowers rather than leaving it to his partner, Kevin. In addition to the bridal bouquet and boutonnieres, he'd made small elegant arrangements for the tables, a larger one for the bridal party's table and two for the front parlor. They were all exquisite concoctions of greens, baby's breath and…roses. With not a single stargazer lily to be seen. And where was the stephanotis? What had gone wrong?

Daphne was supposed to have dealt with this. One quick visit to the florist—that was all she had to do. Roberta could feel her blood pressure rising like a jet taking off from the runway.

She looked at her wristwatch. It was edging toward noon. The bridal party would be showing up for pictures at two. Oh, dear.

She hobbled over to Heinrich as fast as she could. "Heinrich, these are beautiful," she began.

He beamed, obviously pleased with the compliment.

"But where are the stargazer lilies and the stephanotis?"

He stared at her, befuddled. "Lilies?"

"Yes. The bride changed her mind and wanted lilies instead of roses. Daphne was supposed to let you know."

Heinrich went from befuddled to horrified, placing

a hand to his chest as if he was about to have a heart attack. "This is the first I've heard of it."

Roberta was sure *she* was going to have a heart attack. "The bridal party will be here at two. Can you fix these before then?"

He frowned. "That's like asking Michelangelo to hurry up and finish *David*."

Oh, great. Of all times for Heinrich to remember he was an artiste.

He also remembered he was a businessman. "But for you I'll move heaven and earth." He picked up the huge arrangement from the buffet table, obscuring his entire head from view. "I'll take these back to the shop and fix them."

"Of course I'll pay for the flowers you've already used," Roberta said. She'd have to eat the cost; there was no getting around it.

"I wouldn't dream of it."

"No," she said adamantly. "The one who makes the mistake should be the one to pay." And sadly, that one was her. Or rather, her daughter. Honestly, if she couldn't count on Daphne to do this, how could she count on her to take more responsibility for the business?

This was why her daughter had never climbed the ladder of success, Roberta thought as her blood pressure continued to soar through the clouds and into the upper stratosphere. Daphne was incompetent. Sweet and well-intentioned but incompetent. And this was the last wedding she was going to help with. Ever.

She was hobbling out of the room when the culprit came home, bearing two pink shopping bags filled with boxes of Sweet Dreams chocolates. Roberta's displeasure must have sat like a billboard on her face because Daphne's brows knit and she asked, "What's wrong?"

"The flowers," Roberta said through gritted teeth.

Daphne looked around in surprise. "They're not here yet."

"They were here. They were here wrong."

"I don't understand."

"The lilies," Roberta said, her voice rising. "Heinrich had no idea he was supposed to substitute them for the roses. And there was no stephanotis, either."

"How can that be?"

There was only one explanation. "Daphne, you obviously forgot to contact Lupine Floral."

Daphne shook her head. Emphatically. "No. I didn't."

"Well, they weren't in the arrangements," Roberta said testily. It wasn't going to do any good to stand here and argue with her daughter. She started to hobble off.

"Mother, I did go over there."

"Never mind. It's been taken care of." But this was the end of Daphne helping. Every time she "helped," it was not helpful.

"You don't believe me."

The hurt and accusation in her daughter's voice were like fingernails on a chalkboard. *Don't say anything you'll regret!* Roberta took a deep breath and turned around. "Darling, I'm sure you meant to call or drop by. I do that, too, think I've done something when I haven't gotten around to it."

"No." Daphne frowned. "I went over there and talked to Kevin. I'm not completely incompetent, you know."

"Of course you're not." Roberta wished she'd postponed her bunion surgery. "Anyway, as I said, it's all taken care of now." So there was no need to be upset or to fuss at her daughter. But there was certainly cause to wonder what else would go wrong at this wedding.

"I'm glad it is." Daphne's voice was as cold as the

Wenatchee River during spring runoff. "But it should never have been a problem in the first place."

Oh, no. She wasn't going to get the last word. "Why can't you just admit you made a mistake?"

"Because I didn't! And why do you always have to believe the worst of me?"

"Oh, Daphne. I do not."

"Yes, you do. And I'm tired of it." With that, Daphne marched full steam ahead into the kitchen to arrange the chocolates on tiered china serving dishes.

Roberta fell onto the nearest chair, exhausted, unhappy and irritated. Really, at her age she shouldn't have to cope with disagreements and emotional undercurrents. She shouldn't have to walk on eggshells, worrying about hurting her daughter's feelings. Life had been so much simpler before Daphne and all her drama had returned to Icicle Falls.

Was Daphne right? Did Roberta always believe the worst of her? Wanting to help her daughter improve her life didn't mean Roberta saw her as a *complete* failure. She'd been a wonderful mother. Marnie was well-adjusted, happy, successful, and Daphne could take all the credit for that. In addition to raising a lovely daughter, she'd held down the same job for years. She'd been a responsible adult with no addictions or bad habits. Well, except the habit of making poor choices when it came to men. Of course, Roberta was in no position to throw stones, not from her glass house.

Still, it was a mother's job to advise her daughter. And once in a while, when the daughter had fumbled a simple task, a mother should be allowed to feel a little frustration without said daughter climbing on her high horse. Especially since that daughter had fumbled more than one simple task here at Primrose Haus. But, oh, no. Here she was, once again, the cruel, wicked mother, making her daughter's life miserable.

Darn it all, Daphne drove her crazy.

Roberta continued to stew in her emotional juices for several minutes. Then she hobbled past the kitchen, where the atmosphere was decidedly frosty, to the back parlor sofa. She'd barely gotten settled when the phone sitting on the TV tray next to her started to ring. The last thing she wanted was to talk to anyone, so she ignored it. She wished she could ignore the fact that her daughter was in the next room, hurt and angry.

Daphne picked up the kitchen extension. Roberta could hear her talking. "Hello, Heinrich. Yes," Daphne said, her voice softening. "No, no problem. It could happen to anyone. But would you mind explaining to my mother?"

A moment later she was standing next to Roberta, holding out the phone. "Talk to Heinrich," she said brusquely.

"I don't want to talk to anyone right now."

"Well, I want you to talk to him."

Roberta took the phone with all the eagerness of someone reaching for a rattlesnake and said a leery hello. Heinrich had probably returned to the shop and discovered his cooler had no lilies.

"My darling, I am so sorry," he said.

No lilies. The bride was going to come unglued. Del would want a discount.

"This is all our fault."

"You have no lilies," she said weakly.

"Oh, we have lilies. And I'll be able to make your arrangements, but I needed to call and apologize right away. Your daughter did talk to Kevin, and he meant to tell me, but then Hildy Johnson came in and talked his ear off and it went right out of his head. Of course we'll fix this, no extra charge."

"Thank you, Heinrich. I appreciate that."

So Daphne had indeed taken care of contacting the florist. Roberta felt ill. She'd been so determined to blame the problem on Daphne's incompetence that she'd refused to believe her. Why did she always assume the worst about her daughter?

Maybe it was programmed into her by her own mother. *"I'm disappointed in you, Roberta. I raised you better."*…*"Don't think you can come back parading your illegitimate child here. I won't have it. I won't have you humiliate our family any further."*

She'd failed to meet her mother's expectations, and her mother had written her off like a bad investment. She'd never planned to do that with her own daughter, and yet how many times did she find herself feeling disappointed in Daphne? And how many times did that disappointment show? Maybe none as badly as today.

She hobbled her way to the kitchen, where Daphne was busy with the chocolates. It was a short but painful trip, painful on so many levels.

Daphne didn't turn to look at her. "Did you get it all sorted out?" she asked.

Very diplomatic. "Yes." Roberta came closer, setting the phone on the counter. "Daphne, I'm sorry."

Daphne didn't say anything. Instead, she shrugged as if to say it didn't matter and kept on putting out truffles. No "I forgive you" was forthcoming. No hug. Not even any eye contact.

Well, she deserved as much. "I'm terribly hard on you, aren't I?"

Daphne hesitated a moment, then returned to the task

at hand. "I know I'm not the overachiever you wanted me to be."

"Possibly not," Roberta admitted. "But we don't all have to be overachievers." *And we don't all have to be perfect.* "You're a generous, kindhearted woman."

"Apparently, that's not enough." Daphne picked up the tiered plates and left the kitchen.

"Daphne, wait." Roberta hobbled after her.

Daphne didn't wait. Instead, she picked up her pace.

Roberta gave up. It was obvious that her daughter didn't want to talk to her. Her foot was hurting now. She needed to sit down. She needed a pain pill. She wished there was a pill that could make her a better mother.

Chapter Twenty-Two

Daphne, the Queen of New Beginnings

The mayor's daughter got happily and memorably married. The bride was beautiful in her designer gown and her mother, also in a designer dress, was pleased with everything, especially the flowers. The house was packed with family and friends, movers and shakers, and everything went smoothly.

Except for a slight catering crisis thanks to a horde of party-crashers. Daphne saved the day by whipping up some fast and easy appetizers, consisting of crackers and shrimp dip, as well as baking the mini quiches they stored in the big freezer in the basement for such emergencies. She halved the chicken, covered it in sauce and made an extra salad. Lila complimented her on how well she'd handled the situation. Her mother thanked her for all her hard work. It wasn't enough to make her want to stay.

Later that night, with Milo on the bed next to her, she spent some time on her laptop checking out rentals in Icicle Falls. She found a couple that would work, and just as she had when she'd first come home, she went to sleep with tears on her pillow.

The following morning was Mother's Day and Marnie called her on her cell phone while Daphne was still in bed, trying to ignore Milo, who was climbing on her chest, insisting it was time to get up. "Happy Mom's Day," she sang.

"Honeybee, this is a nice surprise," Daphne said, sitting up in bed.

"Why should you be surprised? It *is* Mother's Day."

"Yes, but you already sent those chocolate-covered strawberries on Friday."

From Sweet Dreams Chocolates, of course. They were big and juicy and gorgeous, not to mention pricey, and Daphne had enjoyed sharing them with her mother and Lila.

She'd also enjoyed showing off her daughter's good taste and thoughtfulness. With Marnie, there was a lot to brag about. Unlike her mother, she was doing everything right. She was succeeding in her career. She'd waited until her late twenties to get married and had picked a nice, stable man from a solid family, one with no history of divorce or bad romantic choices. Marnie's life was as close to perfect as anyone's could get. And so was she.

"That doesn't mean I don't want to talk to you on Mother's Day," she said now. "Are you still liking Icicle Falls? 'Cause if you're not, you could move out here with us."

"Oh, your husband would love that, having his mother-in-law underfoot."

"He thinks you're great. So do I."

That little bit of flattery gave Daphne's sagging spirits a much-needed lift. Someone appreciated her just as she was. Of course, maybe that was because she felt the same way about Marnie. She'd never tried to improve her, never hounded her to do more and be better. She'd let Marnie find her own path and become her own person, and she'd exceeded Daphne's expectations. That was more than Daphne could say for herself and her mother.

"What are you two going to do today?" Daphne asked.

"We're going to celebrate."

It wasn't their wedding anniversary. "Did Alan get a raise?"

"He got something," Marnie said, her voice mysterious.

"Okay, I give up. What are you celebrating?"

"You're going to be a grandma."

"A grandma?" Marnie was pregnant? Her baby was having a baby. Lately life had been serving her a lot of lemons. Here was the lemonade that made it all worthwhile. "Oh, honeybee, that's fabulous. When are you due and what are you having?"

"We don't know yet. I just took the pregnancy test."

"Wow," Daphne breathed. "I'm so happy for you."

"You'll come out and help when the baby's born, right?"

"Just try and keep me away."

"I knew you'd say that," Marnie said, a smile in her voice. "Tell Grandma, okay?"

"I will." She had a few things to tell Grandma this morning.

They'd planned to go out to brunch at Zelda's and Daphne had made a gift basket for her mother. She'd been looking forward to the day. Now, not so much. She loved her mother and she knew her mother loved her, but at the moment Daphne didn't exactly like her. With a sigh, she got out of bed.

"Carpe diem," Mother would say. Seize the day, never waste a minute. It was how she managed to accomplish so much. Maybe Daphne should have carpe diem-ed more. Maybe then she would've been a success story, too, like her mother and her daughter. Or maybe success sometimes skipped a generation.

After she'd showered and dressed, she grabbed the gift basket from the dresser and went downstairs to check on her mother, Milo racing ahead of her. She found Mother already up and seated at the kitchen table with her coffee mug, her leg propped on the chair opposite her.

"Good morning," she said. It was tentative, more a question than a greeting.

Daphne set the basket on the table, then bent over and kissed her cheek. Her mother always smelled like Chantilly. "Happy Mother's Day." The words felt awkward and stiff.

"Oh, my. This is beautiful." Mother leaned forward to inspect it. "Chocolates, dusting powder, bubble bath and, oh, I see the latest Vanessa Valentine novel. Daphne, you have such a gift for creativity. You know, you could…"

Daphne cut her off. "Start a gift basket business."

"Well, you could."

"There are any number of things I could do. But right now, I'd like to let the dust from the divorce settle, find out what it's like to be on my own. I've never spent much time doing that." And that could be part of the problem. She'd always been with a man, always felt she needed a man in order to be happy. What she really needed was to learn how to be happy, period.

Mother nodded. "You do have talents. You should explore them."

And then become wildly successful. Anything less wouldn't measure up. Daphne fed Milo, then sat down at the table. "I've been thinking."

"Yes?"

There was an eagerness in that one-word prompt. Was her mother just waiting for her to say she was ready to move out? Probably. Her decision would come as a relief to both of them. "I think it's time I got my own place. I'm going over to Mountain Meadows Real Estate to check out a couple of places this afternoon."

To Daphne's shock, Mother didn't seem relieved at all. Instead, her face fell like a ruined soufflé. "I don't understand. I thought you were happy here. If this is about last night…"

Daphne shook her head. "It's about more than last night. It's about how we work together. Or rather, don't work together." Her mother looked as if she wanted to cry. What was that about?

"Other than our misunderstanding yesterday, I thought we were getting along quite well."

She couldn't be serious. "Mother, we've done nothing but aggravate each other ever since I arrived."

"That's not true," her mother insisted, opting for deliberate blindness. "Don't move out, Daphne. Don't leave, not like this."

There it was again, that moment where her mother looked old, vulnerable. "I'm not leaving Icicle Falls." Not yet, anyway. Although knowing she had a grandchild on the way made the idea of moving east very tempting.

"I was wrong not to believe you," Mother said in a small voice. "I've been wrong about a lot of things." Her gaze dropped to her hands, and she smoothed the skin on them, as if to smooth away the years. "I've done so many things wrong. I'm afraid I turned out to be like my mother, more than I want to admit." She sighed deeply. "I was never good enough for her. She was a hard, selfish woman who cared more about what other people thought than she did her own daughter." Mother lifted her gaze and Daphne saw tears glistening in her eyes. "I hope I'm not that woman. Daphne, I love you, and I'd like to think that's why I've always wanted so much for you. But maybe there was some pride in there, too. Maybe I wanted you to become the most successful woman ever so I could show my mother she'd been wrong to disown us. Either way, I'm afraid I haven't been a very good mother to you." She shook her head. "What a sad thing to realize on Mother's Day."

Now Daphne felt tears flooding her own eyes. Yes, her mother had interfered in her life at every turn, given unrequested advice and often been irritated with her. But she'd always been there for Daphne, offering a shoulder to cry on, lending her money when she needed it, buying extravagant presents for both Marnie and her. She hadn't been a perfect mother but she'd tried. And she'd cared.

"You *have* been a good mother," Daphne insisted. "We're definitely not the same, though. I can't be a version of you. I'll never accomplish as much or be as successful."

"Or as fussy and nitpicky."

Daphne smiled at that. "I hope not."

"I have to admit that when you first came back I thought living together would be a terrible idea. You're right—we are different, and those differences frustrate me sometimes. And, as you may have noticed, I like my independence. But I'm getting older and I could use some extra help around here." She reached across the table and placed a hand on Daphne's arm. "And I enjoy the company."

"You do?" She had a funny way of showing it.

"Darling, I really am sorry about last night. Let's start over. Could we do that?"

The truth was, Daphne didn't want to leave. She

might be fifty-three, but she still wanted her mother's approval. She wanted to try again. If… "Mother, do you think you could be a little less critical?"

"Yes, Daphne. Please forgive me. It's hard to accept your child for who she is when she's not who you want her to be, especially when you see…"

"So much potential," Daphne finished with her, and they both smiled.

"But you know," Roberta continued, "I never measured up in my mother's eyes, even though I always made the honor roll. She wanted me to marry the 'right' kind of man, increase her status. She wanted me to display nicely, like her Dresden figurines. I didn't choose well, and she couldn't forgive me for that because I ruined the facade." Mother sighed. "We could have had a happy life together if she'd ever given us a chance, if she'd seen beyond herself. She didn't, though. She never really saw my heart. I don't want to be like that with you."

Over the years there'd been the occasional mention of Daphne's grandmother but no more than that. When she was small, her great-grandmother had come to see them a couple of times and sent presents at Christmas, and she hadn't questioned the fact that no other family was part of their lives. But when Daphne got a little older she began to ask questions. Her mother had dodged them with excuses such as "Grandmother's busy" or "Grandmother isn't well enough to come and see us." Daphne finally lost interest in the ghost grandma she never saw, and it wasn't until she was fully grown that she learned her mother and grandmother didn't get along. No more details were forthcoming. Hardly surprising, since she hadn't learned about her bumsicle father, either, until she became engaged to Johnny, of whom her mother strongly disapproved. After the way her mother had dribbled out information over the years, her intimate confession this morning felt like a landslide of sharing.

And it explained a lot. "I wish you'd told me more of this over the years," Daphne said.

"I should have. But honestly, Daphne, I don't think I really made the connection between my behavior and hers until now. That doesn't make me a very wise old woman, does it?"

Milo rubbed against Daphne's legs and she picked him up and cuddled him next to her, considering what her mother had said. "I think wisdom comes with experience and with figuring things out. I'd like to believe I'm wiser now than I was a year ago."

"I hope I'm wiser now than I was a day ago," Roberta said.

"Wise or not, I love you."

"Can you love me enough to stay?"

Words Daphne had never thought she'd hear, they poured like a healing balm over her wounded feelings. "It's what I wanted all along," she said softly. "You've always been there for me. I want to be there for you now."

Daphne rarely saw her mother cry. Roberta Gilbert was too strong for tears.

But not today. They flowed in twin rivers down her cheeks. She picked up her napkin and touched it to her eyes. "Daphne, darling, you truly are a wonderful woman."

Daphne gave her a wistful smile, and she, too, picked up a napkin and dabbed at her cheeks. "Even if I don't always keep the kitchen as clean as you'd like," she added in an attempt to lighten the moment.

"There's more to life than cleaning, isn't there?" Mother said, and it was all Daphne could do not to ask, "Who are you and what have you done with my mother?"

Later that morning as they sat in Zelda's enjoying omelets, crepes, strawberries and champagne from the Mother's Day buffet, Daphne revealed Marnie's good news.

"A new baby in the family," her mother said happily. "Oh, how much fun we'll have spoiling her."

"Or him."

"Oh, dear. If it's a boy I'll have no idea what to do with him."

Maybe that wouldn't be a bad thing.

They were just finishing up when Hank Hawkins came in with his mother, a slight woman with salt-and-pepper hair and a stooped back. How had such a small woman produced such a large man?

The large man looked even better in a Sunday suit than he did in his work clothes. His jaw was freshly shaved and smooth and his dark hair slicked back. He cleaned up well.

Someone must have turned up the heat in the restaurant. Daphne took a long drink of orange juice in an effort to cool down.

He smiled at the sight of her and her mother and led his own mom in their direction. "Happy Mother's Day, ladies," he said, stopping at their table.

"Thank you, Hank. Nice to see you, Sal," Mother said to the woman.

"Is this your lovely daughter I've been hearing so much about?" asked Sal.

Hank suddenly looked as if he was the one having a hot flash.

"This is my daughter, Daphne," Mother said and introduced Sally Hawkins.

"Pleased to meet you," Daphne said. She caught a whiff of Hank's cologne, some kind of woodsy virile scent, and she knew she couldn't blame the heat she was feeling now on misfiring hormones. Her hormones were just fine, thank you, and ready to hook up with some nice testosterone.

"How's the breakfast?" he asked.

"Very good," Daphne replied. The best breakfast she'd ever had with her mother. Today was a celebration of new understanding and, hopefully, a new beginning. She smiled across the table at Mother, who beamed back at her.

"It certainly looks delicious," Sal remarked. "Aren't we blessed to have wonderful children to take us out?"

"We certainly are," Mother agreed.

"I guess we'll see you around," Hank said. The look he sent Daphne promised he wasn't about to give up chasing her.

Maybe that was fine with her, after all. Maybe somewhere in the distant future her heart would heal and she'd dive once more into love's choppy waters. "I'm sure you will."

Hank and his mother went back to the reception area to check in with Charley Masters, who was busy seating people. Then, as she led them to their table, he winked at Daphne, turning her internal thermostat even higher.

"He really is a nice man," her mother said. "Not that I'm encouraging you to start dating." This was followed by a guilty expression. "Of course, I don't want to tell you what to do."

"Of course not," Daphne murmured. Her mother would probably never change. She'd interfere in Daphne's life and try to run the show as long as she drew breath. But here was one area she didn't need to worry about. Daphne had finally learned her lesson about love. "I'm in no hurry to start dating. I'm doing fine on my own. And I think that things are only going to get better," she added. Because from now on, she'd be making wiser choices, choices that were right for her.

Actually, she'd already started. Moving to Icicle Falls had been one of the smartest decisions she'd ever made.

Chapter Twenty-Three

Anne, Distracted Wife and Loving Mother

The family gathered at Anne's house for Mother's Day, and talk naturally turned to how the wedding plans were progressing.

"We still have so much to do," Anne said as she passed around slices of chocolate cake. "Invitations need to go out."

"I'm working on that," Laney said vaguely.

"They should go pretty soon." Her daughter shouldn't be procrastinating, and she shouldn't have to keep nagging.

"They will," Laney said curtly.

"At least the save-the-date announcements went out, so people will have it on their calendars," Kendra reminded Anne.

"Bring the invitations over here," said Julia. "We can all help you and have the whole thing done in an evening."

"Good idea," Kendra said.

Laney didn't say anything.

Anne went on with her list of unfinished business.

"The bridesmaids still need to get their dresses. Laney, when are you and the girls going shopping?"

"Probably next week," Laney said, digging into her cake.

She was more interested in the cake than she was in talking about her wedding, and Anne found that disturbing. Lately, Laney seemed rather cranky, too, which was also disturbing.

But hardly uncommon. Planning a wedding could be stressful, so the crankiness was understandable. The lack of enthusiasm, not so much. In fact, it was downright mystifying. When she was a tween and a teen she'd been fascinated by what her mother did for a living, wanting to see pictures and check out links to various sites right along with Anne. Now, when it counted, she wasn't focusing on any of it.

"I want to get my flower-girl dress," Coral, Kendra's oldest, announced.

"Me, too," her little sister, Amy, chimed in.

"Don't worry," Kendra told them. "You will."

"And the bridesmaids' gifts. Have you decided on them yet?" Anne had sent her a couple of different links to check out.

Laney heaved a long-suffering sigh. "Not yet."

"Who's going to be your photographer?" Julia asked.

"I don't know yet, Grammy," Laney said. "I still have time."

"Not as much as you think," Anne cautioned. "We really need to get going." She hated to push, but honestly, they had a lot to do.

Laney made a face. "Jeez, Mom. Stop already."

Stop? As if she was, somehow, being unreasonable in trying to get her daughter moving? "Laney," Anne said sternly.

"Good cake," Cam said, and everyone else at the table happily went along with the change of subject.

Anne sat and stewed. Happy Mother's Day. Hmmph.

"I only want our daughter's wedding to turn out well," she said to Cam after everyone had left. It seemed she'd said that a lot over the past couple of months.

"Everything will get done," he reassured her, leading her over to the couch.

"When?"

"Before the wedding," he said, slipping an arm around her and pulling her close. "Stop worrying."

"Easy for you to say," she grumbled. "All you have to do is show up."

"And, when it comes right down to it, that's all you have to do, too. This is Laney's wedding. She can plan it."

"I know," Anne said. "But the problem is, she's not. She's letting things slide. She needs help."

"Maybe she doesn't want help. Maybe she doesn't care about some of those things."

"Then she shouldn't be having a wedding. She should just elope." Wait a minute. What was she saying?

Cam grinned. "Yeah, I can picture you allowing *that* to happen. Seriously, Anne, let some of this go and make her do the heavy lifting." He disappeared into the spare room that served as their office and then returned with his laptop. "Let's do some planning of our own. How's that sound?"

It sounded better than fretting over her daughter's lack of motivation. "Sure."

He opened the computer and they went online, comparing cruises. "This one with Holland America looks good," he said.

At that moment Anne's cell phone rang.

"Don't answer it."

"It's Laney." Of course she had to answer it.

Cam sighed and slumped against the sofa cushions.

"I'm going to make an event on Facebook instead of sending out all these invitations," Laney told her.

"Sweetie, I think that would be tacky, and not everyone we know is on Facebook. Anyway, Grammy, Aunt Kendra and I are going to help you. Remember?" Since they'd paid for the invitations, it seemed silly not to use them. Cam picked up the remote and brought the TV to life. An action film roared onto the screen and Anne moved to the kitchen. "We'll do it one night this week. Between all of us we can have it finished in no time."

"I guess," Laney said dubiously.

"It'll be fun." Anne tried to encourage her. "Meanwhile, check out the links I sent for your bridesmaids' gifts."

Now her phone was telling her she had another call. She glanced at caller ID. "That's Aunt Kendra. I'll talk to you later," Anne said. As she switched from Laney to Kendra she could see her husband channel surfing, waiting patiently for her to return to planning their anniversary. "What's up?"

"I was going to ask you that. Is Laney ticked at you? She seemed kind of grumpy at dinner today."

"Pre-wedding stress," Anne said. "You know how that goes. But she's fine. I was talking to her when you called."

"Okay. Just thought I'd ask."

She was barely off the phone with Kendra when her mom checked in, also wondering about Laney.

By the time she wandered back into the living room, Cam was involved in a TV show. Or pretending to be. She could tell by the expression on his face that he was miffed. "Okay, now where were we?" she said in her cheeriest voice, sliding next to him.

"*We* were obsessing about our daughter's wedding and ignoring our husband."

"I'm sorry. But, Cam, these things take a lot of planning."

He turned to her, his face solemn. "Anne, I get that you want to help, and I know this is your business, but you don't need to do it 24/7. And like I said, you need to let Laney do some of it herself. It's her wedding."

"I agree. And I am, but planning a wedding is complicated."

He shrugged and turned his attention back to the TV. "Tell me when you're done."

"I'm done now," she said and put a hand to his chin, forcing him to look at her.

He obliged, but he was still frowning.

"Come on now. Don't be mad. This is important. This is our daughter."

He sighed. "You're right. I'm sorry."

"Kiss and make up?"

The frown disappeared. One kiss was all it took to make him forget about the action on the TV and switch his attention to the action on the couch, which started heating up pretty fast, clothes slipping off and Anne slipping into a horizontal position. It was nice to lie here and enjoy her husband's caresses and kisses. She didn't have to spend every second thinking about the wedding to-do list.

Except it was such a long one and they had so many things to check off. Crud, and when she was talking to Laney she'd forgotten to bring up the subject of "Wedding favors."

Oh, no. Had she just said that out loud? Judging by the look on Cam's face she had.

"Now, that's funny," Kendra said the next day as she and Anne perused dresses in Macy's, looking for Anne's mother-of-the-bride dress.

"Oh, yeah. Cam was laughing. I hope my marriage survives my daughter's wedding."

"Your marriage could survive a zombie apocalypse."

Anne pulled out a champagne-colored dress with a nipped-in waist and pleated skirt. It was love at first sight. "I like this."

"Oh, yeah. Try it on."

She did, and the love affair grew stronger. "I'll take it." Oh, that everything would go as smoothly.

But it didn't. It seemed that there was constantly something new to deal with, both at work and on the home front.

The bridesmaids finally got their dresses. So did the flower girls. When Kendra's husband was supposed to be watching them, the girls put on the dresses and played wedding, which somehow resulted in Amy ripping her dress and Coral getting chocolate all over the bodice of hers.

Laurel Browne had two more meltdowns before her daughter's wedding, and on the night of the actual wedding, the caterer was short-handed, the booze ran out and three of the goldfish on the dinner tables did the dead-fish float.

In the end, though, Laurel was so happy with the flowers, her daughter and her new son-in-law that she hugged Anne and thanked her. "Didn't it turn out beautifully?" she gushed.

"Weddings usually do," Anne replied sagely.

She reminded herself of that as she hurried around trying to cover all the bases for Laney's upcoming nuptials. The invitations finally went out, but Laney continued to avoid some of the more minor details.

"Sweetie, you have to decide on wedding favors," she told Laney during one of their many phone conversations.

"I don't know," Laney said, not for the first time.

"What about the bracelets?" Laney had talked about giving away some kind of bracelet since she liked making jewelry. Although now, even with the help of her bridesmaids, Anne doubted she'd be able to get them ready in time.

"No. I changed my mind."

Nice of her to tell her mom. "Okay, then, what about the bubbles?"

"I think using all those little plastic bottles wouldn't be very environmentally responsible. People might not recycle them."

At this rate they'd never decide. "Okay, let's go with the M&M's with your names on them. Everybody likes chocolate." And heaven knew Anne could use some right about now.

"I guess that'll be fine."

She guessed. "Is there something you'd rather have?"

"No, that'll work."

Her daughter's enthusiasm was underwhelming. This was really beginning to bother Anne.

When she said as much to Cam, though, she didn't get the support she wanted. Considering his earlier comments, she shouldn't have been surprised.

"Like mother, like daughter," he said.

Anne frowned at him. "What's that supposed to mean?"

He frowned right back at her. "It means that's pretty much the reaction I'm getting from you about our anniversary. If you don't want to do the cruise, Annie, just say so."

"Okay, fine. I don't want to do the cruise," she said and then shocked both herself and her husband by bursting into tears. Oh, no. Where had this come from?

He was instantly apologetic, wrapping his arms around her and kissing her forehead. "I'm sorry, Annie. I didn't mean to make you cry."

"It's not you. It's just that…"

"I know. You're all caught up in Laney's wedding."

"It's not that I don't want to celebrate our anniversary," she said with a sniffle. She did. Of course she did. "But I'd like to have the time and energy to enjoy planning it. I know you wanted to take a cruise, but I'd rather go up to the mountains and have a getaway, just the two of us, rather than be stuck on a boat with a few hundred or thousand—other people."

"Don't tell me. Let me guess. To Icicle Falls."

"That's not as exciting as a cruise, is it?"

"I don't need to go on a cruise."

"But you want to." He'd been the one to bring it up.

"Not that much. I thought you wanted it."

"*You* suggested it. I agreed it would be nice to get away," she said with a shrug.

He frowned and shook his head. "After twenty-five years, our communication should be better."

Or she should say what she really wanted more often. But she hadn't done that from the very start of their marriage. She'd set the pattern and, for the most part, they'd lived by it. Not that she didn't enjoy the same things Cam did or that she had a problem going along with his ideas, especially when they were great, like those dance lessons they'd taken years ago.

Still, she did have a few dreams of her own, and maybe she should start sharing them more. She sighed. "If I was a rich woman, I'd buy a little cabin on a lake where we could go for weekends, or up in the mountains where we could hike, take the kids for Christmas. But I'd settle for a weekend somewhere quiet." She smiled. "Of course, we could do that *and* a cruise."

He dismissed her compromise with a wave of his hand. "Forget the cruise. I was trying to think of a big-ticket item you'd enjoy and that's what I came up with. I don't care what we do. I just want to give you something special for our twenty-fifth, something to make up for the fact that you never got your big, fancy wedding."

"But I got you. That's what matters," she said, "and our daughter will get the big, fancy wedding." She studied his face. "Are you disappointed?" Maybe he was; maybe he was simply trying to cover it up. Probably not, though. That was her modus operandi.

"Whatever you want. We can decide on something after we get the kids hitched."

She took his face in her hands and kissed him. He was such a good man. "I know I've been…"

"Absent," he supplied. "But I understand, and I'm sorry I was a jerk. You're doing this for our daughter."

In spite of the fact that their daughter didn't seem to appreciate everything she was doing.

She wound up confessing as much to Roberta Gilbert when she made a day trip to Icicle Falls on the flimsy excuse of deciding where she wanted the flowers to go. Really, she just needed the R & R. There was something about seeing those mountains standing guard over the town that eased the stress from her mind and body. The quaint frescoes on the buildings, the hanging baskets and storefront window boxes filled with flowers made her smile. And visiting with Roberta was better than a shrink session.

"I sometimes wonder if my son-in-law would like a picture of me so he can throw darts at it," she said. "He and Laney originally wanted to go to Las Vegas to get married."

"It's a popular place," Roberta said diplomatically.

"I talked them out of it," Anne admitted.

"If they wanted to do it that badly I doubt you could have."

"My daughter always wanted a big, fancy wedding."

"Most girls do."

Anne set aside her teacup. "I plan weddings for a living. I shouldn't be this stressed."

"Oh, I'm not so sure about that," Roberta said. "It's different when it's your daughter."

"You're right," Anne said with a sigh. "I don't think my husband understands that. He's trying, but I don't think he really does. I only want her to be happy."

Roberta freshened Anne's tea. "Of course you do. It's what every mother wants for her daughter. There's nothing wrong with that."

"I should be enjoying this a lot more," Anne said and helped herself to a lavender–white chocolate scone.

Roberta chuckled. "My dear, I've come to the conclusion that anything involving a daughter is a mixture of pleasure and pain. However, you'll both get through this, and as long as the bride is happy and comes away with good memories, that's what counts. Sometimes a woman can get so sucked into all the wedding hustle and bustle, she forgets there'll still be life *after* the wedding."

Anne nodded. Roberta was so right.

"Go home, take a break and take a deep breath," Roberta advised. "Everything will turn out exactly as it's supposed to. We haven't lost a mother of the bride yet."

Anne couldn't help smiling. She'd said as much to a few mothers of brides herself.

She decided it was time to follow Roberta's advice. She called Cam. "I'm on my way home. I'll pick up Chinese."

"Works for me," he said.

Three hours later she walked in the door with their premade dinner and found Cam had a bottle of wine chilling. "Everything set for the big day?" he asked.

She nodded. "Yes, it's going to be fine, and I'm done stressing about the wedding. In fact, I think we should plan what we want to do for our anniversary."

"Nope," he said, pouring her a glass of pinot grigio. "Don't need to. I've already got it figured out."

"You have?"

"Most of it. I have a few details to work out, but don't make any plans for the weekend after Laney's wedding."

Just like that he'd gone ahead and planned what they were going to do for their anniversary? Without asking her? She put down her glass and frowned at him. "Well, don't you want my input?"

He picked up the glass and gave it back to her. "Now, don't look at me like that. Trust me. You're going to like this."

She put the glass down again. "How do you know?" She was the planner, not him.

"I know," he said, sounding both mysterious and cocky. He slipped his arms around her. "I know what you like," he added and planted a kiss on her neck.

"Yeah?" He was doing a pretty good job of showing her right now.

"Yeah." He touched his lips to her shoulder.

"Prove it."

"If you insist," he said and set about doing exactly that.

They abandoned the Chinese takeout in favor of satisfying a different appetite, and this time Anne didn't worry about her daughter's upcoming wedding. She did have one moment when she wondered if they'd ordered enough champagne, but she wisely kept that thought to herself.

Chapter Twenty-Four

Roberta, New and Improved

It was the second Saturday in June, a perfect day for a wedding with only a few wispy clouds floating in a blue sky. But no wedding was happening at Primrose Haus today. Thanks to a runaway bride, the wedding had been canceled.

This was such a rare thing Roberta almost didn't know what to do with herself. Daphne suggested a play day.

"We can start by going over to Bavarian Brews and getting a latte," she said.

"I can't remember the last time I did that," Roberta confessed. She also couldn't remember the last time she and her daughter had gone out and done something fun, just the two of them. It seemed that for the past few years, Roberta had been too busy most weekends to get away, and whenever Daphne had come up to visit, she'd either been with Marnie (always a good thing) or a man (never a good thing).

Bavarian Brews was packed with locals chatting or texting on their cell phones, and tourists wearing novelty hats from the hat shop and armed with digital cameras, ready to shoot pictures of the town's colorful main street and the surrounding scenery. The place was fragrant with the aroma of freshly brewed coffee, and looking at the different concoctions the baristas were making with various combinations of chocolate, coconut and caramel made Roberta's mouth water.

Del Stone and Ed York were there, and after picking up tall orders of coffee, they stopped by to say hello. Del once more thanked Roberta for giving his little girl such a great wedding. "I'll wager you'll be hearing from Representative Wattle. His daughter just got engaged. I told him he couldn't pick a better place."

"Thank you, Del. That's very sweet of you." Del would have her vote in the next election, whether or not those potholes on Pine Street got fixed.

He elbowed Ed. "You and Pat should've done it up right and gone to Roberta for your wedding."

Roberta couldn't have agreed more, especially considering how many years they'd all known one another and how much business she'd given both of them. She'd hoped to get invited to the wedding.

"Pat's daughter insisted on us getting married at her house. It was a small wedding, just family."

At least it wasn't a case of not making the cut. "You have to do what your children want," Roberta said. "I'm happy for both of you," she added to show there were no hard feelings.

"I feel pretty lucky finding a woman like Pat," Ed said. "What they say is true—love is better the second time around."

She'd have to take his word for it.

"After my first time around, I'd sure hope so," Del said heartily.

Roberta shook her head at Del. "You forget I've met your wife."

He smiled good-naturedly, then wished them a nice morning as he and Ed moved off to stake out a table by the window, which offered a view of the street and its various shops as well as Sweet Dreams Chocolates, the town's pride and joy and source of all things chocolate.

"Mother, have you ever thought about dating?" Daphne asked when they settled at a table with their lattes.

"Oh, goodness, Daphne. Why would I want a man at this point in my life?"

Daphne shrugged. "Companionship?"

"I have plenty of companionship with you and Lila and my friends at the chamber of commerce. Besides, no real man ever measures up to the ones in my Vanessa Valentine books. You've learned that firsthand. Although there may be a few out there who come close," she mused, seeing Hank walk up behind Daphne. A shame they hadn't met earlier, before they'd both messed up their lives.

"Hello, ladies," he said, making Daphne jump.

Roberta would've liked to shoo him away, but that would be rude, so she forced herself to ask, "Would you care to join us?"

"Don't mind if I do." He seated himself next to Daphne, whose face was suddenly flushed. "I'm surprised you're not at Primrose Haus getting ready for a wedding."

"The wedding got canceled," Roberta explained.

"Uh-oh. Did the groom have cold feet?"

"Nope, the bride did," Daphne answered. "She'd been married before. She probably decided not to jump off the cliff again."

"You can't fly if you don't take a leap," said Hank.

Roberta could see where this conversation was going,

right into three's-a-crowd territory. What to do? Her first inclination was to stay at the table like a two-legged guard dog, make sure Daphne didn't do anything foolish.

But she'd resolved not to interfere in her daughter's life or tell her what to do, and Daphne had assured her she wasn't going to rush into anything, that she was learning to be happy on her own. Was it really so foolish to have coffee with a nice, hardworking man, a man who, like Daphne, had gotten a raw deal on love? Anyway, if the two of them were going to wind up together eventually, there was nothing Roberta could do to stop it.

So, no guard-dogging. "I think I'll go back to the house. My foot is hurting." Actually, her foot felt pretty good these days. She was off the heavy-duty painkillers and down to ibuprofen, fitting in her morning walks again. She hadn't taken a walk yet today. Maybe she'd do that.

Daphne nodded and began to get up.

Roberta waved her back down. "Stay put, darling. Finish your latte." *Start your new life.*

"We were going to spend the day together," Daphne reminded her.

"We can do that tomorrow." Then, before Daphne could say anything more, Roberta slipped out of the coffee shop.

It was around ten in the morning and by now downtown was buzzing with visitors checking out the various shops. It made Roberta happy to see so many people in town. She could remember when she'd first arrived and the place was almost a ghost town. Thanks to the cleverness and hard work of its people, Icicle Falls had come back to life in a big way.

She caught sight of a couple around her age, holding

hands as they entered Gilded Lily's women's apparel. Their easy familiarity suggested they'd been married for years. The woman had probably said, "Look at that cute dress in the window," and he'd most likely replied, "Why don't you go try it on?"

Roberta sighed. If she hadn't been so bitter, so unwilling to give love another chance, that could've been her. But after two bad experiences she'd given up.

Ah, well. She'd still had a good life, a satisfying life. She'd made something of herself, something her mother should have been proud of. Sadly, her mother never got past her disappointment, valued her pride above her daughter's feelings. Roberta had her faults as a mother, but at least she'd never done that.

She'd done other things wrong instead, always pushing Daphne to do more, be more. Sadly, no one offered parenting classes back when she was raising Daphne. Roberta hadn't had any help. She'd been completely on her own. And she'd stayed on her own, never hearing from her mother, never seeing her again until the end.

2004

Roberta's old friend Nan had kept in touch over the years, mostly with Christmas cards and a few phone calls. One day she'd called to tell Roberta that her mother was dying. "I know you don't care if you ever see her again," Nan had said, "but she's all alone in that place. It's pathetic, really. I think she's sorry she never mended fences with you."

She'd had her chance. Actually, she'd had more than one. Roberta's grandmother had known where she was. Anytime her mother wanted to contact her, she could have. But she hadn't. So let her die alone, choking on her pride.

And what will you choke on someday? came the thought. *Resentment? Bitterness?* Roberta had tasted enough of those emotions over the years. She had to admit that now, at sixty, she'd lost her appetite for them.

And so, on a mockingly beautiful spring day, she made the two-and-a-half-hour drive to Seattle. She didn't tell Daphne she was coming or why. Daphne would've wanted to accompany her, to meet the woman she'd never known and offer Roberta her support. But Daphne still knew very little about her grandmother, and that was for the best. The woman had poisoned Roberta. She hadn't been going to let that poison touch her daughter.

The care facility smelled like a nasty combination of urine and disinfectant. A couple of ancients sat in wheelchairs at the side of the hallway, one a grizzled man who was muttering to himself, the other a woman with sparse gray hair and a caved-in chest, who held out a beseeching hand to Roberta. She had blue eyes and a button nose and in spite of the wrinkles Roberta could tell she'd been pretty in her younger days.

She stopped and took the woman's hand. "How are you?"

"Have you seen my daughter?" the woman asked. "She's supposed to come and see me. It's my birthday."

How many of her own mother's birthdays had Roberta missed? If this woman had been her mother, she wouldn't have missed a single one. "I'm sure she's coming," she said in an effort to comfort the woman.

The sweet face changed into a mask of anger. "She never comes."

The accusation and bitterness hit Roberta like a red-hot poker. "Maybe there's a reason." *Maybe you're like my mother, a selfish, judgmental shrew.*

Or maybe this woman was simply lonely and unhappy. Roberta softened her voice and gave the woman's hand a squeeze. "I'm sure she'll come," she said again. Daughters did. Eventually. Even when their mothers didn't ask for them.

The woman on duty at the reception desk pointed her down the hall to a different wing. Room 27, which her mother was sharing with another patient, a woman in the throes of agony. Roberta could hear her groaning from outside the room. When she entered, she had to catch her breath at the sight of the shrunken form in the other bed. This slack-jawed, sleeping cadaver hooked up to a morphine drip couldn't be her mother. Her mother had been plump, with carefully maintained brown curls and polished manners, always dressed to the nines.

But this was how it ended if you lived long enough. You found yourself riding out your last days in a rickety shell of a body. *This will be you someday.* Except she'd have a daughter who'd come to visit her and comfort her. She'd have a daughter who cared.

She could have been a daughter who cared. She should have tried harder to forge a new relationship with her mother, should have brought Daphne to see her. Guilt overrode the resentment as she pulled up a chair next to the bed and laid a hand on her mother's arm.

"Mother?"

The cadaver slept on.

Roberta tried again, gently tapping the arm, wrinkled and spotted with the bruises of age. "Mother?"

The eyes opened and the head turned. The woman squinted at her as if trying to place her.

"It's me, Roberta."

"Roberta." The sound came out faint and raspy. "What are you doing here?"

"I came to see you."

"I'm dying."

"I heard."

The lips turned down at the corners. "Did you come to see if you're in the will? There's nothing left, you know." The cadaver let out a tired breath and shut her eyes again.

"I didn't come for anything other than to see you and tell you I'm sorry."

The eyes stayed closed. "After all these years?"

"I'm sorry you could never forgive me. I'm sorry we never had a relationship, that you never got to see your granddaughter grow up."

A tear leaked out of one eye. "It could have been different."

"Yes, it could have," Roberta agreed.

"If only you'd listened to me."

So the fault was all hers. Even now, on her deathbed, her mother would bear no blame for those many years of estrangement. "All I wanted was your love."

Another tear slipped out. "I always loved you. You... disappointed me so."

She had; there was no denying it. She took her mother's limp hand and squeezed it. "I'm sorry."

"Why didn't you say that...years ago?"

"Perhaps I was waiting to hear that you still loved me."

Her mother gave no indication of having heard. A breath seeped out and she turned her head away. "I'm tired."

So am I, thought Roberta. Yes, she'd disappointed

her mother but her mother had hurt her deeply. What a sad mess. They should have had a relationship all these years. Her mother should've come to Icicle Falls to spend weekends and see Daphne performing in the Sunday-school Christmas pageant or watch her graduating from high school. She should've been there for Daphne's wedding, should have held her great-granddaughter. Roberta should have come over to Seattle to take her out to lunch. So much they could have done, so much they'd missed. "I wish it could have been different between us," she said.

Too late for that now. The only thing it wasn't too late for was forgiveness. Bitterness was exhausting, and she'd carried hers long enough. "You were never there for me, but I forgive you. I learned from your rejection. My daughter isn't perfect and we've had our problems, but at least she knows I love her."

The eyes stayed shut and the mouth pressed together in a tight, thin line. Her mother obviously had no more to say.

But that was okay. Neither did Roberta. This time the tears were hers. She couldn't help crying for what they'd lost all those years, but she also felt like a woman who had just survived a deadly disease. The fever had finally broken. Now she could truly heal. "I'll do whatever I can to make you comfortable."

"Thank you." The words came out so faintly Roberta almost wondered if she'd imagined them.

She gave her mother's hand one final squeeze. "You're welcome."

Before she left, she made arrangements to have her mother moved to a private room. She lasted another two weeks and then she was gone. Roberta saw to it that she was buried at Washelli right beside her father.

"I hope you rest in peace," she said to her mother when she stood at the graveside. She knew now that she could live in peace.

Roberta gave herself a mental shake. This was such a lovely day. She had no intention of wasting even a minute of it revisiting the past. Instead, she decided to enjoy the moment at hand and take a walk up Lost Bride Trail. She might not make it all the way to the falls, but the scenery would be beautiful and she could look for lady's slippers. She'd bring her walking stick, a bottle of water (and an ibuprofen) and take her time.

Half an hour later found her on a wooded mountain path, surrounded by evergreens and ferns, walking through dappled sunlight, taking in the earthy scent and breathing the fresh mountain air. It had been ages since she'd walked this trail. She really needed to get out more, have more fun.

She eventually made it up to Lost Bride Falls. By the time she got there, she was definitely ready for a break. She sat down on a little wooden bench by the scenic outlook to rest her foot and enjoy the sight of water cascading over a rocky outcrop. What a history that waterfall had. She wondered what had happened to Rebecca Cane, Joshua Cane's mail-order bride, who'd mysteriously disappeared so many generations ago. Had she run away with his younger brother, Gideon, or had Joshua truly killed the two of them in a fit of jealous rage, as so many people had speculated? The lurid story of the disappearing bride had, over the years, turned into something positive. Legend said that any woman who caught a glimpse of the ghost of the lost bride under the falls had a proposal of marriage waiting for her in the near future.

Roberta had never seen the ghost.

She took off her hiking shoe and rubbed her aching foot, then gulped down her painkiller. Even though it was a relatively easy hike, it was probably longer than she should have attempted. She'd go home, kick off her shoes and relax with her latest romance novel.

She'd just put the shoe back on when two strangers came up the path. They were both good-looking men, lean and fit, wearing T-shirts, jeans and hiking boots and carrying water bottles. Roberta judged the younger one to be somewhere around Daphne's age. The other was probably in his seventies, with white hair and plenty of lines to show he'd logged in some hours out in the sun. He resembled a younger version of Clint Eastwood. Roberta had always adored Clint Eastwood.

The younger man said hello, then got busy taking pictures of the falls with a camera that looked very expensive. The older man smiled and said hello. "Nice day to be out," he added.

"Yes, it is," Roberta said.

He strolled over to where she sat. He was a tall man. Put him in a cowboy hat and poncho and give him a cigar and he could *be* Clint Eastwood. "Great view."

"You'd be hard put to find a better one anywhere."

"Do you live here?"

It had been about a million years since a man had been interested, but Roberta hadn't forgotten the signs. "I do," she said and introduced herself.

"My name's Curtis White. This is my son Brian."

"Good to meet you," Brian said and continued to take pictures.

"Mind if I join you?" asked Curtis.

"Not at all." She scooted over to make room on the bench, and he sat down, causing a flutter in her chest.

"We came up with some friends to do a little fishing and hiking."

"This is the place to do it." Roberta couldn't help herself; she had to check his left hand for a ring. Barenaked. A bare-naked Clint Eastwood. *Really,* she scolded herself, *at your age.* Well, what was wrong with feeling the cold embers stir at her age? She wasn't dead yet.

But just because he wasn't wearing a ring didn't mean he wasn't married…

He was checking out her ring finger, too. "Have you lived here long?"

"For years."

"Lucky you," he said. "I've always thought it would be nice to retire over here somewhere, have a cabin, fish every day. Never got around to it."

"It's not too late."

He smiled. The man had a great smile. "You know, you're right."

They chatted for a few more minutes, long enough for him to confirm that she was single and find out she was in the business of providing brides and grooms with a place to get married. She learned that he was a retired banker and had been a widower for five years. And he was in town until Monday.

"Would you like to have dinner with me tonight?" he asked.

"Oh, I couldn't. You're up here with your son."

"And his brother. They won't miss me."

"You can say that again," teased the son.

"Well…"

"I hear there's a restaurant that offers traditional German food. I haven't had schnitzel since I was stationed in Germany. Do you like schnitzel, Roberta?"

"I do, as a matter of fact."

"Well, then, let's make it a date."

Roberta suspected Daphne would have plans for the evening, so why not? They agreed to meet at Schwangau at six. Then, with his son finished taking pictures, the two men said goodbye and made their way back down the trail. Roberta watched them go and wondered what silliness had prompted her to accept a date at this age. Clint Eastwood, that was what.

"Silly woman," she muttered and rose to her feet. Her back was stiff from sitting, and she paused to stretch and take in the view one last time before starting back. The waterfall was a gorgeous, roaring thing, with rainbows dancing in its waters and in that little cave behind the falls... What was that? She saw the figure for only a few seconds. It looked vaguely like a woman in a long gown.

The lost bride!

She blinked and looked again. Of course there was nothing. "Honestly, Roberta, you really are a silly, old woman."

By the time she was halfway down the trail she was limping and chiding herself for walking so far. Then she remembered Curtis White and decided her hike had been worth the pain. But she could hardly wait to get home, pop another pill and put her foot up.

When she got to the house Daphne was back. "I thought you'd be out with Hank," Roberta said.

"No. I came back looking for you. Where'd you go?"

"I went for a hike."

"It hasn't been that long since you had the surgery," Daphne protested. "And you said your foot hurt."

"I thought exercising it would do me good. Anyway, the doctor said I could walk on it now."

"A little. Not a hike. Where'd you go?"

"Up Lost Bride Trail."

"Oh, Mother," Daphne said, her voice a mixture of disgust and worry.

"I'm fine," Roberta assured her and went to the kitchen, trying not to limp noticeably. She got some water and washed down a pain pill.

"I can tell," Daphne said. "Let me get you some ice."

Roberta hobbled to the back parlor and sat on the couch. Daphne was right behind her, carrying a gallon freezer bag filled with ice and wrapped in a towel. She helped Roberta prop up her foot, then laid the ice on it, over the towel. "You're a good daughter," Roberta told her. She was beautiful, both inside and out, and Roberta was glad she'd come home.

"Thank you," Daphne murmured.

"Now, tell me how you managed to get away from Hank. You know he's not going to give up until you go out with him." Whether that was a good or a bad thing remained to be seen.

"I told him I'm not rushing into anything."

"Very wise. I have a feeling he'll wait."

Daphne shrugged. "I do, too. He's taking me to Zelda's for dinner. We're just going out as friends," she hurried to add.

Roberta wished she'd had the good sense to find a male friend to do things with. Maybe she had that afternoon.

"Do you mind? I know we talked about spending the day together."

"I don't mind at all," Roberta replied. "I have plans for tonight myself."

"You do?"

"I'm going to dinner at Schwangau."

"Oh? With who?"

"A very nice man I met while I was taking my walk. He's up here with his sons."

Daphne looked incredulous. "You met a man?"

Roberta scowled. "Old people do make friends, you know."

"I know. It's just that, well, I'm surprised. All these years, you never dated."

She had, for a brief time when Daphne was little, only a casual date or two with a couple of the locals. And then that disastrous affair...

1967

Nobody knew about it. He was a salesman from Seattle. He'd stopped at the diner, soon to become Pancake Haus, for a coffee on his way home from Coulee City and they'd struck up a conversation. Conversation had led to dinner, and afterward Roberta had given him a kiss and her phone number. How fortunate that she'd popped in for a bite on her lunch hour that day!

The next month he came back and rented a small cabin and Roberta got a babysitter. He took her to dinner, to a different restaurant this time, one in nearby Wenatchee, and then back to the cabin, and suddenly her dull life began to sparkle. Love at last!

A month later he was in town again. Janice Lind took Daphne for the night so Roberta could supposedly have a getaway with a girlfriend, and Roberta returned to the secluded cabin.

On Sunday morning she made him bacon and eggs. He reached across the small wooden dining table and said, "It's been a wonderful weekend."

She thought so, too, and went to take his hand. That was when she spotted it, the barely discernible band of white on his left-hand ring finger. Surely she should have noticed that before. "You're married."

Guilt flashed across his face and she pulled her hand away. He tried to cover it with an earnest look. "I am, but it's over."

"Until you go home to Seattle?"

"It's not like that, Roberta. We don't get along. She…"

"Doesn't understand you." The oldest lie in the book.

"It's true," he insisted. "We're separated."

Roberta had no desire to play that game. She'd already been used once. She wasn't going to allow herself to be used again. She could almost hear her mother sneering, "Foolish, wicked girl," as she walked out of the cabin and back to her single life. She was better off alone. The only man a woman could trust was the kind she met between the covers of a book.

"I was running a business," she told Daphne now. *Protecting my heart from further injury.* She'd tried to protect her daughter, too, but Daphne had never listened. She'd kept believing there had to be a good man out there somewhere. Maybe Daphne had been right all along. Maybe Roberta simply hadn't encountered one until now.

"And only this morning you said you didn't want a man in your life."

"A woman can change her mind, can't she?"

"Absolutely, and it's about time," Daphne said now with a smile and an approving nod. "I hope you have a great evening."

"I do, too." It had been years since that disastrous, short-lived affair, and Roberta hadn't been on a date since. She was a female Rip Van Winkle waking up after years of sleep. What was she going to wear? What was she going to say? Was this a bad idea?

Bad or not, she went to Schwangau. She donned a pair of cream-colored slacks, her favorite pink top and floral jacket and her comfiest shoes, and sailed out the door, feeling as nervous as a young girl going on her first date.

Seeing Curtis White waiting for her in the lobby of Schwangau, wearing black jeans and a button-down shirt with a dark blue tie, set her tummy doing flips. She couldn't remember when she'd found a real, live man so attractive.

"You look lovely," he said.

Lovely, at her age. She could feel herself blushing. "And you look… Has anyone ever told you that you look like Clint Eastwood?" *What a silly thing to say!*

He didn't seem to mind. "I get that a lot," he said with a smile. "Normally, I clean up better. I'm afraid I didn't realize there was a dress code at this place. This is the only shirt I had with me. I had to borrow a tie from the maître d'."

"You clean up just fine." Roberta told him. Now, there was an understatement. She should pinch herself to make sure she wasn't dreaming. Except she didn't want to wake up. At this point in life, a woman deserved a good dream or two.

The dream only improved as the evening progressed and they shared a bottle of Riesling and life stories (Roberta's highly edited). Curtis confessed to a love of old fifties doo-wop groups, and then she did sneak a quick pinch. This *had* to be too good to be true.

Nothing vanished. It was still evening and she was still in a fancy restaurant with a great-looking man. "How about breakfast tomorrow?" he asked as they left the restaurant.

"I think I could manage that."

Breakfast was even better than dinner, so they decided on lunch, including his sons and her daughter. "He kind of looks like Clint Eastwood," Daphne whispered as he and his sons walked into Zelda's.

"He thinks I look like Audrey Hepburn," Roberta whispered back. "The mature version," she said with a smile. Of course, other than being slender, she didn't look anything like the famous actress, but she wasn't about to disabuse the man. Let him have his fantasy.

Later that day, after their children had discreetly drifted off, they took a walk on the bank of the Wenatchee River, admiring the view of sparkling blue water wending its way past a forest of pines and firs. He took her hand and said, "Roberta, I've had a wonderful time this weekend."

A little gremlin landed on her shoulder and whispered, *Here's where the letdown begins. He'll say, "But now I have to go back to my real life."*

"I hope you have, too," Curtis went on.

"It's been lovely," she replied, careful to keep her voice neutral.

"I'd really like to do this again."

"You would?"

He looked surprised. "Wouldn't you?"

She smiled. "Yes, actually, I would. But let's take it slow," she added, picking up her daughter's new mantra.

He smiled back. "Okay. But not too slow. I'm not getting any younger, and I'd like to cruise the Greek isles before I die. That isn't the kind of thing a man wants to do alone."

"I'd like that, too," Roberta said. She was sure she would.

"Glad to hear it," he said and kissed her.

It was a kiss filled with both tenderness and promise, and probably the best kiss Roberta had ever had. Maybe life began at seventy-one.

Chapter Twenty-Five

Anne, Mother of the Guest of Honor

The Sunday before the wedding weekend Kendra hosted a bridal shower for Laney. It was a balmy afternoon with the kind of blue skies that made Seattleites ecstatic, and the temperature hovered somewhere in the low seventies. The same pleasant weather was expected for Icicle Falls the next weekend.

In addition to family, Laney's bridesmaids, Autumn, Ella and Darcy, were present, along with her coworkers at the coffee shop and several friends from church. Laney was all dolled up in a green sundress that complemented not only her hair but also the mermaid swimming up her arm.

"She's going to be a stunning bride," Mrs. Ostrom, the pastor's wife, said to Anne as she made the rounds with Laney, saying hello to everyone. Mrs. Ostrom was pushing seventy. She either had no problem with tattoo overload or was too polite to say anything. Probably the latter.

But it was proof of how much everyone loved Laney, and knowing that made Anne happy. Right now it would've been impossible to be unhappy. It had been a race to the bridal finish line, but everything had finally come together.

"You have been busy, haven't you?" Cam's mother said to Laney as she hugged her. "Planning a wedding so quickly."

"I had a lot of help," Laney said, smiling at Anne.

"The best," added Julia, who'd come over to greet her daughter and granddaughter.

Anne smiled at her mother's praise. She was still smiling when Aunt Maude approached, but she felt the smile getting a little stiff. Aunt Maude was one of Cam's aunts, the polar opposite of his mother. She was tall and skinny with a lack of bustline that she accentuated with a horrific blouse in a wild purple print. To complete her ensemble, she wore a faded black, crinkly skirt from a long-gone fashion era. She tried to distract from the wrinkles growing on her face by dyeing her hair a color of red found nowhere in nature. To complete the look, she showed off her perpetual frown with bright red lipstick. She was a walking sour lemon and purveyor of doom.

"Laney, you seem tired," she said, patting Laney's arm.

"She's been busy, Aunt Maude," Anne said.

Aunt Maude shook her head. "Girls these days, they take on too much. I blame it on the women's movement."

No one quite knew what to say to that—and remain polite. Julia turned to Laney and Anne. "Let's get you girls some punch. Excuse us, Maude." As they walked over to the refreshment table, she muttered, "Who invited that woman?"

"I couldn't not invite her, Mom," Anne said.

"*I* could have."

Once everyone had had an opportunity to chat and enjoy a glass of punch, Kendra started a game that involved unscrambling letters to form words that all had to do with weddings. "I love this kind of game," Cam's mom enthused.

"Good for your brain," agreed Maude, who'd taken a seat next to Anne. "Did you know that an estimated 5.2 million people now have Alzheimer's?"

There was some cheery news. "Where did you hear that?"

"I can't remember," Maude replied. "You know, one of the signs is losing your sense of smell," she informed Anne.

Just what she wanted to talk about at her daughter's bridal shower. She found herself surreptitiously sniffing her wrist to see if she could detect the perfume she'd sprayed there earlier. Whew. Her brain was still okay.

They moved from the game to eating, with Kendra's terrier, Barney, posing hungrily in front of various guests, hoping for a handout. "Barney, no!" Kendra commanded. "Don't anybody feed him."

Cam's mother, who was about to share some of her prosciutto, drew back her hand, making Barney whine. Not that he should've been remotely hungry, since he'd already begged several handouts when Kendra wasn't looking.

Kendra the social director soon moved on to the purpose of the shower, giving the bride her gifts. With Autumn on one side, writing down who gave Laney what, and Darcy on the other, forming a ribbon bouquet for the wedding rehearsal, Laney set to work, dipping into gift bags and opening boxes containing everything from margarita glasses to dish towels. The ribbon bouquet began to swell.

"A baby for every ribbon you break," teased Drake's mom.

Laney said she liked kids, then with a grin yanked

off a ribbon, letting it snap apart. Ella folded and stuffed wrapping paper in the ginormous gift bag that had contained a cashmere blanket from Julia.

Barney found this all fascinating. And appetizing. Perhaps it was the fact that he'd been denied that final treat earlier or maybe he was simply being a dog. Whatever the cause, the four-legged garbage disposal, who'd managed to snarf cake off an abandoned plate, now developed a fondness for wrapping paper and began noshing on a piece that hadn't made it into the bag.

Anne watched in disgust as he shredded a bow of pink curling ribbon. "Should he be doing that?" she asked Kendra.

"What?" Kendra turned and saw the last of the paper about to go into Barney's mouth. "Oh, Barney, no!" She took away what was left of it and Barney slinked off to a corner where, later on, as Laney was thanking all the guests for their presents, he threw up both the wrapping paper and his earlier snacks.

"Eeew," said Autumn, wrinkling her nose.

Aunt Maude shook her head. "It's a sign."

"Oh, really, Maude," Julia said, sounding disgusted.

Maude refused to be put in her place. "When things go wrong at a bridal shower, things will surely go wrong at the wedding."

Anne had never heard that before. "Is that a real saying? Where did you hear it?"

Maude shrugged. "I don't remember."

"And how's your sense of smell?" Julia asked, sneering.

Maude harrumphed and took herself off to the refreshment table for another helping of lemon dessert.

"That woman," Julia said, shaking her head. "She's a

regular encyclopedia of misinformation and nonfacts. I never heard such nonsense in all my life."

That's what it is, nonsense, Anne told herself for the rest of the afternoon. When Cam asked how the shower had gone, she replied, "Great." It had been a lovely shower and Laney was going to have a lovely wedding.

She continued to tell herself all evening long, and again when she lay in bed, thinking of everything that could possibly go wrong. Finally, around one in the morning, she took a melatonin tablet to help herself sleep. One wasn't going to do it. She took another and finally drifted off.

And went to Laney's wedding. But instead of wearing her mother-of-the-bride dress, she was prancing around in some skimpy showgirl outfit and sporting a huge, feathery headdress that was so heavy she had trouble holding up her head. This made it hard to keep her balance, and when a groomsman wearing an Elvis-style white rhinestone jumpsuit escorted her down the aisle, she found herself weaving back and forth like a woman who'd had too much champagne.

She toppled into her seat. Cam should have slipped in beside her but he was nowhere to be seen. Instead, Kendra's dog, Barney, jumped up onto the pew, pink wrapping paper hanging from his jaws.

She looked up front and there stood Drake in raggedy pirate garb, a patch over one eye. The "Wedding March" began to play, but it wasn't wedding music. Instead, Elvis, the King himself, appeared, dressed in a white rhinestone jumpsuit, and began to sing "All Shook Up" backed by the Flesh Eaters, who wore zombie makeup. And here came Laney in some kind of serving-wench outfit. Where was her wedding gown?

Anne tried to stand up and demand her daughter

march right back down the aisle and put on her gown, but the heavy headdress propelled her forward and she fell on her face. Barney leaped off the pew and began tugging at the headdress, growling playfully.

"What a disgrace," hissed Aunt Maude, who'd seated herself directly behind Anne. "The woman can't even plan her daughter's wedding. I knew this would happen. Didn't I say this would happen?"

The woman seated next to Maude seemed to be her twin. She whispered back, "I heard they wanted to go to Vegas and Anne put a wrench in it."

"I did not," Anne protested, trying to struggle to her feet.

"Get that woman out of here," said the minister, who looked suspiciously like Jack Sparrow. "She's messing everything up."

"I'm the mother of the bride!"

Drake pointed a finger at her. "She's a Momzilla. Get her out of here."

"I'm going to be your mother-in-law. You can't do this to me!"

But they did. Two burly men in white rhinestone-encrusted tuxes dragged her down the aisle, past the guests. Some stared at her with pity. Some giggled. One fellow showgirl laughed out loud.

"Sorry, sis," Kendra called. (Why was she dressed like a zombie?) "I'll save you a donut."

Down the aisle they went and into the foyer. They pushed open the church door and hurled Anne out.

But there was no sidewalk to catch her. The church gripped the edge of a cliff and she found herself falling, screaming as she went.

She awoke before she landed, Cam gently stroking her arm. "It's okay, Annie. You're having a bad dream."

Bad dream? There was the understatement of the century.

"You all right now?"

She swallowed and willed her heart to stop doing the Indianapolis 500. "I'm fine."

It was just a dream, she told herself. But what did it mean?

Nothing. She was simply suffering from the combined effect of too much melatonin and too close proximity to Aunt Maude. Everything was fine and the wedding was going to be perfect. Anne closed her eyes and snuggled back under the covers.

But she never got to sleep again. Maybe that was just as well.

Chapter Twenty-Six

Laney, Ready for the Big Day

"Just think," Autumn said to Laney as they wiped down counters at the coffee shop, "it's almost your wedding. Tonight we'll be at the Red Barn, dancing with cowboys at your bachelorette party."

It was hard to believe. After all the discussion and planning, the big day was only forty-eight hours away. Everyone would be meeting at the waterfront park for the ceremony, then going back to Primrose Haus for the reception. There would be food and flowers and dancing. No bright lights, no noise and crazy excitement, but they'd have the stars in the sky and they could make their own noise. It would be exactly the wedding she'd dreamed of when she was a little girl.

"Ben told me the guys still don't know what they're going to do up there for Drake's bachelor party," Autumn said. "I think hang out at the river, sit around and drink beer. Talk about boring."

Laney shrugged. "It's not Vegas." Okay, that sounded kind of...off. From the corner of her eye, she could feel Autumn studying her. "I'll take out the garbage," she announced and ducked into the alley behind the coffee shop. It was wrong not to feel more excited about all of this, especially since her mom had worked so hard on pulling everything together for her. And everything had been pulled together perfectly, right down from the donut cake to the DJ. (The Flesh Eaters weren't happy that they'd been bumped from playing at the reception, but Drake had told them about the open-mike night at Zelda's on Sunday, and they were planning to make an impression on the residents of Icicle Falls and maybe get a future booking.) Laney had a wedding gown she loved and was marrying her best friend. That was what mattered, not where or how they got married. Anyway, it was too late to change her plans now. Everything was ordered and everyone was coming.

Autumn was happy to keep the wedding conversation going when Laney came back in. "Are you sorry you guys aren't going to Vegas?"

Laney concentrated on putting a new liner in the garbage can. "My mom's right. This is better."

"For who?"

"For everyone."

"It's not your mom getting married," Autumn reminded her.

Why was she always saying stuff like that? "I know," Laney said. "But this way our family and friends can come."

"They could've come to Vegas. I just got a Visa card. I could go. So could Ben." She grinned. "Let's go."

"Oh, sure," Laney said. "I'm gonna take off for Vegas two days before my wedding."

"I would. If that's what I really wanted."

Laney bit her lip.

"Don't be a wimp, Laney, not when it's something as important as your wedding."

"I'm not being a wimp," Laney insisted. "I want this." She liked Icicle Falls. She liked the river. She liked the old-fashioned house on Primrose Street. So did Drake. Well, sort of. He liked the river, anyway. This was going to be fun, the best of both worlds. They'd have the fancy wedding here and then go to Vegas for their honeymoon. She set aside the image of Drake and her on the Treasure Island pirate ship, shook her head in an effort to erase the beautiful pictures she'd seen on the website.

But she'd *wanted* to get married on that ship. Primrose Haus was beautiful, but in the end, it was just a house and the yard was just a yard. She frowned and told herself to cut it out. Her mom was right, she thought again. She'd have no regrets about the wedding they'd planned.

Your mom will have no regrets about the wedding you've planned.

Where had that come from? It was as if Autumn was still talking to her.

Well, she wasn't listening. Canceling things now would be totally selfish and unfair to her mother.

And so the wedding party left Thursday afternoon for Icicle Falls. Friday morning after breakfast they'd all go rock climbing. At some point during the day, her parents, grandparents, aunts, uncles and cousins would arrive, along with the rest of the guests who would trickle in. There would be a rehearsal on Friday night and then a dinner party for the immediate family and bridal party. Saturday was the big day. It was going to be like Christmas, only better. Yes, she *had* made the right decision.

They checked into the Icicle Creek Lodge and Drake's best man, Ben, said, "This place is something else." Since he'd leaned over to Drake and lowered his voice, she knew he hadn't meant that in a good way.

"It ain't Vegas, that's for sure," Drake whispered back, echoing her earlier words.

Her stomach started churning and that made her cranky. They got to the room and instead of being charmed by the mountain view, she saw fussy furniture she'd never pick and curtains at the window that made her think of her grandmother. Those were antiques. Valuable antiques. And the lace curtains were pretty.

Except she didn't like lace curtains.

This was her bridal suite. This was where she'd spend her wedding night. She burst into tears.

He dropped their suitcases and took her by the arms. "Laney, what's wrong?"

"I don't want to do this," she wailed.

He looked at her in concern. "You don't want to get married?"

"No."

"You don't?" He sounded horrified.

"No. I mean, no, that's not it. I want to get married, just not here. But it's too late."

"No, it's not. Tell me what you want."

She shook her head. Too late, too late. She'd blown it. She'd let herself get talked into something that wasn't her and Drake. Yeah, this had been her when she was ten, when she was sixteen even, but she wasn't sixteen anymore. Somewhere along the way, her tastes had changed. Her mom had meant well, but she'd been wrong and now they were stuck.

He led her into the room and settled them on the bed. "Talk to me."

"We should have gone to Vegas," she said between sobs. "I'm sorry, Drake."

He tucked a finger under her chin and raised her face

to look at him. "Hey, don't be sorry. I told you I'd do whatever you wanted."

"I know, and I thought I wanted this. What I really want is to go to Vegas."

He brightened at that. "Yeah? Then we'll go to Vegas."

"Are you crazy? We can't do that now! It's too late to cancel the reception. My parents have spent all this money."

"We'll pay them back."

"My mom would be so embarrassed." The very thought of humiliating her mother made Laney cry even harder.

There was a knock at the door, and Autumn and Ella ducked in, together with their boyfriends. Darcy and Drake's other pal, Gordy, hovered behind.

"What's wrong?" Autumn asked.

"Laney doesn't want to do this," Drake explained.

"She doesn't want to get married?" Ben asked, shocked.

"No, stupid," said Autumn. "She doesn't want to get married *here*. I told you all along this was a mistake," she scolded Laney. "You're such a wimp."

Good old Autumn, always a comfort. Laney glared at her.

Unaffected, Autumn pulled out her cell phone. "Let's check on flights to Vegas. I bet we can get a red-eye."

"I can't go to Vegas," Laney protested. "It'd be wrong."

"Well, then, what are you going to do?" Autumn demanded.

"I'm going to call my dad." She didn't dare tell her mother what she was thinking.

Her father answered his cell phone on the second ring. "Laney girl, are you guys up there now?"

"Yes, and, oh, Dad, this is all wrong."

"What's wrong?"

His voice was suddenly worried. Great. He was going to be mad; Mom was going to be upset. "Never mind. I shouldn't have called."

"Yes. You should have. Tell me what's going on."

"I don't want to do this."

"You don't want to get married?" he asked, shocked.

"I don't want to get married here. We should've gone to Vegas. I should be happy about this wedding, but I'm just so…unhappy."

"Aw, Laney, why didn't you say something earlier?"

He had to ask that? As if he hadn't been there, seeing all the work Mom was doing, how important this was to her? "Mom." That was as far as she got, but that said it all. She started crying again.

"I know. Your mother really wanted this for you. Sometimes I think that in doing it for you, she's enjoyed planning the kind of fancy wedding we didn't have."

He suddenly stopped talking. Had they lost the connection? "Dad?"

"Don't do anything just yet, Laney. Stay up there. And don't worry. I've got an idea."

Chapter Twenty-Seven

Anne, Mother of the Bride-to-be

Friday morning Anne and Cam got into their trusty little Kia and, after a quick stop to grab some coffee, made their way up the mountains to Icicle Falls. "Don't you love it here?" she gushed as they passed the Willkommen in Icicle Falls sign. "I don't know why we don't come up more often."

"Weddings."

"Oh, yeah, that." Her wedding business did cut into their getaway time. Maybe she should start easing up on her work schedule, take advantage of being empty nesters.

Laney's wedding felt like the apex of her career. It was as if this was what she'd been waiting for all these years. An insistent itch was finally getting scratched.

"Well, this is the most important wedding I've ever planned." She laid a hand on Cam's leg. "Can you believe it? Our daughter's getting married." She felt like a kid on Christmas Eve. *Tomorrow you get to unwrap your presents!*

Cam just smiled.

"Drake's a sweet boy. They're going to be so happy together."

Cam nodded, and Anne turned her attention to all the shops as they drove through town. There was the Mad Hatter, a shop that specialized in novelty hats; there was Local Yokels, a shop featuring all kinds of Northwest treats—everything from smoked salmon to huckleberry jam. They passed Big Brats, the restaurant stand that sold great bratwurst, and Gilded Lily's, the women's clothing shop. She and Kendra would definitely have to do some shopping later, after they'd caught up with Laney and her posse.

They drove on through the town and then down Icicle Creek Drive, where the shops were replaced by woods and an occasional glimpse of Icicle Creek. Off through the trees she noticed a cleared area surrounded by a split-rail fence. A couple of llamas peered out at her. Looking past that, she could see some cabins scattered about—a camp of some sort. The road took a small jog and they wound up on a smaller, private road, Holly Road. It led to the Icicle Creek Lodge, a timbered affair that offered views of Icicle Creek and, beyond that, the mountains.

"Isn't this charming?" she said as Cam pulled up in front of the lodge. "What a fabulous place for a wedding night."

"Annie, I hate to break it to you, but I think they had their wedding night long before this," Cam said.

She frowned at him. "Some things a mother doesn't want to know." Anyway, she was in no position to judge, a fact she'd reminded herself of many times once her daughter moved out.

Her story had turned out fine, and so would Laney's. She wouldn't have a grandchild as soon as her own mother did, though, that was for sure. Laney would be going back to school, and she and Drake had dreams of taking a cross-country camping trip and, after that, buying a house. Ah, young love with all its plans and dreams.

Plans and dreams weren't only for newlyweds. She and Cam had plenty of time left for some of their own. He'd refused to share any details about what he had in mind for their anniversary, but whatever it was, she'd be ready to relax. Organizing her daughter's wedding had taken a lot out of her.

They went inside the lodge and checked in. "We should go see how the kids are doing," she said to Cam as he pocketed their room key.

"They were going rock climbing," he reminded her. "They're probably not back yet."

Good point. "Well, then, later." Meanwhile, they could get some lunch and kick around town as they waited for Kendra and her family.

She'd reserved the private room at Schwangau for the rehearsal dinner, so, wanting something different, they wandered over to Zelda's, one of the other popular restaurants in town. It was less pricey and more hip, decorated with a mixture of Northwest contemporary wood trim and art-deco decor. All the waitresses wore Roaring Twenties headbands and served up everything from salmon and trout to salads with mountain blackberries.

Charley Masters, the owner, seated them and stuck around a few minutes to chat. "Your daughter's having her reception at Primrose Haus? Great place," she said. "I got married in Vegas," she added with a wink. "Different strokes."

The very mention of Vegas made Anne shudder, but she smiled and nodded.

"Anyway," Charley concluded, "I hope you folks enjoy your stay."

"We already are," Anne told her. "I love this restaurant," she said after Charley left to go seat another couple.

Cam smiled. "I think in your present mood there isn't anything you *wouldn't* love."

"True," she admitted. "I'm on a wedding high." She had checked and double-checked every detail. Everything was in order. All she had to do now was enjoy the party.

They'd just finished lunch when Anne's cell phone rang. "We're here," Kendra said. "Where are you guys?"

"We're at Zelda's, finishing lunch. Come on over."

Ten minutes later, Kendra and her family entered the restaurant. The girls were bouncing with excitement. At the sight of their aunt, they let out squeals and dashed for the table.

"Inside voices," their mother scolded, taking off after them, "and no running."

The running turned into hops. Coral was the first to reach the table, but Amy was the first to share the news that they'd had a flat tire on the way up. "And Daddy swore."

"Sounds like you had a fun trip," Anne said, greeting her sister.

Kendra rolled her eyes. "Family fun. Can't beat it. Is it five o'clock somewhere? I think my man needs a drink."

"He needs two," her husband said, coming up behind her.

They slid into the bench opposite and then squeezed in the girls on each side of the table. "Have you seen the bride and groom yet?" Kendra asked.

Anne shook her head. "They're out rock climbing. We figure we'll catch up with them later this afternoon."

"Can I wear my dress to the practice?" Coral wanted to know.

"Not after what happened last time you put it on. It's jeans and T-shirts for the river tonight and your church dress for the party after."

"I like parties," Amy announced.

"That's good," Anne said, hugging her, "because we are going to party tonight."

Roberta's crew was taking care of the seating for the ceremony tomorrow and the other reception details, so all Anne had to do was watch her beautiful daughter take her wedding vows. Life was good.

After a leisurely visit at the restaurant, the men took the girls to the little amusement park that had recently opened at one end of town, giving Anne and Kendra a chance to prowl the shops. "Well, you did it," Kendra said as they examined the antiques and collectibles in Timeless Treasures. "You finally got your perfect wedding."

"My daughter's perfect wedding," Anne corrected her.

"One and the same." Kendra gave her a playful nudge. "Ooh, look at this china mug. I think I need it."

They found several more things they needed as the afternoon wore on—bath bombs from Bubbles, gingerbread boys and girls from Gingerbread Haus and, of course, chocolate from Sweet Dreams. "I may as well get a large box of truffles," Anne said, "since I'll have to share with Cam."

"I'm hiding mine," said her sister.

They met their husbands and the girls at the Tea Time

Tea Shop, where they indulged in purchasing some lavender sugar cookies and chocolate mint tea to take home, and where Anne had a last-minute confab with Bailey, the shop owner who was catering the wedding.

"Roberta's got it all under control. Remember?" Kendra reminded her as they left.

"I know." But once a wedding planner, always a wedding planner.

They got back to the lodge to learn that their parents had arrived.

"Where's Daddy?" Kendra asked once Julia had let them in.

"Off to buy some German beer and check out that sausage place we saw when we drove in." She grimaced. "He does love all that wurst, but it doesn't love him. I'm sure he'll have heartburn by the time he comes back. Where's our bride?"

"She and Drake and their friends were going rock climbing," Anne said. "I guess I'll call her and see if they're back yet." All she got was voice mail. "She must be out of range."

Laney was still out of range at four thirty. "They should've been back by now," Anne fretted as she and Kendra and the girls hung out in Julia's room. "We've got the rehearsal in an hour."

"Try her again," Kendra suggested from their mother's bed, where she was stretched out beside Julia, watching reruns of *Love It or List It*.

Anne did, and again it went straight to voice mail. "Where is she?" Maybe she'd fallen and was stuck in some rock crevice with a broken leg. How would they find her?

Anne was pacing the floor, leaving a frantic message

for Laney to call her, when Cam appeared in the door-way, his brother-in-law behind him. "Looks like we're all here," he said. He cleared his throat. "So now would probably be the time to tell you."

A feeling of foreboding began to sneak up on Anne. "Tell me what?"

"There's been a slight change in plan."

"What's wrong?"

"Well, um, nothing." He cleared his throat again. "Laney and I have been talking."

"Is she back from rock climbing?"

"I don't think so."

"Cam, you're being awfully mysterious," Anne said.

"Well, like I said, there's been a change in plans."

This couldn't be good. Anne braced herself.

"Laney and Drake really want to get married in Vegas."

"Vegas!" Julia repeated.

Anne felt suddenly light-headed. She fell onto the bed opposite her mother. "Vegas?" With Elvis impersonators and the showgirls with the feathers and the chapels of love. And the pirate ship! "Vegas," she repeated, anger roaring through her like a tsunami.

Cam sat down next to her and put an arm around her shoulders. "She had an…epiphany."

"An epiphany! An epiphany is something *good*. An epiphany is not…running off to Vegas the day before you get married." She shot off the bed and went to search through the store bags. "Where's that chocolate?"

"Annie, calm down," said Cam. "They haven't run off. They're still here. They just don't want to get married here."

She had to be hearing things. In fact, she had to be hallucinating. Or dreaming. Yes, she was dreaming, that was it. She shook her head, pinched her arm. Nothing seemed to work. She was standing in the same room, hearing the same shocking news.

Stuffing chocolates in her mouth. "Why can't I wake up?"

"Have another chocolate," Julia urged. "And give me one, too."

"Let me see if I've got this straight," Anne said as she plopped down on the bed and handed over the chocolates. "They're still here but they're not getting married."

"That about sums it up."

"I want to wear my dress," Coral said and burst into tears. That set Amy off, and she started crying, too.

"Oh, boy," muttered Kendra. "Come on, girls. Let's go take a walk." She and her husband ushered the girls out of the room.

Julia stayed behind to comfort her daughter with hugs and more chocolate.

There was no comfort to be had. "I saved for this for years," Anne said, wiping at her eyes. "I wanted her to have something special. And now, just like that, we're canceling the wedding?"

"Actually, we're not," Cam said, and now he was smiling.

She blinked. "I don't understand."

He crossed the room to kneel in front of her and take her hands in his. "There's going to be a wedding here tomorrow, babe. Ours."

"What?"

At that moment his cell phone rang.

"It's Laney, isn't it?" Anne said as he answered it. Their daughter wasn't calling her mother. Probably too afraid. That made Anne both sad and angry.

Cam nodded at her. "Yes," he said to Laney, "I told her. Hang on." He handed over the phone.

"Don't you dare say anything you'll regret," Julia cautioned. "Remember, daughters don't always do what their mothers want."

A not-so-subtle reminder of her own past wedding choice. Anne took the phone and said hello. It was impossible to keep the disappointment out of her voice.

"Mom, I'm sorry. Please don't be mad," Laney begged.

She found it hard not to be. She'd gone to so much trouble to make sure her daughter had a memorable wedding. "Laney, I don't understand."

Laney sighed. "I just… I don't know. We got up here and I realized getting married at the house on Primrose Street wasn't what I really wanted. Neither did Drake. If we went through with it, if Drake and I didn't get married in Las Vegas like we talked about in the first place, I'd always be sorry. I didn't want to have any regrets."

Anne bit her lip. Okay, she understood about regrets. But she couldn't help wishing her daughter had figured this out sooner.

"I tried to want what you wanted for me, Mom. I really did. But the wedding you planned, it wasn't us, even with the raft."

Anne knew she had only one person to blame for how this had turned out, and that was herself. She'd been so determined to give Laney the wedding she'd never had, the one she thought Laney should have, she'd blinded herself to what her daughter truly wanted. And that was something very different from what Laney had talked about when she was younger. Her tastes had changed; they'd veered away from Anne's. Laney had become her own woman and Anne had ignored that.

Still… "If you get married there, a lot of your family and friends won't be able to come."

"But Drake and I will be there and that's what really matters," Laney said. *I'm marrying Cam, and that's what really matters.* Anne's words to her mother floated at the back of her mind.

"I'm sorry I ruined all your plans for me. It's not that I don't appreciate how hard you worked and how much time you spent, but the wedding you planned is the one *you* always wanted. So Dad came up with the perfect solution. You're going to be the bride tomorrow. And I hope I can be your maid of honor."

Anne could barely speak, choked up as she was. This was all so much to process. "That would be lovely," she managed.

"Thanks for understanding," Laney said, and Anne could hear the relief in her voice.

Better late than never. Here Anne did this for a living, yet when it came to her own daughter she'd been clueless. How pathetic was that?

"This is going to be fun," Laney continued, all excitement now. "Happy anniversary."

Anne smiled. "Thanks, sweetie." Okay, so things weren't going according to plan—well, *her* plan, anyway—but her daughter's happiness was what counted.

"I know Dad's excited about this and I am, too. Oh, and by the way, you don't have to get married on a raft. We canceled that part."

Thank heaven.

"I love you, Mom."

"I love you, too." And because she did, she couldn't stay mad, especially since she was the one who'd created this problem. But it was all working out. Her daughter was getting the wedding she wanted.

And it looked as though, after twenty-five years, so was Anne. Everything had changed so fast, she had wedding whiplash. She handed Cam's phone back to him. "I don't know what to say."

He smiled at her. "Say 'I do.'"

Chapter Twenty-Eight

A Wedding on Primrose Street

It was the best kind of day for a wedding—warm weather, blue sky and the sun shining on the bride…who wore a champagne-colored dress with a nipped-in waist and pleated skirt and flowers in her hair. She carried the bouquet that had been ordered for her daughter, and she and her husband were remarried under the rose arbor.

"Do you take this woman for another twenty-five years?" Pastor Ostrom asked the groom.

"I sure do," Cam said.

"And how about you, Anne? Do you pledge yourself to Cam?"

"I do," she said, her heart full.

"Then I pronounce you still husband and wife. I hope your next twenty-five years together are as wonderful as the first twenty-five," said the minister, beaming at them. "You may kiss your bride," he said to Cam.

Cam was happy to oblige. He dipped Anne backward and gave her a photo-op-style kiss, while the professional photographer recorded the moment for posterity…just like every friend and family member present who had a cell phone.

It had been a little embarrassing announcing to all the guests that there'd been a change in plans and they were here to celebrate a different bride and groom, but no one complained. More than one relative was thrilled about Laney's new plan to go to Vegas and begged to be included. "Wish we'd done that," said one of Drake's cousins. "Our wedding was boring." She rolled her eyes. "I let my mom plan most of it. Dumb."

Laney and Anne both said nothing.

Now, with the ceremony over, everyone went to the bar to get down to the serious business of partying.

The crab cakes, Brie and smoked salmon bruschetta, and pulled-pork sliders were a hit, as was the dinner, which consisted of three-cheese stuffed chicken, accompanied by tossed salad, a lobster-pasta salad and crusty rolls. And everyone raved over how clever and cute the donut cake was. The DJ had car problems halfway up the mountain and was still waiting for a tow truck, but the Flesh Eaters were in town and had brought their instruments along and were happy to fill in until he got there. So Cam and Anne did their opening dance to "Give It to Me, Baby, Hard, Hard, Hard," an original song by the lead singer.

"Congratulations on twenty-five years of marriage," Roberta's daughter, Daphne, said to Anne as she proffered a tray of champagne glasses. "These days that's quite an accomplishment."

"It can be done when you've got a good man," Anne said, taking a glass and smiling up at Cam.

"You give me hope," Daphne said with a smile.

"By the way, where's your mom? I haven't seen her," Anne said.

Daphne grinned. "She's in Seattle, visiting a new friend. She said to give you her best wishes."

"Champagne!" boomed Aunt Maude from behind Daphne, making her jump and the champagne glasses rattle. "I love champagne." She took a glass and Daphne slipped away to serve other guests. "Didn't I tell you something would happen?" Maude demanded.

Maude was *not* getting invited to Vegas. "Yes, you did," Anne said. "And isn't it terrific how it all turned out?" Maude scowled.

Julia came up just then. "I think it's time to cut the cake," she said, rescuing Anne and Cam from Aunt Maude. "Well, darling," she said as they made their way to the cake table, "how are you enjoying your wedding?"

Anne smiled up at Cam. "It's wonderful."

"Yes, it is," Julia agreed. "But then, how could it have been anything else with my lovely daughter planning it?"

"Thanks, Mom," Anne murmured.

Cam shook his head and frowned. "I wish I'd known twenty-five years ago how badly you wanted a fancy wedding."

She laid a hand on his arm. "I meant what I said back then. The most important thing to me was marrying you. And under the same circumstances, I'd do it all over again."

Not that she wasn't enjoying her fancy twenty-five-years-after-the-fact wedding. She was. But the simple fact remained. A marriage was about the two people who were making a commitment to each other. How they did it wasn't half as important as *why* they did it. Everything else was just frosting on the wedding cake.

Later that night Cam carried Anne over the threshold into the bridal suite at the Icicle Creek Lodge. "I'm a lucky man," he said, setting her down and putting his arms around her.

"And I'm a lucky woman," she said, reaching up and putting her arms around his neck.

"Thank you for marrying me again."

"I'd marry you again and again and again," Anne said and kissed him.

"Same here." He led her farther into the room, where a bottle of champagne sat next to the king-size bed. The nightstand held a small box of Sweet Dreams chocolates. An envelope sat on one of the pillows.

"You thought of everything."

He picked up the bottle and popped the cork. "I did. I'd actually reserved this room for next weekend, when I planned to bring you up here."

"That was what you'd planned?"

He nodded.

"We can still use it next weekend," she said coyly.

"I don't think we'll need it."

Of course, it would be silly to come back again so soon, she told herself, especially in light of the big blowout party they'd just had.

"Open the card."

She did, and out fell a magazine clipping. She picked it up. It was from some sort of real-estate brochure and featured a rustic mountain cabin perched alongside a river. "What's this?"

"Since we bagged the cruise, I thought we might like to make a down payment on a cabin up here instead. Now that we're empty nesters we can afford it. We may even get it paid off by the time we retire," he added with a grin. "I've got a couple of places in mind and a real-estate agent lined up to show us around. Actually, she was lined up for next weekend, but we moved it to tomorrow."

"A cabin?" Could she have heard correctly?

"Please tell me I got it right this time."

"More than right," she said, then threw her arms around him and kissed him.

The champagne was forgotten. Who needed bubbly when you had a handsome man kissing you?

Later that night as they snuggled together on the big bed, she relived the whole evening. It had been everything she'd ever dreamed of, a perfect wedding—just as Laney's Las Vegas adventure would be perfect for her. Most important of all, the day had been a celebration of love. And in the end, love was all that mattered.

* * * * *

Recipes from Anne, Roberta and Their Friends

Anne's second wedding was enjoyed by one and all. Guests raved over the various wedding cakes, which were made by Cass Wilkes. You're on your own for the donut cake, but Cass is sharing her recipes for the bride's cake and the groom's cake in case you'd like to make one of them for a special occasion. And Anne even convinced Bailey Sterling to share her recipe for Brie and smoked salmon bruschetta. Hope you enjoy them!

Orange Blossom Cake

Ingredients:

2 ¼ cups sifted flour
2 ½ tsp baking powder
1 tsp salt
1 ½ cups sugar
½ cup butter
2 large eggs
1 cup milk
1 tbsp oil
1 tsp orange extract
1 11-oz can of mandarin orange slices,
drained and cut into small pieces

Directions:

Sift flour, baking powder and salt into mixing bowl, then add sugar, butter, eggs, milk, oil and orange extract. Beat just until well mixed. Stir in orange pieces by hand. Pour into two 8-inch greased cake pans or a 9x11-inch greased pan and bake at 350°F for 25 minutes or until a toothpick inserted comes out clean. You can also make cupcakes (bake for twenty minutes). Recipe should make about twenty cupcakes.

Frost with buttercream frosting.

Buttercream Frosting

(Note: Cass makes this more by guess and by gosh, so you may have to tweak the ingredients just a little.)

Ingredients:

*2 ½ cups powdered sugar
(sometimes Cass adds a little more)
¼ cup butter
2 tbsp milk (The amount really depends on whether you end up adding a little more powdered sugar. Conversely, if your frosting is a little too sloppy, throw in some more powdered sugar.)
½ tsp vanilla*

Directions:

Put butter in a mixing bowl and sift in powdered sugar. Add milk and vanilla and cream together until smooth.

Chocolate Zucchini Groom's Cake

Ingredients:

2 ½ cups flour
4 tbsp cocoa
1 tsp soda
½ tsp salt
½ tsp baking powder
½ tsp cloves
½ tsp cinnamon
1 cup oil
1 ⅓ cups sugar
3 eggs
½ cup sour cream
2 cups grated zucchini
1 large handful chocolate chips

Directions:

Mix zucchini, oil, eggs and sugar, then add sour cream. Sift in dry ingredients and mix. Add chocolate chips and stir until mixed in. Bake in a greased 9x13-inch pan at 325°F for 45 minutes.

Brie and Smoked Salmon Bruschetta

*(Courtesy of Theresia Brannan,
owner of East West Catering)*

Ingredients:

*1 French baguette
3 cloves of garlic
½ cup virgin olive oil
Sea salt
½ cup chopped fresh basil
5 Roma tomatoes, deseeded and cut into small pieces
Small wedge of Brie (about 6 oz)
1 pack presliced smoked salmon*

Directions:

Crush garlic, remove skin and cut off woody tip. Chop until fine. Place half the garlic in a medium bowl. Place the rest on a plate and soak with ¼ cup olive oil. Add a pinch of salt. Set aside.

Chop basil and tomatoes (drain off excess liquid from tomatoes) and put into the bowl with the garlic. Mix well and refrigerate.

Cut baguette diagonally into slices about half an inch thick. Brush bread with the olive oil in garlic on the plate. (Any of the oil mixture left over after this step can be added to the tomato mixture.) Slice Brie into ¼-inch strips. Put baguette slices onto a cookie sheet, place Brie strips onto the baguette and put it under the broiler for 2 to 3 minutes or till the Brie melts and the baguette slices start to brown. Remove from oven. Spoon bruschetta (tomato mixture) onto the baguette slices. Place a slice of smoked salmon on the baguette. Serve immediately.

Wedding Tips from a Pro

A wedding is such a special occasion, for both the bride and groom and their families and friends. Here are a few tips from an expert. (Thank you, Megan Keller of A Kurant Event in Seattle!)

Beware of Pinterest. While it's a fantastic tool to begin cultivating your style aesthetic, it can easily overwhelm you. Once you've got the nuts and bolts nailed down about the general design of the wedding, stop there. There's too much pressure these days to create a "Pinterest-worthy wedding" and that's just not what it's about. People will remember how much fun they had dancing or how smiley you looked all night more than the little odds and ends you used to decorate.

Don't feel obligated to talk to every single guest for five minutes. You won't have time!

Don't worry about the details. If you're not having fun, the party will feel like a dud. Conversely, if you're having a great time, your guests will, too. Your energy is contagious.

Most important: enjoy the day. Do what makes you feel happy together. This is the best party you'll ever throw. Enjoy it!

Wedding Adventures in Icicle Falls

You may be wondering what kind of wedding adventures were had by some of the other Icicle Falls residents you've come to know. Here's your chance to listen in as a couple of them remember the unique events that made their special days, well…special.

Roberta Gilbert and Curtis White

October was a busy month for every business in Icicle Falls, due to the many Oktoberfest celebrations the town held, but everyone who was anyone made time to come to Primrose Haus to celebrate the nuptials of Roberta Gilbert and Curtis White.

The grand old Victorian was as packed with people as it was with fall flowers in shades of vibrant reds, yellows and oranges. The bride wore an elegant cream-colored tea dress her daughter, Daphne, had helped her pick out, but what really made her beautiful was her smile. Many a teary eye was dabbed as she said "I do" to the handsome man she'd met in June.

"They make a lovely couple," Muriel whispered to Pat York as they sat side by side with Pat's husband, Ed.

"Yes, they do," Pat whispered back.

Muriel smiled fondly as the groom slipped a gold

band on their friend's finger. "I'm so glad she's found someone after all these years."

Pat nodded. "About time, I'd say."

Pastor Jim from the Icicle Falls Community Church said, "And now, by the powers vested in me, I pronounce you husband and wife. Curtis, you may kiss your bride."

And kiss her he did, to much applause and cheering.

"Wasn't that a lovely ceremony?" raved Olivia Wallace, who owned the Icicle Creek Lodge, as she and her new husband, James Claussen, joined Muriel and Pat and Ed at their dinner table.

They were followed by Dot, her daughter, Tilda, and Tilda's friend from the police force, Jamal Lincoln.

"I've got to say, that kiss made my toes curl," said Dot.

"Mine, too," Muriel confessed.

"Maybe that's a sign you're supposed to get married again," Pat told her.

"Oh, I don't think so," Muriel said. She looked over to the head table, where the new couple sat with his son and daughter-in-law and Daphne. "Two is probably enough for any woman."

"Oh, I don't know," Dot said with a grin. "If Leonardo DiCaprio came along, I'd consider it."

Tilda rolled her eyes and shook her head, and Olivia said, "Really, Dot. You're old enough to be his mother."

"On the outside, maybe," Dot retorted, "but on the inside, I'm still thirty and a babe."

"Who knows, Dot? Maybe one of these days you'll be getting married," Muriel said. She smiled at Olivia and James. "Yours was certainly one to remember."

"Who would've guessed when I came to Icicle Falls for Christmas that I was going to find a treasure at the Icicle Creek Lodge," James said and kissed her hand.

"Gag me," muttered Dot.

"I do love weddings," Muriel said with a sigh.

"And your wedding to Waldo was beautiful," Olivia told her. "The girls as your bridesmaids, the horse-drawn carriage after the ceremony, that lovely reception at the winery—it all went off beautifully."

"Boring," Dot scoffed. "Much more fun to have the kind of wedding Pat had."

"What happened at your wedding?" asked Tilda.

"Well, it was an adventure…"

Pat Wilder and Ed York

"Katie, I really don't think you want to be hosting a wedding when you're so close to having a baby," Pat Wilder said to her daughter.

Pat and Ed had come over to Seattle for Christmas to gather together their children and announce that they were getting married. No one was surprised, as Ed had been pursuing Pat for two years and during the past few months they'd been almost inseparable. Now Pat and her youngest daughter were sitting in Katie's kitchen in her new house, enjoying morning lattes. "Of course I do. The baby's not due for two weeks."

"Yes, but with first babies you never can tell."

"Oh, Mom, I'll be fine. Anyway, we got this all decided yesterday. We need to have it here, because my house is larger than Amanda's or Kevin's. And besides, one of the reasons we got it was so we could have lots of family parties."

"Yes, but not when you're expecting," Pat objected.

"What, like you never did anything when you were expecting? Come on, Mom. I remember you working at the bookstore clear up until the day Kevin was born."

"We should move the date up. How about a wedding in March?"

Katie waved away her concerns. "I'll be fine. Anyway, I love the idea of a May wedding."

Still… "I think we should stick to the plan and get married in Icicle Falls, at Roberta's Primrose Haus. The pass should be okay by the middle of March."

"Come on, Mom. We're just gonna invite family, right? So, let's have it here. You guys don't need to spend all that money."

"It's not as though we can't afford it." If the real reason her daughter was offering to host was to save her money, well, that was just silly.

"Don't spoil our fun." Katie pushed the plate of scones closer to Pat.

Anything to do with entertaining was fun for Katie. In addition to holding down a job as a loan officer and planning her dream home, she honed her culinary skills by hosting a monthly supper club.

Unable to resist, Pat helped herself to a second scone. "I don't like the idea of you girls going to all this trouble."

"For you? You've gotta be kidding. Anyway, like we told you last night, it won't be that much trouble. We've got Manda doing the cake and helping me with dinner, and Shelly doing the flowers. I mean, what's the point of having a sister-in-law who's a florist if you can't get wedding flowers out of the deal, right?"

"You're the best," Pat said, suddenly teary-eyed. "All of you." What had she done to deserve such great kids? They were always there for her, first when she lost her husband, and now, when she was about to take a new one.

"We're glad to see you so happy," Katie said.

Ed had great kids, too, and they'd all be together celebrating as she married a wonderful man. And soon there'd be another grandchild in the family. Did it get any better than that?

She and Ed arrived at Katie and Craig's house early in May, a good two weeks before Katie's delivery date. Even that seemed to be cutting it close, but Katie had insisted both she and the doctor had calculated accurately. No baby until the end of May.

Pat's daughter-in-law had transformed Katie's living room with a profusion of flowers, mixing orchids, stephanotis, roses and baby's breath with delicate ferns and lilac ribbons.

Pat's daughter Amanda showed up with the granddaughters, Adele and Katherine, all dressed up in lilac dresses and ready to stand as junior bridesmaids along with Ed's granddaughter, Clarissa. Both Pat's daughters would be dressed in a dark, rich purple and would act as matrons of honor while her son, Kevin, had claimed the honor of walking her down the stairs and giving her away.

Amanda set the cake out on Katie's dining room table. It was a lofty, three-tiered fondant masterpiece, shaped like a pile of wedding presents, with the "wrappings" done in varying shades of purple. "How's that for gorgeous?" she said.

"The best cake you've done yet," Pat said, hugging her. Amanda indulged her creative streak by decorating cakes. Pat sometimes wondered where her daughters got their culinary creativity. It sure hadn't been from her.

Now Ed was by her side, slipping an arm around her waist. "Look at that cake. Wow. That must have been a lot of work."

"Nothing's too much work for you, Ed," Amanda said and kissed him on the cheek, making him blush.

"Nothing's too much for my bride," he said and gave Pat a squeeze.

Apparently, since he was taking her to Fiji for their honeymoon. Fiji. In her wildest dreams Pat had never imagined herself going to such an exotic place. Her first honeymoon had been on the Oregon coast and that had seemed pretty darned grand. Other than trips over the mountains to Seattle and a jaunt to Disneyland when the kids were little, she'd remained rooted in Icicle Falls. And she'd been perfectly happy to stay that way, running her bookstore and hanging out with her friends. And, of course, seeing the kids whenever possible.

But Ed was determined they were going to enjoy life a little. "I love Icicle Falls, too," he said, "but that doesn't mean we can't slip away once in a while. Our businesses can survive without us for a couple of weeks now and then."

She'd hated the idea of taking off with Katie's delivery close at hand. She didn't want to miss seeing her grandbaby born, and she wanted to be on hand to help Katie.

Katie had overridden those concerns. "Craig's got two weeks' maternity leave. You can come help later, after he goes back to work."

"Just don't have the baby early," Pat had retorted. "I don't want to miss seeing our little Cristabelle enter the world."

"I promise. I'll keep my legs crossed until you guys get back," Katie had said with a laugh.

Pat wasn't so sure about that. The baby had already dropped, which meant delivery could be anytime. And today, in spite of smiles, Katie looked tired.

"Are you okay, sweetie?" Pat asked, watching her daughter press a hand to her back and grimace.

Katie immediately smiled. "I'm perfectly okay."

No, she was exhausted. "I knew we shouldn't have let her host this," Pat whispered to Ed as they moved into the living room.

"I'd like to have seen you stop her."

The doorbell rang, signaling the arrival of the first guests, Ed's daughter, bearing a foil-covered food platter, and her family. "We're so happy for you two," she said to Pat and hugged her. "And wow, look at this great house," she raved to Katie. "I heard you guys designed it yourselves."

"Well, we had an architect working with us," Katie said modestly as her husband took everyone's coats. "Come on. I'll show you the kitchen."

The doorbell rang again, bringing in another in-law with her two sons in tow. And once again, there was much hugging and happiness and oohs and aahs over Katie's new house.

Half an hour later, the house was full and the minister had arrived, and it was time for the ceremony to begin. No one in either family had been gifted with musical talent, so the bridal march, the theme from the movie *Somewhere in Time*, was played on a CD player. Kevin, six feet of young and handsome, escorted Pat down the stairs to the stone fireplace, with its mantel brimming with flowers, where the minister and the rest of the bridal party waited for her. Ed was gazing at her as if she was some young calendar girl. Ah, love was truly blind. And there were her lovely daughters, one of them smiling, the other... Katie didn't seem very comfortable.

"Are you all right?" Pat whispered as she took her place next to Katie.

"I'm fine."

She didn't look fine.

Pastor Jim, who'd come over the mountains to do the honors, smiled at the happy couple. "Ed and Pat, we're all gathered here to celebrate your love, and I thank you both for allowing me to be part of this special day. It is indeed a special thing when God brings love into our lives."

Oh, yes, it was. Who knew she'd find love again? And with a fellow Icicle, someone who appreciated life in Icicle Falls as much as she did.

"And I must say," Pastor Jim continued.

"Oh, no," Katie interrupted.

Pat glanced over at her daughter, who was frowning at her hardwood floor.

"I think my water just broke," Katie said miserably.

"Oh, my God," said her husband. "Babe, don't panic! Where's the suitcase? Where's the car keys?" Without waiting for an answer, he dashed up the stairs toward their bedroom.

"Okay, Jim, we both 'do,'" Ed said. He turned to Pat. "Let's get this girl to the hospital."

"You can't stop the ceremony," Katie protested miserably.

"Sure we can," Ed told her. "We already signed the license. That makes it legal, right, Jim?"

"Sure," said Pastor Jim. "We know you 'do.'"

"Well, then, there you have it."

Katie's husband was running back down the stairs now, taking them two at a time. "Let's go, let's go!" And then he, the man who swore he'd never be like some TV fool, panicking and out of control on the big day, grabbed his wife's arm and propelled her out the door, forgetting her overnight case.

Ed grabbed the forgotten case, and he and Pat fell in behind them.

"But the food," she called over her shoulder.

"Don't worry," said her sister, who'd returned from the powder room with a towel. "Everything's in the fridge. Come on, girls. Get your coats." To the guests she said, "Make yourselves at home. We'll be back. Eventually."

Ed's daughter waved her away. "Don't worry about us."

"Bring Pastor Jim," Katie insisted. "You can finish the ceremony at the hospital."

"And did you?" asked Tilda.

"Actually, we did. It was quite a memorable day," Pat said, smiling at Ed. "And we got back from our honeymoon in time for me to help Katie with the baby."

"That's a great story," Tilda said. "Not as good as my mom's, though," she added, giving Dot a mischievous look. "My dad fainted at our wedding. I guess it was hot in the church."

"Your cousin should never have told you about that," Dot grumbled.

"I still think it's pretty funny," Tilda said.

"Yeah, funny," Dot said, clearly not amused.

Later that evening, as the champagne flowed and the couples started dancing, only Muriel and Dot remained at their dinner table.

"Tilda and Jamal are a nice couple."

"Oh, they're not dating. Just friends, although I'm sure he'd like to be more. But it's awkward, being partners and all. At least, that's what Tilda says." Dot shook her head. "I swear, at the rate she's going, I'll never have any grandchildren." Dot looked enviously at Muriel's daughters and their husbands—and children. Samantha's toddler was adorable, with chestnut hair and big brown eyes. Cecily's stepdaughter was equally darling. Both girls were dolled up as though they were ready for a magazine shoot. And Cecily, who was now pregnant, had that glow that belonged to expectant mothers.

"I'm sure she'll find someone soon," Muriel said comfortingly.

"I doubt it. Tilda's a tough cookie. She's not every man's cup of tea."

"Tilda's special. She just needs a man as special as her."

Dot's only reply to that was a cynical harrumph.

"I do believe there's someone for everyone. Life is so much sweeter when it's shared."

Dot gave her champagne glass a tipsy inspection before downing its contents. "I miss Duncan."

Muriel sighed and stared at her empty glass. "I miss my husbands, too. Sometimes I wish I could turn back the clock, have one more day with each of them. They were both such wonderful men."

"Duncan was a good man, too." Dot scowled at her empty glass. "I wish I could say the same for that piece of garbage I married the first time."

"I'm sorry your first marriage had to end so…sadly," Muriel said diplomatically. There'd always been rumors about Dot's first marriage. She'd tried not to listen to them. Yes, Dot could affect a tough exterior when she wanted to—it wasn't hard to see where Tilda got her tough-cookie facade—but Muriel couldn't imagine her really killing her first husband.

"No loss," Dot said. "Duncan more than made up for it." She shook her head. "Although he did get a case of cold feet right before we said 'I do.'"

"Some men get a little nervous about commitment."

Dot frowned. "This was more than that."

Muriel blinked, unsure what to say.

Dot shrugged. "I may as well tell you." She pointed a finger at Muriel. "But you're the only person I'm telling. If you ever tell another living soul, Muriel, I swear I'll pull that dyed brown hair of yours out by the roots."

"I don't gossip," Muriel said, as offended by the insinuation as she was by the reference to her dyed locks.

"I need more champagne," Dot said. "You might, too. Gosh," she said as she poured them each some, "once in a while I look back at those days and wonder if I'm the same woman who lived that life. If Duncan hadn't come along, who knows what kind of bitter old broad I might've become."

"Ah, but he did. Come along, I mean."

Dot sighed. "Yes, he did. I had a flat tire on Highway 2 and he pulled over to help me. Told him I could handle it just fine on my own but he insisted. He said…"

Dot and Duncan Morrison

"A pretty woman shouldn't have to get all dirty changing a tire."

Dot eyed her rescuer with a cynical eye. His red hair and freckles and sloped nose made her think of Howdy Doody. With that boyish face he looked as though he was all of twenty, and his physique—or rather, lack thereof—had her wondering if he could even lift a grocery bag, let alone jack up a car. But he set to work proving that he did indeed have some muscle.

"You're not from around here, are you?" she noted as she lit a cigarette.

"Nope. Well, not yet, anyway. I just bought a place in Icicle Falls. I'm going up to sign the papers."

"Yeah? I live in Icicle Falls."

He grinned at her in a way that would've been positively lecherous if he hadn't looked like Howdy Doody. "You do?"

She pointed a finger at him. "Don't get any ideas, bub. You're too young for me."

"I doubt that." He bent down to remove the lug nuts. "How old are you?"

"You never ask a woman her age. That shows how young and wet behind the ears you are."

"Okay, then, let's try this. I'm thirty-five. Does that make me too young?"

Dot was thirty-two. It made him just right. But she wasn't sure he was her type. She preferred her men bigger, more manly. More muscled.

Wait a minute. She'd described her first husband. And what a poor excuse for a husband he'd been, the rotten, drunken bully. Of course, when she'd first met Corey with his hot rod and his pack of cigarettes rolled up in the sleeve of his T-shirt, she'd thought he was the coolest thing this side of James Dean.

Oh, yeah. He'd been cool, all right. Too cool to keep any job for longer than six months. Too cool to take her anywhere but the tavern for a beer and some pool. And once his friends showed up, she was always relegated to watching.

None of that had bothered her, though. No, what did bother her was how mean he got after a few drinks. Heck, how mean he got even cold sober whenever she didn't agree with him or do what he wanted. And when she insisted they pay bills instead of blowing money on football bets and booze and old beaters to fix up, well, then he got *really* mean. The day she lost the baby and he said "Just as well. We can't afford a kid" was the day she stopped loving him. The day she told him she wanted a divorce and he slapped her and told her not on her life was the day she vowed she'd leave him. But first she'd make him pay.

"Have you ever hit a woman?" she asked Mr. Scrawny Duncan Morrison.

He gaped at her. "What?"

"You heard me."

"Of course not. Nobody who's a real man hits women."

"Yeah, well, that's not what my first husband thought."

"Your first husband sounds like a winner."

"Yeah, well. He's gone now."

Duncan nodded approvingly and pulled off the tire. "Moved away?"

"Permanently. He's dead."

For a moment Duncan stood there with the tire in his hands as if trying to take in her story. "Gosh, what happened? Car accident?"

"Camping accident."

"Wow, that's…"

"What he deserved."

He looked a little shocked by that, but then he nodded as if he'd somehow sorted it out in his mind. "So, you've been a widow for how long?"

"Three years. I came back here after the dust settled and bought a restaurant in town."

Duncan smiled at that. "Really?"

The way he was looking at her, he probably figured she'd bought something spectacular. "It's more a café, a breakfast place. I call it Pancake Haus."

"Sounds good. I might have breakfast there tomorrow."

"I'll give you breakfast on the house," she said. "As a thank-you," she added, nodding at the tire. After all, she didn't want him to think she was interested.

Except when he came in the next day and they got to

talking, she found she was, just a little. He was the sort of nice guy she'd turned her nose up at when she was young. He didn't dress like James Dean. He didn't even smoke. And he sure didn't drive any souped-up muscle car, just a simple Plymouth Savoy.

"It gets me where I want to go. That's all I care about," he said.

She poured him a cup of coffee. "Where do you want to go?"

"Not far from here. This looks like the kind of place where I could raise a family, do a little fishing, have a barbecue on a Sunday afternoon. I like what they've done with the town. There's a lot of potential for growth, new houses going up. A good place for a guy in real estate."

"Is that what you do?"

He took a sip of coffee and nodded. "Your real-estate office here in town is taking me on as a broker."

Suddenly, and she wasn't quite sure why, Dot was glad this man was going to stick around. Maybe it was his smile. Or the fact that he wanted to be a family man. Or maybe just the fact that he didn't hit women.

She'd found plenty to like about Duncan, and discovered more once he left Seattle behind and put down stakes in Icicle Falls. He was sweet and he loved funny movies and picnics by the river. Mostly, he loved being with Dot, and she loved being with him. When the holidays came, he jumped right in, helping the town's movers and shakers string lights on the giant Christmas tree in the center of town and playing Santa Claus at the grade school's PTA Christmas pageant.

The night before Christmas Eve he proposed to her. "Marry me, Dottie. Let's ring in the New Year planning our wedding."

A wedding, maybe even in a church instead of at a girl-friend's house. With a fancy wedding cake and her sister as her maid of honor. And her stepsister…hopefully out of town. And a real honeymoon instead of two nights at a dumpy hotel out on Highway 99.

They went to Seattle on Christmas Eve and met his family, a normal happy family like on *The Donna Reed Show.* His parents had been happily married for forty-two years and he had two older brothers, also happily married with a passel of children. Not a smoker in the crowd. Would anyone care if she had a cigarette?

As if reading her mind, her future mother-in-law brought out an ashtray. "Duncan tells me you smoke. Please, feel free."

Okay, she really liked this family.

"They're all so nice," she said once she and Duncan were in the car.

"Why are you surprised by that?"

She shrugged. "Maybe it's because I'm not used to normal. I hope my family doesn't scare you off."

"What, do they have satanic rites and drink the blood of goats?"

She made a face at him. "No. They're okay. They're just not like your family." She thought of her hard-faced fairy-tale-worthy stepmother and her bratty younger stepsister. What her father had ever seen in Eunice was beyond Dot. She'd come with a daughter in tow, who was a spoiled brat. Dad never noticed. Dad never noticed much of anything that went on in his house. Or if he did, he didn't care. So their stepmother indulged the little beast, and if either Dot or her sister, Joyce, did anything to make Ronnie cry they were in big trouble with Mom. They'd grown to strongly dislike Ronnie, which made her even more of a brat. Now that they were all grown women nothing had changed, really.

Dad seemed glad enough to see Dottie engaged. "Well, look at that. You found another live one," he joked, pumping Duncan's hand.

Next to him Eunice smiled, happy enough to see Dot find someone and maybe hoping she'd attach herself to her new family and stay out of their hair.

Her uncles were too busy loading up on the spiked eggnog to do much more than wave hello. Her grandfather was busy yelling at one of her nephews, but Grandma was quick to give Duncan a hug and so was Dot's sister.

Ronnie, single after a messy divorce, sidled up to Duncan and sized him up while taking a drag on her Lucky Strike. "And where did you two meet?" she asked and blew smoke out the side of her mouth.

Dot always felt pretty good about how she looked— until she was around Ronnie. Ronnie was stacked and she had a pouty little mouth that she kept ripely red with Revlon lipstick. Ronnie was also a tramp and Dot hadn't been at all surprised when her marriage broke up. Flirting with men was like a drug to her. Which was, of course, what she was doing now. She wasn't interested in Duncan with his red hair and freckles and skinny body, just interested in making him want her.

"We met on Highway 2," Duncan said. "Dot had a flat and I stopped to fix it."

"Oh, now that's truly romantic. You're quite the knight in shining armor."

Duncan, bless him, didn't even realize what Ronnie was up to. He simply blushed and said, "Just thought it would be nice to help."

"What if I had a flat tire? Would you help me?"

"Not if he knew what a spider you are," Dot said shortly. "Don't you need some eggnog or something?"

Ronnie frowned at her. "Cute, Dot." She shook her head. "I can't believe you've found another man to marry you."

"And I can't believe you found any," Dot retorted, making Ronnie toss her ponytail and stomp off. Duncan was looking confused. "Don't mind her," Dot told him. "Every family has a brat and she's ours. She's still mad because her first boyfriend followed me around like a puppy when we were in high school."

"Well," Duncan said, and apparently that was all he could think of to say.

"I thought you said he got cold feet," Muriel said. "It sounds to me like he was pretty determined to marry you in spite of your family."

"Oh, he didn't care about them. What unnerved him was what Ronnie told him." Dot shook her head. "Ronnie never liked me and I never liked her. I guess I didn't help matters when I didn't ask her to become a bridesmaid. She came to the wedding ready to sabotage me."

A church in Seattle had been reserved and the rehearsal dinner was held at Rose's Diner—a popular family-style restaurant outside the city that was famous for its fabulous chicken dinners—in one of the large rooms reserved for parties. Her dad claimed he was too broke to pay for it, so Duncan footed the bill.

It was a June night, unseasonably hot. The men had shed their jackets and the women had given up on powdering their noses. In spite of the warm temperatures outside and the still-warmer temperatures inside, in spite of the fan the owner had going, people were enjoying themselves, standing around chatting before dinner. Dot had slipped away to use the ladies' room. She returned to find her stepsister in earnest conversation with Duncan. Duncan's face was ghost white, his freckles in stark relief.

"Duncan, what's wrong?"

"Nothing," he said, but she could hear panic at the back of his voice.

Dot grabbed her sister by the elbow and marched her to a corner of the room. "What did you say to him?" she hissed.

Ronnie looked at her wide-eyed. "Nothing. I was just telling him about Corey and how he died and how sad it was that so many people thought…" She shrugged eloquently.

"You little bitch," Dot snarled. "I ought to…"

"What? Push me off a mountain? You don't have a life insurance policy on me."

Dot whirled around and returned to where Duncan stood, staring at his Tom Collins.

"She told me you beat him with a baseball bat one night when he was drunk and passed out," he said, not meeting her eyes.

She should lie, tell him Ronnie was a worthless tramp and he couldn't believe a word that fell from her trampy mouth. "No, I didn't."

Relief flooded his face with color and he raised his face to show her a relieved smile.

"I used a frying pan."

The smile did a vanishing act. He set his drink on the nearby table. "What?"

"I'd just found out he'd been cheating on me. He'd already broken my jaw." She shrugged helplessly. "I was only twenty-two." As if age really had anything to do with it. "But to tell you the truth, I'd do it again. He deserved that. And more."

"And did he get more, Dottie? Did you push him off the mountain? Your sister said there was a trial."

"Stepsister," Dot corrected him. "And there was an inquest. I guess I got away with murder, so you'd better not cheat on me," she finished. Ha-ha. Except this was nothing to joke or act cynical about. It had been a horrible, terrifying experience. And maybe she would have said as much if Duncan hadn't been looking at her as if she was some kind of Black Widow.

"All right," her father was saying, "let's all find our seats."

And so they did. Regretful about shooting off her mouth, Dot tried to smile at the good-natured toasts and jests from her father and her uncles, hugged her grandma and her future mother-in-law when the party broke up and tried to think what she should say to Duncan.

She didn't get a chance to say anything. The men dragged him off, insisting on celebrating further on the groom's last night of freedom. He looked over his shoulder at her and his expression was pleading. *Please tell me I'm not marrying the creature from the black love lagoon.*

There was only one monster in the room and that was Ronnie. Dot shouldn't have even invited her to the wedding. As everyone filed out of the restaurant, she grabbed her stepsister by the arm. "What do you think you're doing?"

"I don't know what you mean." Ronnie tried to pull away.

Now Dot's sister had joined them. "What's she been up to?" Joyce asked.

"Up to? Why do you always think I'm up to something?" Ronnie protested.

Dot glared at her. "She told Duncan about Corey."

"You little louse!"

"Somebody needed to tell him," Ronnie said. "He has a right to know what he's getting into."

"Well, and when you bring your next victim around, we'll be sure to tell him how many men you've slept with," Joyce said sweetly.

"I have not…"

"Met a man you didn't like," Dot snarled. "Oh, get out of here before we strip you and strangle you with your bra."

"You would!" Ronnie shot back and hurried out of the room.

"Do you think she has psychological problems?" Joyce mused as Ronnie ran for the door.

Dot sighed. "I guess it was bound to come out. When you've got a past, it always does."

"The only thing in your past you need to be ashamed of was your bad taste in picking Corey in the first place. He was rotten to the core. And the only thing you should regret is not calling me to come over and help you beat the tar out of him that night."

Dot managed a smile. But it didn't last long. "I wonder what Duncan's thinking."

"That he's lucky to have you," her sister said with a grin and hugged her.

She tried to call Duncan at his house a number of times that night but he never answered. She wanted to see him the next morning, but it seemed that every moment was busy with hair appointments and pedicures. All day she kept expecting someone to deliver a note from him telling her never mind, he didn't want to get married, after all, but none came.

That evening, the little church was filled with family and with friends who'd come over from Icicle Falls. The flower girls did their walk down the aisle, followed by her sister, and then her father offered her his arm.

"Okay, kid, let's do this," he said, and she could smell whiskey on his breath.

She looked at Duncan. He stood waiting next to his best man. The expression on his face wasn't that of a besotted groom. He looked like old Howdy Doody would look if someone set him too close to a roaring bonfire. They should have talked. She should've tracked him down. What kind of way was this to get married? She hesitated.

"Come on," her father teased. "Too late to back out now."

Was it? Was that what Duncan thought?

Down the aisle they went. Her father said his piece about giving her away and then sat down next to her stepmother. Duncan held out his elbow. Dot took it, and they climbed the three carpeted stairs to where the pastor stood. It was hot in the church with the evening sun streaming through the stained-glass windows, and Dot could feel perspiration gathering on her brow. Duncan was sweating like a crook under police interrogation.

The bridal party turned to face the minister, who told them that marriage wasn't a state to be entered into lightly. She thought she heard Duncan whimper. She stole a glance at him. His mouth was set in a determined line. This was not the face of a happy groom anticipating his wedding night.

Now it was time to kneel on the carpeted stairs in front of the minister while her cousin Cornelia sang

"The Lord's Prayer." She got as far as "lead us not into temptation" when Duncan moaned and fell over like a toppled tree.

Pandemonium ensued. Duncan's mother let out a cry and his brothers carried him from the sanctuary.

"Get him water," one of Dot's aunts called after them.

As if water would solve the problem.

"We'll continue this in a few minutes," the minister promised.

Dot wasn't so sure. She picked up her skirts and followed the men to the choir room, which had served as their dressing room.

Duncan was just coming around, thanks to a couple of not-so-gentle slaps from his brother, when she entered the room. One look at her and he passed out again. Now one of his aunts had entered with a glass of water.

Dot took it from her and commanded, "Leave us for a minute."

The others exchanged looks, then tiptoed off like people leaving the side of a deathbed.

She walked up to where Duncan lay prone on a church pew and dumped the water on his face, which brought him to, spluttering and shaking his head. "We need to talk," she snapped. "Do you want to marry me or don't you?"

His expression turned mulish. "Of course I do."

She smiled sweetly. "Good. We should be able to live happily ever after...as long as you don't cross me and we never go mountain climbing."

That put him back to looking like Casper the Friendly Ghost.

"Oh, honestly, Duncan. Do you really think I killed my husband?"

"No. I... No."

"So then, why did you pass out?"

"It was hot in there."

"It was hot for *you*. If you can't stand the heat, Duncan, stay out of the kitchen." This wasn't going to work. Duncan was a big chicken and her stepsister was a witch. At the moment, she could happily have choked them both. She turned to leave. "I'm going to tell everyone to take their presents and go home."

He caught her gown. "Don't."

She looked over her shoulder and cocked an eyebrow at him. "I don't see the point in going on. Do you?"

"Yes, I do. But don't you think whatever happened with your husband is something you could have told me about?"

"You'd have run screaming into the night, just like you want to do now."

"I'm not going anywhere. Tell me what happened."

She made a face. "He was drinking. We were up on Mount Rainier with some lousy friends of his and their girlfriends. They were all drinking. We got into a fight." She could remember it all so clearly. The angry march away from the campsite, the raised voices. Corey grabbing her arm and her jerking away. Him losing his balance. "He fell down a ravine and broke his neck, plain and simple. Of course, no one saw it. They only came when they heard me scream."

Duncan said nothing. He sat there on the pew, taking in everything she said.

"He had a life insurance policy. An insurance salesman talked us into getting a policy, told us it would be a good way to save money. I guess it was. I used it to buy my restaurant." Duncan seemed so relieved she could only conclude that he'd considered her capable of murder. She narrowed her eyes. "Of course, I could be making this all up, so we'd better not get married."

Again, she turned to go, and again, he grabbed her gown. "Quit grabbing my gown, Duncan. You're going to rip it." So what if he did? She'd never wear it again.

"You didn't kill him. Of course you didn't. But even if you did, I want you anyway. I love you, Dot. I'll take my chances."

"Yeah? I might kill you."

"Then I'll die with a smile on my face."

He stood up and put his arms around her. "Let's go back out there and finish what we started."

He was either crazy or the most wonderful man in the world. "Are you sure?"

"You bet. But I'm taking off this jacket. I don't want to pass out again. I don't want to miss another moment with you."

Dot raised her champagne glass, toasting her dead husband. "You know what? He did die with a smile on his face. Duncan was the sweetest man." The band was playing a romantic slow dance. She looked out at the couples swaying on the floor, the women with their arms around their partners' necks, smiling at the other. And the bride and groom… If ever a pair looked ready to hit the honeymoon suite, it was them.

Dot pointed in their direction. "Check out Roberta and Curtis. They're grinning like they won the lottery."

"I think they did," Muriel said. "You know, Dot, God gave human beings a lot of wonderful gifts, but love is the best one of all."

"I'll drink to that," Dot said and poured herself more champagne.

Acknowledgments

I had such a good time writing this book! And I'd really like to thank the wonderful people who helped me along the way. Thanks as always to the "brain trust": Susan Wiggs, Anjali Banerjee, Kate Breslin, Lois Dyer and Elsa Watson. And a very special thanks to Megan Keller, event designer and owner of A Kurant Event in Seattle, Washington, for giving me a glimpse into the life of a wedding planner. (I'm sure there are some things I didn't get right, but that's my fault and not hers.) I've seen Megan in action and she plans fabulous weddings! Thanks to my good friend Theresia for the wonderful recipes. Everything you make is fabulous!

Finally, a big thank-you to my agent, Paige Wheeler (you're the best!), my insightful and lovely editor, Paula Eykelhof, and all the wonderful people at MIRA who work so hard to turn stories into books and dreams into dreams come true.

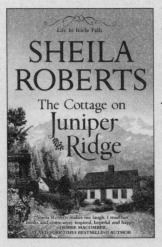

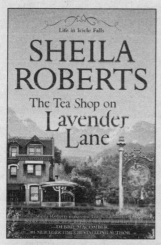

⌁ LIFE IN ICICLE FALLS ⌁

SHEILA ROBERTS

Life in Icicle Falls doesn't always go as planned...

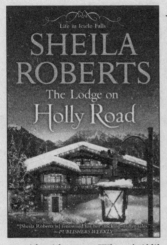

James Claussen has played Santa for years. But now that he's a widower, he's lost interest—in everything. So his daughter, Brooke, kidnaps him from the mall for a special Christmas at the lodge in Icicle Falls, owned by long-widowed Olivia Wallace. Brooke wants Dad to be happy, and yet…she's not quite ready to see someone *else's* mommy kissing Santa Claus.

Single mom Missy Monroe brings her kids to the lodge, too. Lalla wants a grandma for Christmas, and her brother, Carlos, wants a dog. Missy can't provide either one. What *she'd* like is an attractive, dependable man. A man like John Truman… But John's girlfriend will be joining him in Icicle Falls, and he's going to propose.

Of course, not everything goes as planned. But sometimes the best gifts are the ones you *don't* expect!

Available now, wherever books are sold!

Be sure to connect with us at:

Harlequin.com/Newsletters

Facebook.com/HarlequinBooks

Twitter.com/HarlequinBooks

MIRA®

www.MIRABooks.com

MSR1661R